Lofty Mountains

Space Wizard Science Fantasy
Raleigh, NC
www.spacewizardsciencefantasy.com

Publisher's Note: This is a work of fiction. Names, characters, places, and incidents are a product of the author's imagination. Locales and public names are sometimes used for atmospheric purposes. Any resemblance to actual people, living or dead, or to businesses, companies, events, institutions, or locales is completely coincidental.

Cover by MoorBooks
Illustrations by Katie Cordy and Carmen Loup
Copy Editing by Heather Tracy
Book Layout © 2015 BookDesignTemplates.com

Lofty Mountains/J.S. Fields, Heather Tracy.— 1st ed.
ISBN 978-1-960247-14-8

Lofty Mountains

ELEVEN STORIES OF CLOUDY PEAKS, AIRSHIP
ADVENTURES, AND SAPPHIC EXPERIENCES

Edited by J.S. Fields & Heather Tracy

CONTENTS

Introduction

Aaaaand, we're back!

What started as a critique group having fun during a global pandemic has morphed beyond my wildest dreams. The core group of us are all here, of course, but we're joined this year by a crew of incredibly talented authors who have expanded this particular installment of the Worlds Apart series with our best sapphic speculative fiction content yet.

We've got Seanan McGuire's frog-chasing, swamp-loving sapphics and Maya Gittelman's mountain-dwelling, BDSM-loving mountain god. Rosiee Thor helps a broken-winged harpy find love and Robin C.M. Duncan's swashbuckling pirate Vermillion is still wreaking absolute havoc with the ladies. I've traded in my space lesbians for an airship and some plastic dinosaurs, and you can find real dinosaurs in N.L. Bates' story about a salvage mission gone horribly wrong. These authors and numerous others weave stories across mountain tops, wind-swept seas, and desolate, apocalyptic wastelands. There's love, sex, friendship, found family, acceptance, and above all, a broad representation of the sapphic experience.

There's so much, just, absolute *joy* in this anthology. DISTANT GARDENS entwined us with fungus and tentacles (many thanks to Sara Codair for that swamp monster sex scene no one thought would happen), and FARTHER REEFS had us holding our breath over an oncoming apocalypse, or because we were tied to a pirate captain's bed. LOFTY MOUNTAINS sets the reader free to fly with dinosaurs and bees, crash into gardens, flirt with mountain-dwelling mechanics, learn the inner secrets of cats and garden gnomes, and yell at gods.

I can't think of a more perfect set of stories and I am so delighted to have worked with every single one of these authors. Our amazing illustrator, Katie Cordy, has really outdone herself this time, and we even have a couple bonus illustrations for you from one of our talented writers, Carmen Loup.

—J. S. Fields, September 2023

A NOTE ON THE STORIES CONTAINED HEREIN:

Each tale is marked on the title page with what sapphic representation is involved, as well as any content warnings. There is also a "Heat Level" if you wish to read or not read particular sexual content. The scale is as follows:

Low/None: There may be talk of sex, holding hands, or possibly kissing.

Medium: Mention of body parts, touching, and make-out sessions, but all scenes are "fade to black."

Hot!: Has at least one full sex scene, start to finish. You have been warned (or encouraged...).

Don't Look Down

Rosiee Thor

Sapphic Representation: Lesbian
Heat Level: Low
Content Warnings: Coarse Language, Violence

On the first day of featherfall, Charna found a heavy dusting of plumage in her garden. The damn harpies always left her crops in disarray. A carnage of carrots, a ruin of radishes. Feathers pierced holes in cabbage leaves and impaled heads of lettuce. Trying to work with the constant deluge was an exercise in futility. She would be lucky to keep up with cleaning at this rate, let alone harvest anything. Plus, she hated the feeling when the feathers got stuck to her lips, downy and soft and weirdly sticky.

Harpies blanketed the sky this time of year, their wings blocking out the sun as they passed overhead. Sometimes, she'd put aside her ill temper to watch them in begrudging awe. It was a hell of a thing, to see a harpy fly; it was another altogether to see one fall.

"Well, that gives a new meaning to the word *squash*," she muttered to herself as she lost a quarter of her pumpkin patch as a bird hit the earth and rolled.

It would be so easy to head back inside for the day. Charna's solitary log cabin lurked in the shadows of the great pines of the Cloudspine mountain range, so named for the way its peaks arched against the sky, pushing through the clouds like a set of exposed vertebrae. Charna had lived on thoracic seven all her life. Well, she'd lived *in* it for her youth and adolescence. She'd nearly died in it, sequestered too long in the dark caverns her people had carved into the mountain. It had taken everything she had to decide to live—literally. When she left for the brightlands above, she went with the knowledge she would never be welcomed back to the mountain's embrace. At least she could see the sky from here, feel the sun on her face and neck. A worthy trade for companionship, for family, for love. She endeavored not to miss those things. She couldn't have them anymore.

"Oy! Are you dead?" she barked, dragging herself toward the inert form at the far side of the garden.

Her first impression was of silvery wings wider than Charna was tall (an understated four and a half feet). Usually, she thought of a harpy's wings as impressive or invasive, but these feathers were more than rumpled; they were crushed. Charna wasn't an expert on avian anatomy, but even she knew wings weren't meant to bend like that. With a steady hand, she brushed the feathers aside to reveal a few ruined gourds and...a woman.

Sharp-taloned claws made way for a gently sloping humanoid form, waxy skin and tawny feathers colliding in the middle. Thin strands of shimmery hair covered the harpy's face, not so much silver as a collection of hues: lilac in shadow, burnished gold in the sun.

Charna's people had no tales of harpies. They lived inside the mountain, after all. Still, stories found their way to Charna by way of travelers come to trade with the people of the Cloudspines. They brought with them wool and wheat. They left with carts laden heavy with mastersmith weapons and chainmail.

"The farmland's better in the plains," they'd say when they met her. "The mountains are no place for a girl on her own."

She didn't want their pity, but she did want their packets of seeds, so she'd offer to share her dinner and let them tell her of the great adventure that called to them here in the mountains. They'd tell her of the dragon they hoped to hunt and she'd direct them toward the lumbar peaks, then they'd tell her to watch out for harpies.

Birds as big as men. Violent, too. With vicious claws and wings of steel. "But it's the song that'll get you," they'd say. Almost wistful. Almost wanting. "To be taken by a harpy... what a way to go."

A twisted game, the harpies played. Their song was exquisite the way an avalanche was: rolling and wild, leaving only destruction behind. They'd spell folks with their trancing voices, then they'd strike. Lucky were the ones who died quick with a talon to the throat. For most, it was the fall that killed them. Harpies left a trail of dead in their wake with wide eyes and hollow chests. They ate only the hearts. Charna's heart had iced over and then some in the years since she'd surfaced, not that a harpy could tell from the sky, but she liked to think if they ever got ahold of her, she'd give them indigestion as karmic retribution.

Charna was never in much danger. They usually took men. Easier to catch, or so it was said. Still, it was difficult to differentiate with mountain folks on account of all the hair. Charna's beard was not so long as her brother's, but she took care not to adorn it with shiny things to avoid avian attention, wearing only wooden and glass beads in her twists and braids. She'd never been one to take chances.

Now, she stood mere inches from a predator. The scent of iron tickled Charna's nostrils. The harpy had lost a lot of blood. It wouldn't be singing any time soon.

"Let's get you inside." She cast about for a way to do just that, gaze falling on the wheelbarrow a few yards away. "Perfect."

Charna pushed off the ground, but before she could take a single step, fingers closed around her ankle. Below her, the harpy watched through gleaming, russet eyes. For a moment, they simply stared at one another. Then, the harpy threw open her mouth, eyes wild. This was it, Charna thought with an alarming level of calm for someone about to be devoured by a harpy. This was the end.

But the harpy did not scream. Nor did she sing. When her voice came, it was barely a croak, and all she said before slumping into unconsciousness was a lackluster, "Ow."

* * *

The last thing Ruta remembered before she fell was the way her sister Volys said the word *prey*.

"It's only a game," Volys said. "Come now, aren't you hungry? You're a predator. Go catch your prey."

She and the others of their nest were going to catch themselves a man, and what they planned to do with his heart made Ruta want to wretch.

"Remember what the Nestmothers say, 'Confidence is key!' And don't forget the first rule of flying: *don't look down!*"

Easier said than done. Ruta's stomach pitched, then, there was nothing but blurred white as she passed through cloud and feathers and lost control.

The first thing Ruta felt upon waking was the pain. A dull steady ache deep in her bones. She tried to sit up, but her head pounded dangerously.

"Am I dead?" she asked no one in particular.

"Do you feel dead?" came the gruff response.

"No," Ruta said. Pain meant she was alive. And alive meant she was... "I feel hungry."

"Good. That means you're healing."

Ruta blinked and the world around her came into focus. Before her stood a stout woman with green eyes and a mountain of auburn hair on her head and chin. She wore a heavy apron and a heavier scowl.

"Suppose I'll have to feed you, then," said the woman. "I don't have what you're probably used to, but it'll have to do."

Ruta shuddered. "I don't—I'm not—" By the skies, the woman probably thought Ruta wanted to eat her heart. She cast about for the right words, uncertain how best to communicate her distaste for the entire concept. "I don't want to eat you," she said. Directness was probably best, considering the circumstances.

"I didn't think you did." The woman turned her back. "If I'd thought you were a danger, I would've tied you up some."

"Oh." Ruta looked down at her hands. Even if she'd wanted to, Ruta didn't have the strength to take down a rabbit, let alone a fully grown—though short of stature—woman. Someone else might have put Ruta out of her misery. Lucky this woman had decided to spare her. Luckier still, this woman had decided to *save* her. "Who are you?"

"Just a woman in possession of fewer pumpkin plants than I was this morning." The woman didn't laugh, though the words were framed like a joke. "You can call me Charna."

"Charna." Ruta tried the name on her tongue, dragging the softened "ch" from the depths of her throat in mimicry. "I'm Ruta."

"New people don't usually pronounce it right the first time." A smile flashed across Charna's lips like sunlight cracking through thick clouds. "Thank you."

"I like the way it feels," Ruta said. Her vocal cords itched to say the name again. "I don't get to make very many soft sounds back home."

Charna turned away to tend the hearth. She hefted another log onto the fire—her arms a ripple of lean muscle—then crumbled a bundle of dried herbs between callused fingers. The only sounds were crackling flames and the kettle's tinny whistle. A few minutes later, she brought over a wide ceramic mug of steaming liquid. "Peppermint and lemon balm," Charna said. "For the inflammation."

Ruta tried to lift her arms, but only managed to hold them up for a few seconds before the weight became too much.

"See?" Charna's eyes lit with mirth. "You couldn't eat me if you tried."

An instinct rose in Ruta to pounce, to destroy, to prove this woman wrong. She was a danger. She was the menace of the skies. But...Ruta had never been those things, nor had she ever wanted to be. That was her sisters, not her.

"Here, let me." Charna lifted the mug to Ruta's lips and tipped it gently. The tea was bitter and bright. Ruta didn't look away as she drank, gaze affixed to Charna's. There seemed a world within her eyes, rolling hills and mossy glades. She'd heard stories of the mountain folk. Hard to find, harder to catch. No one had ever told her they might be gentle.

Dizzy and a little embarrassed, Ruta lifted her chin, destabilizing the mug so liquid sloshed over the side and onto her neck.

"Sorry," she muttered.

"Don't go apologizing to me. Not my skin you just burned with scalding tea."

"It's fine—doesn't hurt." Not compared to everything else, anyway. Nausea churned in her stomach.

"Be more careful. You've got enough injuries as it is." Charna wiped the spill with the hem of her apron. "Multiple fractures, a concussion, and more bruises than I care to count. Let's not add burns to the list."

Ruta cast off the blanket to see dark contusions on her hips, purple and blue and sickly green swirling together like a storm.

Charna turned away, a pink flush creeping up her neck.

"Sorry," Ruta muttered, pulling the blanket back over her body. "It's not very pleasant to look at."

"Just trying to give you privacy," Charna grunted.

Ruta's gaze swept over Charna's turned back. She wore a thick tunic and loose-fitting trousers, even though there was a fire going. Clothes, in Ruta's experience, were for warmth alone, but it seemed the mountain folk had a stronger sense of modesty. Or perhaps that was just Charna.

"Are you up for something more substantial?" Charna asked, gesturing toward the hearth. "Nothing too heavy. No offense, but I've already killed half my day cleaning your blood off the floor. Don't need to add your sick to the list. You sit back and I'll whip up a broth."

Blood. That wasn't good. Still, Ruta didn't like to be a burden. "I just need a sleep is all," she said, eyes fluttering closed. "If I go tomorrow, I'll be able to catch up to my sisters."

Charna laughed, a deep, throaty chuckle. "You'll be going exactly nowhere, I should think. Not with that broken wing of yours."

"Broken?" Ruta's eyes flashed open. "My *wing*?"

"Afraid so. Don't know much about birdfolk, but if a wing's anything like an arm, you'll be grounded for several months yet."

Ruta blanched. "But they'll be gone by then."

"Your sisters?"

"I don't know the way on my own. I'll need to follow them before they move on." She'd never been good at studying migration patterns. She could just go back to the nest, but then...then she would be a failure. She could almost hear her sisters' jeers.

Little Ruta, such a pest!

Little Ruta, failed the test!

Her fingers balled into fists, the sudden tension in her jaw sending another wave of pain through her body.

Charna was bent low over a pot, face obscured. "Hunting season is short, but harvest season is long." She turned to face Ruta, lips in an unreadable straight line. "You'll make yourself useful if you're to stay."

"S-stay?" Ruta felt winded by the very notion.

"Until your sisters come back for you." Charna produced a wooden spoon from the depths of her apron and hit the flat of it against her palm. "Or I suppose until you depart this mortal coil. Whichever comes first."

Joke or threat, Ruta couldn't tell. Charna had saved her life, but there was a strange outer shell to the woman Ruta couldn't crack, like a nut or a snail. Still, if the alternative was her sisters' unrelenting taunts, Ruta would take the uncertainty of her rescuer any day.

* * *

The harpies came a day later, squawking and spitting and calling her name.

"Little Ruta, where'd you go?"

"Little Ruta, look high and low!"

Ruta cringed at the sharpness of their consonants. It had only been a day, but she liked the way Charna said her name better.

"Harpies," Charna said from her vantage at the window. "Two of them. One's got blueish feathers, the other's are iridescent purple and green. They're approaching."

"My sisters," Ruta said. "They won't hurt you." *Probably.*

Charna wrenched the front door open. "Hello." She nodded curtly. "Got your sister in here. She's bruised up from the fall, as I reckon you can imagine."

Ruta tried to sit up in the bed, but struggled to do more than lift her head. The pain in her wing was still overwhelming when she tried to move. "Hey," she said weakly.

Her sisters only stared for a moment. Pity graced Kima's expression, her feathers waxy and smooth, while Volys's plumage was puffed up, disgust in her gaze.

"You fell," said the former.

"We told you not to," said the latter

"Yes, well, here we are," Ruta said.

"Can you fly?" asked Kima.

"She's broken her wing." Charna moved toward them, but stopped as Volys snapped her head around, leaving her body angled toward Ruta.

"This doesn't concern you, mountain girl," said Volys, eyes sharp, teeth sharper.

Charna looked at Ruta for confirmation. Ruta gave her a weary nod. Best to get this over with.

"I'll be just outside. Holler if you need me."

"Oh, we surely won't," Kima said with a sneer.

The door clicked shut, then there was silence.

Ruta did not resemble her sisters in any familial way. Their feathers were shiny and bright where hers were tawny, and their bone structure was all angles where Ruta was softer. She was not so rounded as Charna in her cheeks and belly, but still there was a sharpness missing from almost everything about her. It was genetics. They had the same nestmother, but not the same birth mother. There was only so much nurture could do in the way of molding her to their image, though Ruta had spared no effort trying.

Volys turned her eyes on Ruta, pinpricks of deepest blue. "Little Ruta failed the game."

"Little Ruta felt the pain," chimed in Kima.

"Little Ruta flies no more."

"Little Ruta, what a bore."

Ruta groaned. She hated their rhyming schemes. "Little Ruta, let me snore."

"Little Ruta, such a chore," Kima carried on.

Volys smiled a wide toothy grin. "Little Ruta, make some gore."

"Stop it." Ruta turned her head, unable to do more.

She wished she had command of her body, her legs, her wings. She would fly away and be done with their taunts. Still, it was more than injury keeping her grounded. She wasn't ready to leave this place where, even if only for a day, she'd felt welcome. There was something unfinished for her here.

"Looks like you won't be completing the hunt, dear sister." There was nothing *dear* in the way Kima spoke. "Indeed, you'll have to try again next year with the nestlings."

Ruta's stomach roiled. It was a humiliation beyond belief to fall, and if she could not catch an earthwalker and take their heart, she would be deemed a failure. She would be allowed to try again, but her success would be expected, not celebrated.

And if she failed again to bring them a bleeding heart, they would be justified in taking hers.

"What about her?" Kima inclined her head toward the door, a hint of mischief in her raspy voice. "It would be easy."

"Yes...let her nurse you back to health. Let her think you are fragile..." Volys held her long fingers wide then clenched them into a fist. "And then you strike!"

Ruta could do that...couldn't she? She was weak now, but in a few months her strength would return. She could fulfil the trial and be done with it. Then, she could ask to be put to work as a nestmother where she would never have to do it again. It would be over, and she could rest.

"Little Ruta, claw and scratch," said Kima in a sing-song voice.

"Little Ruta, claim your catch," finished Volys.

And then they were gone, through the door and back to the sky.

"Nice to have a visit from family," Charna said blandly as she re-entered the cabin.

"Not really." Ruta let out a long sigh and closed her eyes. She would think about killing Charna in the morning.

* * *

Ruta did not think about killing Charna the next day, or the day after that. She wasn't strong enough to think about killing anything larger than a spider, and Charna was quick to deter her from that, too.

"They're good for the garden," Charna said. "Eat pests and the like. And they make such pretty webs. Would be a waste."

Ruta liked the way Charna explained things—perfunctory, but with a touch of the personal not far behind. She was practical, but that didn't stop Charna from being herself.

Over the next few weeks, Ruta became handy with a
trowel and adept at weeding, though she struggled with
what to do with her broken wing when she stooped. It was
awkward at best, terribly painful at worst. A constant
reminder that she couldn't do the one thing all harpies
were born to do. Flight was not an option, so she did her
best to walk, her taloned feet making for uneasy travel
across the ground. But Ruta never complained. She far
preferred the discomfort of walking to the watchful eyes of
her sisters and their ridicule. Here, if she did something
wrong, Charna didn't mock her; she'd just show her how to
do it right and let her try again. It was nice to be taught
instead of expected to know.

They fell into a pattern. By day, Ruta tended the garden,
and by night, Charna tended Ruta's broken wing. Every
day Kima's and Volys's voices rang in Ruta's head, and
every day she resolutely ignored them.

"That's a lot of potatoes," Ruta said as Charna brought
the wheelbarrow around the side of the house.

"Two sets of hands work faster than one."

It was the closest thing to thanks Ruta was likely to get.
"How are we going to eat them all?"

"We're not." Charna pulled a burlap sack from the shed
behind the large glass greenhouse.

"Then why grow so many?"

Charna shrugged. "They're easy to grow up here. Same
with the onions and greens."

"Correct me if I'm wrong," Ruta began tentatively, "but
the mountains aren't exactly a prime location for
gardening."

"Nope."

"Then why do it up here?"

"Cause up here is where I live."

Ruta couldn't tell if Charna's short responses were an
invitation to let the subject drop or just the woman's mode
of operation, so she pressed on. "What can't you grow up
here?"

"Lots of things. Season's too short for peppers, and my tomatoes are abysmal." Charna glanced at the tomato plants currently climbing the wooden trellis by the greenhouse. "I always try, but the yield isn't worth doing more than a few plants."

"If you could grow anything, anything at all, what would it be?"

Charna tilted her head with a curious glaze over her eyes. Ruta leaned in, mesmerized by the way green and gray and blue all came together in her irises like a stormy spring sky or frostbitten flora.

"Citrus," Charna said at last.

"Citrus?"

"Like lemons."

Ruta shook her head.

"You don't know..." Charna's voice faded as her hands came together to form a diamond shape. "Yellow fruit with a waxy outer shell. Looks a might like snake skin."

"And you eat that?" Ruta had eaten many fruits in her day—blueberries, blackberries, salmon berries—but never anything that could be described as a snake berry. "Like an apple?"

"No!" Charna made a face. "It's quite sour. But it's also bright and tangy. It's good for adding flavor to savory dishes with dill or thyme, or you can drink it mixed with something sweeter." She ran a finger over her bottom lip as though tasting an imaginary beverage.

"You should definitely grow that," Ruta said. She was in grave danger of falling into the wistful gaze of her host.

But then, Charna cleared her throat and turned her back on Ruta. "Needs a warmer climate with longer days. No use trying to make it thrive here. Best to grow sensible things."

Sensible things, as Ruta found out, were things like beets, onions, radishes, and herbs. The stockpile grew by the day, and Ruta could not imagine a universe in which that amount of food would be necessary for two people.

"How do you expect all this to keep?" Ruta asked eventually. "Will we dry it all?"

"Some," Charna grunted.

"I've always wondered what a dehydrated carrot tastes like." Ruta had, in fact, never wondered that, but it seemed the thing to say. Charna was not exactly lifting her share of the weight when it came to conversation, but Ruta was not deterred. "What do you use it for?"

"It goes in soups and the like. Not very good on its own." Charna hefted another sack over her shoulder, but this time she loaded it into the wheelbarrow. "Help me with these."

"But we just unloaded!" Ruta's arms tensed at the very prospect. Though she was much recovered compared to her first day there, her wing still ached with a dull pain and every exertion brought new challenges.

"And now we're loading again."

"This is why they named you Charna, isn't it?" Ruta grumbled as she bent to lift another sack, holding her elbow out at an awkward angle to keep her wing from flopping forward.

"Why's that?"

"Because you're all doom and gloom." Ruta immediately regretted saying it. Charna had been nothing but generous to her, providing Ruta with food, shelter, and a healing hand. It was unkind, and it was untrue. "It's actually quite a pretty name, even if it does mean darkness."

Ruta was almost certain she saw Charna's lip twitch. Good. A smile would suit her. But then, a cloud passed overhead, casting the woman's face in shadow.

"It was my mother's." Charna's gaze flicked to a fixed point in the distance between two craggy peaks, heavy with the weight of longing.

"What'd you do, steal it from her?" Ruta asked.

"More or less."

"I'm sorry," Ruta said quickly. She'd only wanted to bring back Charna's smile, not open old wounds. "I didn't mean to pry."

"Not prying. Just don't talk about it much." Charna's voice wavered. "Not usually anyone to talk about it with."

Ruta's eyes didn't leave the space between Charna's shoulders—where wings would sprout, if the fates had sown the seeds. What was it like to have nothing there at all? An absurd urge overcame her to touch the other woman, to place her palm just beneath Charna's shoulder blades.

Tenderness had no place back home. She had known harpies to lie with other harpies, but as she heard it from her sisters, it was meant to be vicious and utilitarian. There were tales of harpies falling in love, but Ruta's sisters were full of derision for that sort of thing. Affection was shown only through barbs and banter, and Ruta had no taste for it. So, Ruta buried her desire for things like romance and companionship, for quiet and love. She would not get it from her life with her family.

Charna moved slowly through the world. She was never in a hurry, and Ruta liked that. She got her hands dirty, but always made time to wash up. Sometimes, she watched the sun as it moved across the sky, like it was wondrous, not commonplace. She taught Ruta with patience, never raising her voice when Ruta did things wrong. She was not liberal with her praise, but when it came, it felt like all the winds had joined together to lift Ruta into the sky.

"You can talk to me," Ruta said, quiet as the breeze.

"Not worth talking about." Charna cleared her throat and dragged her gaze from the peaks. "Now, want to learn about end blossom rot?"

"If I say no, will that make a difference?" But Ruta didn't want to say no. She'd light herself on fire if it was Charna doing the asking.

* * *

Charna didn't want to leave the harpy alone. She was on the road to recovery, her wing healing as well as expected. Ruta would fly again, Charna felt sure. So, the odd churn of Charna's stomach at the thought of being apart wasn't about Ruta's safety, then.

The feeling didn't settle as they passed the days in the garden. Charna found herself checking on Ruta far more than necessary, concocting reasons to interfere with her work.

"Water at the root. If the fruit gets wet, it may split and attract flies."

"When the onion stalks fall, then you know it's time to harvest."

"When pruning, pluck the suckers, not the leaves."

In the evenings, they'd cook together. She'd instruct Ruta in the ways of dicing an onion or peeling a carrot. It was alarming how little the harpy knew of knives. Harpies had their own, after all. Then, she'd watch over twin bowls of vegetables to see if Ruta liked it. Food was a joy Charna seldom got to share. She lived for the widening of Ruta's eyes as she marveled at the flavors after the first bite and the eager way she'd devour the rest.

"Does it bother you to abstain from meat?" Charna asked one night after a particularly satisfying meal of garlic roasted brassicas and potato leek stew.

Ruta paused in her determined attempt to lick the bowl clean. "I hadn't given it much thought."

"I thought harpies were carnivores."

"Omnivores. We mostly ate berries and insects back at the nest." Ruta lowered the bowl to reveal a faraway look in her eyes. "The nestmothers sometimes caught us rabbits, too. I don't mind going without. It's a nice change, actually."

"But you're hunters..." A flicker of something unpleasant crossed Ruta's gaze and Charna quickly added, "or at least most of your kind are, right?"

"Just because they hunt doesn't mean they have to." She swept hers and Charna's dishes into her arms and headed for the wash basin. "Hearts don't even taste good, you know. It's all about power and showing off."

"So, I'm not depriving you of necessary nutrients with a vegetarian diet?" Charna gripped the underside of the table as she spoke, trying not to let the tension show in her face. She'd never hunted before, and she didn't want to start now. But, for Ruta...Charna didn't like to think of the harpy wanting for anything.

"I like your cooking. And it's nice to know my food comes from a well-tended garden instead of from violence."

"I've always thought food is better when you grow it yourself."

Ruta leaned against the wall, hands making lazy circles in the wash basin. "Food is better when you grow it together."

"That can't be true."

"It is!" Ruta straightened. "No one does anything together where I'm from."

Charna could practically taste the melancholy in her words. "But you have sisters."

"I do. You've met them." Ruta chuckled darkly. "What about you?"

Deep in Charna's chest, a thread began to unravel. It was a conversation best avoided, else she'd fall apart in front of her guest. She never should have brought it up. She joined Ruta at the wash basin and reached for the scrubber. Their fingers met, and Charna's brain stuttered to a stop.

"Are you going to let me clean?" Ruta asked, laughter in her voice.

Charna looked at their hands, vying for the scrubber. Heat rose in her cheeks and neck, and she felt sure she looked as pink as a radish. She let go.

"You can finish up."

Charna didn't stop to wipe her hands on the way out the door, leaving sprinkles of soapy water in her wake. When at last she stood alone, blanketed in darkness, she clutched the fabric of her apron and tore the garment from her chest. The seams popped as her breath came in ragged bursts. She felt as though a rockslide had fallen across her shoulders, weighing her down, blocking her path.

Charna was used to solving problems. When her tomatoes were diseased, she added calcium to the soil. When her bread didn't rise, she increased the yeast. When her life had teetered on the edge of shadow, she had sacrificed everything so as not to fall. She knew how to adapt when things went wrong.

But the harpy falling in her pumpkin patch...that wasn't wrong. It was terribly, horribly, achingly right.

* * *

Ruta cleaned only one dish before following Charna. She wasn't nosy, she was just naturally curious. That's what her nestmothers always said. And when it came to Charna, Ruta wanted to know everything.

She raised a hand to protect her injured wing as she passed through the door, more out of habit than necessity. The break was healing nicely, but the closer she got to a full recovery the more uneasy she felt, less like herself. Once she was healthy, there would be nothing tethering her here but the heart in Charna's chest she could take home like a trophy. Her wing twinged as a gust of wind blew through her feathers. Never had she been so glad to feel pain, to know she was not sky worthy yet.

She followed the sounds of Charna's wheelbarrow across rocky terrain, beating a path up the mountain, against an increasingly harsh wind. Eventually, the squeaky wheel of Charna's wheelbarrow came to a stop, and Ruta followed suit. She tucked herself into an alcove between a few rocks to watch.

"It's good to see you," Charna said, voice raspy. "I didn't expect you both."

There was no reply, but Ruta could make out two people of similar stature just beyond. A torch held by the one on the left cast them all in firelight. The torch bearer wore a dark tunic with a bronze belt stretched over a round belly. The other wore more delicate cloth of deep burgundy with a square neckline edged in gold. Both had dark auburn hair and beards just like Charna's.

"I have potatoes." Charna hefted a bag from her wheelbarrow and held it out. When neither reached to take it, she lowered it to the ground. "And dried herbs. I put aside extra oregano for you, Malka, since it's your favorite. And for you, Dvan, there is an extra sack of peppermint for your teas."

The others, Malka and Dvan, said nothing.

"Alright...well...I'll go." Charna laughed bitterly. "You know, there's no one to hear you up top. You could say thank you. I wouldn't tell."

"Come, Dvan, it's late," said the one in chain mail—Malka. "We shouldn't tarry on the surface."

They gathered the potatoes and herbs and turned to go. Neither of them looked at Charna.

Ruta shivered. Charna, who was not very tall to begin with, looked somehow smaller and younger, with wider eyes and a softer jaw. If she hadn't been out of reach, Ruta would have touched her. It seemed an impossibility that she couldn't or that she shouldn't. She almost did it. She almost stepped out from her hiding place. She almost ruined it all.

But then, Dvan spoke, quiet and somber like a grave. "I dropped one, I think. No, go on without me. I'll catch up." There was the sound of boots scraping against rock as Dvan reappeared on the horizon, torch in hand.

For a moment, Dvan only stared at Charna, then she pulled her into a one-armed hug, tipping forward so their foreheads touched. It was an intimacy far greater than words, and still it was not enough. Ruta shuddered where she stood, a silent tear rolling down her cheek as she watched the way Charna's body folded into Dvan's, the tension bleeding from Charna's shoulders at the touch. And then it was gone. Dvan extricated herself from the embrace, gave Charna a last look, and vanished into the night.

Charna stood there a long time in the dark, her body lilting forward. Then, without warning, she took hold of her wheelbarrow and turned around to make the trek home. Ruta darted into the shadows.

She understood what it was to be apart from family—there was an entire sky between her and her sisters. But even when they were together, she didn't feel like this. Charna and her family, separated though they were, still loved one another in a way Ruta and her sisters never had. There was a breakage here like a bone had snapped, a pain she couldn't fully comprehend. But Charna had done her best to heal the break in Ruta's wing without ever knowing that injury for herself, so Ruta resolved to do the same.

* * *

Charna woke one morning to a familiar ache in her joints, a telltale reminder that she could not outrun the dark forever. The cold bit at her muscles all through the day as she and the harpy collected the last huckleberries before the season turned. Her own basket was only a quarter full by the time Ruta found her that afternoon with an abundance of berries, eager to turn them into pie.

"Can't believe I picked more than you!" Ruta said with a smile and a sharp jab of her elbow into Charna's ribs. The harpy looked ethereal against a backdrop of gray clouds, a single ray of light in an overcast world. "What happened? Did you fall asleep or something?"

"Or something," Charna grumbled.

"You haven't been sleeping well?"

Charna didn't have it in her to tell the truth of it. She'd been sleeping *too* well. All she wanted to do was sleep. That was the trouble.

Ruta took Charna's basket and bent to strip a handful of dark berries from a nearby bush. "You shouldn't overexert yourself. Why don't you let me handle the berry picking and you go get some rest?" The harpy shooed her back toward the cabin, and Charna had no mind to argue.

The sweet smell of stewed huckleberries woke her. Ruta tended a pot over the fire, a wooden spoon in hand. She hummed a quiet melody. Charna watched, mesmerized by the gentle cyclical motion as Ruta stirred. The harpy was strangely beautiful, wrapped up in the mundanity of Charna's life. Charna had seen harpies fly and dive, making a ballroom of the sky as they waltzed between clouds, and still she thought Ruta looked most striking wearing Charna's apron with a little smudge of huckleberry on her chin.

It was the song. That was it. It had to be. Ruta might have promised not to eat her heart, but she was still a harpy, capable of stopping Charna in her tracks with a few notes. But then, Ruta stopped humming, eyes bright as they landed on Charna.

It wasn't the song.

"You're awake! Good. I put a pie in the oven, but I thought some huckleberry sauce wouldn't go amiss. We could have it on bread, maybe. Or we could eat it with spoons like soup. I just love them on their own!"

It was difficult this time of year to do much of anything, let alone smile, but Charna did, if only for Ruta. She would do almost anything for Ruta.

"Smells delicious."

"Tastes good, too!" Ruta held out the spoon and gently cupped her hand around it as she crossed to Charna's bed. "Here, try."

As Ruta lowered the spoon to Charna's lips, Charna felt the odd and overwhelming urge to cry. Ruta was so pleased, and Charna wanted to keep on making her so. She would give her all the huckleberries in the world if she thought it would do the trick. But Charna could not move the weight on her chest. It was familiar by now, like a bear come to hibernate in her bones each winter, but just because she knew it was coming didn't make it easier to fight.

"You don't like it." Ruta's voice wavered and her face fell. "I didn't add the right spices."

Charna scrambled to catch the harpy's wrist as she moved away. "It's not the spices."

"Then I cooked them too long."

"No, you didn't."

"Then what is it? What did I do wrong?"

"Nothing," Charna whispered, tugging on Ruta's hand.

Ruta's big brown eyes met Charna's, a tempest of worry in her gaze. "Oh, no. Are you sick?" She leaned over the bed to press the back of her hand to Charna's forehead.

Charna tried to say no, but...if not exactly a sickness, what was it? Just because something didn't cause a fever or a flu didn't mean she wasn't ailing. "Something like that," she finally managed.

Ruta didn't waste a second. She took the berries off the fire and replaced them with the kettle, preparing the tea leaves they'd spent all season gathering. When she was done, she brought over two steaming mugs.

"I hate being sick," Ruta said firmly. "It's terrible."

Charna just nodded and sipped her tea, acutely aware of the way the harpy perched at the edge of the bed, so close to her toes.

"The sore throat, the drippy sinuses, the exhaustion..." She wrinkled her nose. "When all your feathers fall out—though I guess that doesn't happen to you."

Ruta was rambling now, something Charna was happy to let her do. She liked the sound of conversation in her cabin. Her eyes shuttered and her head fell back against the headboard.

"You know what the worst bit is? Being alone. You have to be careful not to infect anyone, so you isolate and hope—when you get better—you didn't miss too much. I don't like to be alone, do you?"

Charna cracked open her eyes at the question, moisture welling in the corners and threatening to spill. "I'm always alone," she croaked, and the tears finally came.

Ruta placed a hand on Charna's knee. Her touch was like a single flickering ember in a firepit long abandoned. Charna curled in on herself, making her body as small as she could. She wanted to put her head down and sleep through the miserable months ahead. She would wake again when the sun's warmth returned.

But warmth was right there. Ruta's weight shifted as she crawled up the bed to tuck herself around Charna. Her hand moved from its place on Charna's knee to wrap around her middle, pulling her close. Ruta's breath tickled the back of Charna's neck, gentle and warm. The harpy's heart beat a bruise into Charna's shoulder, and she hoped it made a mark. Still, Charna shivered at the touch. It had been so long since she'd been held.

Hot tears leaked from Charna's eyes, running messily down her cheeks and into the linens. She wished she could stop. It all felt so silly, to cry over nothing. But nothing was what got her here in the first place. She'd fought nothing and she'd won, but depression was not a single battle; it was a long and tiresome war.

"You," came Ruta's voice, quiet and muffled against her skin, "are not alone."

Charna came undone, unraveling like a poorly knit sweater in Ruta's arms. The harpy's wings unfolded above them to create a canopy as Charna turned to face her. Somehow, it was easier without the gloomy winter world looking at them. In Ruta's embrace, there was no gray sky outside, no pile of dishes that needed doing, no cold creeping into her bones. There was only Ruta.

"You are not alone," Ruta repeated. This time, she was looking directly into Charna's eyes, unblinking. Her fingers traced the line of Charna's clavicle, rounding her shoulder, then up to her throat. "Not while I'm here."

Everything in Charna screamed to look away, to find a distraction. If they never went down this road, it would be simpler when Ruta left, it would hurt so much less. But Ruta had not left. Not yet. She was here, and she was close, propped up on her hip so she leaned over Charna inches away. It would be so easy to just...

"May I..." Charna reached up, thumb brushing Ruta's lower lip.

"Yes," Ruta breathed.

Charna lifted herself up on an elbow until she was nose to nose with the harpy. Then, experimentally touched her lips to Ruta's. It was light and quick. Charna feared it hadn't happened at all, but as she drew back, Ruta's eyes fluttered open. She stared at Charna, lips parted. A beat passed, then two, then, just like she had all those months ago when she fell from the sky, the harpy crashed down toward her.

Kissing wasn't something Charna was accustomed to. It had been longer than she cared to admit since she'd been touched like this. There had been a girl back home under the mountain. They had been all hormones and limbs and tongues and teeth. But then, Charna had slipped into her shadows, and the girl had moved on to someone brighter. Most people Charna met these days were travelers—traders, or hunters. It was rare one was a woman, and rarer still that she was inclined like Charna, but she'd had a tumble or two since leaving home. Once with an axe-wielding dragon slayer and once with a soft-spoken botanist. Neither had stayed more than one night. It was that which Charna craved—not the release, but the steadfast comfort of another person in her world day after day.

As Ruta's lips pressed into her neck, her mouth warm and soft and achingly slow, Charna didn't dare let go, hands finding purchase on the harpy's hips. She felt dizzy with the taste of Ruta on her tongue, the scent of her—pine and maple and huckleberries.

"Ruta," she said breathlessly. "Wait, I—"

Ruta tilted her chin up to look Charna in the eye. Her fingers were knotted in Charna's shirt, her weight pressing low on Charna's belly. Immediately, Charna cursed herself for saying anything at all.

"Never mind."

"No, no, say it." Ruta flexed her hand and eased off Charna carefully.

Charna went with her, rolling onto her side and slotting their legs together, desperate not to lose the warmth between them.

"I was just going to say that I...what I meant is..." But Charna couldn't find the words. Maybe she wanted to tell her how special this was. Not the kissing. Not *just* the kissing. But all of it. The way Ruta dedicated so much to learning Charna's way of life, the way Ruta had helped her all season with the gardening and the harvest, the way Ruta had seen her tired and full of unearned sadness and had sat beside her, never asking her to cheer up. But that was too much. So instead, Charna just said, "Thank you."

A laugh broke from Ruta's chest, high and loud and altogether uncalled for in Charna's expert opinion. That would be it, then. Ruta would laugh at her, pack up her things, and be on her way. The very idea of it left her feeling bruised and weary, but even that was better than numb.

Ruta did no such thing. Instead, she brushed her fingers through Charna's beard and said, "Why are you thanking me?"

"I—"

"You saved my life, remember? You gave me a place to sleep, you taught me to cook and grow things. You let a harpy overturn your entire life and I've done nothing to earn that kindness."

"Kindness? No, that was just—"

"Charna... are you really going to argue?" A fond annoyance twitched across Ruta's lips. "You are so generous and wonderful and the worst thing about it is that I don't think you know."

"No one's ever called me those things." A blush crept into her cheeks, but Charna didn't dare look away.

Ruta traced the outline of Charna's brow. "Well, then let me be the first. And the second. And the third. I will tell you all the days you'll let me."

The kiss came quiet and earnest and full of longing. Charna wanted to wrap herself in feathers and never emerge.

"I didn't think I'd ever meet someone like you," Ruta whispered.

"What, short and callused and full of doom and gloom?" Charna said it like a joke, but the last words, echoes of something Ruta had once said, were like barbs on her tongue.

Ruta paused, hand knotted in Charna's hair. "I'm sorry. I shouldn't have said it."

"It's true."

"No, it isn't."

"But..." Charna let her gaze slip and fall to the linens beneath them. "I *am* gloomy. At least while the weather's like this. Can't snap out of it while it's dark and dreary."

"So...you're like a citrus tree."

That jostled something in Charna enough for her lips to crack into a half-smile. "I'm a what?"

"You need a warmer climate and longer days. You need the sun so you can thrive."

"So, what, I wait until summer and then..."

"You produce profoundly sour fruit!" Ruta tapped the tip of Charna's nose with her finger.

Charna didn't have it in her to laugh. Instead, she let herself fall back against the pillows and said, "I don't live in a warmer climate, though. So, I guess I'll stay gloomy."

"Maybe today you feel gloomy." Ruta set her head down next to Charna's. "And maybe you will tomorrow. Maybe you will feel this way all your days. But you are not the same as what you feel. I see you, Charna. I see a woman who is fiercely capable, who is willing to share more than she's been offered, and who is unafraid to live her life how she wants. That is not doom or gloom. That's..." Ruta trailed off and a smile tugged at her lips. "That's just Charna."

"And... that's what you want?" Charna asked. Ruta had called her unafraid, but Charna had never felt so terrified.

"It is." Ruta placed a hand over Charna's heart. "My sisters...they want action and adrenaline. They want to feel good and powerful and strong. I have always wanted something different. I didn't think I would ever find it. I didn't think I'd be allowed. I want to *know* someone. I want to feel what they feel. I want to lo—"

Charna waited for the rest of the word to drop, but it never did. "You want to...love...?"

Ruta nodded silently.

"Then it's a good thing we feel the same," Charna murmured, quiet as could be. It felt impossible to say aloud. It felt impossible not to. They were from different worlds—Charna of the earth, Ruta of the sky—but here, they were of neither. Or perhaps, they were of each other. "I want you here with me, Ruta. No matter what that looks like. You make me feel alive. You make me feel like I'm flying."

Ruta pulled Charna closer, their lips barely touching. "Do you know the first rule of flying?"

"I don't."

"Don't look down." Ruta gave her a sly smile as she inched down the bed, fingers trailing along Charna's stomach.

"W-why do they say that?" Charna asked, craning to see as Ruta's lips dragged across her belly and lower and lower and lower...

"It's so you don't fall."

The last thing she remembered thinking before Ruta's touch made her mind go blank was that Ruta was being silly with her warnings; Charna had already fallen.

* * *

Ruta woke up angry. Well, first she woke up bleary and content and full of hope. Charna lay beside her, deep in slumber. There had been a thousand little touches between them, and a thousand more affirmations. Seeing Charna's smile felt more like winning than any race against her sisters. Charna looked peaceful with her hair splayed out on the pillow and her hand tucked beneath her cheek— except for a little frown at the corners of her lips. Even in slumber, she was still sad.

Sadness did not belong in Charna's home. Sadness was not welcome here. And so, Ruta decided to drive it out. She was nearly all the way up the mountain to the double peaks in the distance by the time her brain caught up to her.

She passed the place where she'd watched from the shadows to find a narrow path that led to an opening in the mountain, a circular cave entrance lined by unlit torches.

"I'm here to see Dvan," she said to the guard posted there.

They gave Ruta a once over, gaze lingering on her wings, but shrugged and dipped into the darkness. Moments later, they returned with Charna's sister.

"What can I do for you?" Dvan asked, curious eyes sweeping over Ruta from head to talons. "Don't have many visitors from the sky kingdoms."

"Ah, so you speak," Ruta snarled, adopting the lilt and gruffness of Charna's speech by instinct. "Thought maybe you just didn't talk to folks outside your own."

"No, we deal with traders and the like here," Dvan said, eyes narrowing. "Though I know we have a bit of a reputation for being isolated."

"Then why do you shun her?"

Dvan blinked in confusion, then realization seemed to dawn on her. "Not here," she murmured and pointed back up the path. "Let us speak in private."

Ruta led the way back up the path, then turned to face Dvan. In the light, she looked different, older. Lines creased her face in places and there were flecks of gray in her beard. But even with the years between her and Charna, they looked alike. Their eyes were light lichen green, and they had the same divot in their forehead right between the brows.

"Why won't you talk to your sister?" Ruta asked now that there was some distance between them and the cave entrance. "She misses you, and you live so close. Why can't you just be family?"

Dvan sighed and shook her head. "I wish it was that simple. I really do."

"Then make it simple. Go see her!"

"I can't."

"You *won't*."

"You have the right of it." Dvan nodded solemnly. "But you must understand, if I did, I'd be shunned, too. We are not permitted to leave the mountain—not for more than a day at a time, and only when absolutely necessary. It is against our teachings. The mountain is our home, our mother, our god. To leave her is the worst thing one of our people can do."

"Then why cast Charna out? She wants so badly to be with her family. It is all she wants. To not be alone. Why force her to leave?"

"We didn't." Dvan sighed and sat on a large slab of granite. "Charna left all on her own. She chose this path. The darkness of the mountain never suited her. She was always prone to fits of unease. We tried everything—everything except what she needed."

"The sun," Ruta whispered. "That's what she needed, wasn't it?"

Dvan nodded. "There was a darkness pulling her under. I wish we could have made her better but..." She trailed off, eyes distant. "Knowing how close we were to losing her to the shadows, I'm glad, at least, if we had to lose her, it was to the sun. Even if I can't speak to her, knowing she is alive...it has to be enough."

"But it isn't. For either of you."

"No." Dvan shrugged. "But she doesn't want to return. If she did, we would welcome her with open arms. She may not want to be alone, but she will never come home. Of that, I am sure."

Ruta opened her mouth to argue, but Dvan stood and set her jaw.

"It's good that you came," she said.

"It is?" Ruta asked.

"Now I know she is not truly alone. She has you." Dvan smiled Charna's smile and turned away, pausing to say over her shoulder, "I worry for her. It's what us big sisters do."

Ruta swallowed, wishing that had ever once been true of her own.

* * *

Charna and Ruta made warmth in the little cabin all through the cold season, and though Charna's shadows didn't fully recede, they were far less troublesome than they'd been in years past. It was a relief to find the harpy beside her each morning, to know that there was good food, good company, and good sex to look forward to.

When they spotted the first green leaves amid the snow, Charna declared it was time to begin sowing seeds in her greenhouse, and they fell into an easy pattern. The sun slowly returned, and the snow melted away.

And Charna was not happy.

She spotted Ruta on more than one occasion looking up at the sky, as if wishing she were among the clouds. And then, one fateful warm morning, a feather landed in Charna's garden.

"You miss them, don't you?" she asked, almost against her better judgement. "Your sisters."

Ruta nodded. "I suppose, just as you miss yours."

They'd talked of Charna's family, of her exile. She had no regrets, but that didn't mean the wounds weren't still there, raw and untended by years of solitude. They'd pointedly not spoken at all of Ruta's family in all this time, and though Charna sometimes wished it could go on this way, she knew they'd be back soon.

"I suppose," Charna said. "Sometimes I think it would be easier if they weren't so close. It might hurt less if I could just...move on."

"Where would you move?"

"Somewhere warm." Charna smiled at the thought. "Somewhere I could grow things in neat little rows, where the soil's rich and the sun is bright. Somewhere a citrus tree could thrive."

"That sounds nice."

"It does." Charna shook herself. "But it's impossible."

Ruta looked at her with curious eyes. "Is it?"

Charna just shrugged. "Tell me about them," she said eventually. "Your sisters."

"Sisters are complicated." Ruta kept her focus on the weeding. "Mine are...well, they're better fliers than me, both of them. Better hunters, too, I expect. Better at everything, really."

"Now that can't be true. You must be better at something." Charna knelt in the dirt beside her.

"Not really," Ruta said dully.

"Come, now. You can't tell me they're better at gardening." Charna pointed to the rows of spinach and radishes they'd just planted. "Or what about baking pie? Or stewing huckleberries?"

Ruta just shrugged. "If they were here, I'm sure they'd prove skilled at it all."

"Yes, well, they aren't here." Charna laid a kiss on Ruta's shoulder. "You aren't your sisters, and you don't have to be. Trying to be them will only bring you pain."

Ruta didn't look up. She simply finished pulling the last of the pesky weeds and brushed her hands on her apron before stalking off into the woods.

"Don't forget we have a pie baking!" Charna called after her.

There was no reply. Another feather gently bobbed on the wind to land in Charna's outstretched palm.

* * *

Ruta stared at the sky. It was vast and quickly changing from blue to pink to purple with the setting sun.

Soon.

She could feel it in the air, she could feel it in her chest. Her sisters were close.

"Little Ruta, come to play."

"Little Ruta, seize the day."

They descended on her, twin birds of prey, in a cyclone of feathers and talons and teeth.

"Little Ruta, play your part."

"Little Ruta, take a heart."

Ruta couldn't help but smile. "Kima, Volys."

"It's good to see us, isn't it?" Volys crooned.

And it was. Something inside Ruta settled into place and her muscles relaxed.

Kima gripped her shoulder as Volys's fingers closed around the other.

"Little Ruta of the earth."

"Little Ruta, prove your worth."

Ruta sighed and rolled her eyes. "You can stop with the riddles."

"Have you done it yet?" asked Kima. "Have you taken a heart?"

"No," Ruta said.

"But you will." Kima squeezed her shoulder. "You have plans, yes?"

"You will take the hairy woman's?" Volys asked.

"You mean Charna?" Ruta felt an uneasy plunge of her stomach. She wanted so badly to refute them, to stand tall and strong and know it was for Charna. But still, something in her craved her sisters' approval. She shrank under their scrutiny. "I...I suppose I could."

There was a strangled sound and a splat behind her. Ruta whipped around to see the very object of their discussion standing between a pair of pine trees, an upturned pie covering her boots in pastry and filling.

Ruta had only a moment to mourn the loss of such a delicious smelling pie before Charna turned tail and ran. Ruta's stomach churned and heaved. This was so much worse than anything her sisters could levy at her.

"Charna, wait!" she yelled after her, but it was too late.

"Little Ruta must make haste."

"Little Ruta win the race."

Ruta didn't stop to listen, but her sisters' chants followed her as she chased after Charna. Her talons bit into the ground awkwardly as she hobbled over pinecones and needles, but she barely felt the pain. It was nothing to the ache in her chest at the thought of losing Charna. Still, Charna would always be faster than Ruta on the ground...so she would have to try something else. She would have to be a harpy.

She opened her wings, and she flew.

"Little Ruta taking flight."

"Little Ruta time to fight."

Two bodies rose beside her. Sisters, three, side by side. It was all she'd ever wanted from them. But it was too little too late. She didn't want it anymore.

She spotted Charna dashing toward the cabin. With a burst of speed, Ruta beat her there, landing in the space between Charna and the door.

"Charna, please," she said, folding her wings behind her. "I'm not going to hurt you."

Charna panted, hands on her knees. "But you said...you said you were going to take my heart."

"No. Never." Ruta placed a hand over her own. "But mine's all yours, if you want it."

Charna shook her head in bewilderment. "But...your sisters are here to take you home."

"Home is where *you* are, whether that is here on this mountain, or somewhere we could start that citrus tree farm." Ruta took a tentative step forward. "I just...want to be with you."

Charna fell into Ruta's embrace and she let out a tired sob.

"I love you," Ruta whispered into her hair.

Wings beat down on them like thunder, and the taunting voices of her sisters chorused all around. Ruta tried to drown them out. She folded her wings around Charna, a protective circle hiding her from view, and whispered her confession over and over like a mantra. Her sisters' voices reached a crescendo above, toppling down on them like a rockslide of malice and mockery.

"Little Ruta, aim to kill."

"Little Ruta, blood will spill."

"Oh, *shut up*," Ruta snapped, shooting a piercing look at each of her sisters in turn. She extracted herself from Charna's embrace and stepped in front of her, wings spread wide. "And leave this place. I don't want to see either of you around here again."

Volys and Kima snarled at her.

"So, it is to be exile, is it, sister?" Volys asked.

"You won't be welcome back home," Kima said.

"It isn't home to me, not anymore." Ruta's tone softened. It was her choice, and one she knew was right without a doubt, but that didn't make it any less final.

"Then you will be without a flock, a harpy no more," Kima said, a lilt to her voice that was almost sad.

"She has her own flock." Charna stepped forward, brushing past Ruta's outstretched wing to take her hand. "And that is never what made her a harpy. She may lose you, but she has not lost herself."

"Is this truly what you want?" Kima asked.

"It is." Ruta squeezed Charna's hand tight. "It is exactly what I want."

This was it. In all likelihood, she would never see any of her harpy family again. This was goodbye.

"They will speak of you to the hatchlings, a warning tale." Volys sneered. "You will be the shame of us all."

Then again, goodbyes were overrated. "I think I can live with that," Ruta said with a shrug.

Kima shook her head, but Volys let out a cackle. The ground shook as they took off, back into the sky.

"Little Ruta's heart was lost."

"Little Ruta paid the cost."

"Are you really sure?" asked Charna.

Ruta didn't have to think twice. She squeezed Charna's hand and pulled her close. "Absolutely."

Their lips met, and it was like the sun shone just for them.

"So, where is home?" Ruta asked when they parted. "Where shall we make it?"

Charna looked at the cabin behind them, at the rows of little sprouts, and then at the peaks up above.

"I don't know. But I think...I'd like to see what else the world has to offer."

"What about your family?" Ruta asked with a glance back at the peaks in the distance.

Charna kept her gaze resolutely forward. "*You* are my family."

Ruta held out her hand and Charna took it. She spread her wings wide and peered out over the mountain's edge. It was a long way down, but at least they'd fall together.

"Don't Look Down" is a stand-alone short story by Rosiee Thor, whose short fiction can be found in anthologies such as *Common Bonds: A Speculative Aromantic Anthology* and *Being Ace: An Anthology of Queer, Trans, Femme, and Disabled Stories of Asexual Love and Connection*. In longer form, Rosiee is the author of young adult novels *Tarnished are the Stars* and *Fire Becomes Her*, the picture book *The Meaning of Pride*, and the video game tie-in novel *Life is Strange: Steph's Story*. You can find Rosiee online at www.rosieethor.com or on social media @rosieethor.

Piracy is Not A Five-Year Plan

J.S. Fields

Sapphic Representation: Lesbian, Polyamory

Heat Level: Low

Content Warnings: Coarse Language, Violence, Plastic Dinosaurs in Danger

Senna's Moon Avoidance Plan:

√*Year 0 – graduate from Yoint! Federated Airship Academy*
√*Year 1 – pilot's license*
√*Year 2 – buy affordable airship; service appropriately. Follow up on the listing for the VB45 base trim with no extended warranty. Redo leatherwork? Upholstery upgrade? Definitely new balloon. Don't need all the pressurized cargo space, maybe guest rooms?*
(to-do) *Years 3-5 – offer high-end, luxury transport across the globe. Make obscene amounts of money and buy permanent Earth citizenship (is that a thing? Enough money would make it a thing). Home can be a budget airship because anything is better than the moon.*

Captain Senna McBride of the Federated Luxury Airship *You Must Be Daft* jabbed a leather-clad finger onto the screen showing her year-to-date budget. Every column, every account, showed red. Red in the deposit account for her current crop of passengers. Red in the maintenance account that kept her balloon filled with helium and her backup motors serviced. Red in the FOR EMERGENCIES ONLY account that no one knew about but her and her accountant.

Every last account, every last dollar that Senna had earned in the five years since graduating from Yoint! Federated Airship Academy, gone. Just like that. Sure, she'd put off the repeated requests from her accountant to discuss the *Daft's* future so maybe this was partly on her. But all red? All the accounts had been brimming when they'd tethered in Limerick, Ireland. Senna had checked.

And since arriving, they'd taken on new passengers (collecting deposits), and had a few days of shore leave (a cost, sure, but not enough to wipe the aforementioned income). Margins were tight some months, but they hadn't been this month. Senna had checked!

Where in the world had the money gone?

"Money is ephemeral, if you think about it," Alex Biddleman, Senna's accountant, said. She leaned against the wall in Senna's office like she owned the world, her peony-covered tank top showing arms too muscular for spreadsheets. Senna had never cared for Alex's taste in clothing—floral and tight—but she hadn't hired her for sartorial reasons. She might have hired her for her musculature, but no one could prove that. They had graduated the same year from Yoint! and that was enough to douse any potential suspicions. Good captains did not date their employees. It was in the Yoint! handbook.

Alex continued, "Inputs minus outputs. The past eight months we have spent more than we've brought in. The accounts are fine one day, with inputs, but then a big bill shoots them down to the parched ocean floor." Alex paused, considered, then said, "Again, I think you need to consider higher value cargo transport."

Through an overhead speaker, the tinny voice of the *Daft* said, "Captain to Recreation Level 2. Multiple guests requesting departure time."

"Please let them know we're only five minutes overdue, and the port authority can get a touch behind. I'm certain it is nothing to worry about." Senna's airship was idling, engines on, waiting for tether release and airspace clearance. Using her arm unit Senna routed a request to Derrik for a departure update and brought her mind back to the banking problem. "We should be carrying ample balances," Senna said, careful to keep her tone neutral. "We moved into the honeymooners' market, and they've been taking advantage of our bonus amenities packages."

"Nothing yet, Cap'n," returned Derrik through Senna's arm comm.

Not good. She'd have to ping ground control personally to get answers. Her passengers had finished boarding hours ago and were ready for their new adventure, and her crew were waterlogged and ready to move on. Senna saw it on their faces, that sort of antsy jumpiness right before a new voyage, a new continent, a new city. Better for everyone to hit the open air.

"Ughhh." Alex tugged a loose strand of hair, flexing a well-defined bicep as she did so. "It's not about what we *should* have. It's what we *don't* have. Whatever *was* there, *isn't* there. There's been a slow net loss for a while and *something* just, really brought things to a head, you know? Who knows why?" Alex's arms rotated around her head in Muppet-like waves. "The Federation is always raising taxes, you know? Crews spend money. Point is, we need to switch business models or you'll lose your fucking ship, Senna." Under her breath, Senna thought she heard Alex say, "The *Daft* isn't just your home, you know."

"We will not lose the *Daft*." Senna ignored the lack of "captain" in Alex's statement. She would not lose the ship because she could not lose the ship. Growing up homeless on the streets of Chicago, Illinois, the *Daft* was her first ever house, her first ever *home*. Senna had paid her dues, she paid her bills, and she paid her employees. She would find the money.

"Captain to the galley," said the *Daft*. "The peaches have run out in the buffet."

"Tell Chef Chia," Senna said to the speaker. "This should not be routed to the captain's line." With a bright, captain smile and a straightening of her starched Federation Captain's sash, she said to Alex, "I think you might need a vacation. You sound tense. Maybe a walk around the gondola, and we could revisit this conversation later?"

"Oh my god, I don't need a vacation! I need you to listen!"

Senna would not yell and she would not argue. That was not how one got off the streets and into the Yoint! Academy, nor how one graduated third in their class. Good airship captains smiled, and listened to criticism, and diffused situations before their exceedingly few office knickknacks became projectiles. Yoint!—run by the Federation—had tag lines specifically developed for situations of brewing crew hostility. "For potential vacation destinations, I've heard the moon is lovely this time of year. I have a brochure I can give you if you'd like."

What the brochure—given to her by the Federation Tourism Board—did not mention was that the moon was also where most of the world's poor had landed after glacial melt raised sea levels and half of Earth's useable land had disappeared underwater. Senna had been spared that fate, because Senna's parents had gone so Senna could stay and attend the academy. Attend the academy free of charge, thanks to their "volunteering," and, eventually, their death in some unnamed lunar mine.

"I hate you so much right now and stop straightening your damn sash. It looks fine. You look fine." Alex's eyes dropped contact, just for a split second, before she said, "We're not at Yoint! anymore. Would you just *please* consider ditching that damn plan?" Alex pointed up, but Senna didn't need to look. She knew what was written on the stained bar napkin mounted above her head, behind plexiglass, in a waterproof frame.

"As stated in the Yoint! business model, a five-year plan is critical to success."

"Captain?" The voice of Chef Chia rang over the ship speaker system. "The peaches are out of control. I'm out for a bit."

Chia might need a vacation as well. Senna again spoke to the comm. "Chia, there's nowhere *to* go. If you're overwhelmed, I'll be there in twenty minutes after I speak with ground control. We will get the peaches under control."

Chia did not respond.

"Clearly things are disintegrating," Alex countered, crossing her arms and squaring surprisingly broad shoulders. Her eyes narrowed. "Is this just about your five-year plan? Dude, I have a pen in my pocket and I can edit that napkin right now if you let me. Year 1 where you get your Federation pilot license, that's fine. Year 2 get the VB45 airship we're in, sure. It's the years 3-5 that we need to change." A pen appeared, cap flicked off and onto the floor. Alex hopped onto Senna's desk and fingered the plexiglass frame. "Is it glued or something?"

"Stop! Do not touch that, or the desk, or...anything!" Senna said, breaking her captain-cool for the first time in months. She grabbed Alex's upper arm, swallowed down exactly three inappropriate thoughts, and hauled Alex to the floor. Then she took a long, calming breath, and said, "Leave it alone, Alex."

Alex said, eyes bugging, "Where've you been hiding the fire?"

Senna again straightened her sash, then cleared her throat. She was not made of fire, she was made of cool, reflective calm. "The VB45s, the whole VB lines, are antiques."

"I do not care," Alex responded, only half-cowed, bristle returning to her stance.

Senna went back to diffusion mode. "They were originally built for large mechanical transport. But here in 2076, the shipping focus has changed from the air to space. Not a lot on Earth that still needs to be transported in tightly sealed compartments, although the VB45s have enough insulation that they *could* do space, if enough modifications were made. Anyway, those compartments are what you and the guests sleep in. I knocked down the walls, reinsulated, and made the berths. I sold candy bars, bras, electric bikes, every manner of consumable to cover the down payment and the materials for the upgrades. My ship is..." Senna swallowed. "Please don't touch things in my office. It's..." She didn't want to say special, because a bar napkin wasn't special. It was more that the *Daft* was hers according to the Federation, and having her own titled airship was the only dream Senna could remember having since her parents had left. Land she could never afford. An airship though? There was a solid, achievable dream. The *Daft* was special.

"Not trying to mess with your ship," Alex said. "I know how much work you put in, the renovations and such. I live here too, yeah. I'm just trying to talk long-term forecasts because unexpected things happen and I think you should be more ready for them."

Senna snorted—a deeply unladylike sound she instantly tried to play off as a cough and when that failed to settle her, she turned her head. The scenery outside her narrow office window showed grey skies that perfectly mirrored the mood she'd been trying not to show. "I can fit twenty high-paying passengers in the *Daft's* hold, each in their own private two-room suite. We charge for every extra amenity, like the private chef, high-altitude shuffleboard, a repository of holo videos, and the 'adult' floor for the more horizontally-inclined. Our income stream is substantial. The only potential explanation is that the money has been stolen, and I'd need my accountant to help me track that down, correct? Show me the recent transactions. Maybe together we can sort the leak." She turned to glare at the computer console on her desk, which still read *AWAITING CLEARANCE*. "Give me just a moment. *Daft*, do we have a reason yet for the delay?"

"The *Daft's* departure slot has been changed. The Air Port of Limerick appreciates your patience and willingness to move to the back of our departure queue."

They were ten minutes behind now, for a clerical error? "I didn't request that," Senna said as she rubbed her temples. "Can we get our original slot back?"

The *Daft* replied, "The release order cannot be changed once airships are already loosed. Anticipated time to departure, five minutes."

She could live with another five minutes. Senna had a built-in two-hour buffer on any trip specifically for these reasons. "Thank you, *Daft*. Alex, while we are waiting, why don't we track down our potential thief."

Again, Alex's focus flicked, momentarily, from Senna. "Stealing would be...I mean no one is just gonna *steal* from you Senna. Maybe like, *borrow*, but short time frame, if it did happen." Alex's hands moved to her hips, suddenly very much an accountant. "Before we get into that, consider. I have a friend who has some higher value cargo we could haul. Scrap the passengers, the VB45s were never designed for this. These are cargo ships. Well-insulated, well-armored cargo ships. Space markets are opening up, and those markets are hungry for raw materials of a very certain nature. We can't go into space, but we can go a hell of a lot higher than most airships without damaging the goods we're hauling."

Senna blinked. She'd run enough cargo for a lifetime. Having a home meant you didn't need to do other people's errands, at the very least. The *Daft* was a luxury airship, a traveling home where you didn't have to think about your next meal, your next score, and whether or not your bed that night would have cockroaches.

Very firmly and very, very captainingly, Senna said, "No."

Alex's arms all but unraveled. She slumped forward, only for a moment, before righting herself. "You're forcing my hand. Asshole," Alex followed the insult with a hair flip that very clearly was meant to shut Senna down.

"I'm still your captain, Alex," Senna said, swallowing her anger.

"Captain McBride, there is an irregularity in the docking bay," the *Daft* said over the main speaker system.

"Can't Derrik handle it? Does it need a captain?"

"A captain is not required, but human presence should be sent."

"Tell Derrik to get down there. Do we have clearance to leave yet?"

"Captain to the cargo hold," the *Daft* said in response.

"Later. I'm heading to outpost now." She turned back to Alex. "We can continue—"

Alex grimaced, nose scrunched like a pug's. "Listen to me!" Alex stepped into Senna and Senna stepped back, keeping professional distance.

Alex made to step in again, but paused when the speaker once again called out. "Captain to the outpost!" clanged loud enough to disrupt the flight pattern of every migratory bird within three miles of them. "Captain to the bridge outpost. Comm received from the city center. Requesting fingerprint authorization from the outpost for security."

"That won't be a departure clearance," Alex said with concerning certainty.

Senna pushed Alex back, gingerly, properly, with the tips of her two index fingers. She would not get handsy with a woman whose arms could crush walnuts. "You don't know that. We will continue later."

"Uh huh."

Scowling, Senna pushed past Alex and headed to the bridge—a translucent plexiglass bubble on the ship's belly that was lovingly referred to as "outpost" by anyone flying a VB model. Outposts in the VB models had been meant as a sort of reverse crow's nest, installed as a safety measure. Early VB models, lines one through thirty, had done stellar work at floating, just not steering, and a few too many promising captains had skewered their ships on mountain tops. The outpost gave a great view of the ship's stomach and had significantly decreased the number of impaled airships.

Derrik, lead engineer and gardener for the *Daft,* greeted Senna with a grunt when she entered. None on her payroll had ever been particularly chatty, but Limerick weather had made the crew even more taciturn than usual. Senna had caught the group a handful of times now crowded into corners, whispering. It was nice they had each other though, and a berth on a ship they could call their own.

"Comm," Derrik said unnecessarily to Senna.

"How are your tomatoes?"

"Good. New irrigation system works good."

Senna nodded. It'd been her one purchase in the last week. Derrik cared for his hydroponic garden like a creche of newborns, and nothing boosted crew morale like a captain being interested in their hobbies.

Derrik played the message. "Message for Captain McBride of the airship *You Must be Daft*. Upon final inspection we regret to inform you that your tether cable will not be released until your outstanding balance has been paid. Please comm ground control directly to route your account number. You may also use our automated system at any Federated kiosk. Please consider setting up auto-debit so that your ship license with the Global Federation does not lapse in the future."

"Of course this is the moment they try to draft the membership fee," Senna said with a frown.

Derrik sniffed. "Federation membership just keeps getting pricier."

Senna forced a smile. "I'm sure there's a grace period." She again checked the time. Half-hour delay now. Damn it. Her fingers flew across the metal banding on her arm, routing the payment through her personal account and signing what felt like a hundred regulatory documents. "It's a stop gap measure, but that should work until the missing money is found."

"Processing," chimed the computer.

"Great. Now"—Senna opened a comm to Alex—"Alex, come to outpost. I want to run a full accounting report with you here to explain it to me."

"Cap'n?"

"With you in just a moment, Derrik."

"Cap'n err—"

"What?"

Derrik tapped a scarred finger at the screen. "Room two comm."

"Where's Boris? Hospitality is his department."

Derrik shrugged.

"Fine. Put it through."

"...and so I was wondering about the mold. In particular, if there is a spray I can use? They're nice shoes and I don't want to throw them out. I was going to wear them to disembark."

"I'll have someone to you in just a moment." Senna took note of the room number and time and shot a message to Boris. She received no response, but chances were good he was helping another one of the passengers.

"Payment accepted," the *Daft* chimed.

"Wonderful. Now, *Daft,* tell Alex to come meet me down here."

"Alex Biddleman is not aboard the *Daft,*" replied the ship.

"Great, so how soon...what?"

"Alex Biddleman is not aboard the *Daft.*"

Staff disappearing was *not* in Senna's plan.

"When did she disembark? How did she disembark? We are over a mile above Limerick."

"Last body heat scan was taken five and a half minutes ago. Departure was through B gate elevator onto a docked ferry ship named *Doggo.*"

"Heh," Derrik said with a mustache twitch.

"Stop it. Did you authorize a dock? I have to approve those."

"Nah. Prob'lly pirates."

"There are no pirates on the *Daft.* Be serious." Senna's head would explode in the next thirty seconds if the world didn't start making sense again.

"'Kay."

"*Daft,* how many passengers are on board? How many crew?"

"We are at full passenger capacity. All paid at the full rate as the *Daft* is not currently running any promotions. Would you like to schedule a promotional coupon for worldwide, or regional distribution?"

"While you're here Cap'n, I'm supposed to talk to you about the cargo," Derrik said. "And pirates. Lex ever tell you about pirates, Cap'n? Very cool. Low overhead. Stellar hydroponics. VB45s made to be a pirate ship."

"Stop with the damn pirates. This is a cruise line. We should not have cargo." Senna turned, very deliberately, to fully face Derrik.

"*Daft,* who authorized the cargo?"

"Derrik Mulbank."

Senna crossed her arms, fuming as politely as she could manage. "Explain."

Derrik, in his maddening unblinking manner responded, "Plants. Last carrier couldn't do the route so we picked up the old contract. Cap'n. It'll help pay the bills."

"What kind of plants?"

"Space plants."

"What is a space plant?"

"It takes up space."

"*Daft.* What is in our hold?"

"The cargo hold is filled with shipping containers signed for by Alex Biddleman."

"But Alex can't sign for things," Senna said, refusing to stamp her foot. "Only Derrik or I can!"

"The cargo hold is filled with shipping containers signed for by Alex Biddleman."

"Cargo is good bidness, Cap'n."

Had no one read Senna's plan? They all got a copy of it upon signing their yearly contracts but maybe Senna needed to have regular staff meetings? Either way, she couldn't have any more delays. Senna closed her eyes, counted to twenty, moved her sash just a little higher across her chest, and said, "Derrik, you will release that cargo before we untether."

"Tether just got released," Derrik said. "We're rising. Forty-five-minute delay now. You want to extend it more?"

The burning in Senna's stomach silently screamed the words *failure* and *moon deportation* in tandem. The high-end passengers she had spent years cultivating had things to do and were paying Senna handsomely to do them. They would not hesitate to take back that money if she couldn't deliver them, on time, to their destinations. Boris kept the various interactive screens on the *Daft* filled with fun passenger facts. Someone's grandson was getting married. Another had a woodturning conference to attend. One couple was heading to a global shuffleboard tournament. Boris had his own grandkids to see when they landed Stateside. Senna had met all three of them in the last year, and was a godmother to the youngest, having helped Boris's partner give birth when they unexpectedly went into labor while the *Daft* was over the Pacific. She needed to recuperate the lost time.

"Sorry about money troubles, Cap'n. If you need a loan, I know a lady. She's got an eyepatch."

"I have a reputation, Derrik. In five years of service, the *Daft* has never once had a late delivery or drop off, and I have never had to wear an eyepatch. Today will not be a first for any of those, and I will not take money from a loan shark regardless."

"Wadda 'bout a pirate?" Derrik whispered.

"No." She resisted her instinct to grab Derrik's sleeve and haul him from the outpost. "After you show me what's in my cargo hold, we find Alex and I will have a talk with both of you about courting potential administrative action." Silently, Senna mouthed, *If Alex jeopardized my home, those arms won't save her. I will not go to the moon. Ever.*

Derrik grunted but got up. A punch of inertia made Senna bob momentarily as the ship switched from moving up to moving east. The *Daft* said, "Clearance granted on your submitted flight path. Your Federation registration is processing."

"Wonderful." Senna's ears popped. "Moving up and out, and on our way to the USA. Without my accountant and with a near hour delay, but we can make up that time. I'm certain of it."

"Unless pirates," Derrik said.

The thick cord of Senna's patience frayed, a handful of outside fibers snapping apart. She slammed the hatch door closed, grabbed Derrik's elbow, and started jogging toward the docking bay. "Stop talking and start moving. No one on my ship has been or will be, a pirate."

* * *

"Par! Woot woot! Hey dude, watch it. You're stepping on the stegosaurus."

There were a handful of inherent issues in catering to comfort on an air cruise ship. The one in which Senna currently found herself wrestling was four young women on their honeymoon flight turning the cargo hold and the immediately adjacent hallways into a dinosaur-themed mini golf course. Clearly premeditated, one of them had brought at least two suitcases worth of hip-height plastic dinosaurs, a set of clubs, and glow-in-the-dark balls. Another had co-opted the glow panels to bring the interior light down to dusk...or they'd bribed Senna's engineer, Cai Qui, who had a known soft spot for polyamorous couples.

"Your foot?" a tall, willowy blond said again. "You, with the beret and the wild curls, you're on her tail. If we're going to be late going home, we might as well enjoy ourselves, eh?"

Senna lifted her foot and nudged the toy aside. Some six feet from where she and Derrik stood, the door to the cargo area was open. It had been empty for the past year, and Senna had begun plans to turn it into a swimming pool. Currently however, blue plastic shipping containers packed the space, except for a walking strip right down the middle, filled with three tyrannosauruses, a drink cup laid flat, and a flag that read *Hole Four, par two.*

Senna said in her best captain voice, "My apologies, of course. *Daft,* can we get the lights up?"

The *Daft* promptly obeyed. The four women eyed Senna. The blond started to speak but the wife next to her—a taller yet woman with thick black braids—said, "Oh sorry, Captain McBride. Alex said you wouldn't need this space till we landed and hospitality set up the lights."

Senna wanted to snap *Alex doesn't run this ship*, but snark did not endear one to customers. Instead, she said, "You're not in the way at all. We just need to inspect the cargo. I've been hoping to catch Alex as well. Is she around?"

"No, but she said we could give this to you." The blond put down her putter, stepped around a spiny dinosaur that Senna couldn't name, and handed her a crumpled piece of paper.

Derrik leaned in.

"Don't say pirates," Senna said, holding up a hand.

Derrik retreated.

Senna unfurled the note and deciphered the looped, potentially drunk handwriting. The first three lines had been scratched out, but Senna could still read them when she held the paper to the light panel.

~~I am so goddamned tired of your willful ignorance I swear to fucking hell McBride. You can take your plan and shove it in a volcano. You know the job offers I've turned down to be here? You know the salaries they're offering me? We have that same potential and your damn fucking ship is perfect. Why can't you just~~

Look, McBride. Golf don't pay the bills. These women don't, either. It's time to get serious about cargo hauling and the galactic economy. We all count on you, McBride. You've been there for all of us and now we're going to be there for you. And if you're going to have a panic attack about this not being on your old ratty bar napkin, comm me at LEXXA54th on the UNFederated Global Chat and we'll talk. But only when you're ready to listen. I'm not going to let you lose the Daft, so help me god.

"What is Alex talking about?" Senna asked Derrik.

"Pi-"

"Can I mulligan that?" one of the other women said as a golf ball bounced off Senna's calf. Senna felt the bruise bloom and ground her teeth. "We didn't account for your legs in the course. Sorry, Captain. We've got bets riding on this. Could you hurry up?"

"Of course. So sorry." Panic attacks? Senna didn't have time for panic attacks. She forced what had to be a hideous smile and navigated her way to the closest container. "Derrik?"

Derrik unlatched the lid and scooped at the innards. Yellow tufted dandelion heads peeked over the lip. "No worries, Cap'n. Dandelions. One hundred perrrr-cent legal, Cap'n. Good value, too. Short shelf life though so no more delays. They're shot in around a week. But we're meeting the buyer soon. Tight scheduling and such. Distinct place and time."

"You have to treat the dilophosaurus like a water trap!"

Senna sighed and tugged on the end of one of her tight curls. She swallowed bile—the inevitable outcome of anxiety belly. She'd already yelled once today however, and would not be making that misstep again. She could keep her temper reigned in, especially since no one else on the *Daft* appeared to be even remotely worried about current events. "I see. This wouldn't happen to be why it took us so long to leave? Getting shoved to the back of the line, maybe draining my accounts? A lot of work when you could have just asked if we could alter the flight plan enough to load an entire cargo hold of dandelions?"

Derrik took one of the dandelions and a safety pin he fished from his pocket and pinned it to Senna's starched canvas shirt—Federation issue—that read CAPTAIN across the chest. He stayed clear of her sash which was how he managed to keep his hand intact. Senna's will stated that she was to be buried in her Yoint! captain's sash, clutching her bar napkin plan, a homeowner's triumphant smile taxidermized onto her face.

"You're in this with Alex?" Senna prodded. "I told all of you, our primary mission is these passengers."

"This cargo's legal and pays well. They just had a problem with transport," Derrik said, with an upturn on the last syllable. "It's fast and not going to mess with the passengers much. This time. Just wanted to give you a taste of freedom and things."

"What does that mean?"

"Er."

"Derrik." Senna canted her head, elongating the "r" sound of his name like an irritated parent might speak to a cookie-stealing child. "Is this a mutiny? Because I do not have time for a mutiny."

"Nah, it's bidness. Good bidness. Talk to Alex."

"Alex isn't aboard the ship and is, apparently, an embezzling, ship-stealing pirate." The words should have made Senna furious. Instead, perhaps due to years of Yoint! captain de-escalation training, she met the problem with cool facts, a level head, and a creeping realization that she really wanted to see what Alex looked like in a pirate uniform.

"Mebbe. But ask yourself, Cap'n: You know anything about her? She knows you though. That's unbalanced."

"She's my accountant and crewperson."

"You play gin with me every other Monday, at midnight, in outpost. We talk about stars 'n constellations. You bring

Chef Chia regional olive oils every time we get shore leave. You're a godparent to one of Boris' kids. What do you do with Alex, Cap'n? You avoid her. Like this." Derrik clasped Senna's shoulder, leapt a triceratops, and disappeared around a corner. Senna swore she heard him giggle.

"I do not avoid Alex!" Senna yelled, uselessly, after him. "I...don't have a lot of free time. And Alex has...arms." Wow. Pathetic was not a good look for a captain.

Derrik did not return.

"Can we play through now?" the blond asked, her tone further shredding Senna's patience.

"Yes. Of course. So sorry." Senna folded Alex's note into her pocket and picked the same path as Derrik across the Putt-Putt course, and back into the ship proper. Nothing was unbalanced in how she treated the crew. Right? The lot of them had dinner together most nights, sure, but there was only one galley. They had a shuffleboard team, but Senna missed practice more often than not when passengers needed help. She helped them out when she could, and accepted the invites into their land-homes, got them gifts on major holidays, that sort of thing. And that was for all of them. Even Alex. Everything was above board. Especially with Alex. In fact, Alex was more like...an acquaintance. Best they'd ever managed was a Chanukah gift exchange, although how Alex had known Senna was Jewish was unclear.

"*Daft*, are we still on course for the USA?"

"The course remains unaltered, although our altitude is higher than required. We are now one and a half hours behind schedule."

How were they still losing time? "Why is our altitude off?"

"Reroute entered by Sorry-But-Not-Sorry Alex Biddleman."

Control. Control was what Senna needed to get back. A good airship captain was always in control. That was the first class incoming frosh took at Yoint! Keep control of your budget, your manifests, your crew. Senna was 0/3, but she didn't have to stay that way. She had to get more information. Alex's berth, maybe, would be a reasonable starting place. She'd gather information first to potentially maximize leverage, then comm up Alex for a long, long overdue for a heart-to-heart.

"I'm in control," Senna whispered to herself as she started down the hall.

"Fore!" a woman screamed as a blue golf ball whizzed past Senna's head, followed by a pterodactyl.

* * *

Standard VB airship berths were, traditionally, the size of a college dorm bed. Alex, being the first hire, had claimed the largest room—wide enough for a full-sized bed, child-sized desk with yoga ball chair, and a narrow nightstand. Senna had floated Alex the money to buy them the month she'd hired the accountant on. All were now covered in dust and dirty clothing, a look suggesting Alex had not used her quarters in some time.

Senna edged inside, toeing a path amongst the discarded blouses and low-rise leggings. A tote bag sloughed against the right-side wall, half packed and smelling like old cheese. "We have a free, fully functioning laundry service one level up," Senna said to the rotting air. She picked up the duffle by the strap—gingerly, between two fingers—and shook it.

One half-eaten cheese and pickle sandwich fell out, along with two pairs of grungy tube socks. There was a suspicious bulge in the toe-end of one of the socks and Senna, who had pumped the *Daft's* latrine system on numerous occasions when Boris had fallen ill or just needed a break, scrunched her nose and pinched the sock until the whatever-it-was emerged from the end.

Not a liquid, thankfully. Paper. Glossy. Not written on. Senna flattened it on the laminate floor and found herself staring at Alex's beaming face as she shook Senna's hand. Senna had the severe-yet-sensible look to her clothes and hair she'd decided airship captains wore, but Alex...Senna had forgotten Alex smiled. Or wore coveralls. Or had once had hair so long she'd braided down to her tailbone. This was the day Senna had interviewed Alex and promptly offered her a job aboard the *Daft*. Alex had giggled, Senna remembered now, and smiled that giddy kind of smile where her tongue poked between her teeth. She hadn't looked at the pay rate on the offer letter, just signed and tossed the handmade duffle—a gift from Senna for signing on—up the gangplank.

It had been a canvas duffle. Sky blue. The same that currently stank up Alex's room. Why in the world would Alex still have that old—

"Got skies, Cap'n," Derrik said over the comm.

"We always have a sky. Be more specific."

"Grey skies. Not charging the solar and our battery is low from all the waitin'. No movement. Stalled over the Atlantic."

"Are we stalled, or did you stop us?"

"Yeah."

"Would someone please tell me what is going on?" Senna hissed at the ceiling and hopefully also to Derrik.

The comm clicked off, just to click immediately back on. "Captain McBride?"

"This is McBride," Senna said although what she really wanted to do was scream. The comms were not supposed to route directly to her unless they'd gone unanswered at their proper destination. "Who is this?"

"Room Seven. I asked for a shampoo refill yesterday and still don't have it. Not the honey mango stuff, but the coconut, like the next room over has. I can smell it. I want some of that."

"Hold on." She clicked over to a new channel. "Boris? Guests need shampoo help."

"Boris Roeske is not aboard the *Daft,*" the ship responded.

Where in the world had he gone, mid journey? With Alex? "Who in my crew *is* still on the ship?"

"Needs to Rethink Her Priorities Captain Senna McBride, Engineer Derrik Owen."

"I can't run an airship with two people and messing with the *Daft's* title database is unprofessional!" Senna ground her palms into her temples then switched back to the original comm channel. "Ma'am, they may have brought their own shampoo. We only stock honey-mango and passionfruit-lemon. Could I bring you either of those?"

"Oh? Bummer. I thought this was an all-inclusive tour. The lemon then I guess. Room seven. I'll be waiting." The comm clicked off.

The cord that held Senna together snapped.

She screamed.

She allotted herself five full minutes for the breakdown, including kicking Alex's duffle across the room and throwing the cheese sandwich at it for good measure. They needed to get moving, now, or they'd have to start refunding. If they went over a four-hour delay, by Federation law, they had to pay disgruntlement fees. Senna could afford neither without taking a second mortgage on the *Daft*. She'd be on the moon inside of a decade, hands down.

Senna took one final sweep of the room, kicking at the clothes piles, stomping them flat to ensure no other photos lurked. When nothing else turned up she tucked the photo into her thigh pocket and stormed toward the nearest storage room. As she walked, she tapped Alex's username into the chat feature on her arm cuff.

"McBride," said the six-inch holo of Alex that sprang from Senna's wrist. Senna tapped her passcode into the storage room's pin pad, grabbed four bottles of passionfruit-lemon conditioning shampoo, and slammed the door shut. "You know how much we can make ferrying dandelions from the ground to the low-level space transports? The money here is really good. It'll pay off the *Daft.* You can do that expansion you've been talking about. Your quarters first, the crew agreed. You deserve that bigger closet you keep—" She stopped. "Why are you frowning?"

"I'm going to lose my ship and where *are* you?"

"Cool your airship jets. I warned you about the *Daft*, I'm dealing with it, and I'm on a spaceship. A low-level one, as we just discussed. It uh, just happens to be unfederated. We can talk about that later. Right now, I need to make sure these guys can find you and the transfer goes smoothly. You'll want to talk to them, too. Hear what they're trying to do for Earth. This is big picture stuff, McBride. Making a difference. You're going to be all over that, I know it, even if it is with cargo. But uh," Alex sniffed. "I'm sorry about this. You know I tried to talk to you about it but there's like, always a crew thing you have to do, or one of Boris' kids wants to talk to you, or you're rehanging your dirty napkin. You can avoid me all you want, Senna, but I'm seriously doing you a solid here."

The holo shuddered. The *Daft* said, "Forward propulsion has ceased. Upward propulsion increasing."

"Go back on course, *Daft,*" Senna said in a forced calm.

"Awaiting orders from Seriously Awesome Captain Alex Biddleman."

The tiny grip of calm slipped away. "I'm the captain!"

Alex snorted and typed a command into her armband.

"Awaiting orders from The Coolest Captain Alex Biddleman."

Senna shook her arm, disbursing the holo image, which then stubbornly reformed. "Stop playing games, Alex. I don't have time. After I get the passengers delivered, we can talk but I am not hauling cargo! This is my home, and your home, and for a very short period of time, the homes of our passengers, too. It pays well enough, and we do it without bone-breaking, spine-crushing, soul-sucking cargo transport."

"I'm going to help you pay off the *Daft*," Alex said blandly.

"Which I am already doing!"

"Not really."

Senna, in a very immature and un-captainly move, stamped her foot, then brandished the photograph. "You were reasonable, once. And excited to work with me. Remember? Excited to come aboard a luxury transport and do the job? What happened to that woman? Does she need therapy?"

"I do not...*argh*. I understand your whole 'I never had a home so I'm going to give everyone the home I never had' thing, but I'm trying to *help* you, dammit. We all are. Get your head out of your fine ass and meet me at the cargo hold. You have..."—the holo looked off screen—"half an hour to make some good choices."

A blanket of confusion smothered Senna's rage. Yoint! had a three-class series on active listening to employees and Senna had aced it. "Fine ass?"

Alex's eyes found a very interesting spot above Senna's head and stayed there.

"Did you mean...tight...ass?" Senna asked. Had it been an insult? "Get the stick out of my ass, perhaps? Which"—she held up a finger—"is unfair. A schedule and a plan do not make me rigid; they make me efficient." She held up one finger. "Efficiency is the first tenet of airship captaining."

The holo's eyes remained wide for half a second before Alex groaned and put her hands over her face. "Get out of my quarters," Alex said. "Now."

The holo disappeared.

"I do not have a stick up my ass," Senna muttered as she lowered her finger. Although if Alex watched Senna's backside the way Senna watched Alex's arms, they probably needed to have a meeting about more than the mutiny.

"She didn't say you did, Cap'n," Derrik said over the apparently open comm.

Senna groaned, pocketed the tiny shampoos and headed up to the luxury level of her airship. As she walked, she said to the eavesdropping Derrik, "Meet me on level five outside the badminton courts. We're having a discussion."

"Yup."

The crew was determined to give her a heart attack. Senna knocked on shampoo-lady's door. "Ma'am? I have your shampoo."

A short, dumpling-shaped woman answered the door. "Oooh! Did you bring the coconut?"

"I...no. The lemon mix. Here." She stopped short of pushing the bottles at the woman, choosing to drop them into her outstretched hands instead. "I hope you enjoy them."

"I suppose they'll work. I'll let you know if they don't." A crease grew across the woman's forehead. "I don't suppose you have—"

The *Daft* jerked hard to port, sending Senna and Dumpling Woman onto the unforgiving-yet-easily-cleaned laminate floor.

"How did we hit something when we're not moving, *Daft?*" Senna demanded of her arm.

"A docking has been initiated," the *Daft* returned. "In addition, torpedoes from a tailing Federation ship detonated just off the bow. They were likely a warning shot."

Who had the...the *fucking audacity* to take pot shots at Senna's home? "Docking? On whose authorization?"

"Space Captain and Visionary Alex Biddleman."

Ohhh, she and Alex had so, so much to talk about. Yup. And with the *Daft's* Federation registration having only just gone through and likely still processing, the *Daft* probably looked just like the pirate that had docked. "Please excuse me," Senna said through gritted teeth. "There's a situation."

"Will the turbulence affect the water pressure?" Dumpling Woman asked.

"I'll get back to you."

Senna's comm pinged and the audio routed before Senna could shut down her arm terminal. "Hey Captain McBride? We moved to D&D and one of the dinos got 'hungry' and, shush! I'll tell her. Calm down. Anyway, we thought it would be funny if we fed the dinos, so we took some dandelions from the container you opened. A handful of palm-sized Compys fell inside. Is it okay to go in after them? I called hospitality first, but no one answered."

"Please refrain from entering the crates and I will be down in just a moment." Senna slapped the feed off and rounded the corner to the badminton courts. Leaning against the wall, as unconcerned as he'd been a handful of hours ago, stood Derrik.

In a wide stance next to him, arms crossed, barely controlling a grin, was Alex.

"Space Captain?" Senna growled at Alex.

"We have business that can't wait, McBride." Had Alex ever called Senna "Captain"? "You're in or you're out. You want to be in. I know you do."

Another squawk on the comm. "Captain, if a Velociraptor had fallen in too, would that be sufficient grounds to go after them? A Velociraptor and a bright pink golf ball? We reached in to see if we could fish them out but those dandelions are extra sticky. I think they're leaking."

"Just one moment," Senna said to the comm.

"Oh my god just ignore them!" Alex uncrossed her arms, took Senna by the shoulders, and shook her. "This passenger business? It's sweet but small scale. No, put your damn hand down and listen to me for once. The crew has decided it's time for piracy. You're going to help take Earth into the future, McBride, you and the *Daft*, and all of us, okay? And piracy is the way to do it because you can't spend the rest of your life delivering warmed towelettes and smiling at every awful pun someone tells you in the buffet line."

Senna pushed Alex's hands away, but Alex caught Senna's right hand and held it. "Let go of my hand and let go of my ship. It's not yours. Neither are my crew. This isn't how you convince someone you are right. I will not run cargo again. I've been running cargo my whole life, in one manner or another. No one respects you for bringing them a truckload of asparagus or a bra in just the right size. You don't need to be a captain to run cargo. You barely need to be breathing to run cargo."

"You already run cargo! They're just loud, demanding cargo. Dandelions don't demand shampoo. It's the same gig!"

"It is not. The *Daft* is giving people homes, even if just temporary. Little luxury homes in the clouds." Senna had never thought of her job like that until she said it out loud. The words were too close to her heart, too close to a confession. She wanted to swallow them, snatch them from the air and gobble them up like the starving street child she'd been, but they already belonged to Alex and Derrik now, as much to her.

Alex rubbed her forehead and groaned. "Okay well, running my cargo will mean better lives for people who like, actually need homes if you'd just listen to what I have to say. But right now, right now I brought the buyers, Senna. For the dandelions. They're docked and waiting on my spaceship, the fully paid off *Doggo*."

A weight dropped, deep in Senna's gut. "You could have asked first."

Alex's smile faltered. "Don't worry. I'll pay it back with interest. Now I want you to consider that Federated Captain is cool, and like you get a sash that really highlights uh, you know." Alex flushed, shook her head, and made a quick recovery. "Pirate captains could have two sashes though. Three! You know. No rules."

While Alex babbled, Senna brought up an image of the docked ship on her armband. A holo appeared, showing a sleek white space with daisies painted across the hull. The thrusters were a stark, contrasting black with a white skull and crossbones.

"Yo. Senna. Did you hear anything I said?"

Senna had heard plenty. "You're a pirate."

"As of about five hours ago, yes. We all are."

The *Daft* shook again, knocking all three of them to the ground and onto their backs.

"*Daft!*" Senna yelled.

"Another warning shot, with more force. Paint lost on the stern side of the gondola. Three injury reports in progress. Missing pet report from the cargo console for a Velociraptor."

"Delete that one, that's just a toy," Senna said as she again tried to shake loose Alex's hand.

Alex held tight. Alex was sweating like a stuck pig though, so the grip wouldn't last long.

"*Daft,* open a comm to the Federation ship."

"No comm is available."

Senna tried, and failed, to suck in a calming breath. "Try again."

Alex shook her head. "They have a no negotiation policy with pirates, Captain."

"They're firing over dandelions!"

"GMOs," Derrik brushed off his backside, shook his moustache, and got back to his feet.

Senna said, "But GMOs aren't illegal. The only reason Earth could feed its fourteen billion people are GMOs. Well, and draining half the oceans for additional landmass."

"These aren't patented though," Alex said, her voice turning coaxing and calm. "They just came out of a lab in Nova Scotia and overproduce latex, as well as having a full adult dose of Vitamin C per leaf. They're a miracle plant, Senna, but no one will be able to afford them. And no one on Earth needs them. That new generational ship though? The one going to Europa? They need these dandelions, and they're going to get them. Little bit of a transport issue though. No one interested in the haul can get the dandelions from the ground to low space without wilt. No one except a sash-loving, beret wearing, five-year-planning captain of a VB45. If she would remove the stick she put in her own ass."

"Biddleman, can we get the goods?" came through Alex's wrist comm. "Federation allows three warning shots before they start aiming for balloons and thrusters. We need to separate as soon as possible."

"Come on then," Alex said as she pulled Senna down the hall. "You're the one with the codes to open the docking clamps once we're airborne. Why you three-factor authenticated those but not your navigation controls, I do not understand. Just come with me down to the hold, enter the codes, and help me get the dandelions to the *Doggo*. They'll wire the money, fly off, and take the Federated ship with them. The money from that transfer? It'll pay off a full half of the *Daft's* mortgage. Now come on." Alex continued down the hall. When Senna failed to follow, she stormed back over, fists balled at her sides. "Come. On."

Senna didn't move.

Alex tapped her wrist. "We're on our way. Give us five."

"Copy."

Alex took a deep breath, winding up for another round of yelling, then deflated, violently, like a stuck balloon. "Captain," she said, very deliberately. Very softly. "We're going to save your home. We're going to save a bunch of people's homes. Your parents starved to death on the moon, Senna. I know, because you drink and you talk and you're actually a really fucking fantastic person when you stop using the scripts Yoint! burned into your brain. That school was trash, Senna. Brainwashing bullshit. Piracy was the second-best choice I ever made and I'm not going to let the Federation suck you into deep space. Listen to me, to what I am saying right now. No one else, not colonist, not deportee, and certainly not you, has to starve anymore. You can make sure of it."

Senna wasn't entire sure. Everything Alex said made perfect sense and yes, some of the coursework at Yoint! had been over the top propaganda, but life had never provided Senna with an easy way out. "I...," she said, grabbing for the words swirling through her head. "Back in Chicago there were ways to do things. You didn't just start running a restaurant. You had to be a busgirl first, then a server, maybe a cook, right? You didn't, I mean, no part of any of this"—she made a wide sweep with her hand—"has a step that involves piracy. I got the *Daft* by following the rules."

"And the rules only take you so far." Alex sighed, the exhale so forceful that a whistle came from her nose. "How long have we known each other, McBride?"

"Four years, five next month."

"Twelve years." Alex finally dropped Senna's hand. She made two circles with her thumbs and forefingers and held them over her eyes. "Year 1 undergraduate Federation Academy. Cause and Effect Seminar. I had glasses then. Sat two rows behind you. We were lab partners the first day, before you switched sections. You kept everything in a green notebook with spiral binding that you said you found in an antique mall."

"I..." They'd taken classes together? She'd never noticed.

Senna's comm went off again. "Captain, we really are going to need the coconut soap I'm afraid. This smell just isn't what we're looking for."

"Oh my god with this thing, are you serious?!" Alex grabbed Senna's wrist and yelled "Sorry, out of soap!" and killed the connection.

Senna did not reopen the comm. *Second best choice* rang in her head, along with an influx of memory blips. Alex's wardrobe slowly morphing into tank tops. Alex buying her an embroidered "Home Sweet Home" wall hanging for her office, even if she had suggested it could hang in place of the old napkin. Alex requesting, patiently, every week, to meet and go over budgets when any other self-respecting accountant would have been more than happy to have free reign.

Senna asked, very quietly, very carefully, as if the answer might cleave them all in two, "Why did you join my crew, Alex?"

"It was a good job," Alex said without eye contact.

"You could have gotten twice as much on a freight airship. As you've noted many times."

"Better food here though," Alex said nodding at Derrik.

Senna touched her shoulder. "Really?"

Alex screamed. "Oh my god, would you shut up? I'm trying to fucking save you!"

The sentence rang through the plastic hallway, settling as slowly through Senna's mind as dandelion fluff on a windless day.

From just behind Senna, came Derrik's low lilting "Yup." He held out a fist, then unfurled his fingers, revealing a handful of plastic Compys stuck together with yellow dandelion petals.

"They're—"

An ear-shattering BOOM rang through the *Daft*.

Alex's comm screeched, "*Daft?* We have to leave. The Federation ship just shot our main thruster."

"They fired on the other ship," Senna said, eyes wide in disbelief. "Next, they'll fire on *my* ship. My parents died for this ship. I had to sit through thousands of Yoint! lecture hours for this ship. I've put in nearly five years of outstanding Federation service on this ship. And they're still going to *fire on me!?*"

Senna bolted toward the cargo bay. "Talk," she said as they ran. "What's the plan?"

Alex...Alex almost beamed. Or she was just sweating. "World's not going to last forever, Senna. The Irish know how to survive, and we're going to help them terraform the galaxy with these dandelions. Federation had them engineered, then decided not to use them. Cheaper to send the poor to space to do the work. They're disposable, according to the Federation. The people, not the dandelions."

"They promised after the moon they weren't going to do that." Senna tried to breathe through the long-buried rage that bubbled up from her gut.

They reached the cargo bay, now devoid of golfers, one lone T-rex forgotten in a corner. "Australia. The moon. The cycle didn't end with your parents' being shipped off to die and it won't end on Europa, either. But we can help. Your code. Enter it," Alex said. "We have like thirty seconds."

"ATTENTION! THIS IS THE FEDERATED AIRSHIP *GERRYMANDER*. THIS IS YOUR FINAL WARNING BEFORE WE OPEN FIRE ON THE *YOU MUST BE DAFT*."

Senna put in the codes. The hall door to the cargo hold opened at the same time as the much larger bay door on the other end. Normally there'd have been a horrific depressurization but the *Doggo* had already docked with the *Daft*. Dangling from the *Doggo's* port hole were two men in patched brown pants, floppy boots, and overly large shirts.

"Permission to come aboard," Senna said to them.

The men jumped from their idling spaceship into Senna's hold and began hauling the cargo crates across. Senna moved to help but the *Daft* veered to port. Air rushed past Senna's cheeks as alarm klaxons fired throughout her airship. A shipping container was dropped, spilling dandelions and a lone Compy across the hold.

"Outpost breach! Airlock shattered. Computer on backup power," yelled the *Daft*.

Senna reached for her pocket planner. There was no logic behind it, save safety in schedules.

Alex snatched the planner away. "Love will not stop me from slapping sense into you," Alex hissed. "Keep to the new plan. The guys just need a few minutes more."

In a few more minutes, the *Daft* could be plummeting into a mountain. "I think we should talk about this love situation." Senna had just gotten to her knees when gravity spun her, Alex, and Derrik against the far wall.

"Main rudder down. We are no longer capable of propulsion and the Federation ship is coming in for docking."

"Unaffiliated airship *You Must Be Daft*. Prepare to be boarded. Please respond to this message with your docking bay location or we will blow a new one for ourselves."

"Kiss 'er," Derrik loudly whispered to Alex.

"I'm not going to fucking kiss her without consent. Especially not in the middle of a firefight. It's bad enough I look like a long-time stalker who's strong-arming her into piracy."

"How about we call it effective negotiating? I may have done a little stalking myself." Senna nodded deferentially at Alex's right bicep. "Now both of you shut up." Taking advantage of the open comm to the Federation ship, Senna shook free of both of them and said to her comm and, hopefully, to the Federation ship lurking outside, "This is Captain Senna McBride of the Federated Airship *You Must Be Daft*. We are temporarily on suspension for a missed payment, however the money has been sent and should be routing. Please cross reference our serial number DAFT45-G in your databases. You can see the *Daft* has been in good standing for nearly five years. In addition, please reference my parents, Emily Majors and Zach Donahue, participants in Lunar Colony 5. As their child I am entitled to lifelong Federation membership as an individual, so it is technically illegal to fire on me even if my ship is unregistered."

"VERIFYING. HOLD."

Step 1, lie. Step 2, lie some more. "*Gerrymander*, we captured these pirates here, on the *Doggo*. We call first bounty rights. Taking them on our ship now and then we will deliver them to the USA once we cross to North America. We just had to fly really high to capture them. Which we can do, because the *Daft* is a VB45. Which is why I got a VB45, just so you know. To catch pirates."

Somewhere to her right, Derrik laugh-burped.

"COPY, *DAFT. PLEASE HOLD.*" The comm clicked off.

"Now kiss her."

"Shut up, Derrik," Alex said, but the murder had gone from her tone.

"YOU ARE VERIFIED, *DAFT*. WE LOOK FORWARD TO YOUR UPCOMING REPORT."

"Yes, ma'am. *Daft* out." To Alex, Senna said with dripping smugness, "How's that for piracy, eh? Who's flexible now?"

This time Derrik made no attempt to hide his laughter.

Alex, grinning, said, "Fucking amazing. You're *Pirate Captain* Senna McBride. People are going to hear that name and get the shits, instead of asking you to *clean up* their shit. Time to grasp your future, Senna." Then, after a deep breath as she looked down at her shoes, then back to Senna's face. "However much of it you want."

Senna wanted a lot of things in that moment, but the *Daft* had to take precedence. She hooked her arm into Alex's and led her back to the cargo hold. "Let the gentlemen pirates load. You and Derrik, and Boris and everyone else you've stashed away, need to come to outpost and help me strip the Federation coding from the computer. If we're doing this pirate thing, we're doing it right. After we're done stripping, we will all sit down, as a crew, and make a new plan. Together. No one fires on *my ship* without consequences."

A smile bloomed on Alex's face. Just like the picture Senna still had in her pocket.

"About that." Senna held the photo out to Alex. If she could be a pirate, surely she could kiss her accountant.

"I've been remiss in my attention to you. May I rectify that now?"

"Yes."

Thus decided, Senna cupped Alex's cheeks and kissed her top lip—a slow, delicate movement that left her reconsidering her former priorities in their entirety. A home was great. A home was necessary. But Alex's lips, and the way her hands closed on Senna's hips, those were requirements now, too.

"Not bad," Alex murmured, eyes still closed. "Do I taste like a pirate?"

"I don't care what you taste like as long as it isn't passionfruit-lemon shampoo."

Alex giggled, and it sounded better than an airship engine whirring to life.

"I'm not well practiced at kissing though," Senna said. "I'll schedule time to work on that too. First, let's deliver these dandelions. No one else is ending up like my parents as long as the *Daft* can fly."

Alex kissed Senna's cheek. "Knew you'd see reason if I bashed you over the head enough times."

They walked together, arms still entwined, to the outpost. Alex filled the silent halls with nervous chatter, her tongue darting over her upper lip whenever the silence stretched too long between them.

Senna, only half listening, mentally regrouped. *Year 1 – become a pirate and accountant-kisser. Year 2 – pay off ship debt, repair the Doggo and buy a third. Begin a fleet. A space fleet? An air fleet? Retrofit? Keep with the kissing. Year 3... more dandelions. Every world the Federation starts, we will service. Maybe in Year 4, we take the Daft to the stars, find a new planet, and build the kind of world my parents were promised.*

"Piracy is Not A Five-Year Plan" is a stand-alone short by J.S. Fields. You can read more of their science fiction and fantasy work at www.patreon.com/jsfields or check out their website: www.jsfieldsbooks.com

Flight of the Megabee

William C. Tracy

Sapphic Representation: Lesbian, Non-Binary

Heat Level: Medium

Content Warnings: Coarse Language, Violence to Bees

Romara skulked around the edges of the annual winter gathering of the flower valley. They saw human representatives from all surviving cliffhives, their queens and princesses, and the megabees they brought with them. Usually, the huge insects stayed in their part of the hive—with the handlers like Romara—but at the winter festival, the royalty pulled out all the stops, including bringing the giant bees they lived with to the party.

"Come on, Queen Montay will have your hide if you shirk serving duties," Voli said. "We need to put on a good show this year."

"Just because the queen's slowing down doesn't mean we have to make up for her. She doesn't have any children and the old queen megabee didn't lay as many winter larvae as she did last year."

"Get your head out of the hive and start serving," Voli told them, before heading off with a platter full of glasses.

"Mead for the people and honey for the megabees," Romara muttered under their breath. "Maybe I should switch that and see what antics the megabees get up to."

They approached the table reserved for the royalty of the flower valley—the leaders of each cliffhive, who were deep in negotiations about how the nectar supplies would be split up in the spring. As always, Queen Montay of Pointed Hill was seated at the far side of the table from the Queen of Little Head cliffhive. The larger, more aggressive cliffhive had been rivals of Pointed Hill—Romara's home—for ages.

Cliffhives that couldn't negotiate for enough resources didn't last long.

Romara headed to Queen Montay, giving her a goblet of Pointed Hill's finest mead with a little bow. The queen didn't even acknowledge them. Romara skulked off.

"Forgetting something?"

Romara froze. The voice had come from the other end of the long table. They must have passed too close and been mistaken for another cliffhive's server.

"Over here. I'm not going to survive this meeting without a *lot* of mead."

Romara opened their mouth to retort, but words wouldn't come. This must be the princess of Little Head. Long blond hair framed a pale face like a budding tulip, with lips the color of an amaryllis. She was pleasantly padded in all the right places, like a sculpture created specifically for Romara.

And she was princess of Pointed Hill's biggest rival.

* * *

"Did you hear me? I said *mead*," June called to the motionless servant. They were handsome, in a rough way—obviously one of those who scraped the wax from the hive and tended the megabees. It was something June tried her hand at, when she got a chance, but her mother the queen almost never let that happen.

The servant's hands were clenched on their tray, enough to show their muscular arms under...the colors for Pointed Hill.

"Oh! I'm terribly sorry!" June called. She spared a glance for her mother, who was negotiating with several other queens. "Would you mind awfully slipping me a glass of mead anyway? I'm parched listening to them bicker."

The servant approached as if in a trance, but then shook their head.

"I'd be happy to." They offered a glass of mead. "I helped brew this from Pointed Hill's stores myself. Best in the valley."

June accepted gratefully and sipped at the mead. The taste exploded through her mouth, spicy and flavorful and strong.

"What *is* this?" she asked the servant.

"Pointed Head's specialty," came the answer. "We may be a small hive, but our honey is the best in the valley." The servant slipped a glance across the table. "Sorry to run,

Princess, but Queen Montay is looking annoyed at me speaking to you. I don't think it's helping her bargaining position."

"Farewell," June called after the servant as they disappeared into the crowd. She took another sip of mead, letting the complex flavor swirl through her mouth.

The best honey in the valley. June had to find out more about the hive—and the people—who could brew mead this tasty.

* * *

Winter turned into spring, as it was wont to do.

"Romara, Herbert's got into the honey again. The girls are going to throw him off the Hill at this rate. Most of them are bigger than he is."

Romara blew out a sigh and waved a vague hand at Voli, by their side whether training megabees, cleaning wax, or attending the winter festival, though that was months past. Even the memory of the intoxicating princess from Little Head had faded.

Except Voli never went after Herbert. That was always *their* job, to pull the drunkard drone out of the sage honey.

They grabbed a bridle and followed the rustle and whirr of the megabees, stepping across segmented legs and patting furry sides as they went by. Megabees liked to be touched. It was how they kept up their social hierarchy and transmitted information. Romara ducked translucent wings buzzing right above their head. Fortunately, they were shorter than most of the other trainers, and didn't get whacked in the face by one of the bees who decided *right then* was the best time to stretch their wings or do a dance for her sisters.

The annoyed buzzing got louder as they reached the capped honey cells built on the stone wall of a hive passage. Most of those who lived their lives above the brood and honey chambers, away from the colony of megabees they shared it with, didn't know the range of noises megabees made. Romara could tell if a crowd was happy, upset, murderous, on a sugar high, or waiting for the queen to come through. This bunch was definitely annoyed, and Romara knew why.

Even before they got to the wall of wax cells, they could tell from the wide, furry back end—rumbling contentedly—what had happened. Herbert was a small drone, barely larger than a worker megabee, but it was easy to spot his stubby rear end in a crowd of girls.

"Come on, Herbert," Romara said as they hiked themself up on a segmented leg and threw the bridle under the twitching antennae, right in the sensitive spot where they connected to the head. Romara tapped him right behind his wide eyes. "Out of the honey. The sage honey is for special occasions, not for you. You're making your sisters angry, and they barely tolerate you drones as it is. Now you're going to be honey-drunk all afternoon. Why don't you find some nice flowers instead, if you can still fly straight?"

Herbert ruffled his wings, trying to knock Romara off.

"That's quite enough of that, sir," Romara said, easily holding their grip on his back. They pulled back on the bridle just enough to make Herbert back away from the cells of honey. Several workers immediately closed in and began to cap the cells with wax again. Romara pulled back and to the left, making Herbert turn a circle—a little haphazardly—and zig-zag blearily toward the open hangar that was the entrance of the cliffhive.

Once there, Romara put an elbow on Herbert's fuzzy back, shivering in the still chill air. It was nearly spring. They looked out over the dozen or so cliffhives dotting the stony walls of the valley and the giant flowers carpeting the space between them. Pointed Hill had the best tasting honey in the valley, which was why the other cliffhives grew jealous. Negotiations at the winter festival hadn't gone well, Romara heard, and Pointed Hill was restricted to a smaller foraging area. There were fewer new brood than there should have been, as well.

"Why do we even keep you around, Herbert?" they asked the drone, who wobbled on his feet. Probably couldn't even fly straight, with all the honey he'd eaten. "You're annoying as skin mites, don't have a *chance* of mating with a foreign queen—not drunk on honey like you are—and will be dead by the end of the year anyway."

Herbert rumbled and wiggled his antennae toward the flowers in the distance.

"Shame you won't get a chance to go on a mating flight," Romara said. "Only one in thousands gets that chance. About as much as I have of..." They broke off, thinking of the princess from the winter festival. They thumped Herbert's side. "With the other cliffhives boxing in our flightpaths, we likely won't have enough honey for the year. Sugar's expensive, you know. We could even lose the hive." They looked across the valley, to where several previous cliffhives had gone dark the year before.

Herbert rustled his wings, but then settled down under Romara.

"But you don't care about all that, do you? You just have the one simple dream, don't you? Find some princess, make sweet love to her, and die with a smile on your face."

Herbert buzzed happily.

"Yeah, me too, buddy."

* * *

June paced outside of her mother's audience chamber. As usual, all her time since the winter festival had been taken up with caring for the hive.

"Nusa, what's taking so long? We must get back to the queen megabee. She's on a laying streak."

"Peace, girl," Nusa said. "Her Majesty takes precedence even over the queen bee, and she called us here for a reason."

June paced, biting a nail. The queen—the megabee queen, not her mother—had been antsy lately. It was to be expected, with so many queen cells being made. The workers had only just closed them up, and it would be a few weeks until the new queens emerged. Little Head had been expanding, the workers building rooms and rooms of wax cells that the queen immediately filled with new eggs. Her mother had negotiated for a much larger share of flower rights in the valley. She must have some plan, because they would need a lot of honey over next winter, at this rate.

Her mother the queen had prevented a swarm the last few years, and the cliffhive was bursting with workers. With so many new queens in the making, there *would* be a new colony of megabees later this spring, whether or not they found a place to expand. It was fortunate there were several empty cliffhives, but clearing out a deserted hive was a dangerous prospect. All sorts of creatures set up homes in old hives, like mousebears and yellowjackets.

"Junebug," Nusa cautioned, and June stopped her pacing just in time for the doors to the audience chamber to open. June strode in.

"Mother, what's all this about? Why were we called to—" She broke off at what she saw.

Her mother wasn't alone. It was rare megabees were let into the upper corridors of a cliffhive. Even rarer for a small group of the bees to be in the audience chamber. They must have been corralled in here especially. But why go to the trouble?

"Juneifer, today is a special day for Little Head," her mother said. "Thanks to the winter festival, we have the most harvest rights, and by the end of the year, we'll be the biggest cliffhive in the whole of flower valley. It will all be thanks to you."

June took a step back, rebounding off Nusa's solid chest. Her mother had been the master negotiator at the festival.

She had only drunk mead and eyed the servants. "What—?"

"I tried to warn you, Junebug," Nusa said, "But you were taking care of the old queen, and then pacing so much..."

"Meet Capella IV," June's mother said, shooing one of the workers aside long enough to show who they'd been tending.

June drew in a long breath. "But the queen cells have just closed up."

In front of her was the unmistakable form of a new queen megabee. She was only a little larger than the workers, her abdomen not yet distended with eggs.

"It seems Capella III has plans for the colony as big as my own," June's mother said. "She hatched several weeks ago in the lowest portion of the hive. It was only through sheer luck Nusa found the queen cell."

June turned to her friend and tutor, who only gave a shrug with a little smile.

"Capella III is nearly ten years old, and the workers will soon kill her to make room for a new queen," June's mother continued. "I will ride her successor on her mating flight, per tradition. However, *you* will ride Capella IV before that time."

"But where...?" June began. If they were *both* to ride new queens, that meant *two* hives, not one. Her mother was finally going to split the hive.

"When she returns," her mother continued, "you will lead half the hive in a swarm across the valley and take over that dying cliffhive of Pointed Hill. They were the weakest at the negotiating table, and our spies report their honey stores are perilously low. Their queen is even older than ours. You, at the head of a phalanx of our fiercest workers, will invade and take your rightful place. At the same time, you will keep another hive from going dark. We can share our resources, and both hives will prosper through the winter. The hive of Little Head will spread across the valley."

The best tasting honey in the valley. That was what the servant had claimed at the festival. And they had been right. That mead was *excellent.*

"But are you certain Pointed Hill is failing?" she asked. That servant had seemed very...lively. She wished she had gotten their name. She wished she had time to learn more about them before now.

"Their queen is weak, and their stores low," her mother answered. "We would do them a favor by taking over their hive with a new, virile queen."

June wanted to argue—attacking another hive was rare, but if honey stores were low, sometimes it was the only way to get more. She had barely thought to lead a mating flight until her mother had stepped down, though. Now, she would not only ride on her own mating flight, but would be in control of a new hive, forever linked with the line of Capella IV. And she wouldn't even have to fight a yellowjacket in an empty cliffhive. Certainly, she could find one servant when she took over Pointed Hill.

She bowed.

"Mother, it's better than I could ever ask for." She rushed in for a heartfelt hug, then carefully approached the virgin queen. Her attendants buzzed and chittered in hesitation, but let her through. June placed one hand against the warm, smooth abdomen of the new queen. Capella IV hummed and lowered one wing over her protectively.

"A match made by the nectar gods!" Nusa exclaimed. She curtseyed. "With your leave, Your Majesty, I'll take Junebug and Capella IV for training as soon as possible."

"Of course, dear Nusa," June's mother said. "She has much work to do before she's ready to fly. Both of them do."

* * *

The weeks passed quickly for Romara. Spring was in full bloom and there was a flurry of activity in the hive. Though even with the chores building up, Romara remained worried. The old queen wasn't laying nearly enough—she was almost fifteen, ancient for a megabee queen—but the workers hadn't started building new queen cells. At least, none Romara could find.

Their megabees were restricted in the flowers they could pollinate, thanks to Queen Montay's abysmal negotiating skills at the winter festival. Romara's thoughts often turned back to that time, serving mead from their special sage honey to the pretty princess. Romara cursed her heritage. Any time one of the distinctive dark-striped megabees from Little Head were seen, tensions rose in Pointed Hill.

Romara had also dragged Herbert out of the sage honey three more times, and at this rate, they were ready to throw him out of the hive themself.

"Why don't you go fly off with your brothers?" they scolded Herbert, wobbling and drunk on sage honey meant for the summer solstice festival. "They leave the hive every day to go hang out at the drone gathering grounds." Some of the queen's elite soldiers rode them, hoping for a chance to mate with a new queen from Rock Crop, or Seed Basin, or any of the other local cliffhives. Not Little Head, though.

Romara had almost finished scraping wax off the hallway connecting the hive to the human living quarters one day, when the alarm siren blared. They rose and wrinkled their nose as the fruity, sharp scent flowed through the hive at the same time.

"Honey thieves!" came a shout from down the corridor, and Romara shot to their feet, brandishing their scraping tool like a dagger. Pointed Hill's honey was their one claim left to prestige. What underhanded cliffhive would attempt such a thing?

They got to the cliff's main hangar just as the attackers gained a foothold. The workers were frantically buzzing in alarm, many of the sisters' gleaming stingers extended, ready to give their lives for the hive.

The heads of soldiers seated on drones formed a line, but even through the blockade of human and megabee, Romara could see the dark stripes of Little Head workers. Of course it was them. Who else would steal honey from their hive, when they were already struggling after the winter?

"Fiends!" Romara shouted, as they joined the attack. Other workers—human and megabee—were fighting back with legs, stingers, and scraping tools. The metal blades were tools, but doubled as handy weapons. The mounted soldiers had long-handled pikes, much more useful for keeping enraged megabees out of stinging distance. A stinger could run straight through a human.

Romara dodged wings, legs, and mandibles, slicing at wing joints and eyes whenever they saw the distinctive dark stripes.

"The honey stores!" was shouted from the side of the cave, and Romara twirled and rushed in that direction. A line of the Little Head megabee workers had broken through, ridden by well-armored human troops. They rushed down a passage, using the walls and ceiling as well as the floor, sliding through Pointed Hill's workers when they could and stinging when they couldn't. Romara rushed after them, dodging the body of a fallen sister who thrashed in pain from a sting to her abdomen.

"Stop, thieves!" Romara called, but the soldiers of Little Head barely paid attention to them.

"Out of the way, shortlegs!" one cried and pushed Romara sharply, so she rebounded off a cave wall. Through blurred vision she saw the workers and soldiers breaking open capped cells of sage honey as the workers gorged themselves on Pointed Hill's stores.

By the time Romara got back to their feet and soldiers from their side appeared, the Little Head thieves were already done, slipping back around the late guards and out the hangar opening. It had taken only moments, and Romara stared at the sad, ragged cells, empty of honey. No mead for the solstice festival. They might not have enough to survive the summer. They imagined Pointed Hill dead and silent, inhabited only by scavenging yellowjackets.

"After them!" a guard cried, and Romara found themself caught up in the tide. Except, they realized when they got to the cliff edge, they had no guard bee to ride upon.

"Get that honey back!" someone shouted. As the guards took off in formation. Romara turned side to side, searching. Everywhere they saw wounded workers, sisters tending to others or dragging dead bodies away. None of the megabee guards were around. They had all flown off with the human guards.

"Is there anyone left?" Romara cried. They would not stand idly by while Little Head stole their precious honey, even if they weren't a guard. Larvae would go hungry, and their population was already down. Every warm body could help get it back.

"Anyone?" Romara called. They saw no more guard bees.

Herbert bumbled into view, weaving drunkenly, his long, pointed tongue extended to suck up drips of sage honey the attackers had left in their wake. Somehow, he had made it through the fight. Drones had no stingers, and no defense against angry workers.

"Fine. You're my new ride." Romara grabbed a bridle and stalked toward the inebriated Herbert.

* * *

June pressed forward against the thorax of Capella IV. A young queen like this, not yet mated, was a coil of power, frisky and diving through the endless floor of flowers. On foot, a person could go from one end of the flower valley to the other, never seeing the true ground, far below. While flying, they looked like a sea of color. Capella IV had almost unseated June twice, and though she thought the young queen was playing, June held fast to the royal reins and buckled the straps on her seat belt.

Mount and rider flew above and below the flower line, buzzing past foragers from Little Head and the surrounding cliffhives. Some of the foreign megabees whirred their wings in irritation at the smell of unknown queen pheromones, but Capella IV didn't stop long enough for them to catch her. She was a delight to fly, twice the power of regular workers, and with so much more personality.

"We're going to make a good match, you and I," June called to her new queen. As soon as the invasion of Pointed Hill was complete, June would take her place. Most of the existing workers would fall in line with their new queen and the swarm from Little Head. It was rarely required to kill more than a few, once the old queen was gone.

As if the thought was a summons, the whirr and buzz of an approaching arrow of bees and beeriders filled the air with their noise. June tried to pull Capella IV off to the side, but the queen, ever her own bee, rose directly toward the group.

"What are you doing?" June called, pulling the reins to direct her away, but Capella IV ignored the bridle under her antenna.

All too soon, June faced the line of megabees, but relaxed as she recognized the dark strips of Little Head workers. The queen must have sensed her subjects.

But her relief was short-lived. Closing quickly from behind were ranks of unfamiliar bees and beeriders, flying noticeably swifter than those of Little Head. June guided Capella IV to fall in with the riders at the head of the line.

"Did an advance party from another hive attack you?" June called to the soldier in the lead. "How can I help?"

"It's the soldiers from Pointed Hill, Your Highness," the soldier called back, tugging at an imaginary forelock in front of his helmet. "They didn't take kindly to our seizing their honey stores."

June looked across the line of fleeing megabees, flowers flashing past below, only now noting abdomens distended with honey. No wonder the soldiers of Pointed Hill were catching up. The best honey in the valley. Her mother must have known that as well.

"We were supposed to mount a full attack and install our queen—*this* queen." She gestured at Capela IV. "Why steal honey now, when the hive will need it later?"

"Orders from the queen herself, Your Highness," the soldier replied. "She wants to weaken Pointed Hill before the full assault. But I fear we won't make it back without another fight."

"You leave that to me, sir," June retorted. "But tell my mother I will be having *words* with her when I return." She pulled Capella IV up and away before the soldier could do more than give her an anxious look. No one liked to see division in the hive.

June pointed the queen between the fleeing soldiers—no, *thieves*—and the ones from Pointed Hill rightfully chasing their lost property. Property that should be *hers* when she took over the failing hive. They were already halfway between Pointed Hill and Little Head, the flower fields stretching out below them.

It was a risky action. Foreign workers probably wouldn't kill a foreign queen out in the open, and these megabees were currently away from their hive and the influence of their own queen. Susceptible, June hoped.

She held up both hands. "Stop, I beg you!" she called. "I know you have suffered, under my cliffhive's aggression. But I ask you to let these soldiers go for now. They were only doing as told, and I will speak to my mother the queen about returning their ill-gotten gain."

The line of megabees closed. Had the soldiers heard her? Was Capella IV's influence strong enough?

They were nearly upon her when the first megabees faltered, swooping around Capella IV in confusion. The effect grew, as the entire line began to rotate about the virgin queen—a natural swarming inclination.

June patted her mount's back. "Good work, girl," she said. Then to the confused soldiers buzzing around her on all sides, "Please, hear me out! I offer negotiation."

"Why should we listen to you?" someone shouted. It was hard to see who, in the confusion.

"Because I offer parley in good will. We will return your honey. I know your queen is failing. There are other options for our hives." *Ones that don't require theft.*

"You steal our honey and offer it back as a gesture of good will? These are not honorable actions."

Who *was* speaking? Most of the soldiers, in fact, were ignoring her, attempting to wrest their megabees' attention away from Capella IV's influence to follow their quarry. They were *ignoring* her! A princess on a queen megabee!

"Well? What do you have to say for yourself? Still have a taste for Pointed Hill mead?"

June's eyebrows rose as a larger form—though not much larger—came into view between the megabee workers. A drone? With a party of guard bees?

The smallish figure on the drone's back pointed a finger at her. A familiar, muscular form. "That sage honey is for the solstice festival, and to feed our young. Without it, the hive won't survive the summer!"

The summer—when June should be taking her rightful place as the new leader of Pointed Hill. Was her mother the queen trying to ensure June would be no rival until the next year, when Little Head was flush with honey stores?

She eyed the smaller figure, now certain it was the server from the winter festival. She had longed to meet them again, though in better circumstances. Why would a servant fly with the guards? On a drone, no less. Their legs clasped the drone's thorax, flexing as they flew, and their arms showed corded muscle as they fought the reigns. Was that drone...drunk? She'd seen them get that way, gorged on honey.

"I believe we can come to terms peacefully," June found herself saying, though her eyes lingered on the rider. The guards around them seemed to fade away.

The servant had trouble of their own, with their drunken mount surging forward against the bridle, trying to fly nearer to Capella IV. Was she ready for mating already? But surely not with this runty drone from a failing hive!

"There is no peace with honey thieves, even led by beautiful princesses!" the figure shouted back. Then mumbled words that sounded like, "Not now, Herbert."

Perhaps they were distracted. Had they meant that last part?

But June didn't have a chance to ask. The other soldiers were gaining control of their megabees, their rides determining the foreign queen was not a threat, but also not an ally. Several took off after the Little Head soldiers, but June had delayed them enough. Her people would make it back to Little Head.

"I will speak on your behalf with my mother," June called out to no one in particular, though she watched the figure riding the drone, whose eyes seemed to find her own. Braver than the soldiers, to challenge a princess. A fiery personality, indeed. No wonder their mead was so delicious, if they put so much of themself into it. June would find them once more, as soon as she took over Pointed Hill.

She pulled Capella IV's bridle, urging the megabee down into the cover of the flowers before the guards could get any ideas. The new queen obeyed, thankfully, plunging between the giant flower stalks. June turned her charge back toward Little Head, but spared a glance upward for the drone and the figure riding him.

* * *

Romara scraped wax off the walls of Pointed Hill hard enough to flake the stone. The soldiers had faced a larger force of guard megabees near the entrance to Little Head and returned without their honey. Romara hadn't really understood how much larger that hive was, nor how much Pointed Hill had decreased in population.

Herbert bumped their leg with his mandibles, and Romara turned on him. The little drone had stuck to their side ever since they returned, probably hoping for more sage honey.

"Some help you were! You were all over that prissy little queen like a mite after a grub. Don't know what you see in that little firecracker from Little Head. They're so rich they're breeding new queens to expand."

And the princess riding the queen. The gall to tell them she'd figure out how to return the honey, as if it wasn't much quicker to simply demand her subjects to bring their ill-gotten gains back. Just because her long blond hair billowed in the wind like the beckoning petal of a flower. Just because her ample hips, astride the queen's thorax, promised smooth curves and a generous backside...

Romara shook their head and attacked the wall of wax again. Not that it would help.

Fewer and fewer pupae were developing. There was still no sign of a new queen cell. Humans could manually feed a larvae enough high-concentration nectar to turn it into a queen, but the new queen was never well accepted by her colony, as if the megabees could sense she wasn't truly picked by the nurse bees.

They needed another option. What if...

Romara dropped their scraping tool.

They turned back to Herbert, nuzzling their leg.

"How'd you like to go after that queen again, boy? Let me find a saddle."

Herbert's antenna wiggled in excitement, and he buzzed his wings.

* * *

"Mother, you have to let me back out. Capella IV must fly! She must find her mate if I am to take over Pointed Hill."

June had been stuck inside the Little Head cliffhive for the past three days, her queen locked away in a different room of the royal apartments.

"I won't have you risking that queen any longer," Her Majesty the Queen said. "I've moved up the time for the invasion of Pointed Hill since you decided to risk your queen flying amidst the advance soldiers. When Capella IV is fully mature, she will be escorted with a suitable contingent of guards to the best mating site in flower valley, with the genetic line of the drone fully researched. Then you will be installed as the new ruler of Pointed Hill."

"They were thieves, not soldiers, mother," June retorted, her chin raised. "If I am to lead this new colony, I will need resources. Why handicap me by stealing honey?"

"Because we must have it to feed our new brood," her mother said. "We are still expanding."

"But one of the... But what if Pointed Hill doesn't have enough honey even to last the summer?" Best not to mention her encounters with the servant from Pointed Hill.

The queen waved her hand. "Preposterous. Any self-respecting hive is sure to have plenty of stores. Anything less and they don't deserve to be a part of the flower valley."

June curtseyed, eyes down, to hide her frown. Could her mother really *not* be aware of the situation in Pointed Hill?

June considered. How could she be, after all? The last time her mother the queen had left Little Head was the winter festival. She was only concerned with her hive, not the whole valley.

As soon as the queen left, June went to her window—one of the few in the cliffhive, given only to the royal family, situated close to the cliff wall—and pulled a pin from her hair. She long ago figured out the method for unlocking the window. It had been locked for "her protection," but what was that to one who would eventually control a cliffhive?

When the latch *snicked* open, June hoisted her skirts and pulled herself out onto the ledge running along the cliffhive. It was used by cleaners, usually, but she had found it was equally as effective for sneaking out of the palace.

Capella IV was held two rooms down, and the queen buzzed with happiness when June entered her room. The megabee workers attending her made room for June, who carefully checked the queen for any mites or malnutrition.

Three minutes later she was riding Capella IV down the main corridor of the hive, heading to the hangar. She was unbothered until she got to the door of the hangar, where guards snapped to attention on each side.

"Your Highness! Are you supposed to be here?" one asked. Wasn't she supposed to be locked in her room, he meant.

June drew herself up to her full height, on top of Capella IV's back.

"Did you not get the word? The new queen is to have exercise to ensure she is strong enough for her mating flight. Need I return to Her Majesty my mother for her to personally confirm the orders?"

"No, ma'am!" the guard quickly saluted and moved aside. June urged Capella IV past before they could change their minds.

The hangar was a bustle of activity, even more than usual. Besides the foragers leaving and returning with baskets of pollen on their legs, a line of soldiers waited next to their megabee mounts.

"My mother the queen *has* moved up her timetable," June told Capella IV. "This looks like she's starting the invasion immediately!" June directed the new queen to the other side of the hangar, slipping behind workers and out beside several foragers.

Finally, she was free. She would meet up with the soldiers later. For now, Capella IV must mate so she would be ready to take over her new hive.

June let the megabee queen find her own path, away from both Little Head and Pointed Hill. And away from that strange worker who had set her on this journey.

* * *

Every day, Romara had snuck out to scour the flower valley alone for the new queen and her enchanting rider. From Herbert's actions, the queen was ready to mate, which meant she'd be visiting the drone sites. First the winter festival, now this. Romara hadn't been able to get the princess out of their head, as if they'd been fated to meet each other.

They understood why, now. The princess had a commanding presence. Once captured, she and her mount would make good leaders of Pointed Hill, replacing the old bumbling queen, who had given away their pollination rights.

Herbert rumbled under them, sober now the sage honey was gone. He loved the attention, zooming around other drones in the mating fields. Drones from all the local hives—some with riders like them—went there in hopes of being the one to mate with a new queen. Very few ever would.

"A few more hang-out spots to check today," Romara told the drone. They had looked through most of the local spots, maneuvering Herbert through the larger drones. No queens, much less the one they were looking for.

Herbert rumbled again, straining away from the main area of the flower valley. Romara pulled at the bridle, but Herbert ignored the irritation under his antennae.

"We've still got another three left," they told him. "You can't cut out now."

But Herbert took off across the valley, Romara tugging at the lead.

"What's gotten into you?" they called over the rushing wind. Herbert was usually a very laid-back drone. Did drones get withdrawal from sage honey?

But Herbert only flew on, away from the mating grounds, away from Pointed Hill. Romara clenched their teeth against the wind and hunkered down between Herbert's frantic wings, fields of giant flowers passing beneath them.

It was some minutes later when they spotted a lone megabee and beerider ahead of them. They were nearly to the edge of the flower valley, out past most of the dead cliffhives. What was that rider thinking? There were all sorts of dangerous insects inhabiting the dead cliffhives. The bee in front of them was heading straight for a pass between two hills, as if she wanted to leave the valley behind altogether.

Romara could feel the heat from Herbert's wings. He was running hot, trying to catch the megabee in front of them. Romara peered closer. No, the outline was wrong. It was larger than a normal megabee.

They would recognize that rump anywhere. Both of them.

They slapped Herbert's back, "You found her, didn't you? But what's she doing out here?"

Romara raised their hands to shout at the rider in front of them at the same moment the yellowjackets plunged down from the sky.

* * *

June felt the change in air current as the yellowjackets angled into Capella IV.

"Turn around!" she yelled as she jerked at the reins. But Capella IV was already curving her abdomen, her sting extended, ready for a fight.

Yellowjacket raids were rare inside the valley. Patrols kept them at bay for the most part, though sometimes they preyed on the small hives near the edges of the valley. The attackers were about the same size as a megabee, but slightly narrower and longer—in fact almost the same size as Capella IV. And there were three of them.

June held on for dear life as the queen under her zipped to one side, barely evading the first swoop by a yellowjacket attacker. The second one was quicker, and bristled legs scratched against her back, trying to find purchase. June looked up into the yellowjacket's stinger, coming right for her face, as a blur of motion barreled into the wasp, forcing it off June and the queen.

Capella IV looped, and June's hair, which had already come undone from its bun during the first attack, fell around her head, obscuring her vision.

"We must flee!" she shouted, groping for the bridle. But though she was buckled into the saddle on the queen's back, her hands found only air. She tipped back as Capella IV went vertical, buzzing angrily. June felt the wide abdomen under her pulse as the queen's stinger struck home and began pumping venom into her target.

June finally cleared the hair from her eyes to see Capella IV push one of the yellowjackets off her stinger with all six legs. A little farther away, a bulky form with a beerider was fighting the other two yellowjackets. Had one of the guards followed her from Little Head? No, this figure was familiar—had been in her thoughts these last few days. Were they so fated to meet again and again?

They were riding that drone again—with no stinger! They were either braver or stupider than she thought.

A yellowjacket abdomen curved inward, stinger extended, and the Pointed Hill worker made a slicing gesture with what looked like a simple scraping tool. But it must have been sharp, because it cut through the stinger, venom spraying out in a gush to fall harmlessly away.

But neither bee nor rider saw the last yellowjacket right itself and swoop in. She would not lose them before she had a chance to question their actions. And why they kept meeting.

And those strong arms, used to wielding a scraper and maintaining the hive.

"Go, help them!" June screamed, flicking the reins, and this time Capella IV obeyed, diving in to collide with the last assailant much as the megabee had knocked one off her back. While June passed the rider, their eyes locked, and time slowed in that moment, as if each of them transmitted the stories of their lives to each other.

Capella IV bit at the yellowjacket with her mandibles, holding it to sting over and over again. Fortunate that queens were unlike workers, where one sting was enough to end the megabee's life.

The worker from Pointed Hill rose up on their drone's back, sharpened scraper extended. One final blow and the yellowjacket's head fell away from its body. Capella IV let go and the rest of the pest fell into the sea of flowers below.

Now to get answers to many questions.

* * *

Romara gasped for breath, holding a hand out to the ephemeral princess riding the queen megabee. With her hair flowing out to all sides, she looked like some warrior of old, leading an army of bees to battle.

"Are you alright?" Romara asked, still panting. "I thought those 'jackets would kill you for sure."

The woman brushed her hair back with both hands, clasping the queen's abdomen with her knees, then quickly tied it in a loose knot.

"While I am grateful you are here, what reason do you have for following me? We've been running into each other since the winter festival. Are you now tracking down princesses for nefarious means?" Though she tried to hide it, a flush crept up her cheeks.

Romara, for their part, swallowed, not ready for the sudden questions. "I...yes, actually," they managed, then searched for some suave line, but their mouth got there before them.

"I've been looking for you every day. I was going to capture you so your hive wouldn't attack us. Ever since the festival, Little Head has been hemming us in." They cringed as they heard their own words.

The woman's mouth opened, then shut. Then opened again. "So, you are no better than those yellowjackets, coming to attack me?"

Romara raised their hands. "No, never attack. I want you to come back with me. If you and that queen are in Pointed Hill, then the armies of Little Head won't dare to steal our honey again."

Now the woman looked thoughtful, her hair framing her tulip-like face. "I had no wish for your honey to be stolen." She put a hand on her mount's long back. Both bees were jostling around each other, vying for the same space in the air. "Her name is Capella IV," she said. "And mine is June."

"And I am Romara." They tried to give a little bow, but Herbert bucked. "And Herbert, of course. He's been a bigger help than many of the workers, even if he does like to get drunk on the honey stores. He's really the reason why I came after you. He just took off...hey!"

Herbert bucked again, but this time nearer to the queen, Capella IV. The queen—a virgin one, Romara could tell from the abdomen—shimmied away gracefully, but not *too* far away.

"Ah, June, I hate to say this, but we may need to separate a bit," Romara said. "The bees are getting a bit agitated."

June sniffed. "Capella IV would never go for—oh!"

Now the queen bucked under her, approaching Herbert, then backing away again.

"Perhaps you are correct," June said, and pulled on the reins. Her mount did not respond.

"Come on, Herbert," Romara pleaded. "We're way out at the edge of the valley. Can you not get all horny right now?"

But Herbert responded as little as Capella IV had, pulling against the reins and reaching for the young queen.

"I do not believe I can control her!" June cried, and that was when Romara saw the *other* problem.

"Up here, on Herbert's back—quickly!" Watching a drone and a queen together was a rare sight, even for a megabee handler, but Romara understood the positioning of it. June would be smashed flat in the process.

June pulled at her seatbelt frantically. "I'm trying, but it's stuck! When the yellowjacket attacked, it stepped on the buckle and crushed it!"

Romara unbuckled their own belt in one motion and vaulted off Herbert, straight onto Capella IV's abdomen behind June. June, despite riding the queen for half a day or longer, was a vision, hair streaming again as she twisted and pushed her chest against the buckle.

"Hands off!" Romara cried, and when June pulled her hands back, they struck the buckle with their scraping tool, severing it in one strike. "Come with me," they said, extending a hand.

"We're right above the flowers!" June answered, taking their hand without hesitation.

Romara didn't even look. The flowers of the valley were nothing if not ever-present. They jumped off the queen's back, hand in hand.

* * *

June landed on a soft surface and rolled, tangled up in her skirts and in Romara. The bees had been moving fast, and the momentum kept both of them going while June scrabbled and grabbed at flashes of soft yellow that sped past her.

Romara did the same, and as June realized they had landed on the center of one of the giant daisies that grew in the flower valley, she finally grabbed a handful of the yellow florets. Romara went past her, and June grabbed at their overalls.

"Got you!" she said, as Romara's front half dangled between two table-like white petals.

"Don't let go!" Romara's muffled voice came, as their hands searched for purchase. Finally, they found it and pushed themself back up on the center of the daisy. They sat up, panting, and June again admired their strong arms, toned from a lifetime of cleaning wax from walls and tending to a megabee colony. The sun haloed around their head. Queens might be essential for a hive, but the workers were the ones who really controlled things. June wondered if her mother the queen had forgotten that.

"Well, this is a mess," Romara said, their eyes locked on her face. "Are you okay?"

"I am fine," June said, and tried to stand up, but the flower surface rolled beneath her, and she fell forward.

"I've got you." Strong hands clasped around her waist, and June turned to face Romara.

"Finally," she observed. "It took our two hives feuding to bring us together."

Above them, Herbert clutched Capella IV by the hips, similar to how Romara had grabbed her.

"About that," Romara said, dragging June's gaze back to them, "you *do* know what happens to drones after they mate, right? We're...ah...only going to have Capella IV to fly us home. A new Queen of Little Head. A rival hive trying to encroach on Pointed Hill. You have me at a disadvantage, Your Highness."

June licked her lips, trying to determine what to tell them. Then she looked into Romara's eyes. There was only concern there, for Pointed Hill hive, and, dare she hope, for June herself.

"They were not just stealing honey stores," she said, her mouth getting away from her.

"They weren't?" Romara looked concerned, but still held her.

June shook her head. "My mother the queen decided Little Head needed more reserves, in order to expand. In order to bring an entire army of megabees to take over Pointed Hill, with me at their head."

Now Romara dropped their hands, and June found herself missing the touch.

"My mother is even now preparing to invade Pointed Hill."

Romara's eyes widened. "Why tell me this?"

"Because I do not agree with my mother. There is already a new queen in Little Head, so Capella IV needs a hive to run." She sought Romara's hands again, running her fingers up their arms to their biceps, tracing the muscle. "I cannot do anything about it for now, with a virgin queen. However, with a *mated* queen, I may be able to sway the soldiers who attack." She smiled and leaned into Romara. "No matter what happens, we seem to be stuck here, without a ride home, until..."

"Maybe we were fated to find each other," Romara said, lips turning up, and it was as if the sun had come out from behind clouds, though it already shone brightly. "I came to find you. I was going to capture you and bring you and Capella IV to take over from our old monarch, who gave away so much to your mother at the festival. Our queen bee is no longer fertile."

June pressed closer, feeling the circle of Romara's hands close around her back. "Then are we in agreement? Do we wish the same outcome?"

Above them, Herbert mounted Capella IV.

"I think we do," Romara said, gazing into her eyes. "I think we've been moving toward this conclusion since we first met."

"I've thought the same." June folded in closer to Romara, as the megabees consummated overhead. "Perhaps now is the time to get to know each other better, while we're stuck here, with no way back to our cliffhives."

"You know, I've heard one could walk the length of the flower valley without ever touching the ground," they said.

"But who listens to old tales like those?" June said. She looked to the edges of the giant daisy. She could probably jump the gap to the next one if she really wanted, but...she didn't.

Romara followed her gaze. "Best not to test it." Their eyes roamed over June's face, as if trying to memorize it for a painting later. "There must be a lot a humble megabee trainer could learn from a princess."

"First lesson." June leaned into their lips, and Romara stiffened, then melted into her mouth. They tasted of summer honey, with a hint of sage. She was out of breath when they broke apart, but her eyes stayed glued on Romara's. "How to properly kiss a princess."

"Many thanks for the lesson," Romara said, their lips quirking, breathing hard.

"You seem to be a quick learner, but our mounts have set a precedent before us," she breathed. "I should teach you more."

"We must catch up indeed. Who are we to disavow nature?" Romara asked. Their strong arms gripped June's hips, pulling her closer. June plucked at Romara's overall straps, undoing one.

Romara grinned lopsidedly at her and undid the other fastener with one hand. Their overalls dropped, leaving them only clad in a tan linen worker's shirt.

"Are yours so easy to unfasten?" they asked.

"Second lesson: a princess must always be dressed for the occasion," June said, and reached behind her for the ribbon closing the back of her dress. It flowed under her fingers, unraveling, and she shrugged her shoulders until it too fell to the daisy's surface. She wore nothing underneath.

* * *

Romara pushed June back into the soft florets of the daisy: a bed, by any other name. Romara's hands swept down her inner thighs, then up to brush the tips of her nipples.

"You're not too sore from riding all day, are you?" they asked.

"Lesson three: a princess trains to ride for *years*." June clutched at Romara in return, dragging fingernails lightly up their arms and across their stomach. "The question is whether your chest is tired from wrangling that drone all day."

"Drones are much easier to ride than queens."

"Then you shouldn't mind..." Her hands dipped lower, into wetness.

"I had no idea a princess' hands were so smooth," Romara gasped.

"Lesson four: beeswax. It's good for all sorts of things."

"I'm way ahead of you on that one," Romara said. They took a chunk of beeswax from their back pocket, soft and pliable. Easy to mold into a silky-smooth cylinder, long enough for two.

"You know how to use that?" June asked.

"You're not the only one who's had lots of practice riding," Romara smiled, working quickly with their hands to position it correctly.

They rendered June speechless as they pressed deep into her. Then, though a combination of fingers and beeswax, they rendered her very loud for a time.

When the world intruded on Romara again, June sprawled beneath them with their legs intertwined, they realized Capella IV was resting at the edge of the daisy, expectantly. Herbert was nowhere to be seen, but Romara knew what had happened to him.

"Found some princess, made sweet love to her, and died with a smile on your face, didn't you?" Romara said.

"Well, I wouldn't say you're dead yet," June answered. "Feels like you might be able to go a few more rounds, especially if you have more beeswax."

Romara laughed—a bittersweet one, half for Herbert and half for themself. They patted their pockets. "Perhaps I could, but I think the new queen is getting impatient."

June sat up at that, her breasts magnificent in the sunlight, areolas like unfolding roses against her skin.

"Oh, they're done. And...just Capella IV."

"That's right," Romara said. "We'll both have to ride her back."

"Have you ridden a queen before?" June asked.

Romara only stared back, trying to keep a smile from their face.

June's face pinched into a wry smile when she realized what she had said. She smacked Romara's arm. "Pay attention. This is not like riding a drone or even a worker. Queens are individual and willful."

"I've learned a lot about willful queens lately," Romara answered, then relented. "And I learn quickly, as you've seen. You can teach me some more lessons," they said, taking her hand.

June made a cute pout. "So you do. Lesson—what number are we on? Five? A queen needs a consort, especially if they are going to take over a hive," June said.

Romara gave a little bow. "Are you asking, Your Highness?"

"Do you see anyone else out here?"

"Then I'd be delighted to fill that role, if you would like."

"I would like that," June said, and led them to Capella IV.

Romara spared a glance over the edge of the daisy as they mounted behind June's wide hips. The sea of flowers was deep, and there was no chance to see Herbert's body. He'd never have any more sage honey. He was a drone, after all, and had completed his purpose—more than many other drones did. Very few actually mated with a queen, and this way, his line would stay with Pointed Hill.

They leaned into June as Capella IV leaped into flight from the daisy. She obeyed June's commands this time, heading toward the Pointed Hill hive. Romara curled their hands around June's stomach, and she pressed back into them.

Now to see if the megabees there would accept Capella IV. It was a strange thing that the queen of a megabee hive had very little say in her own rule. It was instead the will of the megabee workers. They would accept Capella IV or not, and if they did, the previous queen's life was forfeit. The human queen often stepped down at the same time, as the hive's personality derived from the queen megabee.

* * *

June landed at the edge of the Pointed Hill hangar. They had made it before her mother the queen's army, fortunately. The guard bees at the entrance made room for her, sensing Capella IV's pheromones, the mix from mating with Herbert the drone. The guards must have sent word, because the human queen of the hive—the elderly woman who had negotiated with June's mother at the winter festival—made her entrance to the hangar a few moments later.

Romara hopped off and spoke to several of the human guards, gesticulating wildly back at June and Capella IV. The guards conferred, looking between June and the current queen of the hive. She was happy their long pikes were still held low, and not raised to skewer her.

"You bring new hope with you," said the queen without preamble as she approached. Romara bowed low before her.

"Your Majesty Queen Montay, I bring a new megabee queen to replace our failing one." They didn't mention the human queen's position—that would be rude—but the queen sighed.

"Have you. Then I see the time has come. Truly, I welcome it." She turned to June. "May I ask your name, Your Highness?"

"I am Juneifer, daughter of the Queen of Little Head. Though I know our hives have had their differences in the past, I offer a solution that may be more peaceable than the alternative originally proposed by my mother. If we are quick, I can stop the army that is even now approaching." She clasped her hands behind her back to keep them from shaking. The only way this would work was if she was fully confident.

"I see," Queen Montay said. "From the strength of their negotiations and their raid, I knew we had no chance against the Little Head cliffhive. Perhaps now we do. You come in peace, then?"

"I do," June answered. "Capella IV is also ready." The megabees around her were already accepting their new queen, tending to her needs, and feeding her nectar from the Pointed Hill stores.

"Then I will begin the transfer of power," Queen Montay said, "and I wish you and Pointed Hill the best."

* * *

It was nearly the end of the day when Romara followed June into the royal apartments. As soon as the Little Head megabees sensed Capella IV in residence, they had refused to fight, and the soldiers had no choice but to surrender, betrayed by their mounts. Now Pointed Hill had a sudden influx of new workers, ready to gather nectar for the hive. Romara felt a sense of relief wash through them for the first time this year.

Queen Montay would stay in her rooms for now, but there was a spare suite meant for the royal heir—sitting empty for several years now as the queen was childless. June had immediately appropriated it, deeming the furniture, including a bed, fitting, if dusty.

The rooms had been thoroughly cleaned soon after by an army of servants. Romara would have been beneath their notice the day before, but now they were treated with almost as much deference as June.

Romara carefully shut the door, but turned to find June's face close to theirs.

"We did it," June breathed and leaned in for a kiss.

"Was there any doubt? You certainly didn't act like there was," Romara said with a grin. They had never been near the royal apartments before.

"Lesson six: never show fear," June said. "But being by your side helped. And speaking of being beside one another..."

Romara pulled her toward the newly cleaned and changed bed. It was bigger than any they had seen before. Certainly bigger than their hammock.

"You know, most queens go on several mating flights over a series of days so they can lay new eggs for many years after they get too big to fly."

"I love it when you talk megabee husbandry," June said with a half-grin.

"If you need someone skilled in husband-ing duties, I know where to get more beeswax," Romara said, pushing June back.

"Better follow up on that. I'll have to accompany her if Capella IV goes out again," June said, staring up at them.

"I'm sure she'll want me to come along. You know, if you get bored waiting for her to finish..."

"I'll try to finish at the same time, if you're there with me," June said, and pulled Romara down on top of her.

"Flight of the Megabee" is a short story by William C. Tracy. Want to read more of his works?

Join his mailing list at **www.spacewizardsciencefantasy** and get a free story at the same time!

If you want to read along with his new stories, check out William's Patreon at **www.patreon.com/wctracy.**

Into the Churn

N.L. Bates

Sapphic Representation: Lesbian
Heat Level: Medium
Content Warnings: Coarse Language, Violence, Death

"You want to hire *how* many heliosaurs?" Kirin said.

"Ten," the other woman—Natasa—replied promptly. "Two for cargo plus sixteen crew. It's two to a dinosaur, yeah?"

"And you want to fly them into the Churn."

"And back out again," Natasa said. "We're Wreckers. That's what we do."

As if that would be easy. Managing that many heliosaurs was a challenge at the best of times. Flying those same heliosaurs through the floating islands and violent storms of the Churn seemed downright suicidal.

If Natasa hadn't insisted she could pay up front—and offered to show Kirin the bank notes!—Kirin wouldn't have even looked at her. But training heliosaurs was an expensive business, and the Wreckers were offering ten times what Kirin would normally charge for a four-week trip. So, Kirin looked. Mostly at Natasa.

She was tall, with softer curves than Kirin would have expected from someone in her line of work. But the calluses on her hands said she knew what it meant to earn a living. Her heart-shaped face was haloed by short brown hair, and her clothes, hugging her frame in all the right places, were weather-worn and spattered with mud.

Which was a step up from Kirin's own clothes, at the moment. She'd slept in costume, for one, after the unbearably pompous merchant at last night's heliosaur showing had demanded demonstration flight after demonstration flight before deciding he didn't need a flying dinosaur after all. Then, during this morning's briefing, she'd slopped the contents of a half-empty helio trough down her shirt. So her clothes were ridiculous, and a mess, and she'd made an idiot of herself in front of her staff. Including Christal.

Christal, whose dark hair and wild eyes had caught Kirin's attention from the moment she'd been hired on. Christal, who was completely oblivious to the way her presence glued Kirin's tongue to the roof of her mouth.

Christal, who as one of Kirin's stable hands was definitely off the table as far as romance went, so Kirin would never have to find the courage to say anything to her other than, "saddle that heliosaur, would you, please?"

The Wrecker cleared her throat. Kirin stared into the intense brown eyes of someone who definitely did *not* work for her, and realized she'd been daydreaming.

"Ten heliosaurs," she echoed, ignoring the heat creeping into her cheeks. "That's a lot of salvage."

"That's the hope." Natasa gave her a crooked grin. "The islands that popped up a few weeks ago? They're right over where one of the old ironclads sank. One of the ones with a *steam engine*." She leaned forward, and Kirin felt a flutter of excitement. The woman's enthusiasm was contagious.

It had been more than two decades since ships started disappearing along previously safe trading routes. Tropical storms had expanded to encompass entire oceans. Soon after, the first island punched its way up from the Atlantic, dragging part of a shipwreck with it.

That first island rocketed into the sky, where it stayed. More islands followed. Ocean storms pelted coastlines with detritus and debris. Much of Kirin's childhood had been hard and hungry; her parents' stories of seaside adventure dried up overnight. And with North America struggling to sustain itself, cut off from the rest of the world, nobody was spending much time on experimental tech like steam engines. Instead, a new economy sprung up from the ruins of the old: salvaging the wrecks the Churn dredged up.

"If the Churn unearthed that beauty," Natasa was saying, "shit, I could retire on what that would bring in. We'll have the big firms lining up to bid—we just have to get there first. That's where your heliosaurs come in."

"Wait. How would you have gotten there without them?" Even if it were safe to sail the Churn, the lowest islands were still miles above the ocean's surface.

Natasa raised her eyebrows. "Does that mean you'll hire them to us?"

"I haven't decided." But Kirin found she was smiling. "Humour me?"

"Sure. Imagine a kite the size of you—we call them skimmers. There's lots of updrafts and downdrafts in the Churn, so we strap into a skimmer and the wind takes us where we want to go."

Kirin realized her jaw was hanging open, snapped it shut. "That sounds..."

"Slow? Tedious?" The hint of a smirk touched Natasa's lips. "Impractical for hauling large cargo?"

"Dangerous," Kirin finished.

Natasa was definitely smirking now. "You see why we want the heliosaurs."

Kirin took the hint. "Come with me."

Natasa trailed her out to the paddocks: miles of open fields, with a handful of outbuildings scattered around. "Huh," Natasa said.

It was Kirin's turn to smirk. "Not what you were expecting?"

"Nope." Natasa didn't sound embarrassed to admit it. "Those don't even look like they would *fit* a heliosaur."

"They don't," Kirin agreed. "They store supplies. The helios prefer to sleep outside."

"So, what, you tie them down to something?" Natasa asked, looking around at the distinct lack of chains or hitching posts.

"You could probably find a chain the heliosaurs couldn't break," Kirin replied, "but they don't like being restrained. Good way to get squished." She grinned. Surprising people with how things really worked was always fun. "We feed them."

Natasa blinked. "Say again?"

"Wild heliosaurs fly for dozens of miles a day to find enough to eat," Kirin explained. "We make it so they don't have to. We give them food, water, a comfy place to sleep."

She paused before she delivered the line that always impressed stuck-up dinosaur tourists. "They're here because they *want* to be."

But Natasa was a tougher mark, apparently. "And 'here' is...where exactly?"

Kirin reached for the whistle that hung around her neck. When she blew it, a dark shape appeared in the sky. Kirin heard Natasa's intake of breath.

"Bend your knees," she suggested as the creature hurtled toward them. The force of the heliosaur's landing sent Natasa stumbling back, and Kirin reached out a hand to steady her. "Meet my friend Noble."

Noble was easily three times Kirin's height, even perched on all fours, curious black eyes gazing down at them from the end of a long, swanlike neck. If swans had necks as big around as a person. And that person was a lumberjack.

Variegated wings stretched out from his foreshortened front limbs, almost like a bat's except for the feathers at the edges and tips. His hide was slate grey and leathery, with blue highlights in his feathers and the fleshy wattle under his chin.

"Go ahead," Kirin said to Natasa, who stretched out a tentative hand. Noble extended his neck, snuffling at the Wrecker with a beak as long as Kirin was tall.

"So. Those miles a day, can they do that all at once?"

"They can fly for a day or more without stopping," Kirin replied, "if conditions are right."

Natasa gingerly patted Noble's beak. He snuffled her again. The wind of his breath tousled her hair, which framed her face in a way Kirin could only describe as unfair. "Lots of gasses and such in the Churn. We have respirators, but nothing that'll fit this fine fellow. That going to be a problem?"

"They actually process ambient gasses through their wattle," Kirin said. "It's part of what keeps them aloft.

Changes their flight patterns some, but an experienced handler can compensate."

"I'm sure your handlers have lots of experience," Natasa drawled. Kirin resisted the urge to lick her lips. "Seems like your heliosaurs will do the job. I'm guessing we'll need one of your folks to come along?"

Kirin cleared her throat. "That's right."

"The crew authorized me to make this official." Noble snuffled Natasa once more, then ambled away, fanning out the feathers that tipped his sinuous tail. His talons scored person-sized lines in the grassy soil. "You need me to sign something?"

"Hold on," Kirin said. "I need to understand what kind of conditions I'm flying my heliosaurs into. And my handler, for that matter. What else should I know?"

"Nothing to scare anyone that lets that monster fly them around." Natasa grinned. "I could tell you about the time I caught a bad updraft and wound up halfway to the south pole. Or the time I nearly got skewered when a whole new island popped up underneath me. Or—"

Kirin had to laugh. "You're trying to convince me this is a good idea, not scare off a new recruit."

"We've covered most of it," Natasa replied, more seriously. "Long distances, gasses, heat, cold—they don't freeze up in cold weather, do they?

"Chances of the island thing happening are actually pretty slim," she continued when Kirin shook her head, "and a good crew—and we are a good crew—knows the signs. I won't say it's not dangerous, but we have our safety systems, just like you." She met Kirin's eyes. "So. You got someone for the job?"

Kirin hesitated.

It wasn't, in good conscience, a job she could assign to anyone else. Sure, the Wreckers had safety systems, but Kirin was in no position to judge how effective those were. And no one, except maybe a Wrecker, could be cavalier about the Churn.

And yet.

They were offering enough to keep the stables running for at least a year. Maybe more. And maybe this contract would help her bring the heliosaurs into long-distance transport jobs, instead of cobbling together a business as a novelty farm. No more joyrides barely worth Kirin's time. No more parading around in costumes for wealthy assholes. If nothing else, the money would buy her time to make that happen.

"I'll do it."

"You sure about that?" Natasa asked. "Figured we'd need to hire someone, but you"—and she looked Kirin up and down in a way that was decidedly unbusinesslike—"You seem expensive."

Kirin refused to blush. "You're hiring ten heliosaurs. It's already going to be expensive."

"More or less than those pants?"

She was definitely blushing. "Costume," she muttered, crossing her ankles to hide the embroidery around the hems. "For heliosaur showings. Besides, I made this. It doesn't count."

Natasa's laughter was warm and rich. "If you say so. Besides, it's not like it's my money we're spending. Do you always sew rhinestones on the ass?"

Her face was practically on fire. "Whose money *are* you spending?"

The other woman's face shuttered. "Company named Myriad. Sponsorship deal."

At least they weren't talking about her pants. "Well, that's...good. Right?"

"It got us the heliosaurs," Natasa said. Then she raised her eyebrows. "Did it?"

Uselessly, Kirin brushed at a dirty spot on her shirt, still stiff from the soiled water that had dried into the fabric.

"It did," she said.

* * *

Over the next three days of flight, Kirin watched the landscape beneath them change from prairie, to mountains, to foothills as they made their way to the Wreckers' rendezvous point on the coast. After that, there was just one more day's flight to the ocean. One day's flight to the Churn.

The Wreckers and their tools were everywhere. Kirin saw pickaxes, chisels, and crates wrapped in a fabric she couldn't place. But though the Wreckers couldn't help but notice their arrival, Natasa made sure they gave Kirin space to do her job.

The heliosaurs nipped and chased each other across the fallow field the Wreckers had overtaken, shaking the ground beneath her feet. Almost as soon as Kirin had them situated, Natasa appeared by her side. "Let me give you the tour."

Kirin trailed her dutifully through the camp, giving up on names almost immediately as Natasa introduced the Wreckers in rapid fire:

"Our excavations expert. Do *not* stand in the way of her pickaxe—

"—they can't hold a belaying line for shit, but you'll never see anyone as good with a skimmer—

"—thought he wasn't going to come at all, but Jaan talked him into it at the last minute—" A light-haired man waved as they walked by. "—he was almost as hard to get as you were."

"I don't think I'm hard to get," Kirin said without thinking about it.

Natasa chuckled. "I'll keep that in mind."

Kirin's face flushed as she cast about for a distraction. Happily, a couple of the Wreckers chose that moment to approach one of the heliosaurs, hauling a crate between them. The heliosaur tilted her head curiously, extending her long neck toward them.

Kirin started forward. "Shit. I'd better—"

A voice cut through the din. "Hey! Assholes! You stick one single thing to those harnesses without our flight expert looking it over and that's your seat for the whole trip!"

"And that's Jaan," Natasa said wryly, pointing her thumb toward the source of the bellow. "She's in charge."

Jaan was a tall, wiry woman with black hair and a brisk manner. "Glad to have you, and all that. Forgive the crew. We're particular about how we pack."

"It's fine," Kirin said. "Thanks for reeling them in."

"Of course," Jaan replied. "Now. Do you need to be in a particular position to do...whatever you need to do with the heliosaurs?"

"Not really," Kirin said. "They can hear a whistle cue from miles away."

"It's good to have someone who can perform from any position," Natasa said blandly. Kirin nearly choked.

Jaan rolled her eyes. "I can reel her in, too, if you want."

"I. Um. She's—it's fine." She could handle a little flirting. Especially from Natasa.

"Suit yourself," Jaan replied, but she was smiling. "Natasa, you're on point."

Natasa nudged Kirin with an elbow. "That means we'll be riding together. You can tell me if all your costumes look like that."

"Um. Good?" Kirin managed. Clearing her throat, she added more firmly, "Yes. Good."

Jaan handed Kirin a package that turned out to be Wrecker safety gear: gas mask, heavy overcoat, rain- and heat-repellent cape, and one of the you-sized kites Natasa called a skimmer.

"So how much of this stuff is from your sponsor?" Kirin asked.

Natasa paused.

"Not a jot of it," she said finally. The line of her lips convinced Kirin not to press the issue any further.

They loaded up the next morning. Noble stood patiently as she paraded him in front of the Wreckers. "The harness or gondola goes here, in the centre of their backs. They're secured here, here"—she gestured to the rings at the base of Noble's tail, neck and beak—"and here. Do *not* forget the line that goes from neck to beak."

"Do we get reins?" one of the Wreckers asked. "How do we steer?"

"Absolutely not," Kirin replied. "You leave the steering to me."

Ignoring the resulting grumbles, Kirin showed the crew how to mount and secure a flight harness, pointing out all of the straps and fasteners that had to be done just so. She scolded the crew about double- and triple-checking their tethers. After they were all strapped in, she checked each one herself. Then she made them wait while she checked the harnesses again.

Almost before Kirin realized it, they were flying into the Churn.

* * *

At first, there was nothing to see but fog and ocean. And then, quite suddenly, there was. The fog went from barrier to blanket, pressing on them like a sagging foundation. Beneath them, the ocean started to bubble, froth and, well, churn. Out of the corner of her eye, she thought she spotted a pop of orange-ish light. When she turned to look for the source, it was gone.

There were silhouettes everywhere, brooding dark spots against the fog. At first Kirin couldn't figure out why they were so disorienting. Then she realized it was because they were all around her, level with her on Noble's back or even higher, in places where they definitely should not be. Reaching stalagmites and stalactites with nothing to anchor them down.

The islands.

The smell hit next. Brine, yes, salt and seaweed and rotting fish. But there was something else, too. Sulphur or phosphorus, she thought. Maybe both.

"Do we need gas masks?" she said over her shoulder to Natasa. "The smell…"

"Not yet," Natasa replied. "You get used to it."

The crash and the bubble of the waves seemed too quiet. Kirin's breathing seemed too loud. Even Noble was uneasy, crooning and trilling under his breath. The breeze, at least, was a relief. At least *something* moved in here.

If there was wildlife, Kirin couldn't tell.

"So," Natasa said after a while. "What's with the no reins thing?"

Kirin seized on the chance for conversation. "Remember their wattle? It's the only part of the heliosaur that's really sensitive. Yank a rein around and you could injure them pretty badly."

"Huh," Natasa said. "So, it's whistle or nothing?"

"Some people sit at the base of the neck and steer by putting pressure on the wattle," Kirin replied. "Usually with a lightweight rod. But I'm not a fan. Besides, I'd like to meet the person who could make a heliosaur turn its head if it didn't want to."

Natasa laughed with her. The chill of the Churn became a little more bearable.

"So," Kirin hazarded after a moment. "This sponsorship thing."

"Uh-huh."

"I don't really understand how it works," Kirin said. "People just…fund you to do this?"

That got her a reluctant chuckle. "Not quite that simple. But there's some pretty amazing stuff in the wrecks out here. Old tech, cultural artifacts, stuff that just doesn't make it across the Churn from Europe or wherever anymore. Everyone wants a piece of it, but the big companies? They're goddamn clueless. That's where we come in." Startled, Kirin looked over her shoulder. The set of Natasa's shoulders said Kirin hadn't imagined the venom in her voice. "That's sponsorship. If we fail, it's no skin off their nose. But if we succeed, they get to yell about their contribution to history or technology or whatever, and nobody at the company actually has to lift a fucking finger."

Having already asked one stupid question, Kirin decided to chance one more. "So...why is that a problem?"

For a long moment, they flew in silence.

"It's this way," Natasa said at last. "Most times, they buy you a bit of new equipment, you don't owe them anything in return, their payment is they get to holler about how great they are. No strings attached, right?"

"Sure," Kirin said.

"The bigger sponsorships, though. Suddenly those companies think you owe them something in return. First right of refusal, maybe a cut of the take. Maybe all of the take. Maybe they set those terms up front. Maybe they don't."

Ah.

"I take it that's happened before?" Kirin started to ask, but a gust of wind threw them both forward in the harness. Kirin felt Natasa grab her waist. Even Noble seemed to feel it, flapping his great wings once, twice, before reclaiming his equilibrium with a haughty *screee-ee-ee-e-e*.

"Yeah," Natasa said breathily. "Company offered us some shiny new skimmers, supposedly had better carrying capacity, only they hadn't tested the stuff before they offered it to us. They figured *we* could do that. Bet you can imagine how that ended."

Kirin wasn't sure how to respond.

Fortunately, Natasa didn't seem to expect her to. She chuckled ruefully, relaxing her grip on Kirin's middle. "Not how I prefer to get fucked, you know?"

A flush crept up the back of Kirin's neck. Desperately ignoring the part of herself that wanted to ask how Natasa *did* prefer...certain activities...she settled on a safer question. "So, what're the terms of the sponsorship for this trip?"

Kirin heard uneasiness in Natasa's huffing laughter. "No strings attached."

Somewhere behind them, a heliosaur shrieked.

The air around them was suddenly alive with helio cries. Human curses, too. "It's just a little wave, damn you—"

"—These things are freaking out!"

"I got it!" Kirin yelled to no one in particular and whistled the heliosaurs up and forward. Sometimes giving them a job was enough to calm them down.

But Noble wasn't having it. He tossed his head, rolling an eye the size of a dinner plate back to glare at her. Kirin blew the cue again, and Noble finally huffed and canted his body upward. His nerves were clearly ragged.

"Me too, buddy," Kirin muttered. "Me too."

* * *

They'd been flying for several hours when the sky came alive with oranges, greens, and blues, more colour than Kirin had seen all day in the Churn. "What—"

"Change of plans," Natasa said.

The colours turned out to be flares, signaling a change of route that brought them to a small, rocky island. The island's most notable feature was the broken ship, slimy with dead barnacles and rotting seaweed, that must have attracted the Wreckers in the first place. How they had known it was there, Kirin had no idea.

By the time she had the heliosaurs fed and watered, the Wreckers had broken the ship open, hauling what remained of the cargo out through rotting boards. Off to one side, Jaan and some of the others sorted through a crate of waterlogged textiles. It looked like garbage to Kirin, but every now and then someone would set something aside that they clearly meant to keep. One of the Wreckers poked at a small fire, which popped merrily.

"Are you sure that's safe?" Kirin asked. The air still carried a tang of phosphorous. "The fire," she clarified when the man looked at her quizzically.

But the Wrecker—Amile, that was his name, the one Natasa had said was hard to get—still looked puzzled. "Why wouldn't it be?"

"You mean the smell?" Natasa poked her head out from the wreck. "Don't worry about it. Day or two from now and you won't even notice the whole place smells like farts. Here." She side-stepped through the boards and handed Kirin another half-rotten crate, which Kirin took without complaint. "Got some strength on you," Natasa remarked approvingly, eyebrows rising.

Kirin made herself ignore the warmth rising in her cheeks. Two could play at the flirting game, after all. "You've seen what I do for a living."

Natasa's answering chuckle warmed her as she walked the box over to the fire.

Then there was a triumphant crow from inside the ship. "We've hit pay dirt!"

Pay dirt turned out to be a few sloshing oak casks, large enough that the Wreckers had to roll them out. "Alcohol," Natasa explained, coming up beside her. "Not the most interesting find in the world, but the seal's intact, so it'll sell."

"So, what is?" Kirin asked.

"Hmm?"

"What's an interesting find?" Kirin clarified. "If alcohol isn't it."

"Stuff that tells us how the world used to work," Natasa replied. She gestured Kirin toward the fire, then sat, making herself comfortable. "Old maps, if they're in something waterproof. Old tech. Like that steam engine."

"You think it'll still be intact?" Kirin asked.

"Who knows," Natasa said. "But even if it isn't, maybe someone gets to piece it back together. And if they do, it's because *we* dredged it up."

"And it'll make us rich," one of the other Wreckers piped up. Jaan rolled her eyes.

"That helps," Natasa agreed with a smirk. "Even broken, that stuff gets a good price."

"Figure Myriad will pay a premium for this one no matter what," the first Wrecker agreed. "It's one of theirs, isn't it?"

"Is it?" Something in Natasa's voice made Kirin look up.

"Maybe," Jaan said. "Lots of companies used those shipping lines, before the Churn."

"But Myriad was the only one sending ironclads that way," the same Wrecker insisted.

"And we took a sponsorship from them? That's a bad idea, Jaan," Natasa said tightly. "You know it is."

"I don't *know* anything," Jaan said. "We're speculating."

"*Educated* speculation," the Wrecker insisted. Jaan shot them a glare.

"I'm serious," Natasa snapped. "If they think it's one of theirs, they're gonna want it back. They'll do whatever it takes."

"They can buy it off of us, just like anything we salvage from the Churn." Irritation etched lines across Jaan's face. "This is no different."

"Of course it's different. They've got skin in the game now." Natasa's fingers were stiff on her lap, as if she were resisting the urge to clench them into fists. "Half of us were *on* that crew. We all know they can't be trusted."

"Look," Jaan said. "I went through that contract with a fine-toothed comb. We're not on the hook for *anything*, even right of first refusal. And we already have their cash. It's what got us the damn heliosaurs."

Kirin wished Jaan had left the heliosaurs out of it. She wished it more when Natasa turned to her. "Yeah? What do you think of all this?"

"Leave her alone," Jaan said.

"Why?" Natasa retorted. "She's crewing with us, after all. Did you know, the flunky with the bank notes mentioned her farm specifically?"

"Of course they did," Kirin protested. "I don't think there *are* any others."

"Yeah? Doesn't stop them from offering you a little something on the side."

"Do you seriously think that?" Kirin bit back sharper words. "Nobody offered me anything except this crew, and this contract. You *signed* it. Ten helios and a handler, and that's all."

"Contracts don't mean shit for people like Myriad." Without another word, Natasa stood and walked away.

No one spoke. Kirin hated the silence of the Churn more than ever.

"Sorry about that," Jaan said after a moment. "There was an...incident, back when."

"She mentioned something about it," Kirin said.

Jaan grunted. "I'm surprised she did that much. She lost someone important to her when it happened. Still has a hard time with it sometimes."

"Oh," Kirin said, because she had to say something.

Most of the Wreckers headed for their bedrolls after that. Eventually, the silence of the Churn lulled Kirin into something like sleep.

* * *

Kirin wasn't sure what to expect when Natasa climbed into the harness the next morning, shoulders set. An apology, maybe. But Natasa only said, voice neutral, "So how'd you end up as a dinosaur jockey?"

Small talk was better than nothing. "My uncle was an experimental engineer, before. Flying machines. After, he studied the Churn."

Natasa shifted behind her. Kirin had her attention, at least. "And what, he just lassoed the first heliosaur that stuck its head out of there?"

Kirin laughed, too loud in the dead air. "He actually thinks they were around before that. The Churn just made them more common. So, he watched them for a few years, and then decided to...experiment."

"Sounds too easy." But there was grudging curiosity in Natasa's voice.

"Not nearly. My uncle bores his dinner guests to death with the details." It was on the tip of Kirin's tongue to invite Natasa to a family dinner to experience it for herself. Maybe it would sand away the rough edges between them. "I, uh, I could give you a rendition."

Or maybe not.

"Bet you could," Natasa said. "Because you're the only dino farm in all the world."

Kirin couldn't tell whether that was a jab. "Something like that."

After that, they flew in cool silence.

The cold of the Churn was miserable. The heat, when it came, was worse.

Kirin shivered in her overcoat, sodden with fog and ocean spray, but now the wool became hot and sticky against her skin. Her cheeks, exposed to the bite of the winds, felt flushed. Every breath was an ache in her throat.

Something crawled along her back. At first Kirin thought it was another manifestation of whatever weird fever she must be experiencing. But when she looked behind her, she saw Natasa peeling open the backpack Kirin had forgotten she was wearing. Natasa shook out a layer of glossy black fabric. "Heat protection. Put it on."

Natasa was already wearing hers. That, along with the way Noble's wattle had puffed out around his neck like a frilled collar, finally made Kirin realize the heat was real.

A burning raindrop landed on the back of Kirin's palm. She yelped and yanked her hand back, but not before another raindrop hit her upturned wrist. She could already see the skin starting to blister. Kirin wrestled the protective cloak over her shoulders, pulling the hood up.

Noble shook his great head in irritation, as if dislodging a fly. And then again, and again, as more raindrops hit his wattle.

Kirin turned back to Natasa. "We have this for the heliosaurs?"

"In the gondolas," Natasa replied. "It was too bulky to store anywhere else."

"Then we have to stop," Kirin said.

"It's only a couple more hours—"

"They can't fly long in this," Kirin insisted. "We have to stop."

Natasa hesitated, then finally said, "Bring them up." When Kirin started to protest, she added, "Just trust me, alright?"

Trying to swallow the sandpaper feeling in her throat, Kirin whistled. Natasa pulled a flare out of her pack as the heliosaurs flew upward.

"The heat comes from the ocean. It'll disperse higher up," Natasa said. "I've signalled the stop. Jaan will give us a new heading soon."

The new heading was an island of sand and scattered boulders. As Kirin dismounted, Noble blasted her with a pointed, clicking exhale. "We're working on it," she promised him.

Natasa doused the flare as soon as Jaan started their way. "We need heat sheeting for the heliosaurs."

"On it," Jaan said, and started calling out directions. The heliosaurs huddled together unhappily.

"It's good you spoke up," Natasa said. "We didn't expect the rains to start this soon."

"That happens a lot?" Kirin asked, mostly for something to say.

"Usually not until we're farther out."

Natasa always seemed happiest when talking about the Churn. Maybe Kirin had a chance to smooth things over. "Listen," she said. "I—"

But Natasa looked at her warily, and the words dried in her mouth.

"I have to help break camp," Natasa said finally, and turned away.

Securing the sheeting to the heliosaurs' necks turned out to be no easy task. Finally, one of the Wreckers—Amile the hard-to-get—took pity and offered a hand. Kirin accepted gratefully.

They had just finished when a couple of Wreckers walked past them, carrying a crate. A few more Wreckers followed, similarly burdened. As Kirin watched in bemusement, the Wreckers heaved the boxes over the side of the island.

"What's going on?" she asked.

"We got knocked around during transit," one of the Wreckers called back. "The heat sheeting on our food supplies came loose. Some of them spoiled."

"Oh," Kirin said. "Is that going to be a problem?"

"Not too much," the other man replied. "Just as well you called a stop. We caught it early."

Amile frowned.

Kirin tended to agree. Spoiled food supplies were a hell of a thing to be blasé about. "We should check the helio grains."

The grains were fine. At least there was that.

As she huddled in her bedroll that night, Kirin heard arguing.

"That won't help, Jaan." Natasa's voice, low, angry. "I checked those crates myself, before we left. They were wrapped up tight. If they got unsealed, it's because someone did this."

Jaan, sounding weary. "Say you're right. What do you want me to do about it?"

"For fuck's sake, Jaan."

"Can you tell me who?" And then, when Natasa didn't respond, "If you could, they'd be under my eye. If you could prove it, they'd be off the crew. Since you can't...we can't just start pointing fingers. That's how crews like ours fall apart."

"This shit doesn't just happen," Natasa said, stubborn as ever.

Kirin did not hear Jaan's reply.

* * *

The next few days passed without incident. Amile had taken an interest in the heliosaurs, lending a hand before and after every flight. Kirin talked through the functions of the various cinches and straps as they worked. More than once, she invited Natasa to join these impromptu lessons, but Natasa never took her up on it.

Kirin awoke one morning to a more-orange-than-usual glow and the ever-present odour of phosphorous. The heliosaurs were gamely tolerating the ministrations of Amile, who hadn't waited for Kirin to start harnessing them up. At Kirin's approach, Noble rattled his wattle in an enquiring *crah-a-a-a-ah*.

"No idea," she said.

Amile jumped at the sound of her voice.

"Morning," Kirin said. "Did I miss something?"

"No," Amile replied, too quickly. Then he shook his head. "When you spend as long in the Churn as we do..."

Kirin waited. Amile shrugged. "It's like the heliosaurs," he said finally. "They have moods, right? So does the Churn."

Kirin looked out at the horizon. Pops of light stained the looming islands orange. "What's with the light show?" she asked.

"Another crew, probably." Amile stared into the distance, as if reading the flashes. "Could be the Churn itself, I suppose."

Kirin shivered and turned to the heliosaurs. At least they spoke a language she could understand. "Here, you've got this cinch wrong."

They had almost all the heliosaurs harnessed when the earth rattled beneath her feet.

"What the fuck?" Kirin said, at the same time as Amile breathed, "*Shit.*" The Wreckers were on their feet, grabbing packs and supplies with brisk efficiency.

Kirin looked at Amile. His eyes were as wide as hers must be.

"It's destabilizing," Amile said. "It's going to fall out of the sky."

"W*hat*?"

"We need to go!" Amile shouted, and it was the panic in his voice that finally broke through. "Get on Noble and *go*!"

The island bucked again, nearly sending Kirin flying. Noble was a little ways away, so Kirin grabbed the line of the panicking heliosaur beside her and hauled herself into the harness. She turned to offer a hand to Amile, but he was no longer behind her.

Most of the Wreckers were still afoot, being knocked about by the quake or stamping heliosaur feet. Would the island stay afloat long enough to get the heliosaurs aloft? They would calm down once they were in the air. She could circle back for the remaining Wreckers then.

The island shivered again, and suddenly the question of taking to the sky was academic. Kirin grabbed for the harness as her heliosaur, Argon, launched herself upward. Several of the other heliosaurs followed suit.

But not all. She looked down and saw Noble, along with a few of the others who had allowed training to prevail over good sense. He shook his wattle uneasily, awaiting Kirin's signal as the island's tremors increased to a steady rattle.

Kirin reached for her whistle, but her hand closed on air. The damn thing was as much a part of Kirin's flight suit as her actual flight suit. How had she managed to misplace it?

She'd have to steer Argon from her wattle. If she could calm Argon down, the rest of the heliosaurs might follow.

Too many "ifs," too many "mights." But her options were thin on the rapidly sinking ground.

Kirin reached for Argon's main tether and snapped it into a carabiner on her flight suit by feel. No time to secure the secondary lines. She ran down Argon's back, steadying herself on the line that ran from harness to beak as she started the awkward shimmy up the heliosaur's neck. Beneath her, the island had started to *tilt*.

She had almost reached Argon's wattle when there was a groan the size of the world.

Sudden pressure threw Kirin forward. She felt the tether snap taut behind her, and then, horribly, go slack.

Her shoulders screamed a protest as she gripped Argon's beak line with both hands, dangling precariously over the waters of the Churn. Her hands hurt from gripping the leather as the heliosaur wheeled. "Argon!"

Kirin couldn't even hear her own voice. She wasn't sure if it was the chaos that had drowned her out, or the ringing in her ears.

But somehow, she managed to swing herself upright. Gritting her teeth as Argon juked again, Kirin made herself relax the fingers on her right hand. Not much. Just enough to slide her hand up the line and resume the climb up Argon's neck.

Grip with one hand. Relax the other. Pull up. Grip. Relax. Pull.

There.

Only just, but it would do. Kirin threw her legs wide. Even flattened against the heliosaur's tapered neck, Argon was almost impossible to sit astride. Kirin stretched until her calves ached and managed to press a boot against soft tissue. Not hard. Just enough to bring Argon out of her panicked spin.

Argon banked, pulling herself straight. Pointing her toes, Kirin urged her up. The heliosaur's neck trembled, but she responded, breathing more deeply now her handler had taken control. Kirin swallowed something that felt more like tears than laughter, and finally chanced a glance down.

The island was gone.

There was no debris, as far as Kirin could tell. No rocks or other remnants, no sinking landmark being slowly swallowed by the waves. Just gone.

Kirin took a deep breath and turned her gaze back to the sky.

In the minutes (seconds?) since Kirin had almost tumbled into the watery maw of the Churn, the heliosaurs had scattered to the not-insubstantial winds. She reached for her whistle to call them all back to her, only to remember it was gone.

A blast of cold wind hit her in the face, and Kirin clutched at the leather neck line as Argon shook her head. She needed to secure herself first. Then she could look for the others. With a supreme effort of will, she made herself release a clenched fist, pulling herself hand-over-hand back to the relative safety of the harness's saddle.

She twisted around, trying to spot, she wasn't sure what, anything. But there was nothing. No Wreckers, no heliosaurs.

It was just her and Argon, alone in the Churn.

* * *

It took her a while to stop shaking.

Her first action, after quadruple-checking that all her secondary lines were secure, was to—*carefully*—inspect the harness to see where her tether had failed.

Only it hadn't. It wasn't something Kirin would have spotted at a glance, but one of the supporting cinches had been loose. When her weight was thrown against it, it had simply pulled free.

Even that wouldn't have been a problem if she'd had the time to fully strap in—a single point of failure on a flight harness was never a good idea—but if it had been properly fastened, it shouldn't have come undone in the first place. The fact that it hadn't been seemed strange. Almost deliberate.

Someone did this.

But there wasn't anything she could do about that. So Kirin turned her attention to her other, bigger problem: without the Wreckers to navigate, she didn't know how to reach her destination. Trying to get her bearings, she looked around for any of the others, or at least a spot to land. There was nothing.

At least, sometimes there was nothing. Sometimes, she thought she saw shapes in the distance, sometimes the shadow of an island, sometimes the silhouette of another heliosaur. Once something that seemed like neither of those things, oblong, rounded, with something rectangular hanging from its underside.

Whatever they were, as soon as she turned to look at them, the shapes disappeared. Even the islands. The damn things had been everywhere. Now, it was like they'd *all* fallen out of the sky. She climbed back up to Argon's neck and steered her toward the one low-lying island she could see in the distance, hoping it was close enough.

At least the omni-present odours of phosphorus and sulphur had subsided. Shivering, she pulled her goggles over her eyes, to shield them from the sting.

Kirin lost track of the hours they flew. They didn't seem to be getting any closer. But they were flying through a storm now, and Argon was getting tired. Kirin could see it in her slowing wingbeats, her declining altitude, the deflation of her wattle as she used more and more of her gas reserve to keep herself aloft. The waves were climbing ever higher, hitting with almost as much force as the wind.

Argon shook out her sodden wattle with a protest Kirin could feel but not hear. She spat seawater, fingers numb. The sky darkened abruptly.

A shadow, passing above them. Another one of those damn shapes. Heliosaur-shaped, in fact. But this time, it didn't go away.

An actual heliosaur. With a rider, even, seated on the heliosaur's neck. And the rider was...waving?

The storm fought them, of course, as Kirin urged Argon after the other rider, grasping at them with waves and punishing winds. Argon started to drift lower again, and Kirin dug in with her toes, too hard.

The line of Argon's neck screamed resentment, but she followed Kirin's cue. Up, and up, until she broke free of the storm with a cry.

"We did it," Kirin gasped, throwing herself against the heliosaur's neck. "Good job, Argon."

Now they just had to land. Kirin hoped like hell this rider knew where they were going.

She glanced down, and shuddered. The lashing rain did nothing to obscure the inky, white-capped waterfall that rose from nowhere, pouring back down into the waves below. That was the shape she'd spotted in the distance. Not an island.

A maelstrom.

* * *

Argon settled into the other heliosaur's wake as easily as if she'd been following Noble. It spread the brush of feathers at its tail, its slate blue highlights making it easy to follow.

Actually...Kirin was pretty sure they *were* following Noble.

And the mystery rider was heading for an island. A real island this time, Kirin hoped, not just some trick of the maelstrom.

"Land ho," she said to Argon, giggling.

The mystery rider brought Noble in for a graceless landing, Argon following eagerly behind. When Kirin dismounted, Noble nudged her gently-for-a-heliosaur with his gigantic beak, then turned to Argon and started preening the sodden feathers at her wingtips.

"Good to see you too, buddy," Kirin said, then hoisted herself onto his back to give a hand to the rider labouriously extracting themself from Noble's harness. "Thanks. I owe you one."

"Yes, you damn well do."

Her relief was sharp enough to cut. She knew that voice. Without thinking, she leaned forward to wrap Natasa in a hug.

"Don't go making this into something it's not." The coldness of Natasa's voice stopped Kirin short. "I just don't want your death on my conscience."

Taken aback, Kirin turned her awkward almost-embrace into an attempt to help Natasa unbuckle the harness. "Um, it's this one here. Did you see any of the others?"

"I got it," Natasa said, voice flat. "Just you."

Dread bubbled up inside her. She didn't know any of them well, but she liked Jaan. And Amile. "Shit. I'm sorry. I mean—hopefully they're just regrouping." They knew the Churn, after all. And they had the heliosaurs to carry them to safety. Because if the heliosaurs had carried them to safety, that meant the heliosaurs were also safe.

Natasa yanked on a carabiner, scowling at it as if it were personally responsible for the events of the last few hours. She'd hurt her hand, Kirin saw. She'd wrapped it in scrap fabric.

Automatically, Kirin reached out to unclasp the carabiner for her. "What do we do now?"

Her hand brushed Natasa's bandaged one. She wasn't sure who pulled away faster.

"I *said* I got it." The bite in Natasa's voice made Kirin startle. "The fuck do you mean, 'we'?"

Kirin stared.

"*You*, if you're tagging along, will try your very hardest to stay out of my way." Natasa glared at her. "*I* am going to get us out of this mess. We're still alive, no thanks to you and your damn heliosaurs, so there's a chance."

Kirin winced. "When the island fell. I didn't have time to—some of the harnesses were left undone."

"No kidding," Natasa said flatly. "I don't know what your reason was, but—"

"My reason?" Kirin echoed incredulously. Heat sparked in her gut. "The ground just fell out of the fucking sky, and you think I somehow did that on *purpose*?"

"I'm not talking about the damn island," Natasa snapped. "I *watched* my people fall off your dinosaurs. After listening to you harp on and on about how *safe* they were—"

"It happened so quickly," Kirin said, "there wasn't time to—"

"And I just have to take your word for it, because you're the only dinosaur farm in all the world," Natasa snarled. "I came out here with a crew of 16 people, and we're the only ones who walked away. You really think it matters why? Because if you think I give one solitary shit—"

"It does matter, actually," Kirin fired back. "It matters that you don't think I—that I didn't try to hurt the crew. I followed you here and almost died, and maybe I've lost most of my heliosaurs"—her voice cracked at that—"and if we're going to get out of this mess I deserve to work with someone who doesn't think I'm a murderer!"

There was a long pause.

"Maybe I was out of line," Natasa said finally, in a tone that suggested that maybe she wasn't.

"Yes. Good. Thank you." Kirin took a breath. "So, what do we do now?"

"Stick to the plan," Natasa replied, holding up a hand to forestall Kirin's protest. "It's the only place out here worth going. The others will be doing the same." If they'd survived. "You got supplies?"

"Not much," Kirin admitted. "I lost my saddlebags when the island fell. You?"

"I'm fully stocked." Natasa's tone wasn't accusing, exactly. "Seems like everything on this guy was strapped in just fine."

Kirin swallowed a sharp retort. "Noble's always the first one I harness. I had time to double-check his kit before the island fell."

"Fine." Natasa returned to fumbling with the harness. "Get some sleep. We've got a couple more days of flying yet."

"Let me help," Kirin said. "You've hurt your hand."

"I'm fine," Natasa said, voice flat.

"Don't be ridiculous," Kirin replied. "We need to help each other out if we're going to get out of this."

Natasa pressed her lips together. But she didn't say no.

* * *

The sun, lidded by clouds, peered down at them as they made their way up and east, Natasa seated on Noble's back, Kirin astride his neck to reach his wattle. Even her spare whistle had been lost, or maybe deliberately removed from Noble's saddlebags. Argon, riderless, followed in their wake.

Ahead of them, their destination clawed its way up from the horizon, a collection of strange rocks that jutted up like gnarled fingers. Then they got closer, and Kirin realized what she was actually seeing.

They were corals. Bleached and drying corals. And scattered around, the dull metal remains of the ironclad ship.

It was in poor repair, even for a shipwreck. Its iron plates, themselves overgrown with dead corals and barnacles, had been pulled apart, strewn haphazardly across the island. Kirin wondered how that had happened. It didn't seem possible that the wind could haul such heavy iron pieces around.

"That's us."

Kirin jumped at Natasa's voice in her ear. "Why did you leave the seat?"

"I'm strapped in." Natasa leaned closer. "Listen. The new islands can be kind of unstable. With a crew it would be one thing, but..."

Kirin waited.

"I won't ask anyone to walk into danger with me who doesn't know what they're doing," Natasa finished gruffly. "That's all."

Kirin didn't hesitate. "I'm not getting out of here without you. We'll go down there together."

Natasa didn't reply. But Kirin felt her relax.

Movement caught Kirin's eye. "Look!"

At the base of the coral hills, two huge shapes with feathery wingtips and brush tails ambled to and fro. There was movement in the hills as well, too small to be heliosaurs. People.

"They made it!" Natasa crowed, grabbing Kirin's shoulders. It took Kirin a moment to realize Natasa was hugging her. "The fuckers made it!"

Buoyed by Natasa's laughter, Kirin brought Noble in for a landing. Argon followed behind.

Sand and rotting seaweed crunched under Kirin's feet as she dismounted. She made a beeline for the heliosaurs, and almost didn't see the person coming out to meet them.

"Amile!" Natasa called behind her. "You bastard, you're alive!"

"I am." Amile's face was a study in relief, followed by something too complicated for Kirin to parse. "Good to see you both."

"How'd you bring the heliosaurs in?" Kirin couldn't help but ask. They were both carrying a considerable amount of cargo, although haphazardly loaded. Much of it was in crates or sacks, but there was also a large oblong object, wrapped in familiar black sheeting. The surviving Wreckers had been busy.

Amile held up a small object. Kirin's whistle. "You dropped this when we evacuated. I only got a couple to come back. Sorry." He made no move to give it back.

"The others?" Natasa asked. Amile hesitated, then shook his head.

"You're...you're the first ones." He cleared his throat. "I was hoping..."

Uneasiness pricked at Kirin's spine.

Natasa paused. "*None* of the crew made it here?"

"Natasa," Kirin murmured, keeping her voice low. She didn't want it to be true, but— "There are people in the wreck."

"You've been busy," Natasa said to Amile, eyes flicking to the heliosaurs. "All that cargo. And pulling apart those big iron plates? Had to be a hell of a job all by your lonesome. Have your new friends got the engine out yet?"

Amile stiffened.

"What was your price? A bonus? A bigger cut?" The edge in Natasa's voice could have sheared metal. "Nah, I'm guessing bonus. You were always one to go for the sure thing."

"Natasa," Amile said, his voice thick.

"What about the others?" Natasa continued, relentless. "I'd lay money that they didn't all die out there. You buy them off, or just shove 'em over the edge?"

"*No!*" Amile shouted. Then, more quietly, "No. If they're safe, they're safe. I wouldn't—I'd never hurt anyone."

"You almost got me killed!" Kirin exclaimed.

"Never," Natasa echoed. "Not when our equipment failed at the worst possible moment? Not when we got chucked into the water? I saw some of them go with my own two eyes." Natasa's hands balled into fists. "This is the *Churn*, Amile. Those folks aren't swimming home."

"That was an accident!" There was real pain in his voice. "If the destabilization hadn't happened—"

"Amile." Kirin watched as someone leveraged their way out of the plates of the ironclad wreck above them. "How long have you been planning this?"

Natasa's voice dripped derision. "This entire fucking time."

"*No*," Amile replied. "Not like that. I was only supposed to report back. Then they sent a flare saying they'd changed their plans, they were coming here themselves." Another person had emerged from the wreck. Amile's shoulders slumped. "I was afraid they would hurt the crew if we were here when they arrived. I only meant to slow us down, but the destabilization..."

Part of her wanted to feel sorry for him. Another part of her was dangling from Argon's neck, convinced she was about to die.

The sneer in Natasa's voice was a weapon. "I don't give a shit what you meant."

Kirin opened her mouth not knowing if she was going to forgive him or scream at him. She found she didn't have the heart for either. "So...can I have my whistle back?"

Eyes downcast, Amile reached for his belt.

By the time she'd processed the fact that the thing he'd reached for was not her whistle, Amile had already brought flint to tinder and spark to flare. It popped into the sky, lighting the clouds a fiery orange.

There were shouts from the coral hills. And then a shriek of metal as one of the iron plates rattled down the hill. Pushed aside by those in the wreck, Kirin realized, as the two people she'd spotted earlier were joined by several more.

"Amile." Natasa stalked forward. "What the fuck did you just do?"

"Called for backup. I'm sorry." Amile spread his hands. "They're only here for the salvage, just like we were. Leave them alone. They'll listen when I say you're no threat."

Some of Amile's associates had stopped partway down the coral hills, raising long, cylindrical objects to their shoulders. A sick feeling settled in the pit of Kirin's stomach.

"Just like we were, huh?" Natasa looked at him. Then she punched him in the face.

Amile staggered backward. Apparently, that wasn't enough for Natasa, because she stepped after him, shoving away his upraised hands to reach for his throat.

Kirin was briefly afraid she was about to watch Natasa beat the man to death. Then a boom erupted from the coral hills. Then a second, and a third. Natasa shouted and let him go.

"What the fuck!" Amile screamed. "I said no shooting. They're with me!"

"The hell we are," Natasa snarled.

"Natasa," Amile panted. "Please. I don't want you to get hurt."

"Fuck yourself," Natasa replied.

There were a half-dozen people running down the hill toward them, but Kirin barely noticed. Her eyes were on the people who were clearly reloading what Kirin now realized were coach guns.

Not enough to bring down a heliosaur. More than enough to bring down a human.

"Get on Noble!" she cried to Natasa. Amile had told them not to shoot. Maybe they would listen.

"Kirin." Amile was sporting a bloody nose and a rapidly reddening eye. His voice was nasally, slightly slurred. "They have the heliosaurs chained down. They can't leave. But—Myriad will pay you to bring that stuff back to shore. Maybe future contracts—"

Kirin didn't hesitate. "Not a fucking chance." She reached for the trailing lines on Noble's harness and heaved herself up.

Another volley of gunshots rattled the air. "Fucking hell," she snarled, throwing herself flat against the harness.

Natasa had done the same. Kirin waited a moment, then lurched for Noble's neck, trying to stay low.

"Kirin!" Natasa called. "Good choice back there." And she lobbed something Kirin's direction.

Without thinking, Kirin caught her whistle out of the air.

"Nabbed it from him after I slugged him." Natasa gave her a toothy grin.

Kirin grinned right back. "Get ready!" Gripping the whistle between her teeth and the harness with both hands, she told Noble and Argon to fly.

"You're not tethered?" Natasa shouted over Noble's massive wingbeats.

"I have to get the rest of my heliosaurs," Kirin yelled back. "We're going back in. Just hold on and don't worry, all right?"

The giddy laughter in Natasa's voice sounded like mostly adrenaline. "I trust you."

For just a moment, Kirin felt like she was flying. And not because of the way Noble was driving forward.

Noble accepted the low altitude without complaint. Bracing herself on the line that ran between harness and tail, she leaned over his side. It felt every bit as precarious as when her tether had failed, back when the island fell. As the chained heliosaurs appeared beneath her, she leaned even farther forward.

And jumped.

The drop nearly knocked the wind out of her, and the startle reflex of the heliosaur she'd landed on nearly tipped her over its side. Fumbling for balance, Kirin peered down at the chains holding her heliosaurs down.

They were sturdy enough, all right, but simple. One chain per heliosaur, staked with metal spikes to the broken ironclad beneath.

A single point of failure. Perfect.

The grounded heliosaurs stirred restlessly as Argon, following in Noble's wake, passed just overhead. Raising the whistle again, she gave them permission to do exactly what they wanted.

Go.

With buffeting wings and a shriek of snapping metal, the heliosaurs pulled themselves toward the heavens. The volley of gunshots that followed them hardly seemed to matter.

She spotted movement out of the corner of her eye. In the distance, one of the islands started to move.

Kirin did a double take. It wasn't an island at all, but a large, oblong thing, with fins at its hind end and a gondola under its belly. Her uncle had worked on devices like these, before the Churn, though as far as she knew none had ever flown. A zeppelin.

Now she knew how Myriad had gotten here to begin with. The zeppelin was headed toward them, but it was slow and ponderous, and anyway, Kirin didn't care. She was on Noble, and Natasa was with her, and her heliosaurs were already falling into formation. And then Amile and his people dwindled below them, and they were up, and away.

* * *

Apparently, whenever a Wrecker was lost in the Churn, there was a search. Wreckers from all across the coast participated, just in case there was a chance to bring their lost colleague home.

To Kirin, it felt more like a ritual than a rescue mission. A funeral without any bodies.

She didn't join them. She'd had enough of the Churn. She gave Natasa her whistle, because Natasa had said they were also looking for her heliosaurs. Kirin suspected that was only because Natasa had browbeaten her colleagues into making it so. But still.

By the time the Wreckers had searched the Churn to their satisfaction, Kirin was regretting her decision to wait for them. All she wanted to do was take her diminished herd and go home.

Well, maybe not quite *all* she wanted.

The heavy knock on her waystation-room door was the only sign Kirin got that the Wreckers had returned. "We found three of the crew, actually," Natasa said when Kirin opened the door. "Alive, even." A few more had managed to make their own way home. All told, they'd lost five people and six heliosaurs to the Churn.

"Jaan?" Kirin asked. Natasa shook her head.

Kirin winced. "Sorry."

Natasa shrugged the condolences away. Kirin doubted she had expected anything different. Then Kirin asked the next question, even though she knew the answer. "Any heliosaurs?"

Another shake of the head. "Sorry."

Kirin swallowed. She hadn't really expected anything, but... "Right. Thanks for looking."

"Least I could do." Natasa cleared her throat. "Speaking of which, there'll be a cut of the take for you."

"What?" Kirin asked. "Our contract was for a flat fee."

"Call it a bonus." A slight smile tugged at Natasa's lips. Then she sobered. "I know it doesn't make up for losing them. But if you're worried about the business side of things...we can help with that."

"I...appreciate that," Kirin said. "And that you looked for them." She *was* worried about the business, as much as she hated herself for thinking of it. But she'd just lost over a quarter of her herd, and it was easier to think about losing numbers than companions.

Maybe she should say something to the companions she still had.

"Did you get a good deal?" she asked instead.

"Expect to." Again a little smirk. "Myriad's offering quadruple the value of that whole sponsorship for the engine alone. But since any offer from them comes with an unwritten expectation of 'shut the hell up...'" Natasa shrugged. "Maybe we'll take it. Maybe we'll take the whole lot to auction and let the chips fall where they may."

Kirin nodded.

Natasa cleared her throat. "Hey, you want to know the best part?"

"There's a best part?" Kirin asked.

"That over-sized balloon they trekked out on? They crashed it into the island and sprang a leak." Natasa's grin was positively wolflike. "Myriad's gonna have to pay another crew just to rescue those assholes."

Kirin managed a smile. "Can't say I mind that."

"Yeah. Me neither." Natasa hesitated. "Listen. I owe you an apology."

"An...apology?"

"Yeah." Natasa didn't seem to mind Kirin repeating her like a parrot. "I made some assumptions that you didn't deserve, and treated you like shit because of it." She laughed ruefully. "Made a real ass of myself doing it, too."

"I..." Kirin swallowed.

Natasa raised her eyebrows. "You can say it, whatever it is. I probably deserve it."

"I," Kirin said again.

A tiny smirk appeared on Natasa's lips. "Unless you'd rather just hit me?"

Kirin almost didn't see the tiny flinch in Natasa's shoulders, as if she thought Kirin might hit her after all, when Kirin grabbed her by the collar. And she went altogether stiff with surprise when Kirin pulled Natasa's face to hers.

Then Kirin hesitated. Her hands shook with her need to close those last few millimeters between them, now that she'd finally found the guts.

But still, she hesitated. True, Natasa didn't work for her, and true, they'd done a lot of flirting. But they had argued almost as much as they'd flirted, and Kirin wasn't about to kiss a woman who didn't want to be kissed.

The tension drained from Natasa's shoulders. "Well? You going to leave me hanging, after all that?" The corner of her mouth quirked upward. "And here I thought a dinosaur jockey would be all about the follow-through."

That was all the permission Kirin needed. She pressed herself into Natasa, their lips just brushing at first, then meeting hard. Natasa's tongue flicked, teasing, against her lips, and it was better than the feeling of finally escaping from the Churn. Better than a flight on Noble's back, in unbejeweled pants.

"Good choice," Natasa said, in the space after they'd pulled away. "Been a while since I've done that."

"Apologized?" Kirin asked before she could stop herself.

The vibrations of Natasa's laughter sent little thrills up Kirin's spine. Or maybe that was Natasa's hand, drifting down to her ass. "That too."

"Well." Kirin was suddenly conscious of the volume of her breathing, the rapid fire of her heart. "Maybe we should do it again."

Natasa laughed again, bringing a flush of warmth to Kirin's body. "You saying I need practice?"

"Depends." Kirin traced the lines of Natasa's collarbone with a finger. "What's the answer that means I can kiss you again?"

In response, Natasa pulled her close. Kirin had just a moment to breathe in the scent of her before Natasa was in her mouth, no teasing this time, walking her backward until Kirin's shoulders hit the wall. The faint taste of salt reminded Kirin of ocean. The same ocean that, somewhere behind them, had swallowed her heliosaurs up.

But grief could come later. Right now, it was just the two of them, the taste of Natasa on her tongue, Natasa's lips drawing a tender line along her cheekbone to her neck.

"That one," Natasa whispered, words hot on Kirin's ear.

"Apology accepted," Kirin breathed.

"Into the Churn" is a short story by N. L. Bates. To keep up to date with her work, visit www.nlbates.com. When she's not writing stories about dinosaurs and lesbians, Bates writes and performs music as her alter ego Natalie Lynn. You can find her music at:

www.natalielynnmusic.com.

The Cerulean Princess

Robin C.M. Duncan

Sapphic Representation: Lesbian

Heat Level: Hot!

Content Warnings: Coarse Language, Violence, Abduction, Abuse

1

*By order of the Princex—may their deific steps grace
all the streets of Cardoon, of Lineca, and of every town
in the Hundred Isles—the following rewards:*

- *for authenticated news of the rebel Vermillion's location—five hundred gold farthings;*
- *for capture and return (live) to Cardoon, any member of Vermillion's crew—two thousand gold farthings;*
- *for Vermillion's head—twenty thousand gold farthings;*
- *for capture of Vermillion, her return to Cardoon (i) dead—thirty thousand gold farthings; (ii) live—one hundred thousand gold farthings; (iii) for the return of the star, cruciform, pyramid, diamond paradigms—the title of Earl of Cardoon, and all benefits and properties ascribed thereto.*

- Regal Warrant circulated throughout The Hundred Isles

I soar.

The wind buffets my face. I angle my arms so, tilt my head downwards a fraction, a nod sideways and I plummet towards the ocean waves then—head back, arms out—I climb away from the salt spray back to the heights, to chase the gulls. My name is Astrid Opanimo, and I can fly. Glory to the Princex, I can fly; here above the ocean, or leaping from the Princex's palace—tallest building in our capital, Cardoon—for I am an Eyrsoarer. I am Lineca's last eyr.

This sobering thought returns me to my task. I sweep my arms back, leave the gulls in my wake. For I must reach *Scarlet Sword* quickly. I bring news of the search for Vermillion, reports from the other three ships in our squadron, one of twenty squadrons questing over our island nation. News for my captain, my lover, my heart; Mehdina Taradel. Thought of her blunts my focus. I cant my arms, my path through the cold air becomes unsteady. I've been away from her two nights. I shake. For she makes me quiver, and—even in the stream of cold ocean air that would chill a tern on the wing—she makes me burn.

2

Illustrious and sagacious academicians, surely now, sixty turns after the scurrilous pilfering by heinous Vermillion of the fourth paradigm, we, and thus the Princex—may their reign shine as the sun for another hundred years—must contemplate a strategy for ruling Lineca and the Hundred Isles that does not rely on the glorious paradigms. The power of those relics over the air's aspects is lost to us.

Yes, the Princex's navy pursues Vermillion to the World's end, but government must continue; rising lawlessness must be crushed, commerce must advance. The technological revolution of the age must continue, despite this setback. Foreign raiders must be repulsed by the glorious power of mechanical means. Vermillion will be caught; the stolen paradigms will be restored. Until then, let mechanism be our weapon.

- Maister Flavio Fitanayo addresses the Convocation of
Institutes, Cardoon

Scarlet Sword presents a glorious sight, growing in my vision. Her squadron sisters, *Siren Song, Black Skua,* and *Wavemaster* are mighty warships, puffed up with full canvas, muscled with guns, fast as shipwrights can build, but *Scarlet Sword* bests them, for her captain—even hobbled by lack of her eyrtaster, eyrseer, eyrhearer and eyrsayer—knows the waves like no other, breathes brine, sniffs currents, bestrides the deck as if her feet command the water to carry her. Only one ship is faster.

I curse rising thoughts of Vermillion, our nemesis, who stole the paradigms one by one, as Mehdina's heart grew heavy with failure. The heart that once Vermillion held. In a way, I stole *that* treasure from her, even as she eroded the Princex's power. And I still have *my* paradigm, the only just discovered fifth. Does that gall Vermillion? I hope so.

Sword's scarlet topsail welcomes me home. I bank around it twice out of sheer hubris at my still-growing talents. The crew cheers as I drop to the deck, braking hard, arms outstretched like a gull, to touch down with the lightest of steps.

"What news?"

Ugh. Instead of my Mehdina, I get weasel-faced Lamyn Sakaria, a man of no great stature or grace. Yet he's the Princex's agent; every squadron has one now, to "reinforce" the Princex's stratagems. From what I've seen of this man—who struts the deck like fine clothes could gild a pasty-faced shite—from what I've heard in low discourse with Mehdina's eyrs (for they remain her officers, despite the loss of their powers), he is wily, intelligent, and ruthlessly loyal to the Princex, may they get what they deserve.

"News? That's for my captain, who arrives now." I nod towards the prow from where Mehdina strides up.

In normal course—despite smirking glances of deckhands and crewmates—Mehdina would embrace me, kiss my cheek and neck, strong arms cinching my waist, whisper what new way she's conceived to pleasure me when the lanterns are lit, the dishes cleared away. But my love is as intimidated by Sakaria as her crew, because of what he is—in effect, a spy; what he represents—to wit, censure by the Princex for anything deemed disloyal. He and the dozen guards of his escort.

"Report, Eyr Opanimo," commands Mehdina. Her frustration that messages cannot now be relayed via eyrhearer and eyrsayer is clear. My information is a day old.

"*Siren* and *Skua* put into Moonport during a full-scale riot; protests over the imprisonment of a family suspected of supplying Vermillion. A well-liked family, though. A cargo of cotton was set ablaze. *Siren* suffered damage to rigging, sails, and a large area of her port side. Captain Cujana says *Siren's* seaworthy, but will need repairs.

"After *Wavemaster's* inspection of Fort Garius, Captain Poyallo reports frustration in their crew at the cancellation of all shore leave. *Wavemaster's* platoon disabused the malcontents of that opinion." I nod in ironic deference to his lordship, who gave the order.

Sakaria grunts, the guttural sound clearly intended as approbation. "The country's falling into disarray; indiscipline must be stamped out." His smile thins. "What next, Captain Taradel, Princex's Foremost Privateer?"

He uses Mehdina's full title like ballast to pile atop her responsibility to recover the paradigms, bring the cursed pirate Vermillion to justice. This weight I've seen pull Dina's brow into furrows, or felt as tension when—in her snug bunk—our limbs entwine 'til I've rubbed away her stress with steady hands. Still, after weeks, I wonder about her and Vermillion. Was their love like ours? What words did Vermillion coo in my Dina's ear in gentle hours when the moon paints the shifting waters silver, and the waves' susurration lulls us to sleep? Will I ever know, and do I want to? I mustn't worry about that now; our hunt for Vermillion is all that matters, apparently.

"What next?" Mehdina asks Sakaria. "We keep going south."

3

Vermillion is a thieving wench; her greed laid low the nation;
good captains seek her on the waves; in every port and cove.
And as she fled the rebels rose to fight the weakened Princex;
Lineca soon fell into war; its eyrs weakened sore.

> *Scrub the decks.*
>> *Away with yea.*
> *Pull the lines.*
>> *Away with yea.*
> *Ship the oars.*
>> *Away with yea.*
> *Vermillion is her name, oh.*

Vermillion's lover Mehdina, the Foremost Privateer(e);
she vowed to bring Vermillion back; to face the hangman's noose.
And at Mehdina's side there stood; Lineca's newest Eyr(e);
Astrid Opanimo who can fly upon the wind.

(Chorus, twice.)

- The Ballad of Vermillion (verses four and five) –
Anonymous

Brogine likes Sakaria less than I. But Mehdina's surly first mate and eyrhearer finds novelty in no longer being the least liked person aboard *Scarlet Sword*. We've buried the hatchet since he tried to gut me in the captain's cabin. Enough to keep company over beer, rum or the local hooch in any port's dive bar.

Our duty done till next bell, we slouch in the shade of the larboard rail. We're sailing south, bound for Port Apanto, another place Vermillion might have docked, her old stomping ground. The sun's intent on cooking us 'til we're baked from gut to gizzard. Brogine—constitution doubtless already pickled—sips rum from a tooled leather flask the colour of his weather-beaten skin, while I press a damp cloth to my neck, occasionally throwing it over the side with a string tied to its corner.

"Yon dandy's a frant, *an*' a blagair," Brogine confides.

"Mayhap you're right, Gine. But he's aboard 'til we find the paradigms and bind Vermillion."

He spits on the deck. "Cuwp."

"You've no love for her, then?" I joke. He screws up his face like a lettuce, emboldening me. "D'you think...? Dina and Vermillion... Do you think they...?"

I must have blanched; Brogine chuckles, an unfunny sound. He follows it with an ugly grin. "Used to 'ear 'em at it on late watch. Thought they'd rattle the mast loose. Least yer quieter when *yer* in there stroking each other's kitties." He leers, but I know him enough to take it good-naturedly. I punch his shoulder. Flying builds the muscles excellently. I'm less the gentle flower Mehdina first bedded.

"We'll get Vermillion. Cap'n never surrenders. Yea know that."

"And Sakaria?"

"Heh. He'll get 'is pint o' blood, somehow or other."

4

Tonight I learned my Dina talks in sleep, sometimes,
Whispers dreams aloud that only night may hear,
Witnessing her thoughts it feels like thieving, but I listen,
And fear to hear my love's a lie, but still,
I listen.

- Diary of Astrid Opanimo, Eyrsoarer, Scarlet Sword

I'm coaxed from sleep by Mehdina's fingers. They skate on the sweat-slicked skin of my back. Muggy heat cloaks the cabin.

"Astrid." She whispers it such that I hardly recognise my name. My thoughts swim through the heat. I turn over, fingers reaching for my medallion, the charm that is the winged paradigm itself.

Dina breathes deep and slides atop me, trapping my hand and pendant between our breasts (well, mostly hers). "Astrid, I love you." She breathes it, lips touching my earlobe, teeth closing on soft skin.

"Harder," I say, as her fingers slip down and inside me, and I wet her palm. "Harder."

Only afterwards do I realise the ship's at rest. I hear dockhands calling, brokers shouting offers, drowning each other out. Glancing astern, the windows of Dina's cabin remain curtained, but sunlight claws at the shifting gaps. We're moored at Port Apanto.

Too hungry to think beyond it, Dina orders our repast. We eat oranges till we're sticky, drink fresh water, scarf down some local cake flavoured with spice and dried fruit. The jammy centre explodes in my mouth. We collapse in giggles which Dina quickly shushes. The stain of apprehension marks her beautiful face.

"Don't worry, he can't hear us. And if he does, fuck him."

"That's what Sakaria needs," she opines. "A good reaming."

We chuckle, but the spell that brought us girlish joy is broken.

* * *

Sun clearing the red-tiled rooftops of Port Apanto, Mehdina Taradel strides up a tidy, cobbled street from the harbour, me on her left, Brogine her right. Lord Sakaria treads behind, pace less than ours due to his shorter gait, but his soldiers match stride with him and, reaching the trade gate into the town's government quarter, we must wait 'til he arrives with the requisite authorities.

"I am Lord Lamyn Sakaria, agent of Their August Majesty Princex Apanato, your monarch—may their mercy protect you for as long as you wish. My credentials." He snaps his fingers and his guard captain thrusts a leather folder at the bemused guardsman. The man shrugs, waves us through.

There follow long minutes of chaos in which guards run for clerks, who scurry in search of dignitaries, three of whom arrive and fall to arguing over who should greet Sakaria. Finally—predictably—Mehdina's patience runs out. She steps up, grabs the nearest dignitary by his robe's wide collar.

"Who runs the place?"

"Gah!" says the man, a foot shorter than Dina, already in a tizzy *before* being accosted by a tall, leather-clad ship's captain, brutal sword at her side, enough strength in her whipcord frame to lift him off the ground by his scrawny neck, if my Dina was prone to such vulgar displays of power.

"The mayor," he splutters.

"Get her, now."

"He's...a man," says the dignitary, recomposed enough to be affronted.

"Of course he is," Dina drawls.

Finally, a haughty-looking fellow rolls up plus honour guard of four. The sun's high enough that the mayor's civic splendour is ruined by sweat running through the powder lovingly applied to his jowls. We're escorted to a reception room, but must wait outside 'til his worship composes himself. At least the wood panelled and plastered building is cooler than the sunlit square.

Finally, we're permitted entry. Sakaria wastes no time.

"Sir, have you harboured *Vermillion Lady*?"

The mayor's mouth opens, but no sound issues. Like a fish, he closes it again. He turns to a dignitary, who shakes his head.

"No, we have not."

"You are aware of the royal edict?"

A trick question: to answer "No" would be to invite the noose, but it's a matter of how one answers "Yes."

"Yes," he says, too quickly, without thought.

"Of course," a different dignitary qualifies, waving a parchment under the mayor's nose, which would be unnecessary had the mayor read the edict.

Sakaria's expression remains neutral. He says nothing, like a trap waiting for a victim. Mehdina shifts, rests a hand on her sword's pommel. I glance around, admiring the gilding, marble statues, frescos showing images of conquest, bounty and construction.

"We, uh, will of course take Vermillion into custody should she seek safe harbour here. We are protected by an *elite* fighting force, and our loyalty to the Princex—may they reign for a long time—is unquestioned, sir. Unquestioned!"

"Hmm," says Lord Sakaria. "Well, our inspection of your harbour logs will support your assertion, I'm sure."

"I..." The mayor stops. His neck muscles strain with desire to turn to one dignitary or another with a question to which he should know the answer.

Sakaria's response is smooth as fresh-poured cream. "You have been most helpful in confirming the extent of trust the Princex should place in you. Good day."

The mayor's lower lip jumps to attention. He seems close to rebuking Sakaria for his disrespectful address then realises what a profoundly painful mistake that would be.

I glance at Dina. A tilt of her head implies a shrug. *Scarlet Sword's* contingent departs. No word is spoken as we march down through the town to the harbour, and board *Sword*. Sakaria wants to castoff immediately, leaving Mehdina to explain tides again, as she did in our last port of call.

* * *

The sun's setting as we glide past the breakwater into a sky painted shades of blue and red and gold. Our lanterns are lit, deckhands stride about tasks. Mehdina and I, Brogine and Jantino stand on the poop deck. Jantino waves to some children on the harbour wall.

"Arrest your progress and turn around," says Sakaria, emerging over the ladder's top. "We will fire upon the town."

"We will *what*?" says Mehdina, stepping towards the shorter, robed man. I move to intercept my love, lest she take a step too far. No one's immune from censure, and it was on Mehdina's watch Vermillion—her former lover, mind you—stole four of the five paradigms.

Sakaria tilts his head, corner of his mouth lifting enough to hint at the pleasure he'd take in seeing Mehdina keelhauled under her own ship.

"You witnessed the ignorance of these vapid people to the necessities of empire. I consider their disloyalty confirmed. Even this pit's name is a casual bastardisation of the Princex's name—all hail them. So"—he waves as if to summon a waiter in his favourite bistro—"belay whatever you need to, haul on the requisite ropes, turn this boat around and fire on the town. It is a matter of dispensing the Princex's justice, which you are sworn to do, Captain."

"They're not ropes," growls Mehdina.

"They be lines," Brogine grunts.

"And you bring the *ship* about," I spit.

Dina pushes past me, stands, hands on hips, before Sakaria. The Princex's agent doesn't cower, flinch, or blink.

"Do you protest?" he asks. The glint in his eye suggests he hopes Dina does object. Emotions war on her features. Mehdina does everything with passion; she is commanding, loyal, steadfast and brave. In making love to me she's ardent, abandoned even; but here I see supreme control. Still, tension builds in her limbs. I must act lest she accost him.

"They're not worth our iron," I say. "We must focus on Vermillion."

"*You* must focus on Vermillion," says Sakaria. "I act for the Princex in matters far beyond your understanding. Captain, you will fire on the town."

At least my interjection has calmed Mehdina. She balls her fists, but the tension in her shoulders ebbs.

"Pick a target. I won't fire on houses or inns."

"The town hall will suffice," says Sakaria.

Mehdina gives the order. Brogine repeats the order, slides down the ladder, his shouts putting a fire under the crew. *Scarlet Sword* slows, comes about; three cannon are readied. Sakaria doesn't object to the limitation. The majority of *Sword's* port battery remains capped. His lordship moves to the rail, two of his guards trailing him at their captain's signal.

"Stagger the fire," says Sakaria, already evincing enjoyment. "Two volleys will be adequate; make them think it's a longer barrage."

"Yes, your lordship," says Mehdina through gritted teeth, then shouts the order, "Two volleys! Fire at will!"

One cannon roars, then another, then another. Then the cycle repeats.

ROAR!

ROAR!!

ROAR!!!

The fearsome sound rolls away across the water. The slapping of waves becomes the only sound again as all watch plumes of dust erupt from Port Apanto's town hall. Mehdina trains her spyglass on the building then hands it to me. I find the town hall, what remains of it (*Sword's* gunners are the best in the Princex's navy). The dressed stone walls of the mayor's seat have fallen. The red-tiled roof collapses inward, billows of dust rolling down through sunlit streets.

Lord Lamyn Sakaria lowers his spyglass, nods. "Well done, Taradel. The mercy of the Princex—may their clemency blanket the world—is well bestowed upon you."

Mehdina's not mollified by this slight dressed as a compliment. "Tell me why I just bombarded this town."

Sakaria seems to weigh up pros and cons then deigns to speak. "Years ago, this place was named Port Apanato to honour the Princex—bless their name. Over time, coarse locals and foreigners bastardised the name. This mayor adopted the popular title. Our glorious monarch, in their beneficence, forbore to take action, but the town burghers were informed the change had not gone unnoticed. Still, no correction was made. Another hint has been delivered. Perhaps they will take notice now."

I begin to wonder about our next destination, Mirazel Island, where Vermillion lived for some years. Perhaps—if they escape bombardment—we'll find a sniff of a trace, then the chase will be on.

5

Today served as a salient reminder, lest we forget the power of vengeance. And now, I wonder is it possible Vermillion stole the paradigms purely to spite Dina? Surely not... And is there a risk to mine? Yes, there is always risk.

- Diary of Astrid Opanimo, Eyrsoarer, Scarlet Sword

While *Scarlet Sword's* guns pounded defenceless Port Apanto, our sister ships *Black Skua* and *Wavemaster* visited Dofen Landing and Winter Harbour. Now, three great ships break the waves, forging towards Mirazel. *Siren Song* escorted us to Port Apanto, anchoring offshore, and so remains with us, but *Wavemaster* has not re-joined the squadron. Dina's worried. Not that she'd ever show it, but I see her vulnerability, her passion eating at her control.

"I'll go to *Skua*, learn what I can. Maybe I can find—"

"You'll *not* search for *Wave*," Dina growls, doubtless trying to hide her emotion from Sakaria, but the lord agent has excellent hearing, even through wave and wind. Yet he only watches. "Get me news from *Skua*, report back." Mehdina turns away, strides to the rail, grips it with fingers that might strip out lengths of hardwood.

The sea wind is cool, salt in each breath. I fly to *Black Skua* without pleasure or diversion. I find again that luck's knife slices both ways. There's news both good and bad. *Skua's* captain—Anjo Gaven—cuts a frustrated figure, stomping around his deck in habitual dark blue garb. Face pink with anger (and being unused to these sunnier climes) he rounds on me with a tirade on his attempts to communicate with Mehdina. A young seaman arrives clutching handfuls of coloured flags. Gaven waves him away.

"Maybe I'll persuade you to stay, find an Eyrsoarer in my crew of stumblebums." He steps towards me.

Instinctually, I stand up to him, dare him to try and restrain me. I never could have done that even short weeks ago, still clerking at the Institute of Antiquities, a timid, loveless mouse of a girl. How much Mehdina has changed my life; Mehdina and Vermillion, damn her eyes.

"Tell me the news: *Sword's* cannon are still warm, Mehdina's done with games."

Finally, Gaven spills it. *Wavemaster* was attacked in Winter Harbour, bottles of naphtha thrown into her rigging from a wharf-side granary's roof. Her damage is extensive. Repairs will take weeks, but her crew plan to stay busy hunting down insurrectionists.

I fly back to *Scarlet Sword*, impart the news to Mehdina and Sakaria. Neither's happy, but we sail on. Our mission is set. Hunt until Vermillion is caught.

6

Mirazel, Mirazel, mayhap a princex named you,
But regnal blessings ended there, now denizens proclaim you,
A rufty-tufty bagatelle of taverns and bordellos,
Where questing sailors take their ease, and strain the city's
cellars.
So, if arriving there, good friend, pay caution to your money,
For the thing commending Mirazel is that it's always sunny.
Apart from in the rainy season.

- *From* A Hundred Island Journeys, *by the poet Zorta*
Zuebi

Mirazel Island seems another picturesque tropical place. The sun kisses Port Mirazel's golden stone, quarried from the island's mountainous, wooded core, but there are signs this ducal fiefdom is down-at-heel. The harbour's unkempt. Winter storm damage unrepaired, no scaffold or mason's crew attending to it. Merchantmen are tied up, loading and unloading, but their arrangement's poorly considered. A barque and a brigantine beyond the breakwater await signal or instruction, captains no doubt short-tempered. Mehdina awaits no invitation. We sail in, cutting up a sloop heading to sea. The captain shakes her fist up at us (size matters at sea). Dina ignores her. We moor prow-to, nosing between a barque and a schooner. Departure will be slower, but after weeks of searching, it doesn't take a lover to see Mehdina Taradel's patience running out.

I steal a moment with her as the eyrs—still her leaders on the ship, despite the absence of their powers—oversee our landing.

"Have a care, love," I whisper, glancing around for Sakaria. "Consider *Wave,* her fate in Winter Harbour."

Mehdina's gaze moves smoothly, stops, and I guess she's found the Princex's Agent. "That's why we present a smaller target to the town. We'll get answers here, Astrid, I believe it. In...other days, Vermillion and I lived here. Don't look like that." Her hand comes up to touch my jaw and gently turn my eyes back to hers. "Listen again: She is dead to me. You're all I can see, you, with my eyes and my heart. I strut around and shout the score, but all I can think of is the taste of you, and how many bells till sunset.

"Now," the word—spoken with command—cuts through my yearning. "Ready your shore party. We use the Lord Agent's tactic. He's good for something. The sooner we're done here, the sooner I'll be in bed eating mussels and oysters from your naked tummy, and dribbling brandy on your quim."

"Aye, Cap'n." I salute, spin away, not the least bit giddy, honest! Sweating now, but not from the sun's rising heat.

* * *

Ratter, Faff-herd, a soldier named Corina and I stumble archly through a pub doorway three streets from Mirazel's harbour walk. We left the main street on a side lane, found the alley then the hostelry just where Sakaria said it was. Dina conjectured Vermillion wouldn't be seen dead in the place, but her crew might. And if not, another of *Sword's* search parties roving the town's drinking dens—dressed for spying—hopefully will find word, get us on Vermillion's trail.

The dingy, smelly place is barely half full. I pick a table and drop onto a rough wooden stool. Big, clumsy Faff-herd does the same. I can't tell if he's an expert spy or fell off his stool onto his arse by accident. Either way, plays well with this hovel's regulars, who grunt and laugh. Corina swears like the trooper she is, a stream of filth issuing from pert little bow lips. *Concentrate.* The patrons look like litter blown off the town's dirty streets. Mirazel's dilapidated; if it has a rich quarter, we missed it.

"You're a bully an' a braggart, Faff!" I shout, pushing up, stool clattering to the floor in our prearranged ruse. He lumbers up too, bashes my shoulder, knocking me to the floor. Corina steps between us, blocking him though she's a foot shorter, lean where he's musclebound and powerful.

We swap loud curses, Ratter joining on my side, but we contain our pretended violence, just hand gestures and surly waves so as not to be ejected. Moments later we're dispersed round the bar, grumbling ugly words about our companions, buying drinks for the locals, or letting them win a hand of cards.

Two drinks later—nothing to show for this visit—Corina and Faff leave, him shaking a fist at me, barking like a dog, her dragging him away. I draw a trice and a knight from the deck, slam my cards down and storm out, Ratter hurrying after me.

"You threw a pair o'swans," he protests.

"We're playing different games, Ratty."

Our dubious performance is repeated in three more bars without sign or whisper of Vermillion or her crew. Our next stop's the Duck and Dragon. I pause in the dusty, cobbled street, turning to look back down the hill we've climbed in fits and starts. Baskets and benches clutter the thoroughfare, the odd handcart. We're a mile from the harbour, a hundred feet up. Still, I pick out *Sword's* scarlet topsail like a lover's favour.

The door of the Duck and Dragon bangs open, and two men lurch out, one with a crutch. Their clothes are plain, tatty like the town, worn from long hours in rigging, I'd say. Both wear kerchiefs on their heads to prevent the sun burning scalps painfully white for these parts. Unremarkable for sailors, but the one that isn't lame has a damaged arm, and his sore limb's tied to his chest by a bright, vermillion scarf.

"Hold," I say, Faff stepping to block the lame one. Corina and Ratter corral the other. "That's a pretty sling you have, friend. Where'd you acquire it?"

"Found it," he replies.

"Where did you *find* it, friend?" I step in close. Steel flashes, but I'm quick. I grip the wrist of the evil hand that seeks to slice me. And I'm strong; flying between ships has corded my arms and legs over the weeks. The big man strains against my grip. I see proper shock on his face that a slim girl can restrain him. I give his good arm a tweak. "I can't hear you." I tweak again, he gasps.

"Wha's th'use; she'll boil your eyes, an' flay you for sport. Vermillion left us to heal. Promised she'd pass on the way back an' pick us up."

I pull his arm back slowly. "No! Wha'? I telled you!"

"The way back from where?"

"Easy, Astrid," says Corina, placing a hand on my arm, but I shrug her off.

"Ahhhgh!" His legs go out and he slumps. I let his wrist go, crouching after him, growling—more like a terrier than a hound—before Faff scoops me up by the waist.

"Let 'im talk."

"I need to know! I need an end to this." I need Vermillion out of our lives so I don't have to feel my gut twist every time I hear that cursed name or see the guilt in Mehdina's gaze when I know she's thinking how she failed the Princex, or see her brow clouding with thoughts I *can't* read and she won't speak! I need Vermillion dead.

"Cut—" the pirate stutters through drool and tears, clutching one damaged arm with the other. "Cutter's Landin'."

7

So, while some small residue of power remains, soaked in-to the stone of the paradigm vault here in Cardoon, it is not enough to recharge any eyr's ability. Practically speaking, all eyrs are powerless save Astrid Opanimo, my former protégé, who sails with Captain Taradel. Sakaria, agent of the Princex—may their gaze warm us, dark turn and

bright span—has a duty to see no harm to her, our only
current source of eyr power.

- Academician Hankani, addressing the Convocation of
Institutes

"Now we have a chance," says Mehdina grimly to the
audience of nine around the dinner table in her cabin.

First mate Brogine to her right; me on her left; *Skua's*
Captain Gaven (solidly built—almost dropped him porting
across the gap between the surging ships); and Captain
Cujana of *Siren Song* (much less portly, much more
portable). Lord Lamyn Sakaria, most snide and scheming
agent of the Princex—may they leave us alone for a
thousand spans when this is done—sits, pale face blank and
judging, with his paler guard captain. Powerless eyrs
Sentina, Marin and Jantino complete the guestlist for this
repast.

"Cutter's Landing," says Cujana in velvet tones, belied
by the jaw scar almost hidden by her luscious umber skin.
"Implies she needs repairs. She might be stuck there
weeks. We could have her."

"Or at least get on her heels," says Marin, their eyes
glittering with anticipation of regaining their eyrtasting
ability.

Brogine grunts. My weather eye sees Sakaria nod
slightly. A signal to someone at the table?

"Cutter's is a hellhole," says Dina.

"Aye, cannon-guarded cliffs, hills clear cut for timber 'til
they slide into the water." Brogine considers spitting then
remembers where he is.

"But we'll pursue her, of course," states Sakaria,
intending a command.

"Of course," says Mehdina, curtly.

Dinner is a spicy gumbo of potatoes, fish and beans. The
group eats with an appetite for food, but not conversation.
No wine is drunk, and our guests depart, me flying Cujana
and Gaven back to their ships, which heave close in the

rain and wind-tossed night. I practically drop them on their decks, hurrying back to Dina.

By the time I return, her mood's been tempered by Boravian mescal. She saunters over in a pink silk robe and linen drawers, shucks off the robe, since I'm dripping wet, and kisses me long and slow.

"You make me happy, Astrid, except the times I want to stab you with a dull blade."

"For why?!" I attempt outrage, but she's intent on undressing me—her glass drained and tossed on the bed. Her tongue paints my lips with mescal burn. She doesn't answer, drapes the last of my clothes over her arm, folds, and throws the wet ball towards the door. She's wet now, droplets glistening on her golden-brown stomach, her lean arms, drawers pasted translucent to the curves of her thighs, tempting me into her dark centre.

The garment tries to cling on, but Dina has no use for it, discards it to the door, joins me atop the sheets. She dines out on my body, feasting on my most tender and delicate treats: ears and mouth, neck and lips; she quests across my shoulders to my chest, coaxing tender summits from my breasts that erupt with each surge of the deck and the bunk and my spine. I push her head downwards, but she resists my frantic direction, breaking her journey across my skin—pale here from years in academia—at the whirlpool of my navel, exploring it thoroughly with her tongue.

Suddenly, her pinning hands are gone, her mouth leaves my pelvis bereft. Then she's back, kissing me, mescal dribbling between her lips into my mouth. She moves, dripping spirit on my chest, my stomach, my pubis before a gushing heat lavishes my cunny with tingles, and her mouth devours my resistance; I relinquish all control.

I'm nearly fainted in the cabin's muggy heat, only dimly aware of Mehdina standing, robing herself, moving away, forgoing her own pleasure. I want to call her back, but I don't, for I can sense the storm in her as she stares from the window, the sky dark, the sea surging.

8

To the Governor, Cutter's Landing,
Sir, reports paint a sorry picture of law and order in
your demesne. Report forthwith to the Princex's Secretari-
at what measures you will enact to rectify this situation.

To the Princex's Private Secretary,
Sir, may yer prick shrivel and die, yer wife leave in
disgust, yer children find love on the streets. I choose the
measure o' telling yea to fuck off. Attend to yer mistresses
and leave me to mine!

> *- Correspondence between the Princex's Secretary and*
> *the Governor of Cutter's Landing*

My mother says never sleep on a quarrel. I didn't think
we had, but Dina's mood this morning is foul. Then quarrel
comes.

"You're out of control, Astrid. Corina told me about that
sailor—"

"You'd have done the same!"

"Don't tell me I would torture someone who could
become crewmate!"

She's dressed for deck, me still pulling on boots. She
glares at me, fists on hips. "I am your captain before all
else; your duty is to *obey* me."

"We have to end this, Dina! She hangs over us
constantly, together, apart; dominates our waking
moments, murders our sleep!" How can't Mehdina see
this? Maybe she likes it, still being bound to Vermillion.
"What if it's a trap? Designed to torment us, tease and reel
us in, snare the last paradigm?"

"There it is," she sneers, "all about your precious
geegaw. All about Astrid, Queen of the Eyrs." She storms
to the windows, locks them, stomps to the doorway and

turns. "Stay here. Do *not* leave. That's an order, on pain of binding." She slams the door; it clicks. Locked.

Rage boils in me. I tear the sheets from the bed, throw them down, kick over her chair, snatch up a chart to rip it, then throw it across the room instead, to flap in the air, fall like a dead bird. How dare she?! Like I mean nothing, like Vermillion's poisoned us both. Damn Mehdina, I *will* end this. Maybe then she'll see.

I pick up the fallen chair and advance on the locked windows.

* * *

Cutter's Landing is...I'm conflicted between cesspit and garbage tip. Ladders bridge the gaps rotted through the wooden landing stage. The docks are unremarkable, so—driven by hot anger—I glide inland. Dina will flay me, but I've had enough flailing around. We're closing on Vermillion, all can feel it. Even Sakaria's jumpy; calm reserve punctured by flashes of un-lordly frustration.

And Dina? Does she fear confronting Vermillion, think she can't best her former lover? Is she conflicted by lingering (unwanted?) feelings?

The air's thick in these latitudes; gusting thermals buffet me. The few locals about in the noon sun ignore me. I spy a tower, the tallest building in this grotty place, reaching sixty feet above red-tiled rooftops, pink-brick construction unusual among the ramshackle recycled stone and wood buildings crowding the streets.

A girl waves to me from the tower's top terrace. Long black tresses stream as she moves to follow my path. I bank around the tower, an important building in this decaying town.

Things happen all at once.

A woman joins the girl, a violently red-headed woman.

Vermillion.

The dark-haired girl yells for joy at the sight of me, reaching towards me. Vermillion's features evince a wild glee, gripping the girl's wrist fiercely, pulling her back, for the girl—in her flowing white gown—is trying to mount the railing as if to fling herself into my arms, or to her death.

I circle the tower again. How can Vermillion be here? Where is her ship? Is the girl her lover, her prisoner? What can I do? I have a knife in my boot, but could I best her? Likely not, and what would Mehdina say if I did, if I killed Vermillion?

My third time around, Vermillion has a strong arm around the still-reaching girl's waist. She's wrestled both arms free, and swipes an elbow at Vermillion's head, who jerks away. The girl stamps her bare heel on Vermillion's ankle, swings the other elbow, connects.

I bank hard and up, extending my arms, tipping like a drunken kestrel. I start to drop, have to swoop down then up again to watch what unfolds. The girl's free. Arms windmilling, she launches towards the railing, and over it.

She falls.

I forget Vermillion; forget Mehdina. *Joy of the air, I embrace thee!*

I plunge after the girl who drops, arms spread, the street's packed earth rushing at us. Black hair billows around her lithe form, a cloud along her limbs, arms swelling, bursting with feathers, coalescing into wings. She's...a bird? How—?

Then she's gone.

The street snaps into my vision.

I rear, strain, arch my back, twist my arms, away! AWAY!!

I don't know how, but—back bent near breaking—I drag myself away from the street, and I'm careening at an adobe wall, nowheretogo—

I hit the stone side on, slide and scrape, bruises and cuts my gift for the morrow. I flop in the air, twist up.

Something spangs off the wall beside me. A black cloud descends, blocking the sky, plucks me into the air, carries me away.

"No harm now," says the cloud. "I have you. Bad red is gone."

9

Cannon rip the air apart. Close enough that I must be in the harbour. A generous description for that decrepit jumble of rotting timbers. I roll onto my back, soft wood under me. Bright sky stabs my eyes, but a dark shape moves over me. The girl's long hair hangs around my face, her flanks and shoulders clothed in a crow's black feathers. Her chest is a downy light grey; breasts high, firm-looking, barely human. My eyes drift to her face as her attention is drawn away.

BOOM! Cannon roar again. I twist away. We're on the quayside. Above looms *Scarlet Sword,* her crew scurrying, rigging her for sail.

Vermillion!

Long gone, surely. What did she want with this girl who seemed to be Vermillion's captive, who used my distraction to escape? And she can fly, but not like me. She has wings, is avian in nature. The white dress I saw before was wings wrapped about her.

"Who are you?" I ask, but she rears at the sound of my voice.

"Your folk die." She points out beyond the harbour.

"Astrid Opanimo!" Mehdina yells angrily from above, Sakaria's guard captain at the rail beside her. Then I hear boots. Brogine's clumping down the gangway, swinging a sword around his head like a child's toy.

My rescuer scuttles back, feathers furled, hands and arms distinct from her wings, though they're joined at the shoulder, yet those limbs still are feathered down to the elbow, where the dark fades and copper skin reasserts itself.

Brogine ignores the girl's nakedness. Touchingly, he's intent on protecting me, and I recall again my first days aboard *Sword,* him thinking me a spy, trying to fillet me.

Despite backing away, the girl shows no fear. She laughs, turns, jumps, and soars over the rooftops before Brogine gets near her.

"Yea hurt? Bleedin'?"

"Vermillion," I gasp, the world rushing into my head once the girl departs.

"Aye, her ship's pounding *Skua* and *Siren.* So, how's she in the town?"

"I saw her with..." Uselessly, I turn to where the girl was.

Brogine hauls me up, supports me up the gangway, which is pulled in while we're still on it, jumps to the deck as *Sword* pushes back.

By the time we're gliding past the harbour walls, *Vermillion Lady's* red sails command the horizon. *Siren Song's* topsail, foresail and fore topgallant are holed, and there's a fire on her deck. *Skua's* come around and lets loose, but *Vermillion's* turned by then. *Skua's* volley is ineffectual. I've seen *Vermillion's* gunners work before; I know *Skua's* peril.

Mehdina hollers up into the canvas. "More speed! All speed!" Even Sakaria's agitated, which is unlike the Princex's agent. He can taste the quarry in our sights, but that's different from laying a glove on Vermillion. She *can't* be aboard when I saw her in the town with the winged girl. And if she's not suddenly a witch as well as an oak-bottomed bitch, how will she get *back* on board?

I know the answer, of course, but can't bring myself to think it until the lookout shouts. "Flyers ahoy! Flyers astern to starboard."

She's right. Clear as the sun spanning the sky, two winged women carry a third figure between them. From their passenger's unruly red tresses, it is none other than Vermillion. Not high in the sky, yet enough no shot from us will trouble them.

But I could.

I run to the armoury, rattle down the ladder, run through the ship and back up onto the poop deck. It's the best place to launch but brings me near Mehdina and Sakaria. My new pistol crossbow hangs at my back. Dina sees right through me.

"No, Astrid! I forbid it!"

"Forbid?" That word stops me, not her angry tone. "You forbid it?"

I'm rooted with rage, rigid with it. She closes, clamps her hands on my shoulders. "We've been here before, love," she mumbles. "You've no better chance at her now than in Cardoon Harbour twenty spans ago. Your time will come." She looks up, and I follow her gaze, picking out the receding figures against the sunset. "She'll reach her ship before you catch her. Don't fight me, trust me."

Damn her for being right! I shrug off her grip, wheel around, crossbow bucking on its string. I grab the grip, bring the weapon up, sight on distant Vermillion, and shoot. My bolt falls harmlessly into the sea. Then I turn back to Mehdina. She's fuming, and I wait for fear to roll over me, but it doesn't, my anger remains. Never breaking her gaze, I step close to her.

"I've had enough," I growl. "She stands between us now, and I'm going to kill her."

Mehdina wheels away, hollering aloft. "More speed, damn your eyes!"

Cannon roar again and we watch from our various positions on the poop deck as *Vermillion Lady's* chain shot cuts *Skua's* foremast in two.

10

The damage is done. *Skua* and *Siren* are crippled. They'll repair and refit, but it'll take weeks. Vermillion knows Mehdina won't wait. That should be the only reassurance I need of Dina's faithfulness to me: the look on her face. Anger sets her gaze aflame. The same passion our lovemaking brings out in her, she'd expend on Vermillion as fury. That harridan's humiliated Dina half a dozen times; taken four paradigms under Mehdina's watch—diamond, pyramid, star, cruciform—but it's the bint's use of Dina's heart that pains her the most, I think. Has Dina truly revealed to me the hidden seed of her pain?

And was this Vermillion's plan all along? To get *Scarlet Sword* and Mehdina on her own? Is this a trap? If it is, it's working. Mehdina Taradel is thrashing her crew chasing *Vermillion Lady*. But even the Princex's Foremost Privateer cannot exist without rest. I've been lurking in her cabin through the evening, keeping my head down. Eventually, Dina comes below, slams the door open then closes it gently. It feels like Vermillion toyed with us, but is Mehdina capable of seeing it? A ruse by Vermillion to complete her capture of the Princex's power, the last paradigm hanging around my neck? Now I see this as the all-or-nothing game it is.

"We'll get her, Dina." I'm past caring if she flays me for disobeying.

"What happened in town? You found a harpy? They're from stories."

I relate my tale, ending with, "Feathers, hands *and* claws, with talons for feet. When she took to the air, she...seemed to change. Vermillion—"

"Don't speak of her."

I bite back frustration. "I must; she's all around us, dragging us apart."

"Astrid." She rounds on me. "It's a trap. She means to capture the last paradigm, rip it from your cold, dead neck." The words catch in her throat. She punches the wooden bulkhead.

How long has this been in her head? Since Port Apanto, since we departed Cardoon? "What if it is?" I bark, balling hands into fists. "I've said I'll end her, and—"

A hand pounds the cabin door as the alarm rings loud from above. Dina strides to the door, flings it open.

Sakaria's captain leans in. "Boarders!"

11

A pretty picture greets us up top.

Two bird-girls cower under threat of blades bristling from soldiers and sailors. One bird-girl slumps on her front, arm gashed open, bleeding on *Sword's* deck. The second—also half feather, half flesh—crouches before her companion on pink, clawed feet and bare knees, black talons on dark feathered arms menacing her aggressors, black wings flicking, shadowing the deck. My rescuer from Cutter's Landing.

"Back!" she screams. "Hurt not more! No harm from us!"

"Easy, girlie," says Brogine cooing to her, hands extended, open and empty.

"Hobble them!" Sakaria commands his troops, but I've long since had enough of all the shit raining down on us.

I stride into the fray without pause, putting myself between girls and soldiers. I turn my back on the bird-girls, whose claws could rend me to shreds. "Not on this ship, your lordliness."

Dina holds up a hand to stay the raging tempers, then turns and crouches before the panicked bird-girl.

"What is your name?" asks Mehdina.

The girl flicks her anxious gaze about. Brogine signals lowering of weapons; the girl can't fly without leaving her companion.

"Muto hurt her wing, won't make it home, we need help."

"We'll help as best we can," Dina assures her. "Though we're in a chase."

The dark-haired bird-girl nods. "The red lady runs to Melavorna. She came here from our land."

"Did she, now," says Dina.

I wave the gathering crew away—"Back to work!"—then gesture to suggest (I'm not stupid) Sakaria withdraw his troops. His lips draw tight, but he nods, gives the order with a flick of his hand. Reluctantly, the crowd withdraws, although many watch from a distance. Dina and I, Brogine and Sakaria, remain with the bird-girls. The girl who escaped Vermillion stands tall. "I say yes to your help. I am Loqa."

"This land, Melavorna," says Sakaria. "I don't know it. Tell me more. What resources have you?"

Loqa regards the Princex's agent with narrowed eyes.

"Our land is one. Sky, sea, land: all a gift. We have what we need, do not take more, do not seek more. Of what you want, we have none."

A grimace spreads on my lips. Sakaria's already calculating profit from the trip. Even while the flames of rebellion grow, he quantifies his share of the spoils.

12

It's no news that Vermillion's a sailor unmatched in cunning and skill. *Scarlet Sword* has escaped damage, her crew the best in the Princex's navy, yet *Vermillion Lady* pulls further away each day. Put it down to winds, tonnage, keel design, ballast, whatever you damn please, it's no less galling. Even with her advantage—measured by me flying ahead to spot her—she makes no deviation nor attempt to lose us. She's leading us to Melavorna.

Loqa joins my flight third day out of Cutter's Landing. She laughs behind her feathers at my now clumsy-seeming efforts to slide through the air. She banks in close, dips under me, barrels around me.

"Why stay so near the sea?" she calls, whipping upwards in a long climb toward the clouds. I locate the distant red sails, note heading, then track Loqa as she dwindles, disappears into a bank of white. I've never flown through cloud. How could I? They're so thick, so high. Loqa returns, sweeps her wings back—dripping—dives towards me so fast she must be blinded. She'll hit me and take us both down! No. She twists, throws up shoulders, using her wings like sails, slowing her plunge until she flanks me again.

"I must go back," I shout. "We'll play another time. How far now?"

"She will land near dawn. You half to noon."

Dina will be pleased.

"Your folk know Vermillion then?"

"She left gems in our care."

I nearly stop, nearly fall from the sky. "She left the paradigms with your people?! Where? Are they guarded? Can you show me? Can you draw a map?" We must return to *Sword*. "Come with me now, tell my captain."

"The sad lady?"

"The—? Yes, the sad lady."

* * *

Loqa looks particularly youthful sat in Mehdina's cabin wearing one of her robes pinned up for Loqa's shorter stature. Her friend Muto's wound heals faster than it rightfully should, says Jantino; serving ship's medic now, with her navigation skills lost.

We cannot, of course, conduct such an important discussion without Lord Sakaria, so he's here; silent, appraising.

Loqa's more comfortable in our presence now. She could fly home any time, staying only to watch her injured friend. Muto's more standoffish now than scared, having been well cared for.

"Please, Loqa," says Mehdina. I can see the sadness now, wrapped up in frustration. "Tell us all since you first saw Vermillion."

The girl ponders then nods.

"Red sail came to Melavorna last fire moon." She responds instantly to our puzzlement. "Ten of the moon ago. She gave us a box to keep safe. Five of the moon past she gave a like box, two of the moon ago, a last box. We kept them safe."

"The paradigms," says Mehdina, her eyes downcast. Is it relief?

The Lord Agent nods. "People will hear of your island now, Loqa, that is certain."

13

"Land ho!"

The shout wakes me. Mehdina's gone. I'm up, dressed, out on deck in time to watch Melavorna's mountainous, verdant slopes resolve into an island clearly rich in nature, an emerald gem set in azure skies and sapphire waters. Above lush vegetation, a brutal grey cone rises, smoke trailing from its truncated top. *Vermillion Lady* is moored in the bay, flying flags of truce, gunports closed, signs of a skeleton crew aboard, watching us. Lord Sakaria stands, arms clasped behind his back in prim readiness, his troops ranked behind him. Mehdina stands on the poop deck. Despite sweltering humidity, I've never seen her colder, grey flint gaze locked on the furled red sails of Vermillion's ship.

Her tone is flat. "Drop anchor opposite side of the bay. Ready longboats." Brogine has to repeat the order. Hands rush to, but Mehdina just stands, watching.

I regard the smoking mountain then the shore. There's no trace of habitation. My stomach sinks, feeling impending doom, but whose?

"I should scout ahead."

"Not this time," murmurs Dina.

"The advantage of the air—" I protest.

"Doesn't exist here," Mehdina cuts me off. "Please, Astrid," she mumbles, and my heart clenches. Then, "Loqa, where is your home?"

"Not far," she points into the forest. "Less than half to noon."

"Not closer to the beach?" asks Sakaria.

"No need," says Loqa.

The Lord Agent harrumphs, turns to Mehdina. "We should sink *Vermillion* now. If the locals have the paradigms—"

Dina ignores him. "Brogine, you have command. Ready starboard batteries on *Vermillion Lady*. If a sheet twitches send her down. She'll not escape us."

"Aye, Cap'n."

Sakaria insists on his platoon landing, thus two dozen souls go ashore in three longboats, cutting across the pristine bay. Oarsfolk drive the wooden hulls onto the beach. Fine, golden sand curves away on both sides, the canopy looms above us scant yards up the beach. I pull on Mehdina's arm.

"You can't march in there unknowing. Let me go. It worked at Mirazel, worked at Cutter's Island." I grip her forearms. "Me and Loqa, keep Muto against her good behaviour." Dina's brow furrows, but she doesn't snap. She knows I'm right. She looks into my eyes, and my stomach drops into the pit: She's scared. "Mehdina, trust me."

I see her surrendering. Her eyes close, she sighs. "Protect yourself, and *do not* engage her!"

* * *

Dina's order ringing in my ears, I run up the beach and leap into the air. Loqa's giggling accompanies me as she simply spreads her wings and takes flight. As we leave the coast behind, the buffeting air seems to thicken. Loqa flies with glee, black hair streaming behind her.

It can't be half an hour when Loqa slows. I've seen no buildings, but a wide clearing appears below us, well-hidden at any distance, a ramshackle settlement of bamboo and driftwood circling the space. Before I can speak, Loqa swoops down towards a growing crowd. From the height of the canopy, I watch them greet her. I hesitate. Was this a mistake? Loqa gestures upwards and winged-people take notice, pointing, waving me down. Faced with fifty Melavornans, I have doubts. The winged-folk look friendly enough, I can see no...unfeathered people among them. Still, Vermillion and her crew must be somewhere on the island.

Then I see her, I'm sure of it! A flash of orange in the doorway of a larger, solid-looking building, walls the colour of soil, but crisp, sharp-edged.

Now, all I want in the world is for this horrible feud or pining or fear of Vermillion to end for Mehdina, for me, to be free of her, and I have a knife in my boot, and it's sharp.

It's madness, but it's my chance. I dart down at the doorway, blood and air rushing in my ears. I should stop short, but...

Someone shouts in shock. I form my outstretched hands into fists and spear through the dark doorway, throw down my feet as quick as I can, hands out, I bash into the wall, brace and push off. I twist around, crouch, hand to boot, knife out in time to see Vermillion's fist before—

14

Mehdina slaps my face, not lightly as we do in bed play sometimes, but like she means it. It cuts through the fuzz in my head. I would have stumbled if I wasn't on the dirt floor already.

"You stupid—" She straightens and turns away. Corina pulls me to my feet. I snatch at my neck. The winged paradigm is gone.

"I *knew* this would happen," Mehdina growls, violence coiling in her muscles.

"But still you let her go," says Sakaria.

"Like I could stop her," barks Dina.

Groggily, I glance around the room, well-appointed, stylish, crafted from natural materials without lavish adornment. *Sword* crew and soldiers make the space cramped, outnumbering the winged-folk (three women and two smaller winged-men).

Sakaria addresses the older male. "Where are the caskets Vermillion brought for safekeeping?"

The winged-man looks confused, turns to the tallest of the three women.

"With Melavorna," she says, as if telling an infant water is wet. "In the lap of the land."

"I think I know what that means," I offer.

"The mountain," says Sakaria, "the smoking volcano."

15

"Red lady left in a rush," gasps Loqa, the air whipping our faces, her arms tight around my waist, mine around her neck. "Did not wait for our help."

I nod. If not for my new flying muscles, I couldn't sustain my grip, likely would fall to the trees below. That new strength will fade, if...

"So, we'll win the top first?" I call.

"I hope," she says.

And we do.

I've seen Vermillion move fast through Cardoon's sloping streets. I know she'll swallow the distance, even uphill. Still, after leaving the trees behind and covering long acres of vertiginous rock, we crest the lip of the mountaintop. Loqa drops me on my feet. I stumble, but don't fall. Mehdina lands near me, then Sakaria—falling to his knees (to be fair, I didn't think he'd make the journey)—and a handful of his soldiers, all of us borne up by Melavornans. The soldiers form up on the instant, guarding the Lord Agent in this desolate, exposed place.

"The paradigms?!" Mehdina barks at no one and everyone, drawing her sword, casting about the rocky plateau. Although the dust-blown surface is wide, there's also a feeling of being sucked towards the chasm encompassed by the massive circuit of rock. The crater must be six hundred yards across. We're far enough from the edge we can't see the crater itself, but that's where we're going.

Fearless-seeming—her question unanswered—Dina makes for the edge.

Loqa lands beside me. The other seven Melavornans watch us, wary of these interlopers.

I swallow the fear that I've lost my power forever. Can we win my mother's charm back? Why has Vermillion brought the paradigms here? Maybe the answer is over the edge. I go to stand beside Mehdina, look down into the caldera. The drop is three hundred yards, easy. Fearful-looking yards, now that I'm flightless. A blackened, striated surface stares back, smoke rising from vents across the satin floor. The air down there shimmers.

"Someone speak, tell me!" Mehdina shouts, turns to the islanders, sword held low, but menacing.

"Put down on a rope," says Loqa pointing at the caldera floor. "No one can live in the heat."

"She put them out of reach," I say, knowing Vermillion means to do the same with my charm. "Maybe, if we can wrest my paradigm from her—"

"No!" says Loqa. "The air is dead. You will dry up and die."

"She's right." Vermillion appears over the crater's outer edge, stands on the band of rocky ground, six sailors behind her. "The paradigms are beyond you, Mehdina, beyond your damned Princex—may they rot in hell."

"All but one," snarls Mehdina.

"Take them," shouts Sakaria, and his soldiers attack.

Vermillion levels a pistol crossbow, fires. Mehdina stumbles, clutching her midriff, staggers, inches from my reaching hand.

She falls over the edge.

"Nooooooo!"

I need my paradigm.

The fight is joined, steel clashes, but I have eyes only for Vermillion, though not with such rage or panic that I don't think first. This red bitch is a survivor, a trickster, so there is only one way to confront her. I dart sideways, grabbing Mehdina's fallen sword, then I charge Vermillion.

She doesn't attempt to reload, draws her glinting sword, grins at me. "Perfect."

I swing back, but have no intention of engaging her; she's ten times the swordswoman I am. I throw the cutlass end-over-end. She dodges to avoid it *then* I'm on her, bowl her over, dagger drawn.

Vermillion's knife slices through my shirt, skewers my side. She twists me over, straddles me, traps my knife hand against my burning side. Her next slash is across my throat, but I get my free arm up, take the cut across my elbow. She switches her blade to stab down, and I know I won't survive a third strike. She grins. "Better than killing Mehdina herself."

Loqa's claws sink into Vermillion's shoulders, and she drags the bitch away towards the edge.

"No! Loqa! My charm!"

I reach after them with my good arm. Loqa dumps Vermillion in the dust, loops up away from her flashing blade. Soldiers have gained over pirates, four over two now. Five really; the Lord Agent hefts a blade, knows how to use it, too. I'm impressed.

Three bird-folk have dropped a rope over the edge, and it's pulled tight. *Mehdina!* I dare to hope that my fear is false. My Dina lives, she held on, somehow.

Another pirate is cut down, and the last drops his blade, raises his hands. Vermillion grunts.

"It's over," I say.

"You'll never get the paradigms back. No one can go down there." Her features curve with satisfaction. "The Princex's creeping greed stops here."

I glower at her. "Give—"

Vermillion turns, runs at the edge, jumps for the rope, catches it and drops out of sight, laughing all the while.

Another Melavornan flies to grip the rope, take the extra weight. I wave towards it. "Loqa!"

She understands, darts to take hold as I launch myself at the edge, and over it.

I fall like a stone into frying heat. What if I knock Mehdina off? I scream as I clamp the rope and it burns the skin from my hands. My legs swing down, I grip the line with my knees. Looking down, I see Mehdina on a ledge. Vermillion hangs at the end of the rope, swinging her legs towards the rockface, stabbing at Dina.

"Damn you, tool of the empire!" Vermillion curses, stabs closer, and closer still. Mehdina has nowhere to escape to, stones falling beneath her scrabbling feet, face red, glistening, panting, choking.

"Pull Vermillion away!" I scream up at the bird-folk, but they struggle enough with holding their awkward burden, let alone directing it.

Vermillion kicks Mehdina in the gut, slashes her knife at my love, cuts her leg, swings away again, long and slow then back in as Dina slumps, empty hand grasping.

There is no more time. There are no more choices. I release my grip and plummet down the line.

We're swinging away from the crater wall when I hit Vermillion. She can't have seen me coming; there's no slash at my legs, no curse, nothing. She's near the end of the rope already, and I hit her with force. She loses her grip, slides down, scrabbling, twisting, shouting now, furious, panicked, terrified. We fall off the rope, flailing at the air, clutching nothing.

We fall.

We burn.

I gasp thick, sulphurous air. Only one chance. Tuck knees, head down, straighten legs, try to cut through the heavy air. Inches, inches away from grasping Vermillion.

I have her! Grab her wrist, pull along her arm.

"Paradigm! PARADIGM!"

Horrified eyes find mine, she grasps her neck. Skin's on fire, reddens, prickles.

Fight her hands.

Grasp chain. Pull, rip, break.

Cool silver.

Joy of the air, I embrace thee!

Now, the heavy air's a blessing, buoying me, lifting me up, but my lungs are bursting. I try to lift her. We're slowing, but burning; slowing, burning; skin smoking, we slow, slow, slow, stop, start to rise. So, slowly. So...slowly.

Joy of the air...

Slowly.

I embrace thee.

We rise.

16

The Lord Lamyn Sakaria, agent of the Princex—may they be justly grateful for our service, the wounds we've suffered for them—to my surprise, is all for beheading Vermillion on the spot, but the Melavornans prohibit it. They are peaceful folk, and blame Vermillion for bringing violence to their unblemished island, and violence is not the cure for violence. However, I believe they smell the greed that drips from Sakaria's eyes as he regards the timbered slopes of the mountain, the expanses of glass-making sand, imagines the rich soil resulting from grinding the vegetation into the ground, and building the Princex's manufactories. As a result, the bird-folk are keen to see the back of his lordship, and of all of us.

It's not Brogine who comes ashore; he's aboard *Vermillion Lady*—what a strange notion—putting things to rights, forcing loyalty from the weak, chaining up the strong or duplicitous. Marin brings crew ashore to secure Vermillion, bring her onto *Scarlet Sword* in chains.

"The paradigms?" I ask Mehdina as we're aided aboard the longboats.

She grips my hand, kisses my cheek in front of any who would watch, lingering there, her hand in the small of my back. "Beyond our reach, love," she says with obvious relief, and I look to Sakaria, his expression sour in bitter defeat.

In my hand, I clutch the winged paradigm, the charm my mother gave me, a gift from her father was all she ever told me. She did however call me her princess when she bestowed the gift on my tenth birthing day.

Look at the sky, my darling, look at that blue. Where I hail from, they'd call that colour cerulean, and they would venerate any child born under such a sky. Does it not look good enough to dive into, my sweet? To jump up and soar away to the clouds, and lose yourself there? Perhaps not today, my princess, but maybe another day, just to dive into the sky, to lose yourself, and not come back.

"The Cerulean Princess" is Robin's sixth foray into publication after stories in *Distant Gardens* (2021), *Farther Reefs* (2022), *The World of Juno* (2022), and his novels *The Mandroid Murders* (2022) and *The Carborundum Conundrum* (2023). This story follows "The Vermillion Lady" in *Farther Reefs*. Details and bloggishness at robincmduncan.com and Bluesky @robinski.bsky.social

Mountain Streams

L.R. Gould

Sapphic Representation: Lesbian, Trans
Heat Level: Low
Content Warnings: Coarse Language

I searched the image in the mirror above the bathroom sink for the woman I knew was there. However, stubble shadowed the face of the stranger staring back at me with my own blue eyes. Tying my hair back, I lathered on shaving cream, and removed the cloud hiding the real me with the repeated swipes of a razor. After a splash of water, I re-examined the mirror's reflection. There in the creases of age and behind the hive of welts from my latest electrolysis treatment I saw—me.

My heart rate sped up, pounding in my chest. Light-headed, I spread my hands on the counter to steady myself. An aura crept into the edges of my sight, and I waited for the vision that would come whether I wanted it to or not. At least this time I knew it wasn't a heart attack. The bathroom drifted away in a haze as I disconnected from the world.

I blinked to clear my vision. When my eyes opened the mirror was gone.

I'm standing on the edge of a winding mountain road lined by trees covered in kudzu. Water spills from a metal pipe driven as a tap into the mountainside. It gurgles down the rock-lined ditch into a covert that crosses the road beneath my feet. On the far side of the road, it cascades down the hillside. A panoramic view of a lush mountain valley is visible through the break in the tree canopy.

I blinked.

Rays of sun filter through whisps of hair dancing on a gentle breeze. The gemstones woven into a dangling earring refract the sunlight into a myriad of rainbows that dance on the side of a woman's face. I'd seen her before, knew her, though I'd never met her. I try to focus—to clear the snow of uncertainty from my vision. Hazel eyes stare into mine. I want to get lost in them as I had before, but I force myself to trace the bridge of her petite nose down to soft red lips that move in words I cannot hear despite how desperately I try.

I blinked again.

The bathroom rematerialized.

I held onto the counter, waiting for the lingering waves of nausea to pass. The halo cleared from my peripheral vision and I rubbed the remnants of fog from my eyes. I replayed what I saw in my mind, locking the details into my memory without the stomach-twisting knots—until I became mesmerized by the rhythm of her lips. I shook myself free of her eyes and rushed to my bedroom. Snatching the notebook off my nightstand, I sketched my mystery woman onto the page wishing I had an ounce of artistic ability. I wrote out the more pertinent details I couldn't capture in my kindergarten image.

"Who are you?" My fingers caressed her mouth. "And why do I want you so badly?"

Flipping to the last page of the notebook I added today's date to my expanding log. The visions were becoming more frequent and the nausea worse with each bout. Beside the date, under the heading, *Inciting Event*, directly below yesterday's entry, I added only the day before, I wrote:

Shaving—saw myself in the mirror.

I scanned the list. The first vision came the day my egg cracked while I sat crying in my therapist's parking lot too excited and broken to drive. The second vision came moments after I washed down my first dose of hormones. Another a month later with my eyes closed enduring the repeated stings from my electrologist's hot probe. The common denominator was clear, every vision came with the affirmation of who I was. The two were intrinsically linked.

My knees weakened and I sank onto the edge of my bed. I knew I needed to do something before my visions got worse, and one came while I was driving to work. Valid or not, the thought of discussing my visions with my therapist sent chills down my spine. I confided so much in her, but I couldn't see how admitting that I suffered from hallucinations because of my gender affirmations would result in anything other than an involuntary psychiatric hold. There they would force me to stop hormones while they medicated away the apparitions of my condition. After all that I've been through to acknowledge and embrace my true self, I would not survive putting myself back into that box. I needed to talk to someone I could trust. Someone who would not use my visions to jeopardize my transition.

Sadly, I had few options. Through the years I spent acting out the endless charade of societal expectations dictated to me at my birth by a man in scrubs, I never dared let anyone get too close for fear they would see past that illusion and glimpse my true self. Now that I'd dismantled that façade, I found myself alone with few voices other than family I could turn to for advice.

I ached to call my mom. We'd been so close—before. But after I came out, she hadn't said a word to me without simultaneously thumping me with her Bible. She would see the visions as the proof she needed to get me committed to an institute.

That left me with only one other choice.

My fingers trembled as I picked up my phone and opened the contacts. I scrolled for a person that, for the past thirty years, I'd only seen on holidays and my birthday. Uncertain of what he could offer me, but desperate, nonetheless. I touched the simple three-letter name and waited for the phone to ring.

"Hello?" The deep baritone of the voice on the other end sounded sleepy.

"Dad," I muttered. My voice cracked, losing all hints of the training I'd spent the last few months working on.

"Is that you ——?"

The wrong name cut deep into my soul. I made a small acknowledging squeak around the rock of anguish lodging itself into my throat. I came out to him on my birthday in a pages-long text where I bared my soul and explained everything. His lone reply, *I don't understand, but I will always love you,* had the brevity of a too-long-didn't-read response. In the months that followed I heard nothing else. Not that we ever had a close relationship. Unsure why I had expected more, I thumbed the red cancel call icon.

The phone vibrated in my hand. I checked the caller ID and debated answering his call. It rang a second time. Numbly I pressed the green icon and slid it to speaker phone.

"Umm, Lindsay, I'm sorry. I'm still waking up. Is everything alright?"

He called me by my name. That small gesture freed my larynx. "No. Dad, can I come see you?" I asked, pitching my voice too high.

"Uh...sure. Sure. How about coffee?" I could hear a slight hesitation in his voice, and I tried not to read into it, but my mind still questioned what I was doing.

"Yeah, that...that sounds good."

"Okay. Let me hop in the shower and get dressed. I'll see you in about a half-hour at Grit Coffee on Libbie?"

"Thanks, Dad." I placed my phone down on the dresser and fought back the instant panic as I tried to decide what to wear to meet my dad as me for the first time.

* * *

Cars much finer than the rust-encrusted, duct taped, patched relic I drove filled the small parking lot beside Grit Coffee. I circled through the packed lot and eventually found a street spot a block and a half away. Checking my makeup in the rearview mirror, I took a settling breath to calm my nerves, tucked my hair behind my right ear and opened the door. Swinging my legs out, I adjusted the skirt of my dress over my knees and stood. The breeze immediately pulled the lock of hair free from my ear and whipped it across my face. Ignoring the loose hair, I slung the strap of my purse over my head, shut the car door, and made my way to the coffee shop.

"Welcome to Grit," a staff member greeted blindly over a burst of steam from the espresso machine.

Glancing around the room, I tried unsuccessfully to find my father among the handful of customers. Hopefully I was simply early. I considered ordering a drink while I waited. That was until I did a mental accounting of the meager holdings in my bank account. They would barely put enough gas in my car's tank to get me to my next payday. I settled into one of the leather chairs, did my best to cross my knees properly, and I tried not to stare at the door.

"Lan...um Lindsay?"

The aura narrowed my vision and I blinked.

The coffee shop vanished.

I am in my car sitting in the broken asphalt parking lot in front of a paint-flaked two-door mechanic's shop. The flickering neon sign over the doors reads Angel's Automotive Rescue. A tap-tap sounds on my driver's-side-door glass. A woman dressed in overalls leans down to the window. The rays of the setting sun behind her refract off the gems in her earring.

"No." I mashed my eyelids closed. "Not now," I growled, willing the vision to go away.

"Lindsay? What's that?"

Cautiously, I opened my eyes and twisted in my seat. Behind me, standing only a few steps away, my father wrung his hands hard enough to iron out the wrinkles.

On trembling legs, I stood, thankful I wore my ballet flats instead of my heels. "Dad?"

"Lindsay." The corner of his mouth fluttered then crooked up in a hesitant smile. "You look good."

The simple compliment eased the tension in my shoulders.

The aura returned. I forced myself not to blink. To not lose this moment.

"Can I buy you a cup of coffee?"

Cotton filled my mouth and all I could do was nod. However, before he took a step for the register I leaned in and wrapped my arms around him. His hands slowly came up my back and pulled me in close. Tears filled my eyes and ran down my cheek as I laid my head on his shoulder. My eyes burned, but I refused to blink. I would not lose my father. Not now.

He held me, remarkably, not pulling away.

I let go first and lifted my head to wipe away the tears with a thumb. He reached over to one of the tables and pulled a napkin from the holder.

"Here, your mascara is running," he said handing it to me. "Go to the restroom and freshen up. I'll get us some coffee."

"Thank you." I dabbed my eyes with the napkin, barely able to see past the aura. "But I'd prefer a chai tea if that's okay."

"Sure."

I locked the bathroom door behind me and—blinked.

I am sitting on the bench seat of an old truck. The woman whom I'd seen so many times before drives with one hand on the wheel and the other on the shifter between us. The truck drops, then bounces out of the rut in the road. I brace myself with one hand on the dash and the other I plant firmly on the seat to steady myself against another jolt. A smile curls her lips as she reaches over and grabs my hand, sending a spark of electricity through my skin.

I blinked.

Tracing the back of my left hand with a finger, I could still feel her hand on mine. The aura was gone, but when I closed my eyes, her lips were all I saw. Holding onto the sink I took deep slow breaths waiting for the nausea to pass and for my heart to slow. When I finally felt stable on my own feet, I wet a paper towel and cleaned away the mascara runs before touching it up with a tube from my purse.

I found my dad sitting at one of the high tables with two steaming cups in front of him. Pulling out the stool opposite him, I sat and wrapped my fingers around the cup he passed me. He waited patiently while I took a sip of tea.

"Thanks," I said managing to keep my voice steady.

He held onto his cup with both hands and didn't quite look at me. "You're welcome."

"Um...I didn't ask you here just so I can come out to you in person. I've been having...um. I've been having visions." I waited for the burst of shocked horror. For the rant about mental illness. About how my being trans all makes sense now—I'm just delusional. But none of that came.

My dad took a long drink from his coffee cup then peered into the black liquid as he placed the cup on the table in front of him. His lips parted twice before any words came out. He swallowed then ran a pensive hand across his face. "Tell me about them."

I took a long gulp of tea and nearly burned my mouth. "Right." Placing my purse on my lap, I pulled out my notebook and walked him through the sketches I had created. The mountain road. The woman. The mechanic's garage. Then I flipped to the back of the notebook and walked him through the date log. "Over a dozen different episodes. At first, months passed between visions, now— I've had two today. Dad, I'm scared."

He leaned forward and grabbed my hand, holding it in his. "Lan...sorry, Lindsay. I swear I'll get used to the new name. Have you told you mother about this?"

I scoffed pulling my hand back. "I can't. Mom..." I choked on the tears welling in my eyes. "Mom won't even look at me. She calls me an abomination, a pervert. I can't even talk with her without her quoting the latest bigoted rhetoric from whichever far-right talking head she gets it from."

"That sounds like her." He sighed. "You know, she didn't always used to be that way. I remember her before she found her faith."

"I wish I did."

"It was before you were born. Actually..." He glanced up at me. I dabbed at my tears with a fresh napkin, trying not to smear my freshly applied mascara. "Never mind. When she ran to religion isn't important."

"Then what is?"

"The why and why now that you are getting these visions. When I first met your mother, there were rumors about her family. The kind that are only spoken late at night around a campfire or when someone has had too much to drink. Some claim they are witches that fled the witch trials in Salem and made their home in the Appalachian Mountains. Others say that they are descendants of Romani who immigrated to America to flee European oppression and for a price they'll tell you your future. The one thing that all the rumors agree on is that the women are all clairvoyants."

He brought the cup to his lips and finished it off. "I was a sceptic. I never believed the rumors. Not until after I married your mother. She managed to hide her visions from me at first—then she became pregnant with you. As the pregnancy progressed, they got stronger and the nausea got worse. She would hardly eat and what she did eat she couldn't keep down." The memory of his past worry clouded his face. "I still remember the profanity-laced argument she had with the doctor when he proclaimed you'd be a boy. According to her visions she carried a girl who would inherit her curse." He barked a hoarse laugh. "Guess her visions were right after all.

"Anyway, your mom ended up on bed rest with an IV in her arm and the doctor pulled me aside and told me to be prepared to lose you both. That's when, against your mom's wishes, I wrote her mother, your Mawmaw. She came down and I don't know how, but she helped your mom manage the visions and the side effects. You were born a month early, underweight, and oh so small, but you both survived. When the doctor handed you to your mom with a smug *I-told-you-so* smile, she cursed your Mawmaw and sought out religion to purge her demons."

"But why does mom hate my transition?"

My dad shook his head in regret. "Because it proves her visions were right. It forces her to reconcile her faith against the truth, and I'm not sure she can do that."

Despair at knowing mom would never accept me made it hard to breathe. "Dad, what do I do?"

"About your mother?" He sighed heavily. "Nothing. I'm not sure there's anything you can do. Only time will tell. About the visions? All I can tell you is what your Mawmaw told me. The visions are personal. They only reflect your future—no one else's. You have to be affected by it in some way. Other than that, I can't help you. But considering what your Mawmaw did for your mom, she might be able to."

"I've never even met Mawmaw. Mom never talks about her."

"Yeah. The visions weren't the only thing your mom ran to religion to get away from." He pulled out his phone and scrolled through his contacts. "Your Mawmaw never had a phone, but considering her visions, I guess she didn't need one. I think I still have her address though. I can't promise she's still there, but she used to live up in Sterling Holler near Waynesboro. People don't often move in the hollers. Ah, here it is."

* * *

With a little help from my dad, I jumped on Interstate 64 with a full tank of gas and headed for the mountains. Thanks to an air conditioner that gave out under the last presidential administration, I rode with the windows down despite the knots it worked into my hair. It didn't take long for sweat to form and roll down my back in the hot summer air. My bra dug into my sides and my dress stuck to my back. The hair whipping in the wind stung my eyes no matter how many times I tucked it behind an ear or redid my ponytail.

"Argh," I hollered into the road noise. My frustration broke into a crooked smile. "Nothing like twenty-first century woman problems."

I blinked.

A collection of old cars lines the edge of the broken asphalt lot I stand on. I peer over the handful of buildings lining the small-town street and look up to the mountains. Tears roll down my cheeks as hopelessness clouds my thoughts. A hand rubs my back and...

I blinked.

Miles had passed and I tried to get my bearings while I fought the nausea. To my left, across the eastbound lanes of traffic, I could see the lower lookout at the bottom of Afton Mountain. Red lights suddenly bloomed through the slug of traffic ahead of me. A pair of eighteen wheelers drag racing each other up the seven-mile climb created a rolling road block. I stepped on the brakes with both feet and popped the shifter into neutral to avoid becoming a permanent attachment to the car in front of me.

Shifting the car back in gear, I let out the clutch, and stepped on the gas. The engine revved, but the car acted like it was stuck in the mud and failed to accelerate.

"No! Not now!" I lost sight of the Dodge Ram's grille behind me as it moved forward, offering to push me up the hill whether I wanted them to or not. "Come on, girl, you can do it." Letting off the gas, I patted the car's dash in encouragement, then eased my foot back down on the accelerator. The clutch finally engaged, and the car lurched forward.

Refusing to risk shifting gears again, I crested the mountain in third gear and rode my brakes all the way down the other side. A few miles later I had no choice but to downshift as I descended my exit ramp. At the bottom of the ramp, I put it in gear and played duck, duck, goose with the gas pedal until it took. Three red lights later, the clutch gave out completely and I coasted into the first service garage I saw.

I set the emergency brake, cranked the windows closed, and leaned my head against the steering wheel. I wanted to cry, but the repeated rap of knuckles on my window stopped me. I lifted my head to see who it was. The setting sun silhouetted the woman outside my door and light wove through her earring casting dancing rainbows on her cheek. My breath caught. I knew those hazel eyes. Those lips. It was only then that I bothered to read the flickering neon sign over the garage doors—*Angel's Automotive Rescue.*

Grabbing my purse and my bag, I opened the door. It protested the movement with a loud screech. I swung the door closed putting all my pent-up frustration into the swing. It crashed with a bang. I waited for my rust-bucket of a vehicle to give up the ghost and completely fall apart right then and there, but it didn't.

"So, what did she do to you?"

"She stranded me here." I turned to face a woman a few years younger than me wearing combat boots and service station overalls. A smudge of black grease obscured her name tag. Strands of violet hair escaped her loose bun and fell over an undercut.

Her brows scrunched together. "Do I have grease on my nose again?"

"Um, sorry. Ah...Um...No." I pushed a smile onto my face. "You just look really familiar." I slung my purse strap over my head to force myself to break my stare. "Have you ever been to Richmond?"

"Not since I was kid," she laughed, and I about melted at the melody. "I think I had a field trip to the capital once."

"Must be a doppelganger then." I chuckled.

"Must be." She walked up to my car and ran a caressing hand along the hood. "Your baby here has seen better days."

"I'm sure she has. But she's the only thing on the lot I could afford."

She glanced back at me, and I diverted my eyes from her to the tape holding the back window in place. "Wait? Someone sold her to you—like this?"

"Yeah, the dealer promised it would get me from point A to point B. I guess I should have asked about the return trip."

"Probably," she laughed her beautiful melody again. "Plenty of folks around here drive worse. Though in their cases, it's usually a hand-me-down. I'm happy to help though." She spun and sat back against my car. "What's going on with her?"

I tilted my head, staring at the earring from my visions if only to keep from staring at her eyes. They call it love at first sight, but was it really first sight for me? Over the past few months, I'd been falling in love with the woman of my visions, but more than that, I knew I could trust her. I described the driving through mud feeling when I let the clutch out as best as I could.

"Sounds like the clutch pad is burned up." She checked the watch on her wrist. "Unfortunately, the shop's closing for the night and tomorrow is a Sunday. So, I can't get the parts until Monday. That's if they have them in stock, but worst case it won't be more than a few days."

My heart sank as I mentally calculated how many meals I could stretch out of the fifty dollars my dad gave me; let alone how I was ever going to pay for the repair. I turned, looking over the small village to the mountains for strength and only feeling more lost.

"Hey, Darling, it's ok." A comforting hand warmed my back. "We can get her fixed."

"I...I can't afford it," I confessed unable to hide my tears.

"Honey," she said pulling a rag from her hip pocket, "don't you worry about that. My momma raised me right." She reached up and wiped a tear from my cheek. "Mountain folk don't walk away from someone in need, not when they can help." My hand rose to hers. She placed the rag in my hand, but held onto my hand a moment longer. "I'll get her fixed and we'll figure something out."

"Thanks," I whispered. "Maybe I can work it off or..."

"Ack, we're not going to worry about that now. Do you have a place to stay tonight?"

I shrugged my shoulders, hope and desire mixed with my worry. "I was on my way to my Mawmaw's up in Sterling Holler. But she doesn't even know I'm coming."

"I know that holler. You're not old miss Margret's granddaughter, are you?"

Only when I heard her say "granddaughter" did I realize she never once gave my broad shoulders a second look or balk at my imperfect voice. She saw me and treated me like the woman I was. New tears welled in my eyes.

I blinked and the shop disappeared.

I am standing before a large wooden barn. Its red paint weathered closer to almost brown. The white-trimmed door is propped open with flower beds flanking it on either side. I turn. Over the green hood of an antique truck, I see a white farmhouse. A pair of rocking chairs adorn the deep porch. From one of the chairs, a silver-haired woman lifts a wrinkled hand and waves me to the house.

I blinked, returning to the garage and my car. My knees gave out, but my angel caught me.

"Yep. You're definitely Miss Margret's granddaughter."

I held my breath not wanting her to let me go and waited for another vision that gratefully didn't come.

"Come on," she said escorting me to a green pickup truck straight from a '50s movie. "I know how to get there."

* * *

The dirt road winding up the mountain made me grateful my car decided to quit when it did rather than abandoning me with nothing but sky and trees to keep me company. My chauffeur drove in silence, bouncing in the seat whenever the truck came across a maze of potholes too complicated to navigate on the narrow road.

"Um, I never got your name," I asked to break the silence.

"And yet you got into my truck and let me drive you out into the sticks," she said giving me the side-eye.

"I...um..." I stuttered, uncertain how to explain why I trusted her.

She lifted her hand off the shifter and waved me to silence. "It's fine. I'm Angela, but everyone just calls me Angel. You may have noticed the name on the garage. But, girl, you've got to be more careful. Don't get into people's vehicles unless you know them and always make sure someone you trust knows where you are going. And on the rare occasion you don't have a choice, like today, then you get a name, you take a photo of the license plate, and text them to someone you trust with a time you'll check back in."

"I...uh thanks," I said sheepishly bracing myself with one hand on the dash and the other midway on the seat beside me as we hit another pothole.

Angel's lips curled into a grin and her hand drifted across the bench seat to find mine—electrifying my skin. "It's ok. We all learn it one way or the other. Some of us learn it the hard way. I'm just glad you didn't have to." She pulled her hand away to down shift. I could still feel her lingering touch. I didn't move hoping she would take my hand again.

The truck drifted to the side of the road and stopped. Angel winked at me, "Come on. I've got something I think you'll find interesting."

I gave her a questioning look. "You want me—to get out of the vehicle—on the side of a mountain? What was that safety lecture you just gave me? Why don't you give me a second to make a phone call." I pulled out my phone long enough to see I had no reception and put it back in my purse. "Or not."

"Right. Sorry about that. Here take the keys." She pulled the keys from the ignition and placed them in my hand with a smile. "I'm going right there. To that break in the trees on the left. There's just enough sun left to see the valley. It's beautiful at sunset."

Angel stepped out of the truck and went to exactly the spot she pointed to. I waited a moment longer debating what, I wasn't certain. I wanted to follow her to be close to her. I wanted her to hold my hand again, so why was I hesitating? The visions showed me her. Her garage. Even her truck—though that would only be true if she took me all the way to Mawmaw's. I got out and made my way along the ditch to the front of the truck. To my right I heard the gurgling of falling water and smiled when I saw the pipe driven into the mountain. I stepped up beside Angel already knowing what I would see and the view did not disappoint.

"You're right. This is beautiful!"

Angel leaned toward me and bumped me with her hip. "I thought you would like it."

"Thanks." I hooked a thumb over my shoulder. "What's up with the pipe back there? Are we tapping the mountain like a keg?"

She barked the cutest laugh. "Basically yeah. It flows year-round and it's some of the best drinking water you can get. Actually, I have a couple jugs in the bed of the truck, I'm sure Miss Margaret would appreciate some."

She gathered the jugs from the truck and filled the first one halfway before handing it to me. "Here, try some."

I eyed the container skeptically. "What straight from the bottle?"

She laughed that wonderful melody again. "Next you're going to tell me you've never drank from a hose either."

"Um, actually I haven't," I said, feeling my cheeks heat in embarrassment.

"Oh, you are going to be fun. I'm showing you around the holler tomorrow."

The mischief and joy in her smile were infectious and before I could stop myself, I said, "As long as it doesn't end with us skinny dipping in a pond, I'm all in."

"If you insist, I'll remove it from the itinerary." The *your-loss* twinkle in her eye made me instantly regret my words. "Come on let's get you to Miss Margaret's."

We loaded the filled jugs in the truck and continued up the mountain. A mile or so later, Angel rounded a bank of mailboxes mounted on a wooden rail. She stepped on the gas and the truck kicked up stones as it sped up into the holler. At the end of the drive, we pulled up to an old barn. It matched my vision in every detail from the weathered red paint to the half-open door.

Angel pulled the keys from the ignition, letting the engine rumble to a stop. My eyes remained fixed on the barn as I got out of the truck. I turned, peering across the hood of the truck seeking confirmation of my vision. A woman with frosted hair raised a welcoming hand beckoning us to the front porch of the farmhouse.

"Angela, so nice to see you," the woman said pushing herself up out of the rocking chair. She shuffled across the wooden planks and wrapped Angel in a hug. "My Donna is in the kitchen making chili. Would you mind giving her a hand?"

"Yes, ma'am." Angel gave me a warm encouraging grin before she disappeared into the house.

I shifted my feet at the bottom of the steps, unsure how to introduce myself.

"Alright, dear, don't make an old lady climb stairs she don't need to. Get on up here and give your Mawmaw a hug."

I stared dumbfounded. "But...how did you know?"

She placed her hands on her hips and tilted her head. "I think you know exactly how I knew that my only granddaughter was going to be visiting me today."

Tears welled in my eyes. I stood before a relative who welcomed me and gendered me correctly without my mother's open condemnation or my father's mental delay as he adjusted his language. My Mawmaw simply saw me. I rushed up the steps and fell into her arms.

She wrapped me into a fierce bear hug crushing me against her. "So, young lady, what do you call yourself?"

Before I could answer—I blinked.

Standing beside a willow tree with its branches drooping down to the river I slid off my shorts and hung them on a branch. Angel was already in the water inviting me in.

"Mountain Streams" is a stand-alone short by L.R. Gould. Find out more about her at www.LRGould.com or follow her at LRGouldWrites on Facebook and Instagram.

The Aerial Gardeners Shop

Rebecca Kim Wells

Sapphic Representation: Lesbian

Heat Level: Low

Content Warnings: Gnomes in Danger

By the time Mara Windward had seen twenty winters she was quite good at the usual things—minor enchantments, solemn incantations, and the like—and those with which she had only middling success were too minor to bother with anyway. Having graduated from the local college at the top of her class, she was deemed ready to go and seek her fortune.

Ever a self-starter, she took to the task like the proverbial duck to water. The first few months went splendidly—a few good deeds to crones standing at crossroads in gloomy forests led to a favor to the local innkeeper, which started out as a hunt for a rare spice for a nearby lord's evening soup and culminated in a quest to the top of Third Mountain, where she successfully traded an enchanted silver bracelet to the roc living there in exchange for a vial of goldtongue. The goldtongue went to a cursed princess making a play to retake her throne, and Mara had been handsomely rewarded. All was proceeding as it should.

And then, somehow, it had all gone so wrong.

Right now she should be doing something else impressive, like negotiating a diplomatic solution to a small city's unexpected griffin problem. Instead, she was sitting behind a dingy off-white counter under glaring overhead lights as the door to the Aerial Gardeners Shop swung forcefully open.

The door chimed—a screechy rendering of the first few notes of "Battle Hymn of the Seven Tree Sisters"—and a spindly shadow advanced down Aisle 3 toward the service counter. Mara stood up without bothering to look at her coworker. Fi never did anything besides read her magazine and lean on things if she could help it.

The spindly shadow was attached to Constantina Brevwit, a spindly woman of indeterminate age and odious temperament who was, unfortunately, a regular customer. Mara fought to keep her expression neutral as Constantina reached the counter. The woman had clearly come to the Shop in a huff—she wore a feathered dressing gown and had her hair in curlers—but it wasn't obvious why this was such an urgent errand.

"Ms. Brevwit. How can we help you tonight?"

Constantina reached into her handbag, pulled out a messily wrapped package about the size of a book, and slammed it down on the counter with a thunk. "I demand a refund!"

The package wriggled.

"Oh!" Mara stepped back in surprise. "Um. What is that?"

"Defective merchandise!" Constantina snapped. She ripped off a corner of the paper wrapping, exposing a furious bearded face. The face, complete with angry red cheeks and a green cap, gawped up at them for a moment. Then it opened its mouth and started to yell.

At the other end of the counter, Fi glanced up from her magazine. "What *is* that?"

"I repeat, defective merchandise. *Your* defective merchandise." Constantina looked down her nose at them. "I want a refund."

Now that she was over the surprise, Mara saw that the face bore a striking resemblance to the gnomes currently on display near the greenhouse entrance. "Have you modified it, though? The garden gnomes don't usually...move." *Or yell,* she thought. She tilted her head, trying to concentrate. The yelling was thin and high-pitched and in no language she recognized.

Constantina sniffed. "I bought the useless thing to keep out garden pests, but it didn't work at *all,* so I thought I might enchant it into...running around a little. And then *this* happened."

Fi snorted. "So you wanted the gnome to come to life, but you're upset that it did."

"I don't appreciate your tone, young lady," Constantina said. "I wanted it to *move,* not do *this.* And you haven't seen the worst of it yet. The cursed thing *flies.* So now I have this gnome flying around after me wherever I go, yelling incessantly and making lewd gestures. I can't have that. I won't."

"Because of the enchantment that you put on it," Mara said timidly.

"No, because I was sold defective merchandise. Gnomes are supposed to be pest-repellent. *Clearly* this one was not, since I was forced to enchant the thing myself. So this is your fault, and I insist you take it back. Refund. Now."

"Well..." Mara swallowed. "I'd have to ask a manager about it? Seeing as how it's not in the same condition as when you bought it? Since they're not really meant to be enchanted?" she finished on an almost-whisper.

Constantina's nostrils flared. "Do that." She folded her arms across her chest. "I'll wait."

For a moment Mara imagined Constantina standing at the counter, squinting suspiciously at her for the next five hours. The thought almost made her laugh—it was either that or cry. "The manager won't be in until tomorrow, but I can keep the gnome here so he can inspect everything when he arrives."

Constantina drew herself up to her fullest height. "Fine. And *I* will be here to give your manager a full report on how I was treated tonight. You can depend on that." With a final sniff, she turned and flounced performatively out of the store.

"Battle Hymn of the Seven Tree Sisters" mingled with the gnome's incomprehensible yelling. Mara felt her teeth clench. "What am I supposed to do about this?" she said, mostly to herself.

"Constantina?" Fi didn't look up. "That's probably the best you could have done with her."

"No—the *gnome.*"

"Easy. Put it somewhere for Howard to look at."

"But—the *yelling.*"

"Somewhere behind a door, then. Like Howard's office."

"Do you think it actually flies?"

"I think that I doubt the righteous Constantina Brevwit would lie about something like that. So yeah, it probably flies. And it's probably a good idea to make sure the wrapping is secure."

Fi was right. The wrapping in question did not look particularly secure. "Any thoughts on the best way to do that?"

"No."

So helpful. Mara gingerly scooped up the gnome and, holding it at arm's length, fast-walked it back to Howard's office.

* * *

The Aerial Gardeners Shop perched precariously at the edge of a crumbling lookout about three quarters up Fifth Mountain. Despite the fact that its supports had to be propped up every year or two or else risk simply falling off, it was a treasured local institution. This had more to do with its ownership than the quality of its selection or service. After all, it wasn't every day that one could say they had bought silbur bushes at the shop owned by *the* Gavin D'Olndaria, the best cloud cultivator in all the Five Mountains. (It didn't seem to matter that Gavin himself only made an appearance at the shop every few months.) Most people would say it was a very pretty shop.

Mara hated it.

It hadn't started out this way. When she had arrived two months ago, the shop had charmed her too. She'd first heard about Fifth Mountain from a bartender after she'd banked her pay from the goldtongue job and was considering her next move. The eagles had caught her attention first. "Right terrors," the bartender had called them, eagles taller than humans that roosted atop the mountain—and yet humans lived there too. Apparently this had always been the case, but over the last decade humans had moved higher and higher—and it was all because of Gavin D'Olndaria. He had tamed the weather, softened the rain, plucked the sting out of the mountain winds.... In short, he'd made living on Fifth Mountain more than possible. He'd made it pleasant. "The greatest cloud cultivator in the Five Mountains. Maybe in all the world," the bartender had said reverently. *Weather magic*, Mara had thought. *I like the sound of that.*

In retrospect, the ease with which Mara acquired an apprenticeship should have been a warning sign. After climbing the mountain and waiting at the Shop for Gavin to make an appearance, she'd expected to plead her case. Instead, Gavin had leaned back in his chair—Howard's chair, she'd later learn—placed his muddy boots on top of the desk—Howard's desk—tossed his cape over one shoulder in a manner he clearly considered rakish, and proclaimed, "Of course, my intrepid girl! That is, as long as you don't mind paying your dues. Every apprentice of mine starts out in the Shop."

Despite being less than thrilled by the sobriquet, Mara was very pleased by the offer—and what was a few weeks working at the shop when she would learn weather magic from the master himself?

Unfortunately, nothing had gone to plan since then. "A few weeks" turned into "we'll see," and before she knew it she was stuck on the night shift with Fi, whose idea of work was occasionally deigning to raise an eyebrow or point a finger. So Mara was left to deal with the night customers—the worst kind, she quickly learned. Night customers tended to be the sort that viewed every gardening mishap as an emergency, no matter the hour, and they acted accordingly.

Mara shouldered open the door to Howard's office. The gnome was squirming even more now, and she clamped it between her elbow and torso while she searched for something suitable with which to bind it. Eventually she settled for a roll of tape on the desk, which she wound several times around the gnome before taping the whole thing to the chair. She wrote a note for Howard explaining the situation, then made sure she locked the door behind her. The gnome probably wouldn't escape its wrapping, but one couldn't be too careful.

Fi was still reading her magazine when Mara got back to the counter. Mara slumped into her chair. Day clerks weren't allowed to sit, but Howard made an exception for the night shift, probably because the average night saw about two customers.

Constantina Brevwit was awful, but at least she'd broken the monotony. Mara glanced at the clock on the opposite wall. Four hours and fifty-six minutes left in the shift, and not a single thing to look forward to. She could almost feel her brain atrophying.

She slumped further, putting her head down on the counter. "What do you think Howard will do about the gnome?"

She heard a page flip before Fi replied. "Not my problem. Not yours either. Neither of us is getting paid enough to care."

"But it's upsetting, isn't it? She's the one who brought a gnome to life and now she's making it our problem? There's a *live* gnome tied up in Howard's office! That doesn't disturb you?"

Fi shrugged. "Serves him right. And the gnome's not really alive. Just enchanted."

Right. Enchanted. What with the moving and the yelling and the facial expressions, the gnome really did look sentient. But that was just how enchantment worked—Constantina's enchantment had made the gnome conform to her own expectations of what a gnome should do. It *wasn't* alive. Although... "How could anyone think that a gnome would fly?"

"Gnomes are made up to begin with. Who's to say they couldn't fly?" Fi flipped another page in her magazine.

Mara turned her head so her other cheek rested on the counter. If Gavin had been her greatest disappointment since arriving, Fi was the second greatest. They were about the same age, and Fi was pretty—very pretty, Mara sometimes thought grudgingly—but her initial attraction had been immediately tempered by the fact that Fi had said an entire three words to her—"Hi. I'm Fi."—during their first shift together. Not to mention that her idea of customer service consisted of such blatant apathy that Mara was stunned she still had a job.

From Howard's office, the gnome's yelling grew louder.

Two months of appeasing unreasonable gardeners and she still hadn't seen even a single eagle, let alone had a lesson with Gavin. Not that she was desperate to throw herself into the path of an eagle's talons, but they had sounded so majestic. She'd hoped to see them in flight. Now, the longer she went without spotting one, the more it felt like the mountain was playing a cruel trick on her.

Was this it? Had she climbed Fifth Mountain for nothing? The counter, which had been cool when she first slumped against it, was warming under her cheek. She was more than this, wasn't she? She'd accomplished things. She still could. But not like this.

* * *

Howard was already on his way out the door when Mara arrived the next day. He was a nervous whippet of a man who looked over his spectacles at Mara when she inquired about the gnome, then looked quickly away. "Oh, don't worry about that. It's taken care of."

"Really? Did you disanimate it?"

Howard ducked his head. "Never you mind about that. Now, be polite next time you talk to Constantina. She was really quite disappointed in your conduct when she came to see me this morning."

Of course she had been. Mara cleared her throat. "There was nothing wrong with the gnome before she decided to enchant it. The Shop isn't at fault for her misunderstanding." *Or her poor enchantments.*

"Don't let her catch you saying that. Here, the customer is always right. Especially if that customer is Constantina Brevwit. We sent her home with a new gnome, so you can expect not to see her for a little while. But it's something for you to keep in mind for the future."

Hot anger flashed through Mara's veins. No, the customer was *not* always right. People got emotional! Illogical, even! Just because a person wanted something didn't mean it was reasonable to give it to them. And besides...if she was being mercenary about it, she also had to mention—at least privately, to herself—that the Aerial Gardeners Shop was the only garden shop on the entire mountain, and that was before taking into consideration that it was owned by *Gavin D'Olndaria*. What was Constantina Brevwit going to do if she didn't get her way one pitiful time, go all the way down the mountain for her garden needs?

But she didn't say any of that. Instead, she said, "She probably *will* come in, if she realizes this gnome isn't pest-repellent either. Since none of them are. By default."

Howard's eyes slid away from hers. "Well—I did put a little enchantment on it. Just enough that the good lady won't complain."

Aha! So he knew just as well as she did that Constantina's complaint was nonsensical. He had just chosen to take the easy way out and appease her. It was infuriating. Doubly so because there was nothing to stop another criminally entitled customer from haranguing her today. And tomorrow. And the next— *No.* She had to stop thinking about this, because if she kept it up, she was going to lose it.

Fi was already parked at the counter with her magazine when Mara arrived.

"You're late," Fi murmured.

"So?" Mara snapped.

"Just mentioning it," Fi said mildly. "I've never seen you late before."

"Well, I didn't realize I was being observed so closely for potential workplace protocol violations, but I'll keep that in mind for the future." Mara dumped her bag on the floor and grabbed her shop vest from the hook on the office door. She yanked it on and sat down, fuming quietly. In two months, she'd learned that most insect infestations in the area could be treated with Most Unusual Soothing Treatment (Aisle 4, next to the sparking hoses), and that in order to replace the lightbulbs in the shop, you had to first bribe the pixies that crowded around them with candy, or else they would bite. But did any of that have anything to do with learning weather magic? Of course not. What was she *doing* here?

"Here. It's terrible, but it'll pass the time." Fi slid a magazine across the counter toward her. It had one of those covers that changed images from time to time, highlighting different articles that promised gasps and scandal within its pages.

Mara stared down at the magazine. She couldn't decide whether she was disgusted or appalled. "You...enjoy this?"

"Oh, these are my *favorite*. How else would I ever know how to tell if my coworker is flirting with me?" A rare glimmer of a smile broke across Fi's lips, and she winked at Mara. "Look around. It's not as though there's much else to do."

Was Fi—? No, she shouldn't finish that thought. Not now, when she felt all jagged on the inside. Better to let it rest, come back to it in a softer mood. She smiled at Fi and opened the magazine.

* * *

When Mara had done all the quizzes and sniffed all the scent samplers, Fi passed another magazine down the counter without saying a word. It was a quiet night. The only customer had been surprisingly pleasant, an insomniac who wandered up and down the aisles before buying a chocolate bar on the way out. After they left, Mara emptied the cardboard candy box and restacked the bars. There was one bar too many to form a neat layer, so Mara dug a coin out of her pocket and took it for herself.

There was caramel in the middle of the chocolate, Mara's favorite. She neatly peeled open the wrapper and broke the chocolate in half, then offered a piece to Fi.

"Thanks," said Fi.

For a moment they ate in companionable silence. Fi turned another page of her magazine.

Mara finished her chocolate. She looked at the clock. She looked at Fi. She let her head fall against the back of the chair. "So...what are you doing here, anyway? It seems pretty obvious that you aren't interested in gardens. Or customer service. How are you going to stand out to Gavin if you don't...make an effort?"

Fi looked up from her magazine, her eyes wide. As Mara watched, her lip started to tremble. "Wow, Mara. That's a little harsh, don't you think? I'm doing the best I can."

"Oh no—I'm sorry, I didn't mean—"

Not just a smile—this time Fi actually laughed. "Relax, ponytail. I'm kidding. And to answer your question, I'm here for the money. Night shift pays better than day. Plus, you can sit down, and there are fewer customers to deal with. All pros in my book."

"But—what about Gavin?"

Fi snorted. "I remember when he was first starting out and he couldn't master a single substitution spell. I doubt there's anything he has to teach that you don't already know. I heard about the trade you made on Third Mountain."

She had? Unexpectedly, Mara felt warmth rising on her cheeks. She tried to ignore it. "But he's the best cloud cultivator in the Five Mountains!"

"Is he?" Fi said, raising her eyebrows significantly. "Have you ever actually *seen* him do it?"

Mara stared at Fi, speechless. She'd thought several ungenerous things about Gavin recently, but she'd never heard anyone else say a single word against him, much less insinuate that he was incapable of doing the very thing he was famous for. She opened her mouth to say—well, to say something, though she honestly didn't know what—when the Shop door banged open.

"Help! I need help!"

"The Battle Hymn of the Seven Tree Sisters" warbled loudly as a man staggered into sight. His face was bloody and he carried a large, thrashing burlap sack. Behind him the door shuddered, as though something heavy had crashed into it.

Mara turned to Fi. For once, she actually looked concerned. "What happened?" Fi said quickly. "You should go to the lift station—an emergency medical car can take you down the mountain tonight."

"No!" The man limped to the counter and heaved the sack on top of it. "You don't understand. My face, it's superficial. It's these bloodthirsty decoys. You have to help me."

Decoys? Mara mouthed at Fi, who let out a minuscule shrug before addressing the man. "At least sit down, let me get you some water."

"No, there's no time. I came to warn you—the owl decoys you've been selling, they're coming to life. They attacked me tonight! I barely managed to trap one, and then they chased me all the way here! I wanted you to see it, so you could—well, I don't know..." The man trailed off as he looked between Mara and Fi. "You look a little—well, is there someone else I can speak to? A manager?"

"Sit down," Fi said firmly. "Mara, go get the first aid kit from the office. Now sir, tell us what happened."

The man lowered himself into a chair, but he kept his grip on the sack. "I heard something shuffling in my garden last night, so I went out to see what was going on. I've had issues with mice recently—that's what the decoy was for. But the moment I set foot in the garden, it attacked!"

He kept talking as Mara went back to Howard's office. The first aid kit was on the bookshelf. She took it down and was turning to leave the room when she heard something strange—a high-pitched whine coming from the back of the room. From the closet at the back of the room, to be precise.

Not my problem not my problem not my problem—but she couldn't stop herself from walking over and opening the closet door.

Mara generally tried to avoid the closet. Everyone did. It was the dumping ground for everything Howard didn't want to deal with, from the broken vacuum cleaner to three boxes of lawn treatment that had been recalled due to its unfortunate tendency to turn the ground bright pink where it landed. (Why anyone was trying to landscape a manicured lawn this high on a mountain was beyond her.) In the last few weeks, it had also developed a slightly disturbing glow with no obvious source. Unfortunately, it was also where Howard kept the lost and found box.

Right now the box held two jackets, five umbrellas, and one voluminous hat—and the package containing the enchanted gnome, which Howard had clearly just thrown on top of everything else.

Mara knew the gnome wasn't actually alive. The only thing animating it was Constantina's poorly executed enchantment. But she still couldn't help feeling it shouldn't be left like this. Chances were that without intervention, it would still be here next month—or as long as Howard could put up with the whine. Maybe one day he would simply open the office window and throw the gnome off the side of the mountain.

She picked up the package and carefully folded down the paper so the gnome's face was exposed. "Look," she said, feeling silly the whole while. "I'll take you out of the closet, but you have to be quiet, all right? I've got a lot of things to do."

The gnome fell silent. While this was what Mara had wanted, she couldn't pretend she wasn't bothered. An animated gnome statue was annoying. An animated gnome statue developing sentience was disturbing. But she didn't have time to waste on untangling that particular conundrum. She slipped the gnome into her pocket—it *barely* fit—and went back to the front.

* * *

"What took you so long?" Fi cried. She was wrestling with the burlap sack, which was thrashing even harder now. The man was nowhere to be seen. "Get a shovel, hurry up! Aisle six!"

Mara dropped the first aid kit and ran around the counter—the man had collapsed to the floor, she saw as she ran past—and retrieved a shovel. "Now what?"

Fi grabbed the sack by one end and dragged it off the counter onto the floor. "What do you mean, *now what?* Bash it!"

Fi's insistence cut through Mara's hesitation. Mara raised the shovel and brought it down as hard as she could on the burlap sack. *Thwack!* The sack lay still. Fi slumped back against the counter. Mara lowered the shovel. "What *is* that?"

"An owl decoy. According to Elgar here, anyway. Want to see if he's right?"

Mara didn't particularly want to—she had her suspicions about whether whatever was in the sack was actually defeated or was just pretending—but Fi opened the sack and upended it before she could object. Splintered wood fell into a pile on the floor. The last to come out was, unmistakably, a carved owl's head. Mara tightened her grip on the shovel, but it appeared that the first blow had worked. Nothing moved.

"Yep," Fi said. "That's definitely one of ours."

"But how? Why? Did he misenchant it like the gnome?"

Fi started scooping the remains of the decoy back into the bag. "He said he didn't. And considering he caught a nasty gash from it, I think it's likely he's telling the truth. Which means that this is Gavin's problem."

"What do you mean?"

The shop door shuddered again. Mara flinched.

* * *

"There are more of them right outside, and since it seems unlikely a ragtag band of gardeners all misenchanted their decoys in the same way, the common denominator is the Shop. Gavin owns the shop. Ergo, it's Gavin's problem. So we're going to patch up Elgar's head, dump this sack on Howard's desk with a note, and not worry about it."

Mara couldn't argue with Fi's logic, but logic wouldn't prevent the decoys from attacking them or anyone else unlucky enough to catch their attention. "We can't wait for Howard. If the decoys are attacking people and they come from the Shop, it's our responsibility. We have to do something about it now!"

"Like what? Are you going to go after them one by one with the shovel? How many do you think you'll get?" Fi opened the first aid kit and started wiping the dried blood off of Elgar's face. "It's Gavin's fault, so it's Gavin's problem to fix. We're just the people who take the complaint."

Gavin's fault? Wait. Gavin's fault meant something very different than Gavin's problem. "Fi," Mara said slowly, "are you saying Gavin knew the decoys would do this?"

Fi didn't reply. She placed a bandage neatly over the cut on Elgar's temple and smoothed it down. Then she reorganized the first aid kit and handed it back to Mara. "You can put this back now."

Mara stared at her. "No. Not until you tell me what's going on."

Fi rolled her eyes. "Trust me, you'll be happier if you don't know."

Mara folded her arms over her chest. "Trust me. I won't."

* * *

"That is...the most ridiculous thing I've ever heard."

Fi sighed and took another bite of her chocolate bar. They had gone through five at this point. Well—Mara had gone through four herself as she couldn't quite bring herself to believe what Fi was saying. "Look, I know you think Gavin D'Olndaria is amazing. But the only amazing thing about him is the way he's been able to convince everyone in the Five Mountains that he knows how to cultivate clouds."

Mara unwrapped her fifth bar and stared sadly down at the chocolate. "I don't know what to say."

"Don't you think it's strange that he promised you an apprenticeship and you've been stuck here for two months instead? There's a reason for that. He can't teach you cloud cultivation. He put you here to make you so miserable you quit."

"But what about the weather? *Someone* is doing the cloud cultivation."

"It's eagle magic," Fi said, her words muffled as she chewed. "They're the ones with the power."

"If that's true, where are they? I've been here for months and I haven't even *seen* an eagle."

"They're here. I used to see them all the time when I was a kid. It's just been this way since Gavin came. He struck some sort of bargain, and part of that must have been that they keep a low profile. And if I were to guess why the decoys are suddenly coming to life, I'd guess it was because Gavin has somehow reneged on his side of it. It's not just the weather, see. All the enchantments in the shop come from eagle magic. If they wanted to, they could make everything in here go haywire."

"But why would the eagles agree to be used like this? And to hide on their own mountain?"

"Beats me. Also, not our problem."

"Fi. There are owl decoys swarming right outside our door. Unless Gavin walks in *right now* to deal with it, it's our problem."

"I've got magazines and a fully stocked candy rack. I can wait them out." Fi leaned back in her chair and put her feet up on the counter. Mara smacked them down. "Hey!"

"*No,*" Mara said. Her body thrummed with anger. Her heart pounded with it. Her fingers *trembled* with it. "No, you listen to me. I've been jerked around for two months by a fraud of a wizard, and I am not about to stand by while he puts the entire mountain in danger. I'm going to do something about it." Fi opened her mouth—Mara held up a hand to stop her. "No buts. I'm going to find the eagles and figure this out, and you're going to help me—unless you want me to tell them that you were in on this with Gavin from the beginning."

Fi went quiet. It was a different sort of quiet than Mara was used to from her. Usually she was quietly ignoring everything around her, in a mocking sort of way. This, though. This was a focused quiet. A serious quiet. A quiet like Fi was looking at her and seeing her, for the very first time. After a moment, Fi nodded. "All right. But if we're doing this, you might want to bring the shovel."

* * *

Mara had gone through several impressions of Fifth Mountain in the time she had lived there. At first, she'd been awed by the natural landscape, the wind that always seemed on the verge of taking her breath away, the way she could see for miles, all the way to the other four mountains, on a clear day. Once she was put on the night shift the mountain lost its mystique. What did she care how the mountain looked when she trudged about the path in darkness and spent most of her day sleeping? Boredom, disillusionment, resignation had all followed. But she had never been afraid—not until she and Fi were standing at the front door of the shop, interior lights off, peering through the glass out at the night.

Mara tightened her grip on the shovel. "Do you think we can make a run for it?"

"Hardly. It's a long way to the eyrie. If the decoys intend to attack us, we'll never make it. Again, I vote for staying inside. Where it's safe."

"Not happening," Mara said. But Fi was right about the decoys. They couldn't leave the shop unless the owls stood down.

Mara gingerly touched the door handle. The shop must have sold at least twenty of the decoys over the last few weeks. And now they were out there, waiting.

Fi pinched the bridge of her nose. "Okay, I'm not saying this is going to work, but—" She reached past Mara and pulled open the door, just a crack. "Um, attention, owls? We want a parley? So if you could maybe stand down so we can come over to the eagles, that would be great?"

Silence. Fi opened the door further—and was met by an eerie screech. She forced the door closed and leaned against it just as something battered the other side. "Guess that won't work," she gasped.

Mara felt something move at her side, and looked down to see the gnome poke its head out of her pocket. It looked up at Mara and said—something. She still couldn't understand anything it said. But its tone sounded...positive? It pointed to the door.

"When did that thing end up in your pocket?" said Fi incredulously.

"Not important," Mara replied. "But it's trying to tell us something. I...think it wants to go outside." She was trying really, *really* hard not to think about what it meant that the gnome seemed to understand what was going on enough to have an opinion.

"So the gnome is on their side? Perfect," Fi grumbled.

"No, I think it wants to help." And Mara was inclined to let it. It wasn't as though she had any other ideas for how to get past the owls. "What's the worst that could happen if we let it out?"

"It tells the owls how to break through the windows. The owls get in, we get maimed, we die."

Mara glared at her. "Not helping!"

"Fine, fine. I really hate that I'm saying this, but sure, let's make this night even weirder. Why not."

Mara took the gnome out of her pocket and lifted it so their eyes were level. "You want to go outside to talk to the owls? Is that right?"

The gnome nodded curtly.

"Okay, then. Let's do it. On three. One, two—"

Fi pulled open the door and Mara reached out far enough to set the gnome down on the stoop before they slammed the door shut once more.

The gnome cut quite a lonely figure on the stoop. Mara felt oddly protective watching it. Had she done the right thing? What if the owls ripped it to shreds?

The gnome started to speak, its odd speech barely audible through the glass. Then it lifted off the ground and *flew*—up, up, and out of the range of the tiny stoop light.

"So it's abandoned us. Nice," Fi said. "We should probably start building a barricade now."

Mara rolled her eyes, though she kept the shovel handy. Maybe it was just wishful thinking, but she really thought the gnome had wanted to help. And if it hadn't, then what had all that noise been before it took off? Explaining it was a neutral party and requesting to leave? Well, now she was just thinking like Fi.

She was about to suggest they try sending a message to Howard or Gavin when the gnome came back into view. Flight was perhaps not the right word for what it was doing. Instead of flapping its arms like wings, it simply floated through the air as though gravity had no effect. Either way, it descended gently to the stoop. As it landed, wooden owls dropped out of the night behind it, landing on either side of the path.

"I guess we have our answer," Mara said. "Let's go."

Mara dropped the shovel and stepped gingerly outside. When the owls did not attack, she picked up the gnome and tucked it back in her pocket, adding a reassuring pat on its cap. She would have to thank it later.

The wind had quieted and everything was still—except for the decoys. Owl heads turned as she and Fi walked past, their scrutiny raising the hairs on the back of Mara's neck. They were silent as they took flight. It was easy to imagine one of them swooping down upon her, claws tearing into her skin, and difficult to stop her shoulders from tightening.

The owls led them through the village, then higher up the mountain. Past a certain point, the trees grew sparse and scraggly, and the night cold. When Mara exhaled, she saw fog in the clear night—and above her, the stars. So many stars, splashed like liquid across the sky.

She had never been so far up the mountain. The only thing out here was Gavin's workshop, and she'd never received an invitation. But now she felt a certain rightness—the same sense of peace and purpose she had felt as she ascended Third Mountain. Why had she waited so long to climb?

Fi climbed next to her, silent save for the sounds of her exertion. Mara watched her out of the corner of one eye.

She had been outraged to learn about Gavin's duplicity, but now that the shock had settled, she had to admit that she wasn't surprised. What else had she truly expected by the man who didn't appreciate the work of his employees, who never appeared at the business that bore his name? The person she was surprised by—surprisingly—was Fi. Fi, who *did* care, Mara was beginning to realize. She might have preferred to leave everything well enough alone, but she had taken care of Elgar's wounds. She had told Mara the truth. And she was walking next to her now, side by side.

"Why didn't you tell anyone what Gavin was up to?" Mara asked.

Fi shrugged. "I only learned any of this because I'm so unimportant—it's easy to hear things when no one remembers you're there. If I told anyone it would be my word against his, and who would believe me? He's the great Gavin D'Olndaria. I'm just a clerk in a shop."

On impulse, Mara took Fi's hand and squeezed. "I'm sorry."

"*You* didn't do anything wrong," Fi replied, but she squeezed Mara's hand back. "Now let's get moving. I don't want to freeze to death out here."

* * *

Fifth Mountain's twin peaks were separated by a sharp chasm. The owls herded Fi and Mara right up to the edge of the first before Mara saw the bridge—a spindly contraption of wood and rope that looked as though it might collapse if someone so much as breathed on it. Lone lanterns lit each end, showing the chasm to be *extremely* wide.

Mara stumbled back. "No. Oh, no. Definitely not." It was one thing to climb mountains with one's feet planted firmly on solid ground. Trusting one's life to a fragile bridge strung over depths of nothingness? That was another thing entirely. She looked at Fi, then at the owls surrounding them. "Can't—can't we do this here? Or maybe one of the eagles could carry us across? Do we *really* need to—need to—" Her chest was tight—she felt as though she couldn't get a full breath. Her vision went spotty and she crouched down, closing her eyes tightly. She couldn't do this. No one should do this.

"I don't really think we're in a position to argue." Fi's voice came from somewhere very far away.

Mara shook her head. "I can't do that."

"Yes, you can." A reassuring weight came down on her shoulder—Fi's hand. She sensed movement next to her, and a tentative finger brushed her face, lifting her chin. "Look at me." Mara opened her eyes. Fi crouched beside her. Her face was shadowed by the night but Mara could feel Fi's breath on her cheek. "It's going to be fine," Fi said. "The bridge will hold. We'll have our audience with the eagles. But not if you don't get up now."

"No."

Laughter crept into Fi's voice. "Look, I've got one more chocolate bar in my jacket, and I'm going to be really disappointed if you make me eat it alone on the other side of that bridge."

Mara's lips quirked up, though her heart was still pounding. "Half a chocolate bar? For crossing that bridge, I should get fifty. At least."

Fi's fingers traced Mara's cheek before she swept a stray hair behind Mara's ear. She leaned in, whispering. "Tell you what. If you make it across that bridge, I'll kiss you."

"You—what?"

But Fi was already up, and Mara couldn't look away as the other girl practically danced across the bridge. The wooden planks shuddered and the ropes strained, but the bridge held. Just like Fi had said. And then she was on the other side, waving back at Mara.

There it was again, that thought she had set aside. Fi-shaped and winking and unexpectedly sweet—except she couldn't think about it now because of everything else crowded into her mind. The frustration of two months of drudgery. The injustice of Gavin's actions. The visceral terror of the bridge before her. The knowledge, bone-deep, that this was what needed to be done, and that she was the one to do it. She had to.

I'm going to die, Mara thought, as she placed her hands on either side of the bridge. She stepped out on the first plank and immediately regretted it. Her eyes squeezed shut and she immediately regretted *that* too, so she opened them again, straining to focus only on the lantern in the distance and *not* on the swaying planks underfoot, and the unending blackness under *that*.

"Come on, Mara!" Fi called in the distance, and it was silly that such a small thing helped, but it did. Strangely, so did the owl decoys. They were circling overhead, waiting. For her.

Her legs threatened to collapse with every step. Her knuckles were white with the strain of gripping the ropes. She couldn't tell if her vision was narrowed because she was focusing so hard on the lantern or because she was about to faint, but somehow, *somehow*, she took one step forward, then another. The bridge swayed every time she moved, but she was walking, the muscles in her legs straining as she edged down toward the center of the bridge and its turning point, then rising once more as solid ground loomed ahead of her and the lantern grew in her vision. And there, at the end of it all, was Fi. Fi taking her hand and pulling her forward, off of the bridge onto solid ground once more. Fi's arms around her, holding her as she shook. Fi's murmurs in her ear, Fi's laughter as she joked about the chocolate—and then Fi's fingers in her hair, Fi's lips on hers.

Was her heart pounding because of the bridge or the kiss? Mara only knew that kissing Fi was surprise and sweetness, like the first moment of flight on a skyship, like seeing a shooting star. It was wonderful and it was over too soon.

Fi smiled against her lips as she pulled back. "Never say I don't keep my promises," she said. "Now, let's go meet the eagles."

* * *

By the time they arrived at the eyrie the adrenaline had drained from Mara's body, leaving her wobbling and exhausted. This didn't stop fear from shooting through her chest at the first sight of the eagles—dozens of them, each taller than a human by at least half, looming in a circle around the nest. And at the center of the circle lay a man.

It must be confessed that Mara's first thought when she saw Gavin's prone body was not concern, but contempt. Once she would have seen rescuing the best cloud cultivator in the Five Mountains as an opportunity. Now that she knew he was nothing but a lie, there was nothing stopping her from leaving him to his fate. But the people who lived on Fifth Mountain didn't deserve to be terrorized because Gavin had broken faith with the eagles.

The decoys led Fi and Mara to the center of the nest. Mara looked from one eagle to the next. Their wings were brown and gold and white flecked, their eyes bright, their beaks dangerously curved. They were *beautiful*. She could so easily imagine them filling the sky.

Fi spoke, her voice clear and carrying. "Eagles of Fifth Mountain, we come in peace. We have seen what your anger has wrought, and we ask what we can do to make this right."

One of the eagles shrieked, cutting white pain straight through Mara's head. She gasped, falling to her knees. Fi fell beside her.

"Enough!" came a voice that quieted the circle. An eagle stepped forward, bowing its head in the moonlight. Mara tried not to shiver as its beak drew her gaze. "Humans, this business is between us and this pitiful excuse for a life form. Not you."

Mara swallowed. "Then we agree. This man is a liar."

"Mara, please," Gavin moaned from the ground. "Help me..."

Mara looked down at him. His cape was torn and his jaunty hat was missing. He was clearly terrified. *Well, good.* She turned back to the eagles. "We are here only on behalf of the other humans who live on this mountain, to ask what we can do to make this right. I am Mara Windward. My companion is Fi."

"A trick," called an eagle behind her.

"Gavin tricked me too," Mara said, speaking louder. "I came here because I hoped to learn from him. I only discovered the truth about your magic tonight."

The rumble of discontent grew around them. Mara reached for Fi's hand and squeezed it tightly.

The first eagle raised its wing, and the eagles went silent. "Very well, humans. I am Scaw."

A name. That had to be a good sign. "We are honored to meet you," Mara said.

Fi echoed her words, then added, "I understand Gavin bargained with you for the use of your magic. What did he offer in return? How did all this go wrong?"

An eagle's hiss sent shivers down Mara's spine. "What did he *offer* us? Treachery!"

"Quiet, Qhoot!" Scaw snapped. Its yellow eye fixed upon Mara. "Long ago, our precious egg was stolen from us. The human promised that he could find and return it, if only he could draw upon our power. For many years he promised this, but we were fools to trust him. Now he has found the egg—and thinks himself powerful enough to threaten us with it himself. For this treachery he will die. But the egg—" Scaw's voice cut off, and it let out a furious shriek. "The egg may be lost to us. It is near to hatching now—it may already be glowing! But he has not given it up. We know not where he has hidden it."

Mara's heart sank. Gavin could have hidden an egg anywhere. Even if they were given the chance to look, they would be lucky to get farther than Gavin's house before the eagles lost patience. They wanted Gavin dead—which seemed fair, in all honesty. But in the meantime, the owl decoys had already hurt a mountain resident. If everything sold by the Aerial Gardeners Shop started acting up, there was no telling how much damage might be done. So if there was a chance to make peace with the eagles, Mara had to try.

Mara's pocket twitched and she flinched in surprise. Fi looked at her, puzzled. Scaw drew back, its eyes narrowing. "What is the meaning of this?"

The gnome! In the midst of everything, Mara had forgotten it was there. "I'm so sorry, I meant nothing by it. I forgot I had this with me, and then it moved. I was just startled." Slowly, carefully, she drew out the gnome.

"That is not an egg!" cried another eagle. "Do you mock us?"

"Of course it is not the egg, Magdah," Scaw said wearily. "We all have eyes to see that. And the human will explain, I am certain."

"Thank you," Mara said. "I apologize. This is..." What *was* it? An enchanted gnome? It had started out that way, but it was more than that now. Mara was certain of it. "My companion," she said finally. If the gnome wanted to be, of course. But the words felt right—righter than most of her time on Fifth Mountain, anyway.

The eagles peered down at the gnome. The gnome craned its head as it looked back at all of them, looked up at Mara, then dove back into her pocket. She couldn't blame it—it must seem much safer in there than out here. The gnome probably wished it had stayed in the depths of Howard's closet. Howard's *glowing* closet. A door no one opened unless they were forced to—and even then, no one ever really looked inside. She looked at Fi. "I have an idea."

* * *

Mara had never considered herself particularly lucky. In fact, after the last two months, she would have called herself quite *un*lucky. But thanks to Constantina Brevwit's infuriating attitude and magical incompetence, she was lucky that night. For there in Howard's office, under the eagles' careful watch, she dug past the lost and found, past the recalled lawn treatment, behind the vacuum cleaner and a hundred other bent and broken items that had accumulated over the years, and unearthed, at last, a cardboard box. It was unmarked and nondescript—aside from the white glow emanating from its seams. Warmth traveled up Mara's fingers the moment she touched it, and when she opened the box there it was—one precious egg swaddled in newsprint and rags, glowing so brightly it hurt her eyes to look at it.

Scaw took the egg and passed it to Magdah, who spirited it immediately away.

The eagles didn't thank her, not by word. But once everyone was clear of the shop, the full convocation landed in a semicircle around it. They spread their wings under the rising sun and sang. And slowly—majestically, even—the Aerial Gardeners Shop lurched sideways, fell from its perch, and plummeted off the mountain. It fell so far, Mara didn't even hear it land.

Fi stood next to her, their shoulders touching, as the eagles took flight. They were beautiful, just as Mara had imagined. She hadn't asked what would happen to Gavin. She didn't need to know.

"So what are you going to do now? The eagles might teach you weather magic if you asked."

Mara shuddered. "Maybe in a few years. Right now I've got to get the taste of the last two months out of my mouth, and that's not going to happen on Fifth Mountain." She wasn't worried. So the cloud cultivation thing had turned to rubbish. She'd made her way before, and she'd do it again. If all else failed, the gnome had given her a few ideas about enchantment and sentience that deserved further pondering. Maybe she could find a position that would let her do that at leisure. Court mages got a lot of time to experiment, and that cursed princess *did* owe her a favor.... Of course, the most important thing was that she was never, ever going to work in a retail store like this again.

"You're leaving, then." Fi spoke in classic Fi tone, the one that said she couldn't possibly care less about the conversation. This time, though, Mara could tell she cared quite a lot.

"Yes," Mara said, threading her fingers through Fi's. "But I'd love it if you came with me. You're much too interesting to stay on one mountain your whole life, anyway."

The eagles in flight were beautiful. But nothing could compare to Fi's surprised smile as Mara's invitation sank in.

Three days later Mara and Fi started down the mountain. The gnome sat on Mara's shoulder, quiet for once—and smiling.

"The Aerial Gardeners Shop" is a standalone short story by Rebecca Kim Wells. For stories with more queer magic, fury, and joy, check out her novels Shatter the Sky, Storm the Earth, and Briar Girls. Find out more at rebeccawellswrites.com.

Climb Every Mountain

Carmen Loup

Sapphic Representation: Lesbian, Bi/Pansexual, Polyamory
Heat Level: Hot!
Content Warnings: Coarse Language, Violence, Xenobiology

Chapter 1

"I have to assassinate the Superior Mother of the Rhean Order of Ultra-Physicists," Yvonne announced, loudly, to the entire bar.

She went on to say, "I don't know why...they just said I had to."

"Huh," replied the bartender.

She realized she had said that out loud and quickly fished for an explanation. "Uh...that was a joke."

The comm device The Third Option installed in her head clicked on.

"Idiot," Olnbaim whispered to her over the comm device.

Olnbaim, her commanding officer.

He watched her from a dark corner of the bar, threateningly sipping a drink. The drink was for cover, only. Olnbaim disdained alcohol; he disdained anything that made life livable, Yvonne often thought.

She slipped a finger under the decorative tracking collar he had locked onto her neck, trying to get some airflow to the sweaty skin under the band.

Fortunately, the bartender believed that it was a joke, albeit a massively unfunny one, because she was very, very inebriated.

"That's enough for tonight," he said. "I hate to turn down extra crystals in this economy, but I don't think my conscience could handle serving you anymore perception modifiers." He was a handsome Rhean, and obviously young. Bartenders around these parts typically overcame their conscience early on in their careers.

Yvonne didn't fight him about closing out her tab. She couldn't afford it, anyway. She'd have to find a way to sneak out without him noticing.

"You know, you remind me of my last lover," she said with a goofy grin, her mouth continuing to leak every thought that flashed across her mind. "They were Tuhntian, though. Blue and very pale, not like you. They used to cut me off, too, the poslouian-slug-grass-eating-coward."

"Is that right?"

"Yep—" Yvonne gazed out the bar's dusty window, so full of alcohol her eyeballs seemed to float along with the low clouds. The mountain where, she had been told, she would find the hidden location of the Rhean Ultra-Physicists, an unassuming primitive monastery. "Though if I had taken their advice and not joined the zuxing rebellion I wouldn't be here in this...what is this place, a town?"

"It's a valley."

"Yeah, but it's a town in a valley, right?"

"No, ma'am, just a valley."

"Isn't it organized under some kind of government?"

"No, ma'am. It's just a valley. No taxes in this area, so there are lots of bars. No laws either, so there are lots of other things."

"Then why's the Rhean Ultra-Physics' HQ here?"

"No taxes."

"Oh."

"No laws, neither."

"Right. What are they doing up there?"

"Ask them yourself," the bartender nodded his head to the opening door, then went to sanitize the steadily growing tower of used glasses and snack orbs.

Yvonne slowly turned around. The room was already spinning in one direction, and she had to somehow make it go the other way.

A small group of Ultra-Physicists entered the bar, their outfits setting them far apart from the other bar-goers. They were barely drinking age, wearing crisply draped grey robes with neatly tucked head cloths. They looked as if they were ready to perform either a sterile surgery or a sacred ritual. Any member of the Rhean Order of Ultra-Physics was always prepared for either. The two really weren't that different, anyway.

Five of the six rushed, reservedly, to the bar, but one tucked herself into a booth near the back, scanning the bar left to right and back again like an AutoSanitizer, her eyes wide and curious. Her position by the door would be perfect cover for Yvonne to slip out without paying once she found out where their Superior Mother could be found.

Yvonne tripped off the barstool, caught herself, composed a reasonably sober-looking gait and leaned over the newcomer's table, drawing her shoulders together to emphasize the pillowy qualities of her boobs. What came next, she was already quite accomplished at, sober or not.

It was time to flirt.

"What's a gorgeous Monastic like yourself doing in a seedy bar like me?" Yvonne winked.

Her efforts were met by a subtle, silent head tilt.

"Like...zuut. I mean like *this*. This one. Blitheon, I've had a rough couple of rotations, I'm sorry. I'm usually zing up to caliber at this." Yvonne looked up hesitantly. Fortunately, her deep purple cheeks hid her blushing, but her face still radiated the heat of embarrassment.

The corner of the Monastic's thin, dark lips drew a dainty smile across her periwinkle face.

"'Zing up to caliber' at what, exactly?" she asked.

"Uh...just getting to know people," Yvonne said because she didn't want to come right out and say that she had been trying to flirt. Before the war, she'd been the King of a burlesque troupe. Flirting had paid her way through higher schooling. Now that she was using it for a sinister purpose, however, it fell a touch flat. "So...why are you here?"

"The Superior Mother sent all the monastic youth down to the valley to explore. She said we needed 'airing out.'" Her delicate finger tapped a button on the table, placing an order for a glass of water.

Yvonne swallowed at the mention of the Superior Mother. The one she was ordered to kill for reasons beyond her station. She laughed to loosen her voice again. "Airing out, that's funny...So, do you uh...you come here often?" Usually alcohol improved her abilities, but under the circumstances it had only made her feel horribly vulnerable.

The miniature teledisc embedded in the table glowed brightly, then materialized the water the Monastic had ordered.

"No. I have never been here before," the Monastic sipped the water. "I am not sure I like it," she added, using the corner of her sleeve to remove a smudge from the glass.

Yvonne turned the wooden chair around and sat on it backwards, a move she hoped made her look confident. It would've worked if one of the chair legs hadn't come loose and sailed across the grimy floor. She clambered back to her feet, moved the mop of curls which hung like golden Spanish moss out of her eyes, then gently laid the chair aside, choosing instead to squat beside the table. "I'm Yvonne, what's your name?" Yvonne asked, finally getting around to the really vital question.

"I am Ix under C'Zabra of The Rhean Order of Ultra-Physics. I am more typically called 'Ix,' though." She sipped her water, and Yvonne got the vague sense that she was displeased that no one used her full name and title. Yvonne was mistaken, however. It was simply true that she was typically called "Ix" and so she had said it.

"So, Ix under C'Zabra of The Rhean Order of Ultra-Physics. How did you get into Rhean Ultra-Physics? I hear it's pretty advanced stuff."

Ix looked down, giggling softly into her shoulder. "You may call me Ix, if you would like. I was raised in the care of the monastery. Advanced Ultra-Physics is advanced, but the rest of it is not."

"I guess that should've been obvious, huh?" Yvonne stacked her hands on the table and rested her chin on top, looking up at Ix. "Can I sit next to you? My chair broke."

"Ask—tchk—about the Superior—fzzzz!" The device implanted near her ear was cheaper than glotchbur fur muff and worked half as well. Olnbaim was, of course, watching her defective flirting.

Ix's eyes darted toward Yvonne's ear and Yvonne smiled tightly. "Translation chip's acting up," she said. "That was a lie, sorry. I uh..."

"Blitheon's tits, you're bad at this," Olnbaim hissed.

"Who is speaking to you?" Ix asked. "And why are they asking about our Superior Mother?"

All the warmth generated by Yvonne's drinking and flirting dropped out of her, leaving an icy chill and a fevered cacophony of curse words in her ear. The device was designed to be undetectable to outsiders. She was promised it would be!

"How—" Yvonne's partially formed question was interrupted by Ix's surprisingly strong fingers slipping a laserblade under Yvonne's tracking collar, slicing through it and chucking the device into the middle of the room where it promptly exploded, scattering a dozen bouncing globs of sticky pink which splatted around the bar. The pink blotches might've been comical had they not, seconds later, burst into flames.

Ix was already up, collecting her colleagues and seeing that each in turn swiftly exited the premises. The rest of the bar-goers surged to the door, catching Yvonne in the current and pulling her into the tsunami of bodies flooding outside.

Pink exploded beside Yvonne's head, splinters of wood bouncing off her skin, a wall of flame blocking her exit. She felt something tickle the back of her elbow and she swatted at it, thinking it was a bug, but felt liquid on her fingers.

"Zuut," Yvonne cursed at the sticky, dark blood dripping down her fingers, glistening in the light of the fire. She felt her right shoulder with her opposite hand and discovered a dagger of wood from the booth explosion piercing her shoulder.

She squeezed under a table in the corner farthest from the fire and quietly cursed Olnbaim and all his ancestors. When cursing Olnbaim stopped helping, she moved on to cursing the "Great Powers That May or May Not Be" in Rhean alphabetical order from O'Zeno to Blitheon, on down.

"Curse Blitheon's infected nipple blisters," is what she was whispering when Ix came into earshot, having ducked beneath the table.

"That will only make the pain worse," Ix admonished. "Repeat after me. 'Dook ah sarva dook ah maya om,'" said Ix's ethereal face, silhouetted against the fire, particles of ash blooming in the angelic aura around her body.

Yvonne's brain tingled. She could actually feel every cell of her body falling in love with this mysterious monastic. It was, of course, only adrenaline mixed with the dizziness of smoke inhalation and some lingering intoxication. It felt better to call it love, though. Yvonne desperately wanted to feel something which wasn't fear, helplessness, or anger, the only emotions she'd been privy to since signing her life away to The Third Option Coalition.

"What does that mean?" she asked.

"It means 'Dook ah sarva dook ah maya om.'" Ix gripped Yvonne by the waist and slung Yvonne's uninjured arm around her neck. She dragged Yvonne right through the flames and out of the charred bar door, mysteriously untouched.

The other bar-goers, including Ix's fellow monastics, just stood around watching the flames consume the building, mesmerized by the carnage, but Ix took Yvonne far from the flames and sat her down on the rocky ground beside a derelict building. Yvonne leaned gratefully into the cold concrete wall.

"Allow me to help," Ix said.

"No, no, you should go," Yvonne said. The collar had been thwarted. Olnbaim would be looking for her to finish the job.

"You are injured. I have studied medicine," Ix said, inclining her head cutely, Yvonne thought. No, now was not the time to indulge her libido!

"Listen, this is serious. You have to go! I was sent here by The Third Option Coalition to infiltrate the monastery and murder the Superior Mother."

Ix blinked, sat back on her ankles. "That is silly. I thought you said this was serious."

"Silly?! I just admitted to trying to kill your Superior Mother!"

Ix laughed lightly, shaking her head. "No one can kill the Superior Mother. It *is* silliness. But you're hurt, you should come back to the mountains with me. This is an excellent excuse for us to stop being 'aired out.'"

"Agh, that's what he wants," Yvonne said, hissing as she tried to move her arm. "I'm sure they're still tracking me with the comm device they installed. If you take me up to the mountains, someone from the coalition will follow us. Maybe several someones!"

"Then we will treat them as honored guests." The coin-sized mark on Ix's forehead lit up—a thought-controlled headlamp. She crawled around Yvonne, lifting her hands and shaking them each time like a cat shaking water off its paws. "The ground is filthy," she whispered, kneeling behind Yvonne to get a good look at the shoulder wound.

"Warn me if you're going to—Zuut!" Ix had already yanked the wood chunk from her shoulder, which gave her very little time to worry about it.

"Dook ah sarva dook ah maya om," Ix reminded her, tossing the shard aside.

"Dook ah sarva dook ah maya om," Yvonne repeated dutifully.

"Yes, keep going. It will help."

Yvonne heard Ix shuffle around in the cloth bag at her side and produce a simple roll of gauze. Funny, she thought, that an Ultra-Physicist privy to the most mind-boggling technology still packed a roll of gauze when light-seal sticks were so commonplace.

Ix mindfully unrolled the gauze, held one end up to Yvonne's forehead, and began snuggly wrapping her top-down, leaving a slit for Yvonne's confused eyes.

"It's just my shoulder that—"

"This is tele-tape. I am packaging you."

"P-packaging me..." Yvonne said feebly as Ix reached her shoulder, the part that actually needed attention.

"Prepare for teleport," Ix said, then tucked the tail end of the gauze into the wrap. Yvonne's atoms were ripped asunder and sent hurtling into the mountains.

Chapter 2

The room Yvonne woke up in ballooned endlessly around, despite being quite small. It was as if she'd been put behind an invisible fish-eye lens. A small hint to what was going on ran in pale text along all the middle line of every wall, "Objects in room are closer than they appear."

A new perspective, the Rhean Ultra-Physicists had found, was in fact the best medicine, and so the infirmary rooms were all fitted with a subtle perspective scrambler. The cool, soothing gel of the aloe vera plant—found on any planet in the universe whose inhabitants had developed skin—was also a pretty good medicine, and so while Yvonne had been asleep, a massive wad of the gel had been applied to her wound and covered with a heavy square bandage.

After a good while of waiting for further instruction, Yvonne had hazarded a cautious "hello" into the empty room.

No answer came.

"Olnbaim?"

Silence. Either the comm device was busted, or Olnbaim had been killed in the fire he started. It didn't matter much, though. Nothing could get her out of her contract with The Third Option Coalition.

The first option she'd been presented with when war broke out between her home planet, Tuhnt, and Rhea, where she had been hatched, was to watch all her friends—natural-born Tuhntians unlike herself—get drafted and killed one-by-one while she helplessly came up with new routines to keep her burlesque act fresh despite the rest of the troupe being gone.

The second option had been to go back to Rhea, get drafted herself, and fight against Tuhnt because the Tuhntian military would never let a Rhean get beyond filling out an application.

So, desperate to somehow end the war, Yvonne had been easily sold on The Third Option, a coalition of

Rheans, Tuhntians, and a few busybodies from other parts of the galaxy who purported to seek a peaceful end to the war.

Funny that the peaceful end had somehow involved murdering the head of the Rhean Order of Ultra-Physicists, but "Peace cannot exist without war" was The Third Option's motto and Yvonne had to admit it made sense.

Sometimes.

Sometimes she felt as if nothing would ever make sense again.

Flirting with Ix had made sense. It hadn't gone well, but it felt far more natural and honest than anything Yvonne had agreed to do since she joined The Third Option.

The door creaked open and Ix entered holding a stack of grey linens, startling Yvonne out of her brooding. She went back to doing what made sense.

"This is the first time I've ever had to get skewered to get invited back to a cute larv's place before. Worked though!" Yvonne tried to shimmy her shoulders enticingly, as she'd done a thousand times before, having forgotten about her recent shoulder wound. It was still stiff, but already mostly healed.

"'Cute larv'?" Ix asked, the neat stack of linens she had brought to the room sagging slightly between her hands. "You are attracted to me?"

Yvonne nervously tucked her lips away, wishing she had even a modicum of control over them. Too late to backtrack now, she decided to tell the truth. "You *are* cute, but I just ended a pretty serious relationship and I kinda told him I wanted to focus on doing my part to end the war and the war isn't over, so it would be sorta rude to get into another relationship right now..."

The sweet tension Ix's question had introduced between them dissolved into Yvonne's ramblings, and Ix set the linens on the table near the bed. "I understand. Thank you for the compliment. I would return it if I could."

"If you could?" Yvonne asked, stung. Was she not cute? "I used to get paid to wiggle my bits on stage, you know. Not long ago, either. Back on Tuhnt, I am a very desirable—"

Ix's gentle laugh cut her off. "I'm sorry, I should've explained. I cannot return the compliment because I do not engage in special relationships. My prime allegiance is to the Superior Mother. I am certain your...bits wiggle well."

Yvonne peeled the large bandage off her back and folded it indignantly. "They do," she affirmed and defiantly set the folded bandage down on the bedside table, once again finding that she had embarrassed herself in front of this simple, pure-minded celibate.

"I am not simple," Ix said.

"Wh—" Yvonne began to defend herself, but wasn't sure what she was defending.

"You must be careful what you think here," Ix explained. "The perspective field in the infirmary rooms heightens telepathic awareness to allow for more accurate medical care. And I don't think my mind is as pure as you're imagining." Her cheeks blushed mauve, and she hurried out of the room, shutting the door behind her.

* * *

"Pardon me, but may I please see your Superior Mother? You know, the one I was sent to kill. I'm really feeling much better, and I think I ought to complete my mission and get off your mark," Yvonne said for the tenth time to the image of herself reflected in the mirror which hung in her room.

She was practicing.

She had not heard from Olnbaim, but even if he was dead, The Third Option would be after her, and the radio silence had only made her mind more restless. Silence allowed too much space for thought, she craved stimulation.

Stimulation, she thought, wouldn't be such a bad thing. She glanced at the bed, then at the door. Were they watching her? If not, perhaps she could whip a quick clutch out on her ovipositor. If so...well, to be honest that would make it even more enjoyable. Yvonne was nothing if not an exhibitionist.

No, she decided, at last. She was a full-grown Rhean with a serious assignment.

Now was not the time to masturbate.

She resolved, instead, to go exploring.

The door to her room popped open at her touch, introducing her to the hallway which was, in comparison to the bright and round infirmary room, blindingly dark. The walls of the hallway were hewn out of rock, its only light the yellow bioluminescent skrum which clung to the ceiling, undulating leisurely along the length of the tunnel.

A pair of monastics who were not Ix sped by Yvonne, walking at a serious, practical clip. They ignored her entirely. So, she wasn't a prisoner. She wasn't even a person of interest.

She turned to watch the pair disappear down a corridor on the left, their already soft footsteps quickly became inaudible. Yvonne followed. Fearing that calling after the pair might startle them and make them disappear, she kept quiet.

She turned the corner and came nose to nose with Ix, nearly knocking the tray of food and drink out of Ix's hands.

"You are up," Ix noted. "And you are wandering," she said, a hint of annoyance in her voice.

Yvonne's resolve melted at seeing Ix again. She needed to communicate to Ix that her Superior Mother was in grave danger, but if she spoke out loud, her betrayal would be found out. Telepathy could come in handy here. Yvonne grabbed Ix's forearms excitedly, jostling the plates and cups on her tray again. "Can you hear my thoughts out here, too?" Yvonne then thought carefully about her predicament with The Third Option for Ix's benefit.

Ix breathed in and out slowly through her nose before answering. "I cannot. Please let go of me."

"Sorry," Yvonne said, stepping away from her awkwardly.

"I believe you are trying to communicate something to us about The Third Option Coalition. It is under control. There is nothing we do not know. You need not worry."

Yvonne was worried anyway.

"Come with me," Ix said, gentler now, inclining her head in a way which she always intended to be friendly but often came off as pejorative. "You need food and fresh air."

Yvonne glanced down at the tray, which she now realized Ix had been bringing to her. A bowl of warm, mashed something, a dish of water for cleaning, an infusion carafe filled with hot water and pungent herbs, and two small empty clay cups.

"You are nervous," Ix said. "The gardens will relax you. Follow me." Ix pivoted around and led Yvonne deeper into the tunnel. The skrum-light became thinner, but it was still enough for Yvonne to notice that Ix's head remained still as she walked, as if she'd had a gyroscope installed in her easefully swaying hips.

Typically, Yvonne had some dignity, and she would avoid staring when someone caught her eye. Now she had several other thoughts she really wanted to avoid swirling around in her brain. Simple, carnal pleasure made a worthy distraction.

The tunnel ended in a short flight of stairs, smoky blue light from outside competing with the dull glow of the skrum as they ascended. The exit to the tunnel was delicately carved with sweeping lines and curves, geometry which looked at once sacred and mundane.

Yvonne's eye-line was just about level with Ix's legs now, and the long slit in her robe allowed her periwinkle calf to peek out with every step up. "The architecture's beautiful," Yvonne said. Ix did not reply, but Yvonne could hear her start to chant something under her breath. The chant—though Yvonne could not have known this—was designed to help whoever practiced it resist temptations of the flesh.

They emerged on a platform and a blast of damp, cool air washed over Yvonne. The platform overlooked a sprawling courtyard hedged with tall blue-grey conical trees, tangling vines, flowering bushes, and the occasional silver statue. The garden ended at the cliff edge which opened on to an eye-wateringly vast vista. Three mountain peaks, the middle one rising just slightly higher than the other two, perfectly framed by the garden's foliage. Dense, cold clouds completely obscured Rhea's sun, diffusing soft blue light into every corner.

The scene was so strikingly bright after the dark tunnels that Yvonne had to blink several times to get her eyes to adjust. She wanted to say something, but the things which came to mind, "It's beautiful" or "Wow" or "That's neat," sounded a little dull in comparison to the grandeur of the mountains. So, she quietly followed Ix down the understated steps which led into the garden.

Ix stopped at the edge of the plateau, a sheer cliff plunging into the mists below. She tugged the handles of the tray and four hard-light beams appeared beneath it, turning it into a short table which she set on the ground beside the drop-off. She then sat down next to it, feet dangling over the abyss.

"Blitheon, is that safe?" Yvonne spoke now, shocked out of her awed silence.

"Perfectly safe."

"But what if you fall?"

"I will not fall."

"How do you know?"

"Because," Ix said as if it were obvious, "if I fell from this height, I would be killed." She poured a herbaceous, dark blue-green liquid from the carafe into each of the cups. "Come, sit," she encouraged.

Yvonne took a step back, wishing to sink back into the protective garden.

"I can't," she said. "Heights."

"What about heights?"

"I...I don't do them. I wouldn't trust myself not to fall."

Ix shifted, turning herself around to fix Yvonne with the totality of her judgmental gaze. "You would intentionally throw yourself over the edge?"

"Well, no...I mean...it would be an accident."

Ix seemed to prepare her argument, to further convince Yvonne that she was not going to topple over the edge, but she stopped herself. Instead, she nodded and began to pour the tea back into its carafe. "This is for the best, then."

"What is?"

"I wanted you to sit beside me and observe the mountains. I should not have wanted that, and so it did not happen. I will escort you back to your room where you may dine in peace. I apologize for my impropriety."

The only thing which could overcome Yvonne's fear of heights was her fear of missing out. She defiantly plopped herself down next to Ix, somehow convinced that if she were to fall, Ix would be more than capable of catching her. She curled her legs beneath her, deliberately but gently touching Ix's thigh with her own.

Ix glanced nervously up at her.

"There. I'm sitting on the edge now," Yvonne said, her pounding heart gave her voice an undeniable tension. "You don't have to let your fear stop you, either. What are you so worried about?" Yvonne asked.

"Accidents," Ix whispered, gaze shifting to Yvonne's lips.

Ix looking at her lips was her invitation. Yvonne leaned in, trailed her fingers down Ix's long, smooth jawline, and brought her mouth close enough to Ix's that a light breeze could have pushed them together.

Ix didn't wait for the breeze. She pressed her lips into Yvonne's and her fingers explored her mountain of soft curls. Ix's motions were inexperienced and hesitant, but vibrated with desperation.

Yvonne complied heartily. This was nothing new for her, and she quickly scooped Ix's slender body into her arms and began exploring her mouth deeper.

Ix tensed, placing a firm hand on Yvonne's sternum.

"Be careful," Ix said.

"I don't like to be careful," Yvonne said with a saucy wink.

Ix gracefully scooted away, the cups clattered when she bumped into the tray. "Then you should not come so close to the edge." She tore her gaze from Yvonne and refocused herself on the mountains, quietly repeating that phrase again. The one designed to resist temptations of the flesh.

Yvonne inhaled, preparing to retort, but decided not to press the matter. She scooted back from the edge and sat cross legged, watching the mountains which Ix clearly found so much more interesting than her.

"All things pass, you see?" Ix said. "Like the clouds flowing over the mountain. All things pass. To hold on to anything would be foolish."

"And what's so bad about being a little foolish when you've got something nice to hold onto?"

Ix's head tilted to the side, but she didn't turn around. She needed to process the question.

Quiet.

Enough quiet that Yvonne's thoughts again turned to Olnbaim. The threat of The Third Option had seemed so far away up there. That was a problem for the valley, not a problem for the mountains.

"I will take you to see the Superior Mother," Ix decided out loud, having run into a mental feedback loop which required additional external input.

Yvonne became blazingly alert again. "You will? But why? I mean...should you?"

"I must ask her something. And meeting her may assuage your concerns. Please, eat. I will be forgoing food for a while." Ix shifted the tray closer to Yvonne, keeping her gaze on the mountains. She began her chant again, though with slightly less conviction, Yvonne thought.

* * *

The skrum was much thinner here in the core of the mountain. Sound didn't reach, either. Warmth and light were also right out, and Yvonne swore she didn't usually pant this hard after just a few flights of steps.

"You are breathing loudly," Ix noted.

Yvonne almost laughed over her embarrassment, but decided not to waste her breath. "Sorry."

Ix stopped walking and inclined her head at Yvonne, her gaze studying, scanning Yvonne's body slowly. "You are breathing wrong," she asserted, at last.

"Oh well...I mean it's worked for me so far," Yvonne shrugged, continuing to breathe incorrectly.

"When the oxygen content is low, you must use your vestigial lungs to draw more air."

"I thought I was..."

Ix smiled, shaking her head slightly. "You are only using the top thirty percent of your lung capacity. May I touch you?"

"Uh, yeah. Have I not made that abundantly clear?"

Ix placed a hand under Yvonne's last rib. "Your inhale should move my hand," Ix said.

"Okay," Yvonne said, breathing even more shallowly now, her skin beginning to excrete a thin mucus to increase its oxygen permeability. Under Ix's touch, her limbs vibrated.

Ix lifted an eyebrow. Her hand did not move. "You are beginning to asphyxiate."

"I realize," Yvonne wheezed.

Ix removed her hand.

Yvonne bottled her disappointment.

"Here, try this instead." Ix collected a sizable glob of skum from a crevice in the cavern wall and offered it to Yvonne. "You can eat this. It will oxygenate your blood."

"Thanks," Yvonne dipped her face into Ix's hand and lapped up the skrum. Ix had intended for her to take a fingerful, not to lick her hand clean. Though, if she were being truly honest with herself, she didn't mind Yvonne's smooth, warm tongue tracing over her palm. She spun on her heel as soon as Yvonne had finished and began leading her swiftly and silently onward.

Yvonne still felt lightheaded, but now for a different reason.

Light was the first hint that something had changed, then oxygen, blessedly. And then sounds Yvonne could not name began to emanate from whatever the tunnel ended in.

"It's the sound of information," Ix explained, not because she could hear Yvonne's thoughts here, but because everyone she brought down there asked.

The sprawling garden above was a side salad compared to what Yvonne saw next. At first appearance, the mess of vines and leaves appeared completely random, but as Yvonne got closer to the wall of vegetation, she discovered that it was all part of an intentional pattern.

She stroked a broad, ribbed leaf and the gentle cooing of the forest changed ever so slightly, as if she had strummed a stringed instrument. This thought occurred to her: *The largest organism in existence is the Morbean Bropopalif. Its body spans the entire coast of the Morbe continent on Udo. Although most don't know of its existence, it does not experience loneliness, because it is always with itself.*

"It is unwise to elicit unfocused information." Ix paused as if she were done speaking, but her curiosity got the better of her. "What did it say?"

"Just something about a lonely giant." Yvonne hurried away from the leaf. "Hey, is this like the IFI?"

Ix laughed, leading Yvonne on again, in both senses of the word. "The IFI you have used is a very small and imperfect sampling of the information provided by an Ocular Forest."

"You came here to find out more about Olnbaim and The Third Option, didn't you?" Yvonne whispered, ducking under a vine which, when she accidentally brushed it, informed her that on average twelve million mosquitos hatch every minute on a planet called Earth.

"No," Ix said. "I am not worried about them. The Superior Mother cannot be killed, as I said."

"But I can! And you can!" Yvonne grabbed Ix's wrist to make her listen. She wanted Ix to be as worried as she was.

Ix gently patted Yvonne's hand. "We are safe here. If you'd like, you can ask the Superior Mother about it. I can't guarantee she will tell you everything, though. She sometimes refuses information for our own benefit."

"What are you asking her, then?"

Ix stopped and chewed her bottom lip, searching the ground as she asked herself the same question. "That's private," she said, finally, and walked on.

The plants became less dense, their stems getting thicker, more tree-like. Eventually they came to a tree trunk twice as wide as Yvonne was tall.

"Blitheon, that tree's so thick you could hold an orgy in it," Yvonne said, immediately regretting it. But Ix giggled.

"Some of the monastics have," she said.

"I thought you all were celibate."

Ix shrugged. "Not all of us. Some are more dedicated to their studies than others," Ix said, placing a gentle hand on the tree trunk's DNA entry pad as if in greeting. A sonic field emanated from tiny metal implants surrounding the tree's base.

Ix stepped through the sonic field and entered the tree, disappearing behind its bark.

Yvonne did not.

"What the trok?" she said out loud, to no one. She looked around, waiting for Ix to reappear, or for a gaggle of laughing monastics to tell her it had all been a prank.

Neither happened.

And so, Yvonne followed Ix, finding the inside of the tree completely dark.

Or, more precisely, Yvonne's eyes did not work inside the tree. Of course they didn't. They couldn't see what was now a part of them. The sonic field had broken the bonds that tied Yvonne together just enough that she could merge with the tree, but not so much that her consciousness was totally dispersed.

It felt like getting trapped in a teledisc.

That had been a fairly traumatizing event in Yvonne's larvaehood, and she quickly shut her eyes to try to rid herself of the sensation. It worked, but through no effort of her own. With her eyes closed, Yvonne saw a lot more.

"Greetings, larvling, I am your user interface. How would you prefer to see me?" asked a swirling cloud of what Yvonne could only describe as blueish glowing nanobots, though they weren't nearly as real.

Yvonne thought for a moment, trying to push aside her actual preference to instead imagine something more professional.

"I understand," said the presence with a warm giggle as it rearranged into a light-infused image of Ix. "But I will be keeping her clothes on, for her sake." She winked.

"O'Zeno," Yvonne whispered. She really was infatuated. "Are you the Superior Mother?"

"That is what the monastics call me," she nodded. Her voice was not Ix's voice. It was indescribably vast, though it sounded like it was coming through a long tube.

"Look, you're in great danger," Yvonne began. "There's this coalition to—"

The Superior Mother raised her hand—or was it Ix's hand?—to stop Yvonne's rambling. "I'm aware. Ix told you it would be okay, and it will. Olnbaim is currently in a dire condition due to his burns. He may or may not live."

"What do we do if he does? He's going to kill me! Then you!"

"You will climb that mountain when you come to it, larvling," said the Superior Mother. "You have another mountain to climb at this moment. You are attracted to my Ix."

Yvonne squirmed, heat beginning to rise in her belly. "I don't think she's attracted to me, though. And I'm in too deep with the coalition. I can't drag her into that."

"You are right on only one of those accounts. You *are* in too deep," she touched Yvonne's cheek with her hand. It felt more like a fizzing, carbonated beverage than solid flesh, but the gesture was comforting anyway. "Reach your left hand out," said the Superior Mother.

Yvonne obeyed, finding something warm and almost solid in front of her. As soon as she touched it, the image of the Superior Mother was replaced with a thin, old Rhean with incredibly high, sharp cheekbones and incredibly low, sharp breasts. The Superior Mother wore a thin fabric gown and a metal circlet around her head. She was speaking to Ix. The real Ix.

"You have committed your life to inner exploration," said the actual Superior Mother. "But one cannot live in a vacuum. Why not test yourself in a different external circumstance?"

"Uh, hi," Yvonne announced her presence quietly, not wanting to feel like she was spying on Ix's conversation. Ix turned and the Superior Mother vanished behind her, leaving Ix and Yvonne alone in the tree space.

"Sorry," Yvonne smiled awkwardly. "I didn't mean to interrupt—"

"I want to study you," Ix interrupted quietly, desperately. Ix had studied her own body and mind for so long, she craved additional external input.

Yvonne tensed. The impetus was in her sphere, but she had suddenly forgotten what to do with it. Ix stepped forward, her body almost but not entirely solid. As she moved toward Yvonne, the robe she had been wearing seemed to melt off, merging with the molecules of the tree itself, revealing first her even, small shoulders, then her modest breasts, the peak of her prominent hips which dipped into the valley between her thighs, flooded with softly rippling pubic hair.

"Blitheon..." Yvonne whispered.

"You don't seem happy," Ix noted, drawing back slightly, concern crushing her eyes.

"Oh, no, I am! I was just...stunned, I guess. How did you do that fancy little strip?" she said, trying to walk forward out of her own clothes but failing.

Ix crossed her arms over her nipples and she shrunk in on herself as she shrugged her uncertainty.

"Doesn't matter," Yvonne said, grinning like a h'undow in heat. She peeled off the tight Layflex top, feeling her own breasts catch on the edge of the top then bounce as they dropped free of it. She shimmied her hips out of the shorts she'd been wearing and, hopping on one foot, kicking them away. It wasn't the best striptease she'd ever pulled off, but she *had* pulled it off, and that is what mattered.

"Alright, study partner. Where do we start?" Yvonne breathed excitedly.

Ix chewed her lower lip again, this time more with excitement than trepidation, and reached a hand out to caress Yvonne's shoulder. "Subject appears to be fully healed," she said before gently squeezing Yvonne's firm mound of shoulder muscles. "And well designed."

Yvonne snaked her other arm around Ix's waist and cinched her close. "Well, I worked hard on those shoulders." She took Ix's hand and guided it down to her body, setting it on the roundest part of her ass. "I worked hard on that, too."

Ix buried her fingers in Yvonne's hair and their lips connected almost magnetically. Ix pushed Yvonne down with unexpected force and they landed in pillowy nothingness, as if cradled in a pool of salt water. The solidity of Ix's skin on Yvonne's seemed to dissolve, the space between their atoms giving way to each other.

Yvonne's ovipositor twitched desperately within her, and she obligingly released it along with the three smaller grasping tendrils which coiled around Ix's thighs and pulled her hips closer. Ix gasped and Yvonne felt her pull away slightly.

"Too much?"

"No, but..." Ix dropped her head into the crux of Yvonne's shoulder and Yvonne marveled at how perfectly she seemed to fit. "I've never released my ovipositor before."

Yvonne smiled and kissed her forehead. "I'll teach you," she said and held Ix's hips in her strong hands, rolling her thumbs along the edge of Ix's pelvis, absently counting the characteristic sex ridges as she always did. She had never counted this many, though.

"You're a six?!" Yvonne tensed, pushing Ix away now. "You're a queen?"

Ix squeezed her eyes shut. "That's why I've never mated. I am almost guaranteed to impregnate anyone below sex number four."

"Oh, larvling," Yvonne said with a laugh. "I don't care! I've got a diaphragm installed. Those eggs won't make it into the sac. Now relax and let me help you." She gently pressed her thumbs into the soft swell of Ix's lower belly and rubbed down, coaxing Ix's tense member out of her cloaca.

Ix's lust overcame her. She hungrily grasped Yvonne's lips in her own and pushed her tongue into Yvonne's mouth, her ovipositor slipping around Yvonne's before entering her, snaking up into the warmth of Yvonne's body where it undulated with pleasure.

Yvonne responded in kind, slipping her own ovipositor under Ix's and pressing into Ix with gentle, deliberate movements. That was a technique she'd have to teach Ix later, for now she was just happy to be full, and of a six, no less! She'd never been with anyone whose ovipositor could reach far enough up to impregnate her. Her previous lover had only been a four, although they'd been known to go into heat occasionally which allowed their appendage to nearly reach her egg sac.

Ix, like most queens, had a naturally high libido and her body took to Yvonne's with ease. She sunk both hands into Yvonne's thick, sensitive hair, tugging so that Yvonne's entire scalp tingled with pleasure. Ix's three long tendrils snaked up Yvonne's hips, one curling around her waist and squeezing while the other two toyed with her nipples.

"O'Zeno," Yvonne gasped, taking the Lord's name very much in vain.

"It's Ix," Ix whispered in her ear, then nibbled at Yvonne's earlobe.

"Oh...Ix," Yvonne moaned, struck by Ix's forcefulness. She was so used to being the assertive one, this was a pleasant role reversal. She relented to Ix's will, letting herself be teased, coaxed, kissed, probed. Studied.

At last, Ix seemed satisfied with her assessment of Yvonne's entire body and, shivering, implanted a thick gel of miniscule eggs deep within her.

Yvonne orgasmed immediately.

It was like nothing she'd ever experienced before. The blinding light of orgasm she was used to, but she *was* the light now. And Ix was the light, too. And together their atoms exploded out in all directions, expanding to encapsulate the entire universe.

She was everything and then nothing, and then slowly, in stages, she became herself again, entwined still with Ix's slick, hot body. She felt as if she was breathing her own spirit back into her body and she needed it to get in there deeper, so she breathed into the very bottom of her lungs.

Ix laughed gently near her ear. "You're using your vestigial lungs properly, now," she said.

"You're a good teacher." Yvonne withdrew her ovipositor back into her own body and Ix did the same. "Was that...uh...I mean did you enjoy that?"

Ix laid her head on Yvonne's chest. "It was as I had theorized it would be," she said.

"Zuut. You're honest," Yvonne laughed and ran her fingers gently through Ix's silky grey hair.

A buzz in Yvonne's ear brought her fully back to her body. A click. A voice.

"Maintain your position. We are coming."

Chapter 3

Ix fell asleep in Yvonne's arms, floating together in the warm nothingness of the Ocular Forest's inner space. She had never before had such a perfect complement of inner and outer peace. In her past, external comforts had always brought immediate regrets.

"Wake up, my larvling. It is morning outside," Ix heard the voice of the Superior Mother, not Yvonne. Yvonne was gone. Now the Superior Mother crouched before her, watching her with eyes like pools filled with absolute compassion. Despite her concern that Yvonne was not there, she felt comforted by the presence of the forest.

"Where's Yvonne?"

The Superior Mother sat cross legged now, an odd look for someone of her apparent age, but her body wasn't exactly real anymore, so it could do whatever her will demanded of it. "She escaped the monastery in the middle of the night, undetected."

"Why?" Ix blurted, though she knew the answer. She knew every possible answer the Superior Mother could give. Essentially, because it was her path. Because she had to. Ix buried her face, embarrassed by her outburst, embarrassed that she had given in to temptation so easily. Embarrassed that she had enjoyed herself so much. "This was a test, wasn't it?" Ix asked quietly. "And I have failed."

Ripples of light energy traveled down Ix's arm as the Superior Mother stroked her. "There are no tests in life, my larvling. Only experiments. The way you reacted tells you something about yourself that you needed to understand. There are no failures in science."

Ix looked tearfully up at the Superior Mother who was as serene as always. Unbothered. She wanted nothing more than to be unbothered in that eternal way, too. She could pretend, most of the time, that she was. But now she had tasted her forbidden fruit, and she was damned to want more.

"Whatever gave you the idea it was forbidden?" the Superior Mother responded to Ix's thoughts.

"Because eating it caused desire! And that desire has led to suffering."

"And that is as it should be," said the Superior Mother. "You can choose to suffer more, much more, in this lifetime my larvling, and your spirit will grow. Or, instead, you can choose to remain here and deny your own desires to the end of your life, never moving another step forward along your path."

Then, in Ix's mind, the Superior Mother conjured a mess of passion, disappointments, horrors, losses, explosions, reunions, healing, growth. A whole life with Yvonne. A scary, hurtling kind of life. Years of solitude and longing. Years of frustration and fear. Years of peace and beauty. On and on. Never ending.

"Eat the fruits which have been presented to you. You cannot renounce that which you don't understand," said the Superior Mother.

"Where is she?" Ix asked. And, again the Superior Mother conjured a scene in Ix's mind. Yvonne, lost in the mountains...

"The Third Option will find her. And if you are with her, they will find you, too," warned the Superior Mother. "If you leave, you will set in motion something which you will be unable to stop."

Ix was already standing and dressed. "It has already been set. I cannot stop it even now," she said and left the Superior Mother for the last time.

* * *

"Maintain your position. We are coming," they had said.

Though Yvonne very much wanted to maintain her position beside Ix, floating in the pleasant nothingness of the tree, she would not lead them directly to the Superior Mother. So, she bolted, leaving Ix and her clothes inside the tree, tearing through the vegetation which chattered meaningless facts in her brain.

The planet Yutternog is the only planet in the universe which produces the gaseous metal yutteflite. Most water in the universe is sentient, but prefers to communicate with other liquids. Nothing, objectively, exists.

Yvonne ignored these facts and more. Her mind was otherwise preoccupied. The voice in her ear hadn't belonged to Olnbaim; it was someone else. Someone new. Her case had been escalated to someone with a higher command. That stupid, cheap implant in her ear had led The Third Option directly to the Superior Mother. Whether or not the bodiless presence inside the forest could be killed was beside the point. Every monastic who protected it certainly *could* be killed.

She burst into her large/small infirmary room, wrestled her slick, sweaty body into the extra Layflex suit from her satchel, and scooped up every sheet, towel, and blanket she could find.

The monastery was still an impenetrable maze to her. The only way out she knew was over the cliff edge. She would repel down as far as she could. Hopefully far enough to find solid ground.

The hallways were clear, and no one stopped her as she dashed through the gardens. It was the middle of the night, why was she hoping someone would stop her? She tied the sheets together, corner to corner, tugged on the knots, tied one end to the sturdiest tree near the edge and wrapped the other end a few times around her fist. She looked down.

It was a dizzying height, but there, over to the left, a snowy mountain pass could be seen glittering in the moonlight, peeking out under the rock. Thank Blitheon there was a triple moon tonight.

Yvonne tugged once more on the sheets and stepped down, sideways, allowing herself to be held in the tension as she inched down the cliff side.

The rope was shorter than she had expected, the drop would be nearly twice her height. She could survive that, but once she released the rope, there would be no climbing back up to the safety of the monastery.

She let go, setting in motion something which she would be unable to stop.

Yvonne landed heavily, her knees unenthusiastically taking the brunt of the impact. She began to walk down the gently sloping path, choosing the problems of the valley for herself with single-minded acceptance.

The night morphed into early dawn, though in the fog of the mountains, the transition was so subtle Yvonne barely noticed the change. She kept her gaze a few feet ahead of her on the path, kept her mind focused on one step, then the next.

The sun rose above the clouds, illuminating the valley below in orange, purple, and yellow beams. Not the valley she had come from, this one was on the other side of the mountain. Good, she thought. That would take The Third Option farther away from the monastery. That was the best she could do.

She tucked herself into a small alcove in the rocky mountain side, taking a moment to rest. Trying to convince herself that this wasn't the last sunrise she'd ever see. At least it was a good one.

"Yvonne!"

Yvonne peeked out of the alcove. Ix walked steadily down the pass toward her, a large camping bag saddled with provisions on her back, a wide, toothy smile dawning across her serious face.

"Ix?!"

At the sound of her name, Ix began to run. They met in an embrace, Yvonne purposely placing Ix's head in the crook of her neck, the spot that seemed to be made for her.

"Why did you follow me?" Yvonne asked.

"Because you are on my path," Ix said, smiling, tears streaming down her cheeks.

Yvonne looked confusedly down at the mountain pass she had been walking. "Oh, sorry, this is your path?"

Ix laughed and kissed Yvonne's cheek. "You're being silly again. I meant that I have chosen to face these obstacles alongside you."

Yvonne winced. "They might kill us," she said quietly.

Ix pulled a glass bottle filled with water from her pack and handed it to Yvonne. "We all must die of something. Besides, the Superior Mother told me they will not kill us," Ix said as Yvonne hydrated herself.

"Oh, that's good," Yvonne said when she'd finished drinking.

"They will do worse," Ix told her, casually, re-sheathing the bottle.

"Oh...that's not as good." Again, Yvonne began to breathe with only the top thirty percent of her vestigial lungs.

Ix put a gentle hand to Yvonne's sternum and looked up at her lovingly. "Dook ah sarva dook ah maya om."

"Dook ah sarva dook ah maya om," Yvonne repeated, her breathing relaxing a little. "What does that really mean?"

"Suffering is everywhere, and suffering is an illusion." Ix took Yvonne's hand and, together, they headed for the valley where emissaries from The Third Option awaited them.

"Climb Every Mountain" is a stand-alone short by Carmen Loup.

Want to know what happens to these doomed alien lovers? Find out in The Audacity series by Carmen Loup at CarmenLoup.com!

Bonus alien anatomy diagram, for the curious 😄

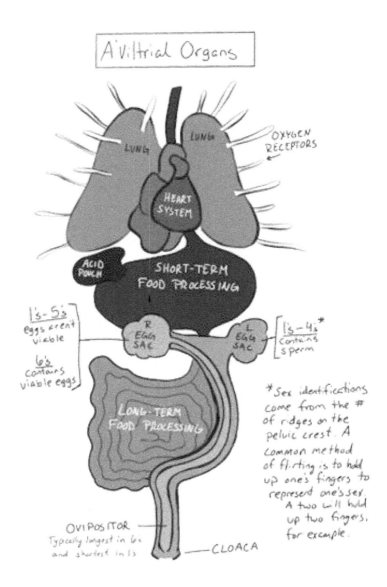

Featherton's Claws
Sara Codair

Sapphic Representation: Lesbian, Non-binary

Heat Level: Low

Content Warnings: Coarse Language, Violence, Death, Danger to Cats

Mira's gradebook was missing, and the cat wasn't helping. The contents of her messenger bag lay strewn across her desk. There was her planner, her leather-bound journal, a half-eaten brownie and bag of nuts, hair ties, folders full of student papers, letters from the feline rescue society, pens and pencils. There was no gradebook but there *was* Gideon, a plump, fluffy ginger cat, pacing back and forth, exacerbating the mess.

There were lots of cats at Featherton Academy for Young Mages, as they were very efficient at controlling pests like rats, poltergeists, and stray tentacles. Gideon, however, was unashamed to admit her own laziness. She'd never killed anything bigger than a moth. Gideon looked down, saw a pen that dared to exist beneath her paws, and swiped it off the table, where it joined a pile of pens and pencils on the floor.

Mira took a deep breath and glared at the cat. "Is that really necessary?"

Gideon plopped forward and headbutted Mira. *Mira, pay attention to Gideon! Something isn't...*

The thoughts cut off when Gideon walked past Mira and stopped touching her.

Despite working at one of the most renowned magic schools in the world, Mira's only magic power was the ability to talk to cats that were touching her. In elementary school, her teachers had claimed she was a promising young mage, until she did a spell on a dare, messed it up, and lost all but this tiny fraction of her abilities. Perhaps rightly so, as it had been absolutely ridiculous of her to attempt Rite of Three Stars at ten years old, but she'd been so confident she could pull it off, and she really wanted impress Mary Harlowe.

But instead of conjuring three super-hot tiny stars that would've floated around the room and proved her coolness to her crush, a horribleness had welled inside her, broken, and a heartbeat later, her magic had (mostly) gone.

She loved being able to talk to cats, but she longed for other magic. If she could cast a tracking spell on her gradebook, or could've used a duplication charm to make copies of it, she wouldn't be at risk of losing her job and housing. And if she got fired from Featherton because she couldn't properly keep track of her student's grades, *no one* was going to hire her. Even if she could convince the community college she used to teach at to take her back, it wouldn't pay a high enough salary to afford housing on her own.

Back when she'd worked for lower pay, she'd been married to someone with a high paying job. Now, she was single, and too afraid to talk to anyone who might change that. She loved the idea of talking to her more magical co-worker, Penny, but every time they talked, she'd make awkward small talk, embarrass herself, and find an excuse to leave. Still, she had a feeling if she could just talk to Penny for more than five minutes at a time, they'd hit it off.

Mira reached out and scratched Gideon under her chin.

Feels good. Gideon purred. *More chin scratches. Please. And treats. Cheese treats.*

Cats didn't actually think in words like humans, but Mira's brain was very wordy, and her magic translated cat thoughts to words as best it could. And in turn, it translated her words into cat-think.

"Gideon, what were you trying to tell me before you walked away? Is something wrong?"

Gideon sat with her paws in the air, giving Mira mere seconds of warning before she jumped into her arms and nuzzled her head in Mira's sweater.

Trov forgot my morning treats!

"The school is getting ready to move. He's probably busy trying to wrap up all his experiments." Mira looked out the window. Mountains marched on for miles, their snow-covered peaks kissing the sky that enveloped Featherton's Academy. The lower peaks were bathed in red, orange, and yellow, but the higher ones were white with snow. Soon, the harsh winter weather would render the flying school's protections inefficient, and it would have to move south toward more populated areas. This meant they couldn't jettison labs, or even the whole bottom section of the school, if something went wrong.

And things did go wrong when a bunch of magical academics were required to do magical research in addition to their teaching responsibilities. That meant instead of just focusing on teaching, they split their attention, which lead to substandard magic work. Not to mention teaching and research were two separate skills, and not everyone at Featherton had mastered both. Like Penny, a brilliant magician, and researcher, and the most fascinating person Mira had ever met, but their classroom was pure chaos. Just last year, they'd had to jettison the whole lower level because it became infested with interdimensional tentacles. Mira shuddered. Maybe she couldn't do a tracking spell, but at least she didn't need to worry about accidentally conjuring monsters from another dimension.

Trov smelled funny, said Gideon. *Followed him. Sir Iron Claws guarded his lab. He gave Sir Iron Claws treats but Sir Iron Claws didn't eat them. Must be sick. Cats can't reject treats.*

"Sir Iron Claws was probably full from eating mice." Mira took a deep breath, trying not to worry about Sir Iron Claws. Cats not eating was a serious problem, but maybe Sir Iron Claws just didn't like that flavor treat. Some cats were pickier than others.

Full? Gideon is never full! Gideon would like treats, please.

"Do you know who stole my gradebook? I'll give you lots of treats if you help me find it." Mira couldn't deal with a sick cat on top of a missing gradebook. How would she submit grades at the end of the term if she couldn't find it? How would she prove grades if students challenged them, and she didn't have evidence of what they got on their first two essays? She'd be canned for sure!

Her breaths came fast. She was going to be in so much trouble if she didn't find the damn thing. She needed a tracking spell.

Napped in the library all afternoon. Gideon saw nothing. Gideon hungry. Mira have treats? Gideon squirmed away, jumped to the floor, and started hitting pens around the room.

"Who do I ask for help, Gideon?" Without proof, the administration wouldn't take her seriously. They'd think she lost the grade book and didn't want to admit it. But she hadn't lost it. She'd put it in her bag this morning and not taken it out since.

If Trov was busy enough to forget Gideon's treats, he probably couldn't help Mira. And she had to admit, he had seemed preoccupied this morning. He'd walked away with Mira's tea instead of his own, and got mad at her for pointing it out, even though was the one who left her mug all slimy with whatever gunk had been on his hands, probably from whatever experiments he was doing in his lab.

"Should I ask Penny? Or Alina?" Penny, a fellow cat-lover, was probably the most powerful mage at the school, but also the most scatterbrained and attractive, and sometimes Mira got all jumbled when talking to them. Alina was the librarian, and had always been kind to Mira, but it was hard to have a conversation with her about anything other than her special interest of the moment.

Gideon rubbed against Mira's legs. *Go see Penny! Penny has treats! Penny doesn't forget my treats.*

Mira decided to listen to the cat, even though she knew Gideon's reasoning did not extend beyond Penny having cat treats in their pocket. Mira never turned down an excuse to talk to Penny. And sitting around wasn't helping her find her missing grades, either.

* * *

Mira found Penny in the library, buried under a stack of ancient-looking books, one of which was engaged in some kind of whispered argument with another. A third book had teeth bared at a cat that was gnawing on the pages of a fourth, which was crying.

"Grouse, what have I told you about eating paper?" Mira scolded, momentarily forgetting why she was even there.

Penny jolted up from apparently trying to read three books at once and smiled. "Mira! It's good to see you!"

Penny's hair, a feathery copper pixie cut, was sticking up in different directions and they had a pencil tucked behind their ear. Ink smudges on their face. Their grass green eyes were bright. The top button on their shirt was undone. One pant leg was tucked into a boot and the other went over it.

"Good to see you too, Penny. How's the project going?" Mira asked, hoping that was acceptable small talk for a conversation leading to her asking for help. And while Mira wasn't sure what Penny's current project was, they were always working on something in their lab.

"It's going." Penny straightened and winked at Mira. "You brought Gideon! She has the best fur of all the library cats, but she likes to bite me."

Penny had a hand extended for the cat despite knowing she would probably bite them, like her orange fluff was just too tempting not to touch.

"You can only pet her under the chin," said Mira. "She has arthritis in her back. She likes me because she knows I won't touch the sore parts."

"Does Marcy know about the arthritis?"

"Marcy?"

Evil monster who pokes me with needles!! Tell her nothing!!

"She's one of our healers, but she's better with animals than people. You should tell her about Gideon's arthritis. She can give her something for it. Did you not meet her at orientation?"

"The year's orientation was over by the time they hired me." They had hired someone else for this job months earlier, but that person had backed out at the last minute after accepting a seven-book contract from one of The Republic's premier publishers. Mira had been qualified enough and able to start on short notice, but she felt like people didn't see her as a proper replacement for the more magical novelist. "Penny, um, I need help with something."

"With what?" Penny asked, their head tilted.

Mira plopped down on the floor and hoped neither the books nor the glaring cat bit her. You never knew what was going to sink its teeth into you in this library. "A thing. I would prefer it to stay between us."

"As long as keeping the secret won't do harm, it will stay between us." Penny closed their book and scooted closer to Mira. A whisker closer and their legs would be touching. Mira's cheeks flushed. Did Penny move closer because she liked Mira? Or was she like that with everyone?

"My gradebook is missing," Mira blurted. "I'm afraid a student stole it. Several are failing because they don't think non-magical subjects are important enough."

Penny frowned. Their forehead wrinkled and it made them look a little like a French bulldog. "Is there a particular reason you're coming to me and not the administration?"

"I don't want to go to the administration unless I have solid evidence it was stolen," Mira said hesitantly. "And even then, depending on who stole it, I'm not sure I want to report it. I don't want to get anyone expelled."

"The disciplinary committee loves expelling scholarship students, crusty old bastards," said Penny.

"So, you'll help?" Mira was hopeful.

"I will, but I will need your assistance in exchange."

Mira wasn't sure what a powerful mage like Penny could possibly want from a barely magical nobody like her. "With what?"

"One of the cats who guards the potions storage room has been acting strange and hides from the healer. Marcy can't get near him, and the one time she got close, well, she needed to be tended to by the other healer afterward."

"Which cat?" Mira asked.

"He goes by Sir Iron Claws."

Mira frowned. Maybe she shouldn't have brushed Gideon off earlier. "If Marcy couldn't get close, there is no guarantee I could either."

"All I ask is that you try." Penny reached out and took Mira's hand. "I'll help you even if you fail, as long as you try."

Mira looked down at the spot where Penny's hand touched hers. Warmth radiated from it like a slow spell breathing life into an ailing garden. Mira wanted to feel more of that warmth. "That I can do."

She just hoped she wasn't going to lose an eye, or a hand, in an attempt to get her grade book back...or get herself in trouble trying to impress Penny.

* * *

Penny insisted they head down to the labs once the students' curfew had passed. The instructors who taught non-magical subjects were not required to be fully magical, and therefore not expected to supervise magical children. And Penny, well, they got off from all kinds of duties because of their research. So, while many of the other faculty and staff were busy wrangling a bunch of rebellious magical children, Mira and Penny crept down the stairs into Mira's least favorite part of the school.

The school itself was a strange contraption that had no right to fly. Sure, it was shaped like a dirigible, but where dirigibles were made of cloth and all but the bottom passenger parts were filled with gas, here there was no balloon.

The upper "balloon" was mostly wood and glass, all carved with enchantments that made it lighter than air and strong enough to withstand the worst storms the mountains could muster, even projectiles flung from rare tornados. The detachable lower section was metal and stone with very few windows, more like slits than anything else. After the last time it was detached, the tentacle monsters had supposedly all been crushed or frozen to death before the structure was replaced but Mira was still cautious. What else might the faculty and their students have conjured?

As they entered the dim hall, Mira couldn't help but keep an eye out for tentacles. She thought she saw one too, but an annoyed meow revealed it to be a cat's tail. It was a sleek, black tail. The cat they were looking for, Sir Iron Claws, was gray and fluffy.

Still, this one, if it was willing to talk, it might be able to tell Mira where to find Sir Iron Claws. The cats in the lower part of the structure were a clowder unto themselves. The cats in the upper level chased moths out of the library and mice out of the kitchens and dormitories, but the lower level cats often had to deal with the results of summonings gone wrong. So the upper cats who Mira talked to knew of these cats by reputation, but a library or kitchen cat seldom interacted with one from the lower levels.

"I think Sir Shadow Murder is around," whispered Penny. They took a bag of treats out of their pocket and shook it.

The cat appeared in front of them and came purring toward Penny.

"How is the handsome killer who saved my mandrake roots from that nasty poltergeist?"

Sir Shadow Murder's purr deepened as he approached, his chest puffed out and head held high.

"My friend here can talk to cats when they let her touch them," Penny continued.

Sir Shadow Murder sat and looked at Mira with his head tilted.

Penny tossed him a treat. He gobbled it up, looked at Mira, then rubbed against her legs.

Tuna treat good. Real tuna better.

"Have you seen Sir Iron Claws?" Mira asked, focusing on her magic's connection to the cat.

More treats. I tell.

"He wants more treats," Mira told Penny.

Penny tossed him three more. "He always wants more treats."

Mira sat down on the cold stone floor. Sir Shadow Murder climbed right into her lap and started kneading on her sweater.

Good fabric. Soft.

"Where is Sir Iron Claws?"

Sir Shadow Murder doesn't know. Sir Iron Claws hunting big game. Won't share location or details or food. Won't cuddle. Was good cuddle. Best fur. Better than sweater. Kept Sir Shadow Murder warm!

"Where did you last see him?"

Skulking by feeding station, wouldn't touch good food.

"Did he smell sick?"

Smelled like dust and magic. I sneezed.

"Do you have any idea what he is up to?"

If he did, she never got an answer because the squeaking of a rat got his attention, and he was off chasing it.

After reporting the conversation to Penny, they decided to check out the feeding area. But that meant venturing further into the chilly depths of the lower levels. Mira walked close to Penny, so close the tips of their fingers brushed together. There was that warmth again, accompanied by a fluttering in her stomach. What would Penny do if she did more than brush their fingers? If she took their hand and held it? Did she dare ask?

"We're here. You okay?" Penny stopped and turned to Mira. Their soft smile and bright eyes lit up the room.

"I'm good." Mira forced a smile, not wanting to admit to Penny she was afraid of the lower levels, and focused on the scene in front of her.

The dungeon cats were mostly fed kibble in large feeding stations in the heart of the lower level. Their lifestyle was very different from the library cats individually fed chicken on tiny plates in rooms by themselves. Those cats would eat themselves sick were they free fed. But the lower cats got most of their meat from the creatures they hunted, and the kibble just supplemented it.

Mira carefully approached each one, offering treats before gently touching them to ask about Sir Iron claws. No one had seen him, though the cats did complain of strange smells coming from Trov's lab. Strange smells weren't unusual down there, though.

"I didn't think he'd be so hard to find," said Penny.

"Is there a spell you can do to track him?" Mira asked with little hope. She couldn't perform tracking spells, but everything she'd read about them said they required an object that had a strong connection to the subject or even a piece of the subject. Still, she hoped a mage as powerful as Penny would have a way around that.

"I'd need a piece of him, like some fur." Penny looked down at clumps of fur drifting across the floor like tumbleweeds. "Some of this is probably his but I don't know which pieces belong to which cat."

"The cats probably know though. They can smell the difference." Mira bent down next to one of the eating cats and gently stoked its back. "I know you didn't know where Sir Iron Claws was, but can you tell me which piece of fur is his?"

After eating, the cat thought without pausing its munching.

Mira didn't push, and instead sat in silence, fretting about whether or not she should try to make some kind of conversation with Penny. Was the silence a bad thing? A good thing? Silence could be comfortable, but it could also be awkward, and Mira wasn't sure which one this was. Penny was staring at her. Did that mean they were waiting for her to make conversation? Did they find her as attractive as she found them? Was her hair sticking up funny? What would happen if she reached out and touched Penny's hand? Or traced the freckles scattered across their cheeks? The air between them felt thick and magnetic, like it was drawing them together, but Mira was afraid to move.

After what felt like an hour but in reality, was probably only three minutes, the cat left the bowl of kibble and started sniffing around the floor. Mira tried not to hover, but wanted to be able to easily reach out and touch the cat. Finally, it meowed and rubbed up against her legs.

Sir Iron Claws ball of fluff, it thought before batting at a tumbleweed of gray fur.

"Use this," Mira told Penny.

Penny held the fur in their hand, rolled up their sleeve and touched a magnifying glass that had been tattooed on their forearm. They rubbed the fur over the tattoo. Ink wasn't necessary for magic, but it made it easier, and a lot of mages opted to get tattoos for spells they did over and over again. Mira found it interesting that Penny used a tracking charm enough to have it inked into their forearm. Maybe they lost stuff all the time.

After muttering a few words and furrowing their brow, a translucent green arrow rose out of the tattoo on Penny's arm. "Let's hope this is for the right cat."

They followed the arrow through a labyrinth of dark halls filled with enchanted mops and brooms moving, sweeping and mopping, held up by magic Mira couldn't see. She wondered if Penny, with all their power, could see the threads of the spells holding the cleaning devices together or if they looked just as haunted to them.

She swore the halls got darker as they trudged deeper into the structure, passed the regular classrooms into the faculty-only labs where experiments were allowed. The arrow directed them into one that was locked. Mira thought it was a dead end when Penny didn't have a key, but after making sure no one was watching and waving their hands in the air, they dismantled the locks and the wards, claiming no one would ever know they'd been in there.

"Are you sure this is a good idea?" Mira asked as they crept into the room.

"If something in here is making Sir Iron Claws sick, then we need to know."

Mira agreed, though she hoped it didn't cost her this job. Not only did she need the money and housing, but she enjoyed it, and more importantly, she enjoyed the company of a certain co-worker.

* * *

The door creaked open to an empty lab. *Empty.* No counters or chairs or beakers or cabinets. It was suspicious. There wasn't even a speck of dust, and certainly not a cat. Yet, the arrow on Penny's arm was urging them forward.

Mira was afraid to step in the room. She had goose bumps on her arms. Something felt wrong and she didn't have enough magic to know exactly what was wrong. What if there was some magical booby trap she couldn't quite detect?

"What do you see?" Penny's whisper was so close it tickled Mira's ear.

"An empty room." Mira turned and found her face a breath away from Penny's smirk. How easy would be to kiss them?

Mira shook her head. Now was *not* the time.

Penny reached an arm behind Mira's head and snapped their fingers. "Now look."

Mira did.

The room blurred.

Mira blinked.

On the edge of her vision, something unraveled. A rainbow of threads frayed and snapped, revealing a room that was not, in fact, empty at all.

Overturned tables and open books were strewn across the room. Feathers, gray fur, and red smudges Mira hoped weren't blood covered the floor. And in the middle of it all, Sir Iron Claws lay on Mira's missing gradebook, licking something red and sticky off of his claws.

Mira lurched forward, ready to rush to her gradebook and snatch it out from under the suspicious feline, but Penny grabbed her, pulling her close. For a moment, Mira was overcome by the feeling of Penny. Strong but small arms wrapped tight around her, pulling her into a soft chest. Cinnamon and ink and the leather of old books filled her nose. It was warm and fuzzy and Mira would have lingered in that embrace forever had a ceiling tile not crashed down a few feet in front of them—one that probably would've landed on her had Penny not caught her.

Sir Iron Claws looked up.

"Let me finish deconstructing all the enchantments," Penny whispered softly, like they were worried about the enchantments hearing them. Mira supposed the caution was warranted. You never knew with enchantments. Maybe they could hear.

Penny worked like they were conducting an orchestra, occasionally glancing over their shoulder at Mira. But the problem was, the cat had noticed what Penny was doing and decided they were enough of a threat to care. His ears went back. His butt wiggled. He let out a yowl and launched himself at Penny. Mira, in a fit of rare athleticism, jumped between Penny and the cat, and somehow managed to catch Sir Iron Claws. She held him at arm's length.

Kill! Intruder! Kill!

"*Stop!!*" She thought and shouted with all her magic. "Don't kill, tell me what is going on here! Trade. Tuna, chicken, steak, for information!"

The cat stilled.

Human! You hear me!

"Yes, and I promise you all manner of delectable treats if you give me information and don't murder anyone."

I want steak!

"Then you shall have steak!"

Sir Iron Claws purred. *Steak! Spill secrets for steak!*

"Who put you up to murdering the intruders?" Mira asked.

Steak first. Then secrets. Sweater soft. Let Sir Iron Claws cuddle your sweater!

Mira let Sir Iron Claws climb onto her sweater while Penny unraveled the remaining enchantments, fingers dexterously untangling strands of energy Mira couldn't see. By the time Penny was done, Sir Iron Claws—after sending Penny detailed descriptions of his favorite cuts of meat—was sound asleep on Mira's shoulder, claws tangled in her sweater. Mira hoped they stocked ribeye and filet mignons in the school kitchens. She was a vegetarian, so she did not pay attention to what kinds of meat were served.

"It's safe to go get your gradebook now." Penny wiped sweat off of their brow.

Mira took tentative steps forward and picked up the grade book, which had bits of rat fur, feathers, and blood on it, but she flipped through and was very thankful at least the inside did not appear damaged or altered. So, what was the point of stealing if not to alter it? Had a student temporarily stashed it here? Or had it been taken for a more sinister reason? There were spells that could be cast upon a person through their personal belongings. But what could Trov possibly want with her?

"Is that..." Penny walked over to a purple mug. "I was almost late to teaching this morning because I was looking for this mug!" They turned to Mira. "How did you get Sir Iron Claws to calm down? Is he okay?"

"We owe him some prime cuts of steak," said Mira. "He promised to tell me everything after we pay up."

"Any chance he'll give us the info first?"

Claws dug into Mira's shoulder. "No."

"Alright. I'll take a magic recording of the state of this place and do some poking around, but I don't want to stay here too long in case Trov comes by after he's got his charges settled into the dorms for the night. We can go back to my rooms and order some steak."

Yum! Feed Sir Iron Claws Ribeye!!

* * *

In some ways, Penny's rooms were as much a disaster as the lab, but minus the mysterious blood and fur. But where the lab felt creepy and cold, their room was cozy. Maybe it had something to do with the lack of blood. Maybe it was the huge window overlooking the mountains. Maybe it was all the blankets haphazardly thrown across furniture, the roaring fire in the hearth, or all the books stacked in random places. Nothing made a space feel cozy like piles of blankets and books.

Perhaps, the cozy, warm sense of contentment brewing in Mira's heart had nothing at all to do with the space she was in and everything to do with the person it belonged to—the person who filled it. How could a space inhabited by someone as charming and quirky as Penny not be cozy?

Mira's cheeks flushed. Yesterday, she would've been nervous about starting a conversation with Penny if they ran into each other in the hall. Now she was in their *room*.

"Let me send a message down to the kitchens." Penny picked up the phone and called down to the kitchens, placing an order for enough meat to feed a small army. "Anything specific you want for yourself?"

"The vegetarian ravioli, extra sauce," said Mira since she had missed two meals today over the stress.

When Penny was off the phone, they eyed Mira's gradebook, which she had clutched on her lap. "I'll inspect that while we wait for the food to be delivered."

"You ordered it to be delivered?" Mira never did that. Food was included as part of their salary, but delivery wasn't, and instead of being sent a bill, any charges faculty and staff incurred from the school were deducted from their pay.

"I hate going into the dining hall. Way too much noise. Too many random people talking to me and asking me favors and questions."

"I'm sorry if I became one of those people." Mira cringed as guilt chilled the warmth in her chest. Her lack of magic meant she'd needed help. And she'd liked that the help had come from Penny because it turned into an excuse to spend time together. But feeling that she'd been a burden...

"You're not. You are helping me with something in return. Most people just want free labor and knowledge out of me." Penny smiled and rested a hand on Mira's shoulder. Warmth chased away the cold and cringe. "Now hand over the gradebook."

"We have it back. Why do you need to inspect it?" They'd gotten it back. They were done. They just had to feed the cat and enjoy each other's company.

"I want to know if a student stashed it in Trov's lab or if he took it himself. Something has seemed off about him lately. I assumed he was just stressed, trying to wrap something up before the move, but after seeing his lab...something is wrong. And I want to know if your grade book is part of it. Plus, I need something to keep me busy while we wait for the food and the information it will buy."

Mira handed over the gradebook, letting her fingers brush Penny's just long enough to hopefully communicate to Penny that she was interested in them without having to find the right but awkward words to explain her feelings.

"The spell I'm going to do is quite simple," Penny continued, seemingly too caught up in their investigation to reciprocate Mira's touch. At least, that's what Mira told herself. She wasn't ready to admit Penny might not be interested. "It searches for traces of sweat, dead skin cells, and even droplets from breath, and lets me know who has touched the object."

Penny placed the gradebook in a circle and started making strange hand motions. A tattoo on their arm glowed. To the NMs, it looked silly, but Mira had vague memories of seeing and feeling magic when she was working a spell. She thought she could see a faint glow around Penny's hands, something a NM wouldn't detect. Little things like that made her wonder if her magic was really as far out of reach as she thought, but after all this time, she didn't dare let herself hope.

The traces of energy brightened. They turned into a wild storm of flailing light and coalesced into a blob of purple tentacles and teeth.

Mira jumped back, heart racing.

Sir Iron Claws arched his back and hissed.

Penny waved their hand and the image faded.

"Did you do the spell wrong, or did a tentacle monster steal my gradebook?"

Before Penny could answer, there was a knock on the door.

A confused-looking server delivered four covered plates, each containing a large cut of meat, and a fifth with Mira's vegetables.

As soon as the servant left, Penny slammed the door shut. "I didn't do the spell wrong. Hurry up and feed Sir Iron Claws so he talks. I need more information."

Mira's hands shook as she cut up the steaks and hand fed them to Sir Iron Claws. He only ate a fraction of it, and Penny stored the rest in a magic-powered refrigerator, something Mira did not have the luxury of having in her rooms, and turned to the cat. "You've had steak. Now, what can you tell us about what was going on in that lab?"

Sir Iron Claws plopped down on Mira's lap and proceeded to take a bath and flooded Mira's mind with thoughts. He must have been sitting high up on a shelf, looking down. There was Trov and two students, busy in the lab, muttering things that sounded like gibberish in Sir Iron's Claw's memories, either because they were speaking spells Mira had never heard or because cats didn't have the best memories for human speech. Mira was never sure how much they understood of people talking to them without magic and it seemed to vary from cat to cat.

"Is there a way for me to share memories with you?" Mira asked Penny. "He's showing them doing magic-looking things in the lab, but it doesn't mean much to me."

In the memory, there was some kind of explosion of color and smoke. Things blurred as the cat presumably jumped off of the shelf and down the floor. For what happened next, Mira could only see people's feet. They moved around a lot. There was screaming. More words she couldn't understand, then there were strange smells, something else was in the room. It had big claws and Sir Iron Claws knew he had to stay hidden and quiet, for this was a predator bigger than him. There was blood and screams. The two students fled and based on what little Mira could see through the cat's eyes, the thing with claws and tentacles ate the teacher and became him.

"Oh shit!" Mira barely managed not to jump up. Nausea rose in her throat and her heart felt like it was squeezed in a vice grip. "Something...something...at...ate Trov!"

"What?" Penny got up from whatever they were fidgeting with in the fridge and then the memories consumed Mira again.

The thing, now wearing Trov's skin, skulked around the room, sniffing until he found the spot where Sir Iron Claws was hiding. His voice sounded off as he spoke, but magic flowed with his words, translating them to something Sir Iron Claws could understand.

Tell no one what you saw here. Guard this room. Kill any intruders. I will keep you well fed and happy. Betray me and I will eat you.

Sir Iron Claw's agreed to the terms.

But you told us what happened, for one meal of steak, Mira thought of the cat. *Are you afraid of what it will do to you?*

Creature bad and too big for a cat to kill. Thought I couldn't handle it, but couldn't. Sir Iron Claws sent back to Mira. *Steals things from faculty. Planning something bad. Want out. Need help. But wanted one last good meal in case humans can't actually help.*

"We'll do everything we can to help," Mira said, hands clenching into fists, wishing she was as powerful as Penny, so they'd have a better chance at defeating the monster.

"Help with what?" Penny asked, now kneeling next to Mira and the cat. Their face was pale and they were biting their nails. "You haven't said anything out loud since 'ate Trov and wore his skin.'"

When Penny said it out loud, the sheer horror of it finally dawned on Mira, who had been so caught up in the cat's memories and the magic of it that what she had witnessed hadn't really registered in her brain. Her stomach roiled and she barely made it into the bathroom before she vomited and was reduced to a sobbing mess of tears.

A person had been eaten.

Eaten.

And some*thing* was parading around the school as him, doing gods-only-knew-what.

That thing had taken one of her possessions...it had been in the hallway alone with her this morning. It could've eaten her! Was it going to come after her? What did it want with other people's stuff? Mira's mind spiraled with all manner of horrible rituals a tentacle monster might perform. Was it going to try to control all the faculty? Eat their hearts? Steal their magic? What would happen if it tried to steal *her* broken, all-but-non-existent magic?

"Mira, what is going on? I need to know." Penny waved her hand and the vomit disappeared–both the stuff in the toilet and what had gotten in Mira's hair and shirt, and gently rubbed Mira's back.

Reassured by Penny's magic and touch, Mira rinsed her mouth out at the sink and did her best to compose herself, and not let her mind think too much about the poor person who had gotten eaten. She was very good at boxing things away when needed, but sooner or later, the feelings would catch up and overwhelm her. For now, she could hold them at bay.

She took a few deep breaths, walked out into the main room, and started telling Penny, as best as she could, what Sir Iron Claws had shown her. Before she was even done, Penny was up, waving their hands around the room. Tattoos glowed on their skin. Runes glowed on their walls. The scent of magic cracked in the air.

"What are you doing?" Mira asked.

"Reinforcing my wards so Sir Iron Claws stays safe while I deal with the monster poor mislead Trov and his students summoned by accident." They did a few more hand waves and muttered some words. Then turned back to Mira. "I'm going to need to know who the students who saw were and then I am going to need you to convince all the cats to evacuate the lower level in case we have to jettison. Last time some refused to leave, and we lost three. I really don't want to lose more cats if we have to jettison again."

"What about evacuating the students?" Mira asked, wondering if they should be more concerned about the human inhabitants of the school.

"They know to follow the protocols, and the deans won't go through with the jettison if they know there is a kid down here. They don't care about the cats as much. I'm going to alert the school. They'll take care of the students and staff. You make sure the cats get out. You are literally the only one here who can have a complete, two-way conversation with them."

"Alright, got it."

"And I've configured the ward so you are allowed in here and my lab, but do not under any circumstances let anyone else in, and don't let me in unless I tell you the word 'Goblin-shit' and can perform the Rite of Three Stars. You know what that is?"

"Does it have to be *that* spell?" Mira snarled. Rite of Three Stars was extremely dangerous to pull off and relatively useless, so few mages learned it. For those who did, it was a symbol of status and personal achievement. Yet, the three stars it created—little seven-pointed, sparkly balls of fire—did relatively nothing other than cause risk for burns and sometimes explode if they weren't done right. Or, in Mira's case, render her unable to do any other spells.

"Even if the monster somehow gained access to my memories when it ate me, I doubt it will be able to pull it off," Penny said. "You know how difficult it is, right?"

"A botched attempt left me unable to *do* other spells at all," Mira said through clenched teeth. She'd never said that aloud to anyone at Featherton. It was easier to let people think she was born like this than that she lost her magic thanks to her own arrogance. And while Penny was a very capable mage, thinking of Penny doing the spell made Mira worry.

"If that's true, there might be a way to get it back." Penny's eyes met Mira's in a way that made Mira feel like Penny could see right into her head, and if it was anyone else, she would've cringed. But with Penny...Mira wanted Penny to perceive her in every way possible. "If we survive tonight, I'll find a way to fix your magic, assuming you want magic."

Mira opened her mouth to say that dozens of mages had tried, that her parents had gone broke hiring the best healers to fix her magic, but nothing had worked. She was going to say she was okay without magic, that she was content just talking to cats, but the words snagged in her throat. She'd had a taste of magic once and lost it. She missed it.

"I am going to inform the headmistresses of what happened and engage appropriate protocols. You focus on making sure the cats are out of the lower level." Penny took Mira's hand and squeezed it, making Mira feel far more secure than she thought possible given the current situation. And even if Mira did have some doubts about whether Penny could actually fix her magic, she'd decided it was worth letting them try. It would be an excuse to spend more time basking in the warmth of Penny's attention.

Penny grabbed a cloak, a staff, and was out the door.

Mages like Penny didn't need staffs to do magic, and most mages either used them as crutches to focus energy, or used them when there was going to be a fight and they needed to be able to quickly sling raw energy around. Mira wondered if Penny had ever been in a magic battle before.

She stuffed her gradebook in her bag—she wasn't letting that out of her sight again, slung the bag over her shoulder, and was off to the creepy part of the school, hoping the people-eating monster was not down there quite yet.

She hadn't walked more than a few yards away from Penny before she started to miss them, not just because Penny was a powerful mage who made her feel safe, but because she was finally having real conversations with Penny that weren't awkward and she wanted more. She wanted to see Penny do more magic, hear the excitement in their voice as they discovered new things, and know what it felt like to touch more than just their hand.

* * *

In theory, Mira knew she was in a flying school. She could even feel it moving. The whole thing had lurched a few minutes ago and the walls hummed with magic. Now Penny had alerted the faculty to the situation with the tentacle monster impersonating Trov, the school would be climbing. The students would be locked in their dorms and the school would rise until it was several hundred feet over the pointiest, coldest, stormiest, most cursed mountain in the range. The faculty would lure the monster down to the lowest levels, where they'd fight it, and if they failed to defeat it there, they'd seal it in and drop it on Mt. Winnifred.

Still, Mira felt like she was underground.

Had the lower-level halls been this dark earlier today? Had it been so cold? Was that slime dripping underneath the lantern? Soft fur brushed up against Mira's leg, and she would have screamed had it not been accompanied by soft purring and a plea for treats.

"You need to leave the lower levels," Mira told the cat. "Do you know where the others are?"

The sleek feline twined around her legs. *Hunting? Napping? Why leave?*

Mira did her best to describe the situation. "We need to get all the cats to the library."

Library cat came here, looking for you! Gideon!

"Where is she?"

Looking for you!

"Where did you last see her?"

Feeding station.

"Go to the library," Mira said, then headed to the feeding station. With any luck, Gideon was still there. That cat had an endless appetite.

Fur brushed against Mira's leg. *I help.*

The calico she'd just talked to trotted ahead of her, nose to the ground like a dog.

Mira knew better than to argue with the cat and followed her. When cats had their minds made up, they were hard to change. Plus, this probably would go quicker with one cat to help her sniff out the others. Ideally, they'd all be out of here long before Penny and their team of faculty lured the monster down here.

The problem was that each cat they found wanted to help. Mira wasn't sure whether it was a fault in her magic, or the cats weren't listening, but they seemed to think this was a pest they could hunt, not a monster that could swallow them in one bite. They sounded brave now, but Mira feared one look at the monster, or one whiff of its scent up close, would send them all into hiding.

By the time Mira got to the feeding station, she was surrounded by six cats. Sir Shadow Murder was nibbling some kibble, but there was no sign of Gideon.

Mira put a hand on his back. "Have you seen Gideon? A floof from the library? Smells like books and chicken?"

Ate till she puked and ate some more. Library softy.

"Where did she go?" Mira asked.

Further down. Penny's lab.

"Thank you! You all should head up to the library. I'll find Gideon and the others."

There were meows and chirps and when Mira walked on, all the cats followed. "I'm not giving anyone any more treats until you're in the library."

Still, they all refused to leave, meowing that it was their *job* to keep vermin away.

They didn't listen when Mira told them this monster was too big for them to hunt.

They sniffed out their last three clowder members and found Gideon napping in a broom closet.

Mira shook her awake. "What are you doing?"

Too much food. No Penny. Need nap.

"We need to leave, now."

Gideon rolled over.

Mira scooped her up, no patience left. They had to get out of here.

But as soon as she set food back in the hall, she heard shouting.

A scream.

Terrible gurgling.

More shouts and screams.

Too late. Smells wrong. Too big.

Hide.

The fight was here.

Close the door!

Hide!

Hide!!

Mira gave into the cats' urges and closed the door.

She'd wait for the fight to pass her, then sneak out.

With no magic, Mira couldn't do much, could she? She had to stay with the cats and shepherd them to the library. They could still get out before the lower levels got jettisoned. Maybe they wouldn't even need to jettison. The mages just needed to figure out the right way to kill the thing.

The sounds got louder.

Then Mira recognized Penny's voice.

"Stop slinging spells, you idiots. None of them work!"

"But it's a...ahhhhh."

"Alina!!"

There was a gurgling roar.

Screams.

Mira's heart raced. If she stayed quiet, the monster might not know she was there. It might go past without hurting her and she might be able to sneak out before they jettisoned. Or no one would know she was down here. What if the other faculty perished and the dean jettisoned with her in here? She'd plummet a thousand feet down to the pointy cursed summit of Mt. Winnifred.

And what if the monster could smell her? The broom closet door was flimsy, un-enchanted, and crammed in here with all the cats and brooms, she could hardly move. She pictured its long tentacles reaching in, wrapping around her, and dragging her and the cats out to its massive toothy maw.

She didn't have any magic, but she had arms.

And brooms.

And an army of cats.

"We need to fight!" Mira could hardly believe the words as they came out of her mouth. "Magic isn't working. We need to help fight!"

No fight! Just hide! Predator too big!

Hide!

Hide!

"You hide, I'll fight. Better, I'll distract the monster and you run past the fight to the library." Mira grabbed a broom and before the cats could talk her out of it, she opened the door and ran. She nearly tripped over a fallen librarian groaning on the floor, clutching a bloodied leg. Ahead, Penny was backed into a corner, swiping at tentacles with a kitchen knife.

Mira didn't stop.

A tentacle twined around Penny's leg.

The monster was so focused on Penny that it didn't notice Mira behind it until the broom handle hit it and sank into its gelatinous gut.

The monster made a sound like a tea kettle and let go of Penny, flailing its tentacles at Mira.

She ran.

And she tripped over the wounded mage.

She thought she was done for when the tentacles flailed toward her, but a black cat leapt up and latched onto the tentacle, kicking it.

Mira wasn't sure if the cats were actually coming to save her, or if the flailing tentacles were too enticing not to chase, but soon all thirteen of them, including Gideon, were attacking. The more the monster moved, the more they leapt, swiping at tentacles, biting, and latching on and kicking. They always let go and leapt away before they got too close to its mouth, but as one leapt away, another would jump on.

We kill the pests! one said as it brushed by her.

"It used our stuff," Penny gasped, wobbling. "To make a charm that made it immune to our magic. It activates upon touch. Mira, you're the only one who can kill it, because your magic is...."

Penny collapsed.

* * *

Mira ran.

The tentacle monster slithered after her.

Every time a tentacle got close, a cat would leap out and swipe at it with sharp claws, allowing Mira to stay just ahead of the monster. She wasn't in the best shape though and wouldn't be able to keep running for long.

Luckily, she didn't need to. She just needed to reach Penny's lab.

She could see the door, the one plastered with rainbow flags and stickers.

She reached out her hand.

A hot, slick tentacle wrapped around her ankle. She went down hard. Air rushed out of her lungs and pain shot through her ribs. Something tugged inside her. An electric hook, groping for her magic, but it wasn't finding anything to hook onto. Where a well of power should've been, there was a wall of electrified briars, a dam holding her magic back, and when the tentacle tugged at it, a spark leapt through. Mira cried out as it kept tugging. Then something snapped. The dam busted. Fire blossomed inside her and magic flooded past in a torrent that pushed the tentacle out.

Panting on her hands and knees she could see the protections on Penny's door.

She could *see* the protections on Penny's door!

Glittering squiggles and sigils covered it. There were glowing lines on the walls and floors. Veins pumping magic through the school.

Tears glistened in her eyes. She hadn't seen magic so vivid in over twenty years. Whatever the monster did to render others' magic inert must have had a reverse effect on her.

She started laughing at the absurdity of it. The power was useless. She'd hardly learned any spells before she lost her magic. She could feel power coursing through her veins, but she had no clue what to do with it. The only spell she fully remembered was the one that locked away her power—The Rite of Three Stars.

A yowl caught her attention.

An orange blur—Gideon—leapt at the tentacle around her ankle, biting and kicking it. But the rest of the monster was here, more tentacles encroaching.

Mira managed to pull her ankle away and grabbed Gideon. She had just enough time to open Penny's door and sidestep the monster. Its momentum carried through the door.

Now Mira just needed to figure out how to make it eject.

There was a spell to do it, but of course, Mira didn't know it.

But fire...out of control fire could trigger the school to purge the lab.

Mira took a deep breath, uttered the only spell she remembered. If it stripped her power again, well, as long as it didn't take away her ability to talk to cats, she'd be fine. She didn't *need* magic. She was plenty capable without it.

Her heart beat fast as the words came out and her hands, steadied by the sound of Gideon's purring, seamlessly performed the motions they'd messed up decades ago. Three white hot stars appeared in front of Mira, and she willed them forward. They collided with the monster just as it tried to push back through the door, and it exploded.

A wall of fire rushed at Mira, stopping just shy of her as it hit an invisible barrier, and fell.

A shimmering wall of light made Mira shut her eyes. When she opened them, the door was closed. The tiny window didn't show a lab beyond, but a brilliant sunset over rocky, snowcapped mountains. A ball of fire collided with the pointy, cloud-swathed peak of Mt. Winnefred.

* * *

Mira stood next to Penny, holding their hand, shivering on a bare mountain top. As much as Penny's mere presence warmed her, this summit was *cold*. Debris from the lab surrounded them, and stray magic occasionally forked in the air like mini-rainbow lightning. They couldn't stay out here long, but Mira needed to see for herself.

"Over here," someone called. "I found it. Definitely dead."

Mira and Penny walked over to the person in a big furry parka and followed their gaze to part of the tentacle monster. It wasn't moving, and it was impaled by several pieces of debris.

"Better incinerate it, just to be safe," said Penny.

"You sure you don't want to study its corpse?" Alina the librarian limped over with a crutch. She'd been injured in the fight with the monster.

"No." Penny muttered a few words and white flames enveloped the monster until it was mere ash.

Mira was sweating in her parka by the time it was done.

"We should get back to school," said Penny. "Even my protections have their limit on this mountain."

Mira took Penny's hand and together, they walked back to the school. Now, Mira could see the glass and stone airship in all its true glory. Lines of magic in every color shimmered across its surface. Mira didn't know what the different colors and symbols meant, but she intended to learn. And Penny had offered to help. Penny was the most magical part of it all, not just because they were literally magical, but because after months of Mira being afraid to speak to them, talking to them was just so easy now.

"You want to share a meal tonight? After lessons?" Penny raised their eyebrows. "In a date kind of way?"

"I'd love that," Mira inched closer to Penny. Her only regret was that she'd waited so long to talk to Penny.

Mountain morphed into airlock, and airlock became hallway. They stepped into a shadow, into an empty classroom, and shared a kiss. For a moment, Mira was lost on the softness of Penny's lips. The taste of peppermint on their tongue.

Then soft fur brushed against her leg.

Gideon hungry. Why feed Penny but not Gideon? Give Gideon treats!

Sara is the author of an odd assortment of novels and short stories. Learn more at **www.saracodair.com**. Follow Sara on Twitter and Instagram **@shatteredsmooth** for updates, cats, and dogs.

Cloudbreaker

Maya Gittelman

Sapphic Representation: Lesbian, Bi/Pan, Non-Binary
Heat Level: Hot!
Content Warnings: Coarse Language, consensual BDSM

The morning sun slips slow through the kapa-kapa at the window, dappling the soil-dark wood of Mari's bedroom and easing open the eyes of the mortal splayed beside her in a tangle of Mari's third-best sheets.

Mari gazes at the stirring woman with familiar, distant fondness. The bites and bruises the girl had begged for blossom prettily on her throat and thighs. She'd given as good as she'd got—it had been the sort of night that made Mari almost wish she could keep a wound from fading longer than a day. To catch sight of herself in the mountain lakes or her mirror-rooms with evidence of a lover's passion on her body, connection written into her very flesh.

A foolish dream. Her divinity heals her too quick for anything to leave a real mark. Mari knows this. It's always been this way. It always will be.

"Good morning, my lady." The mortal says it with the needy, breathless awe she's used on Mari since she found her way up to Mari's lodgings. The raw hunger of her longing sits sweet and thick on Mari's tongue.

"Now it is, darling," Mari rumbles. She leans over the girl, preening internally at the urgent sparks of delight in her eyes. "Now that you're awake."

The girl—Sara, her name might be, but it might be Kara or Lara—flushes a sweet pink. She's lighter than Mari but only just, and Mari feels a familiar heat lazily blossoming within herself. Mari *could* exert some minor magic on her own memory to be sure about the name, but doesn't bother. It isn't necessary. It rarely is.

"My lady honors me," maybe-Sara says shyly, but it's tempered with an earnest eagerness that makes Mari shift in guilt. She indulges in a crooked grin, twisting her fingers absently to summon a fresh rain cloud from the mountain lake for the girl's morning bath.

This is the seventh dawn they've shared together. Mari knows what that means, she always does.

Sara should too. Mari's reputation precedes her—defines her, even. No one makes their way up the mountain to the palace of the cloud goddess unless they want something from her. Long ago, it had been ghost-pale men. They sought to steal the resources that belong by right to Mari, her fellow minor diwatas—the ancient deities who shaped the islands at the beginning of time—and the many mortal communities of the islands who prosper in mutual service. The violence of the pale men wounded the islands so deeply, even the very soil still must grow around the scars.

Mari knows they will come again. Every diwata does. Perhaps not for hundreds of years, but Mari will still be on her mountain when they do, and they will. Again, they will fight. Again, mortals will die, for pale selfishness and cruelty. Again, she will call upon the might of her powers to do what she can to protect the life that flourishes in her mountain range. The blood will slow, and the storms of Mari's clouds will, presently, wash it away.

And so it goes.

Most of the other diwata cope by settling into their divinity: meditating for decades at a time, performing little miracles in their villages and cities, abandoning their posts when they can thieve a fortnight in order to visit other diwata and share tales of their good deeds.

Mari tried it.

All of it.

Time and time again.

This is the only distraction she's found thus far that makes her near-eternal life half worth living.

* * *

Sara steps into the bathing pool. Behind her, Mari's domain sprawls, vast and lush. The sun casts her range in a brilliant glow of gold and a thousand shades of emerald, more precious than any jewel cultivated by mortalkind. The roll of the mountain takes the shape of Mari's own form on earth, a reclining woman in a protective, alluring sprawl.

Mari as she was at the earliest creation of the islands, that is. She's spent the last century or so planning targeted squalls to chip away at some of the mountain's fuller curves without her siblings or the higher deities noticing. She hasn't told anyone. The neighboring diwatas she might call "almost friends" love to play by the rules; they would be horrified that she's intentionally disfiguring her domain.

It's so *embarrassing* as it stands, though. Creation had coincided with Mari's *highest* femme phase thus far. Tits out and everything. Nothing like the close-shorn crop she sports now, shaved close enough to her skull that she shivers when girls scrape their fingernails across it. And Mari often binds or pads her chest with cirrocumulus beneath her garments, cutting a stockier, sturdier figure than the curves of the mountain suggest. The look of the landscape makes Mari rankle, like finding a picture of yourself in an old photo album that reminds you of a time when you liked who you were and you didn't know anything different, and you look at that girl now and hate her just because you're *not* her, anymore. You never will be again.

Mari doesn't need any more reminders.

She joins Sara in the pool, beckoning a fluffy cumulus to sprinkle fresh sun-warm lake water over their sweat-slick bodies.

Mari kisses her before she can think on it further. Drinks deep of Sara's wanting, her desires to be treated firmly but without violence, pleasure pressed upon her without threat of cruel retribution, stolen liberties. Her thighs part in the clear water, and Mari flashes a wicked grin before ducking her head and basking in the immortal pleasure of not needing to breathe.

She takes Sara apart until the pool is hardly clean enough for bathing, then hauls her onto the dewy clouds on her chamber floors and does it again, and again. She refills the pool and bathes her, dotting kisses on the soft skin below her arms, the hollows of her throat, then holds her down and crooks her fingers and *gives,* til Sara's sobbing in exhausted relief. Mari hardly has time to grin at her, triumph surging through familiar pathways in her brain, before Sara's begging her to the bed, clutching hungrily. Mari does not deny her. Were it cold enough in Mari's chambers, the woman's very breath would conjure little wisps of cloud. As it is, her cries come with only sweat, want, and a needy frailty that nearly makes Mari wish, distantly, that they had days left together instead of mere hours.

But Mari established this rule for herself long ago. It's the one thing she holds to. She won't keep any mortal among her clouds for longer than seven days.

Sara moves clumsy and terribly earnest, and Mari indulges in her offered, fumbling pleasures.

Here is magic. Here is beauty. Here is what makes life worth living. The sweet staleness of a lover's breath, the press of their touch, the urgency of their need.

Brief, impossibly tender, and finite.

It's almost enough to make Mari feel human.

* * *

"Another week."

"Darling."

"I won't get in the way!" Even as she stands at Mari's doorway, her things in a tidy bundle, Sara's cheeks flush with emotion. The twist of guilt in her gut is a familiar flagellation. It almost feels good. "Another day, at least— I—*my lady*—"

"You're ready," Mari says. She lets an air of command prickle through her voice. Sara likes a firm hand, Mari knows, so long as it has her best interests at heart.

That sort of hand takes trust that's hard to come by. It'll be easier, now. Mari's blessing protects Sara from that sort of harm, which allows Mari to justify any of this to herself.

"But what of you?" Sara sniffs. "I'm leaving you all alone here again!"

For a moment, Mari wants to snap at her. She feels her restraint cracking, hears it in a roll of vicious thunder, churning leagues away, summoning the angry snap of lightning to mirror its mistress's ancient rage.

Instead, she chooses another sort of violence.

"Oh, darling," she grins. "I won't be alone for long."

Sara blinks at her as she takes in what she means. Her look of earnest desperation recoils, twists into surprise, then dismay, and resignation. She knew, of course she knew. They all know what they're in for when they seek out Mari. Mari makes it clear: Maria Makiling lives alone.

But each girl thinks she can change her. That as Mari gifts them what *they* want, they can be the one to rescue the legendary mountain diwata from her own loneliness. Each one hopes. They want to be chosen. Not even because they care about her, really, for how could they? Mari is never the same thing to more than one person. She shifts to give each girl what they need: respite, relief, a sanctuary, an escape, a fight.

"Yes, my lady," Sara says softly. Something that isn't quite satisfaction curdles in Mari's gut. It digs like a fingernail into a scar that's healed and opened again and again.

"Go back to your own life," the goddess tells the mortal woman. "There is nothing for you here."

"No," Sara says. "I suppose there isn't."

Mari takes a deep breath. This bit is important.

"Hey, hey, darling," Mari says, pitching her voice soothingly. An echo of the tone she uses during aftercare, which makes sense. "Remember what you've learned, when you return to your village." She touches her thumb to Sara's lower lip, and the girl lets her, even as it trembles. "You deserve to live as fully as you can. You deserve adventure, and a life that brings you joy. With the fertile rains you'll bring home, you and your people won't be beholden to your leader's selfishness any longer. You will flourish, my darling. You will live a whole, mortal life." You won't stay stagnant, Mari doesn't say. You won't rot to your immortal soul while your reflection stays lovely.

Sara opens her mouth, then closes it.

Mari smiles. Kisses her on the forehead. And sends her down the mountain.

She knows Sara, or Mara, or Kara, will look back.

She doesn't wait to see.

* * *

Once Sara has safely gone enough down the mountain that the sound will seem like distant thunder, Mari shrieks. She takes a breath of west wind that billows her to her spirit form, releasing the trappings of mortal-like flesh that house her. It's more comfortable, really, to be a size that fits the earth, but every so often when a girl leaves, Mari's approximated humanity feels like a joke.

She fills into a cumulus the size of her mountain, rising above it. She sails herself over jungle and river, village and road, until she hangs heavy above the sea, at the edge of her jurisdiction. Calls the sweet near-eternity of water with a curl of her fingers, a flex of her wrists. It swirls around her, breathless and bright—and powerful, but only because of her. On its own it's stranded there in the sea.

Mari wails eldritch lightning. She thunders claps of futile rage. She spreads and rolls, gazing up into the bright expanse of sky. So many stars up there, just beyond the glare of the sun. But so much more of it is void. Vast, endless, and ever-emptying.

What does that mortal know of loneliness?

What could that girl, in a life measured by months and years, know of eternity on a planet that will continue until it doesn't? Humans seek purpose: diwata are created *for* a purpose. Mari knows hers. This is it. There is nothing to strive for. There is nothing to build. There is nothing to hope for, and nowhere to go. There is the way a storm comes, and what grows after. Mari helps it happen, and nothing happens for her. Or to her. Or at all, in any way that matters.

To be fair, some of the mortals who understand loneliness best are the ones who seek Mari out.

The girl will carry the blessings of the cloud diwata to her people. She will live the rest of her days touched by the divine. Her crops will flourish, her soul affirmed. When the major diwata call forth floods—as they do every year—her people will be protected. Mari can do that much.

It seems cruel, Mari knows. She has no need for what they give her. She would not withhold the grand routine of her blessings if mortals stopped the pilgrimage to her mountain. But she will not turn away the needy, delectable morsels who seek her out, who pass along myth and rumor of the strange diwata and whisper to other aching women that they might find what they seek if they follow the curved path of Mari's mountain.

The sky churns gray, and the goddess laughs. The sea rises to meet her whining wind, crashing in on itself. Mari's fingertips prickle with each bolt of lighting she calls down from the heavens to drown in the sea.

She takes solace in the knowledge that she's not, really, taking her ennui out on the mortals she serves. Mari truly does her best to protect everyone in her jurisdiction, to nourish the land and its peoples. There are a handful of other bored minor diwata who wield their powers for cruelty in the service of their own pleasure. They deceive, they betray, they torment. Mari would never.

At least, though, when a mortal finds her way to Mari, she knows what she's looking for. Mari gives it to her. The runaway makes a *choice,* to seek out the lady of the clouds, the rumored diwata who changes women's lives for the better. A few men used to come, but rarely enjoyed their stay as much. The extent of Mari's malleability ended with allowing men to exert real control over her, and that's what too many of them wished. If you trusted the rumors *they* brought home, you'd get the sense the only thing you'd find on the mountain was a woman who looked and behaved, to them, too much like a man for them to enjoy. Mari's heart was never in it with most of them anyway, and now it's only women, though women of every shape and body.

Mari doesn't lie to these women.

She just lets them see what they want to see in her.

It's what she does best.

...well. It's one of several things she does best.

A raw howl wrenches from her, the roiling cumulus thick with shameful want.

Sara had felt good, when she touched her. They don't always, necessarily—never *bad,* it's just that the ones who find her don't typically know much about what it means to touch someone shaped like a woman, that's why they're here in the first place. Sara didn't, but she learned quickly, within a week.

And now she's gone and Mari has no bruise, no bite, no scar. She shifts, restless with the wind and she lets herself go broad, coating her mountain in heavy, gloomy fog. It feels like a good stretch gone on too long. This sort of behavior is not befitting of a diwata.

But no one ever cares. No one minds. The higher deities know Mari won't let anyone drown in her emotions. They've got more pressing matters to attend to than a minor diwata having a tantrum.

The girl before Sara had arrived six weeks prior. The one before, two months earlier than that—she'd been a scrappy thing, eager to prove herself, that had been a nice week. Half a year before, a timid maiden who required, at least, more of Mari's concentration to attend to. Tenderness had never come easy to her, despite what the soft, lounging rolls of her mountain seemed to indicate.

Another will come, eventually. Mari will take the shape of what she needs, just as she does for her domain. And then the mortal will leave.

Mari deepens the fog, forces more power into the hammering rain. She roars into it, booming thunder over her domain. The trees shudder with her heaving fury. She watches mortals scurry, human and animal alike. Tiny things. Everything must feel so urgent when you're so small.

The rage is almost refreshing. It's a different sort of ache, and Mari is, evidently, starved for difference. Enough so that she lets herself feel a hint of shame at her own tantrum. She allows herself to storm until guilt gets louder than indifference.

With a sigh, she diminishes to her person-sized shape. Clears the skies. Conjures sweet cirrus wisps to reassure her people that their cloud diwata has not forsaken them.

Yet, she thinks darkly.

Mari sets off to her lodgings for a good, less destructive sulk.

Except, to her extreme surprise, there's already someone there.

* * *

The first thing Mari realizes is that the person standing at her entryway is not human. She can't tell *what* they are—they're certainly not a diwata.

The second thing she realizes is that they look irritated, which is equally unexpected.

Though to be fair, they're *extremely* bedraggled.

The person looks at her and frowns.

"Is this yours?" they say, gesturing to Mari's palace.

Mari blinks.

"No one comes here unless they're looking for me," she says slowly.

"Tough shit," says the not-human, not-diwata. "Any port in a storm, right?"

The storm. Right. She supposes she might have gone a bit careless with the details. Mari schools her face impassive, jutting out the sharp lines of her jaw.

Still, this is unusual. Everyone in her territory knows what her mountains are.

The uninvited guest wrings their waist-length hair all over Mari's wood floor, their face etched with irritation. Mari frowns. Without thinking, she jerks her wrist, banishing the puddle through the entryway and up into cloud.

The person's jaw drops.

"Oh, god," they say, somewhat ironically. "You're Maria of the Mountain."

"Yes," Mari says, crooking a brow. "And who are *you?*"

"I'm soaked is what I am," they grumble, turning their wringing to their clothes now. "Is this your fault? I'm Kahuyan. Kayan if you're friendly, which I'm assuming you're not."

Mari blinks. No mortal talks to her this way.

"Kahuyan," she repeats, a question in her voice.

"Forest nymph," Kahuyan answers, dismissive. "I take it to mean that yes, this *is* your fault. Could you help, then?"

Rarely is Mari called upon for something as mild as *drying clothes.* She has half a mind to call a mudslide to wash the intruder away.

The other half feels staticky at the sheer newness of it.

"I know every nymph and spirit in my dominion," she drawls. "I like to think I would have remembered you." She wrenches the wet from Kahuyan's clothes and hair with more power than she usually bothers for something domestic. Kahuyan stumbles, and something warm flares within the cage of Mari's ribs. *Pride,* she registers with surprise. She hasn't wanted to be impressive in a long time. She hasn't needed to. Everyone is already impressed.

Kahuyan regains composure quickly.

"I'm not *from* your domain, thanks. I've got my own."

Well.

"Then what brings you here?"

"Your *storm*—"

"Wouldn't have passed beyond my territory," Mari cuts in. She hadn't been *that* careless. "Which you were in. Why, exactly?"

Kahuyan glares at her.

"Because when a princess runs away, the whole point is to leave behind the land that belongs to her. Which necessitates entering a land that *doesn't.*"

Mari blinks.

"*What?*"

"And now that I'm dry," Kahuyan continues, loudly, "I'll be on my way."

"Where?"

"I—" The princess blushes, and looks furious about it, cutting her gaze away. Interesting.

"You can pass the night here," Mari offers. "Proceed on your path to nowhere at dawn."

"I don't need your charity."

Mari snorts.

"It's hardly charity, but if you want to pick your way down the mountain in the muddy dark"—for the sun was sinking, Mari's tantrum had apparently taken up most of the day—"be my guest. Turn down the offer to share a god's quarters."

Kahuyan eyes her with unmasked suspicion. It prickles. Mari is accustomed to, quite literally, nothing but reverence. The nymph princess from beyond her jurisdiction owes her none of that, and has no qualms about making it clear.

"I don't want to fuck you," Kahuyan says bluntly.

"Excuse me?"

"Look, I've heard the stories." Kahuyan's gaze trails down Mari's figure. The nymph is tall in this form, taller than most human women. Mari finds she's glad she's got her cloud binder on, which is an odd feeling—she does that for herself, she never cares what she looks like to her visitors. "I never really *believed* them. I assumed the girls who came back were lying to cover up affairs, and the families of the ones who didn't convince themselves their daughters were safe in the arms of a diwata, instead of fleeing their abusive boyfriends or what have you." Something seems to occur to Kahuyan. She stiffens, glancing around herself as if expecting to see a pile of bodies. "What, um. What *does* happen to the ones that don't return?"

"I eat them," Mari says, keeping her voice impassive.

It doesn't work for even a moment; in fact, it seems to set the nymph at ease. She laughs, lovely and surprisingly husky, pitched lower than her speaking voice.

"Oh, good," Kahuyan says. "I worried for a moment there that you were a monster."

"The men are the monsters," Mari says, not joking now. "Boyfriends, husbands, sure, though none so much as the ones who feel jilted. Not only men, either—enough girls have fled the confines set by mothers who refuse to let them lead a life they felt had been barred from them." A muscle in Kahuyan's jaw twitches. "The ones who don't return are pursuing a life that suits them best. They find their direction here, and I give them enough of my blessing to seek it where they can."

"By fucking them and sending them away after a week?" Kahuyan says bitingly, and that's really quite enough.

"Look, princess," Mari says, losing her temper. "Do you want to stay or not? Because unless you've heard of someone returning with hate or horror for the time they spent with me, there's no reason for you to speak to me like that, much less in my own palace."

Kahuyan's lips part, then close. Mari gets the sense no one's spoken to *her* like this either.

Mari ignores her. She sets about readying her chambers for the evening with a bit more force than absolutely necessary. She'll have to conjure clouds for a guest mattress—she's got plenty of rooms, but no overnight visitor has refused to share her bed.

By the time she's got everything settled, the nymph has made a little chair for herself out of Mari's floorboards, winding the wood to fit her body.

Mari *has* chairs.

This girl is showing off just as much as Mari is.

"I respected it," Kahuyan says at last, breaking the quiet.

"I very much doubt that," Mari says dryly. "You, respecting anything."

"When I thought they were using you to cover up affairs, or to escape without being pursued." Kahuyan doesn't look at her. She picks at the arm of her chair. As fussy as Mari is about her floor, it's sort of nice to see something in her palace *change,* for once. Her floorboards make a lovely chair, it seems, twining mahogany that Kahuyan's shaped neatly for the comfort of her curvy body. "I thought it was a great idea, a thing humans so rarely have."

Mari snorts despite herself.

"Sorry to disabuse you of the notion." She furrows a brow. "I forget. Do nymphs eat?"

Kahuyan's face spreads into a grin, the first smile Mari's seen on her.

"Occasionally," she says. "It's not necessary all that often, but—I like food."

Mari rolls her eyes. She hopes she successfully passes it off as irritation; the truth is it leans closer to odd fondness. Mari is the same. She likes food too, though she doesn't need it. She doesn't often indulge when she's alone.

"C'mon, then."

Kahuyan doesn't hide her relief when Mari leads her to the room that serves as her banquet hall.

"I knew you were eating those girls," she breathes. "You fatten them up and then devour them. Of course." She takes one moment to stare in wonder before digging in with her hands at the piles of lanzones, dragonfruit, ripe banana, pastry, and more, the fruit fresh preserved in the coolness of Mari's kitchen cloud. Mari finds herself pleased that she hadn't set aside her mortal provisions after Sara yet, she usually does it right away. There's even most of a lechon, kept fresh. Kahuyan tears into it with her teeth, not a care in the world for the mess or the sauce on her face.

Mari hides a smile.

The princess conjures another chair instead of opting for Mari's bench, but this time it's a simple thing conjured with the flick of her wrist. It appears that some of her posturing, at least, falls away in the face of a thorough meal. It's been so long since anyone was around Mari without trying to impress her at every turn, without trying to secure their desired blessing. She's not entirely sure how to act. It's disarming. It's a bit anxiety-inducing.

It's...well. Mari won't give it *exciting*. But at least it's something.

She allows herself to pick at the food too, finding the turon tastes sweeter than it did last night with Lara. She's got more of an appetite than usual. Something about Kahuyan's unbridled delight in the food makes Mari strangely hungry.

Minutes pass where neither speaks, except to navigate the meal. Night's settled velvet over the islands. Birdsong lilts, insects and frogs cry and croak. Brief little things. Calling out into the world with everything they have, begging to be less alone.

Mari pokes at her rice. She's not used to eating without flirting, or coaxing, or something of the sort. It's...nice. *Companionable,* her mind supplies, and that makes her feel so silly it itches.

No, Kahuyan is not a lonely maiden who sought Mari's attention.

That doesn't mean she's not going to leave.

In fact, it means she's not even going to stay anywhere close to a week, judging by her behavior so far.

"So," Mari says presently, in part to interrupt her own thoughts.

"So what?" Kahuyan says through an artless mouthful of pork. Mari's nostrils flare.

"You said you were a runaway princess."

"I did." Kahuyan shifts, as if unsure she should have. Mari pauses, but Kahuyan doesn't elaborate.

"Where are you going?" Mari says at last, as if it should have been obvious.

Kahuyan looks away. Her warm, bark-brown skin doesn't show a blush, but Mari can half-feel it in the air.

"All right," Mari tries again, "then what is it you're looking for?"

The nymph frowns. Shovels another mouthful of pork and rice into her mouth and reaches for the gulay.

Mari seizes her wrist. Not hard, just enough to get her to look Mari in the eye. Kahuyan's gaze burns like daybreak. Mari doesn't look away.

"I think I've earned that much," she says mildly, and releases her. Kahuyan's hand hovers above the table for a split second before settling on the gulay. "If you're going to stay in my quarters. If you know so much about *me* already."

A muscle works in the nymph's throat.

It's really quite a throat. Now that Mari's had a chance to look at her properly, she's not surprised the nymph comes from woodland royalty. She's clearly accustomed to being well-fed, to getting what she wants. There's a music to the curves and lines of her body. While Mari's curves are usually a source of irritation and misunderstanding, Kahuyan wears hers with a sort of sharp, lovely defiance. As if she knows she's beautiful, and dares you to notice. There's something untouchable about her.

Mari isn't used to the concept.

Kahuyan takes several contemplative bites of the gulay before she speaks. Mari waits, though patience has notably never been a strong suit.

It's a funny thing, to see a tree spirit eating leafy vegetables.

"So I don't know exactly where I'm going," Kahuyan says in a rush.

Mari blinks. Of all the things—

"What?"

"So I haven't figured out what I'm running *to,* all right?" Kahuyan says, and oh, that anger is tinged with...*embarrassment.* Mari knows *that* well enough. "I just needed to run away."

"I thought you weren't one of the maidens fleeing from her life into my arms."

"You wish," Kahuyan returns easily, flicking buko juice at her. Mari's jaw drops. She flecks a grain of rice back. Kahuyan grins again. It makes the deep brown of her eyes gleam gold.

It dulls, when she starts talking again.

"I just left. Didn't pick a direction, really, and then I got caught in your storm and here we are. I don't know. Maybe it's different for diwata." Kahuyan exhales hard through her broad nose. Mari tries to look at her without staring. "Nymphs don't age either, but—we can be killed." Her knuckles go white. She nearly pops the lanzone she's holding. "It's happening, in other parts of the world. Nymphs who've been alive as long as I have, their forests felled for greed, their souls cut down alongside." She looks at Mari with big eyes. "Haven't you ever been...restless? Ever felt like you've done everything you were meant to do, found your way to the biggest moments in the life you've been given, and now the rest is just...waiting?"

Mari's so surprised to hear her own thoughts spoken to her that she barks a laugh.

"Sorry, I just—*yes.*"

She says it with enough vehemence it takes Kahuyan a bit aback. She regains composure quickly, but something in her expression softens with understanding.

"I don't want the world to end before I've felt something new," Kahuyan says, her voice soft as rustling leaves. "And I wasn't going to find that where I was."

Mari stares at her.

"Right," she says, rather foolishly. Fuck. When was the last time she didn't know what to say?

A *princess,* though. Her people, her forest. Who's tending to it now? The one constant Mari has in her life is her purpose. She's never considered leaving. How could she?

Kahuyan shifts uncomfortably, as if she could read these thoughts in Mari's face.

"I'm tired," the nymph says abruptly.

"Right," Mari says again, after a beat. "Ah. I'll get the room ready." She rises, beckoning a wisp of cloud from the night. "It won't be wet unless you're into that sort of thing," she promises at Kahuyan's dubious look. "Just soft. And it'll keep you cool in the morning sun."

"Thank you," Kahuyan says. She has toyomansi sauce on her cheek. "Really, Maria of the Mountain. I do appreciate this."

Mari shakes her head with a crooked little smile.

"You're welcome, princess. And please call me Mari."

"I—" Kahuyan starts to protest, perhaps to atone a bit for her earlier bluntness when she was drenched in Mari's storm.

"Don't worry, it doesn't mean we're friends," Mari says. "I don't even mind Maria much, though it doesn't quite fit right. I just *hate* hearing my full title."

Kahuyan worries her lip with a fingernail. She looks as if she wants to say something else, but she doesn't.

"Thank you, Mari."

Mari's smile broadens despite herself. It's been a long time since someone didn't simply defer to *my lady.* "You're welcome, princess," she repeats, and retires to her chambers before she thinks better of it.

* * *

Mari half-expects Kahuyan to be down the mountain at the first light of dawn. Instead, she's helping herself to more of Mari's food—and has forsaken her dry clothes for one of Mari's cloudspun robes. The audacity makes Mari go hot at the back of her neck. She's wearing one too. They *match*.

"Sleep well, princess?"

"You know," Kahuyan says, her mouth full of sweet rice and mango, "if we're not doing titles for *you*, why don't we avoid the one I've fled from, yeah?"

"Fair enough," Mari says. "Kahuyan, then." The name feels warm and round on her tongue. "It suits you," she says before she catches herself.

Kahuyan grins and jerks her head in thanks.

"I see you've taken it upon yourself to decide my robes suit you as well," Mari says.

"Don't they?" Kahuyan shoots back, entirely undaunted. She shimmies in her seat, the cloud fluffing lazily around her. She looks like a forest thick with fog, all rich browns and heady magic things, ready to grow.

Mari shakes her head like she's exasperated, but Kahuyan's grin only broadens knowingly in her silence.

No one moves like this in Mari's chambers. There's confidence, yes, but there's also a sheer *brazenness* to it that makes her head buzz, makes her want to push and tease. Mari doesn't know how to act on any of that. She's used to being worshipped. She knows how to give what she's asked for.

Kahuyan swallows her mouthful and breaks the quiet.

"I slept well," she says. "Loud bugs."

"You must be used to that."

Kahuyan grins.

"I am. Yours are different, though. Louder."

"Sorry."

"Don't be," Kahuyan says. "I like it. My forest was too crowded, but traveling on my own was..." She trails off, and shakes her head. "I like the sounds of the night. Makes me feel alive."

"I get that," Mari says, and Kahuyan shoots her a look. "What?"

"You're not trying to seduce me, are you?"

"*What?*"

"Isn't it what you do? Is that why you've been so nice? Why you're...*relating?*"

Mari bristles at that.

"And here I thought you knew the stories. I don't seduce *anyone.* They come to me."

"All right," Kahuyan says, chastened. "Sorry."

The morning sun blares through Mari's chambers. She's got to bring some water in from the overflow of her storm and send it into the sky for a gentler mist of rain before it floods.

"If you're leaving after breakfast, take whatever food you want." Mari shoots her a look as she prepares to take flight. "Don't take my robe with you."

"Wait," Kahuyan says, "where are you going?"

"To do my job," Mari says, more tersely than intended. If the princess is going to walk out of her life, she'd prefer not to be around for the moment of parting. She gets enough farewells as is, thank you very much.

Kahuyan gets to her feet. She is *clumsy* for a nymph. Mari works very hard not to find it charming.

"Can I come with you?"

Mari has never heard those words in her life. Which is probably why she says—

"Okay."

* * *

"I didn't know diwata could lose their hearing, but you're sure giving it a hell of a try, pri–Kahuyan."

"I'd scream less if we were on *solid ground.*"

"What on earth made you think a cloud diwata's job meant *solid ground—*"

"Shut up and don't you *dare* drop me."

"If I were you, I wouldn't be telling me to shut up when I'm the only one between you and—"

"*Mari.*"

"Sorry, sorry. Don't worry, I've got you."

Once the nymph gets over the shock of flight, she actually takes to it quite well. Mari's in her human form as she rises into the clouds, so she can cradle the princess in her arms like a bride. Since her hands are full, she points with her lips to channel her powers. Kahuyan giggles.

"So gods do that too."

"I think everyone on these islands do," Mari says, "and I think anyone would if their arms were full of nymph."

"Fair enough," Kahuyan says. "*Whoa.*"

They've reached their peak. Mari's taken care of the rivers, and a gentle, nourishing mist settles over her domain. The sky is still tinged pink and gold with dawn. It casts a warm glow on Mari's mountains. The clouds around them are as big as mountains themselves, sweet fluffy giants, some of Mari's favorites.

It *is* quite pretty. She hasn't noticed in a very long time.

When they land back at the palace, Kahuyan doesn't ask before heading to the food, and Mari doesn't stop her. She doesn't bother eating, either. Just sits on her chair while Kahuyan sits on the one she made for herself, and watches her eat. The novelty of it—a morning guest she hasn't fucked, or at least pleased in some way—feels something akin to what Kahuyan must have felt when she was in Mari's arms in the sky.

The nymph peels an orange, and tells Mari about herself, unasked.

Mari listens.

"My life is to root," Kahuyan says, bitterness staining her tone. "I was *made* to root. And all I ever want to do is run."

Mari waves her wrist, summons the cloud with fresh nata de coco, and the tension in Kahuyan's brow eases.

"It makes sense, though, doesn't it? A forest spirit. You move slow, but you move. You grow." Not like a mountain.

Kahuyan scoffs, fingernail digging too deep into the flesh of the orange.

"Hardly! I stay planted, Mari!" Mari gets the sense Kahuyan's been wanting to talk to someone, anyone, about this for a long while. "I am the steady creep of time," she says, "moss on a log, a forest made to *endure.* To withstand. I don't change with the seasons, like my brethren in other parts of the world, and I think that's beautiful, but that doesn't mean I don't get *tired* of it."

"You're allowed to travel, some. Just as we are."

"Not when you're a *princess,"* Kahuyan says, bitter again, and then the whole story comes out.

Yes, she has a people to return to. They're good to each other and good to her, largely, which complicated things. But she doesn't want to lead, she never has. Her brother, Dakila, would be a far better ruler in her estimation: he's younger, but he's always been more popular, and he has a penchant for domesticity. He's been with his lover for centuries now, they've raised generations of sapling nymphs. Kahuyan's people appreciate her, but they *love* Dakila and his partner. They're good at growing things. They *want* to root.

But Kahuyan is the eldest, and that means she's meant to stay.

Mari blushes when Kahuyan details the more sordid details of a bored nymph princess, running her hand through her close-cropped hair. The princess has never wanted for lovers. She's had hundreds, she's bored of them all.

"I'm even bored of my own *hand*," she says in irritation, and Mari does her best not to picture what she'd done and how much she'd done of it to tire of pleasure.

They talk late into the day. Mari finds herself sharing her own story. She finds she has more of it to share than she realizes—an earth's history of storms and sunsets, the growing things of her mountain she loves dearly.

It starts off clumsy. Mari is out of practice talking about herself in a way that doesn't fill in the missing piece of a lonely woman's life. But it eases, because Kahuyan *listens*. Rapt at times, teasing at others.

Mari likes talking to her, she realizes.

...fuck.

* * *

Night comes again. Kahuyan helps herself to another meal, then retires to the guest room.

Three days pass like this, then three more.

Every morning, Kayan's up before the goddess. She's taken to patching up parts of the palace Mari hadn't realized needed it, parts that cloud can't fix. She coaxes the bowed rafters straight again, chastises the termites from the walls, whispers conspiringly to the moss until it fluffs itself into something softer and cleaner.

None of it is strictly *necessary*. But, begrudgingly and privately, Mari admits it's pretty.

If it wasn't for the uneasy knowledge in her gut that she won't be able to keep it this way once the nymph leaves. At least not for long.

After breakfast each day, Kayan insists on tagging along with Mari's duties. She's taken so well to flying she doesn't need Mari to hold her anymore, clinging to her shoulders like a rucksack and hooting in glee as they duck around shrikes and sea-birds.

The days pass differently when there's someone traveling alongside Mari, yet demands nothing of her time aside from sharing it. They're longer and shorter at once, the sun sinking seemingly swifter yet the hours more full than Mari remembers.

It's not only time that feels different, it's Mari's domain, too. Kahuyan clambers over the various patches of Mari's mountains with clumsy, ruthless curiosity. She doesn't ask, only squats by a forest brook to taste the rainwater mingling with salt, crashes her way through the underbrush to let a waterfall drench her and drown out her peals of laughter.

Mari doesn't know how to be what Kahuyan needs, because Kahuyan doesn't need her. Kahuyan freed *herself*.

So all Mari can be is *her*self, the way she is when she's alone.

She's starting to figure out she's not entirely sure who that is.

On the fourth day, Mari brings Kahuyan to a festering lagoon at the edge of her domain. There had been construction on a nearby roadway, and the company left behind concrete and chemicals clogging up the water, choking the fish, the turtles, the life.

The air is thick with rot. Mari can feel Kahuyan's rage as clearly as her own.

"If you fix it," says the nymph, easing a trapped butterfly free from beneath a branch, "they'll only come back, won't they?"

"Maybe," Mari says. "Probably." She kneels at the shore, trembling with loathing at the sludge-strewn waters. The butterfly flits eagerly to Kahuyan, alighting on her shoulder. "But I'll fix it again, and again, and maybe they'll pick another spot next time. Maybe they'll take their shit with them."

"*Maybe*," Kayan says, watching the butterfly stretch its wings.

"Well, yes," Mari says. She hasn't thought about this for a long time. No one's ever asked. "But before they do, if I fix it, everything they hurt will get to live. Just a bit longer, but it will, and when it dies it won't be because a human was careless." She looks up in time to see Kahuyan stare at the butterfly as it lifts itself back into the arms of the jungle. "It's not enough," she says, because it isn't. "But it helps."

Kahuyan doesn't say anything, but when Mari raises her arms to beckon a rush of clean water from her clouds, Kayan steels herself, and raises hers too.

The nymph's magic smells like static soil out here. Bright and furious, she drags the banyan and balete roots deeper into the earth until they reach something cleaner. Mari makes the water rise, and Kahuyan gives the jungle her fierceness and her strength. The rain drenches their clothes, their hair. Mari lets it, and Kahuyan doesn't ask her to stop. The shifting roots make the ground tremble. The wet earth opens to swallow the harm, and they push until the last of its poison is buried beneath the mountain.

Without a word, they turn. They beam at each other as this corner of the world writhes in the storm they made, together.

The next morning, there are birds again, and the lagoon teems with sparkling life.

* * *

On the seventh day, Mari wakes jumping out of her skin with sick anticipation.

Sure enough, she finds Kahuyan staring at the clothes she arrived in with a frown.

"Leaving, are you?" Mari says, keeping her voice light. Kahuyan doesn't respond. Mari shakes her head. "Have you decided yet? Where you're going to go?"

"I—"

"Take what you want from the kitchen. Who knows when you'll happen upon a decent meal again."

Kahuyan stares at her.

"Why are you being so blunt all of a sudden?" she asks.

"You're one to talk."

"*Mari.*"

Mari stands at the window. Looks out over her beautiful domain. She feels sick, a thing she should not, by rights, be at all *able* to feel.

"I hate goodbyes," she says in a clipped voice.

To her surprise, Kahuyan laughs.

"If you hate goodbyes so much, why do you live like this? Seven days of companionship at a time?"

The back of Mari's neck heats.

"What choice do I have?" she snaps. "You want me to ask a human to spend the rest of their short days in this gilded purgatory with me?"

"It's not—" Kahuyan breaks off, flexing her thick fingers. When she lifts her gaze, Mari realizes what she's about to say before she says it. The heat spreads, down her throat, her heart, her hands, lower. It takes root. Or, rather, Mari lets herself feel just how deep those roots go already, the way they've wound around the veins of her. "What if...it wasn't a human, necessarily? Would you ever consider that?"

The truth is no. How could she have? How could anyone have predicted this absolute lightning storm of a princess—of someone who doesn't need her at all, but *wants* her? This nymph, who she wants to follow into forest magic the way Kahuyan follows her into the sky? What would it feel like to be the one who grows, instead of only the one who sends the water? What would it feel like to trust that you too deserved to be saved from a life that doesn't let you get close to anyone real? It's not that no other human was deserving of a lifetime of Mari's company—it's that she couldn't bear to let anyone get close for longer than a week, because she knew the farewell was coming. A year or seventy. No human lasts.

"How could you condemn yourself to a lifetime of this?" Kahuyan says, stepping closer. It's not a question. "It's a punishment you haven't earned."

Mari lets out a half-hysterical laugh.

"Haven't I? If I ever didn't deserve it, don't I *now,* after everyone I've pushed away?" She shakes her head. "Just go. Go find your purpose, or your people, or whatever."

Kahuyan steps even closer, crowding into Mari's space when she tries to turn away.

"Don't *do* that," she says, and for the first time Mari hears the princess in the command of her voice.

"Do what?"

"Tell me what you think I need to hear!" Kahuyan's breathing heavily now. She's taller than Mari, though only just. Her fists are balled again. "This is what you do, isn't it? I should have known. That's the thing with clouds—you see whatever you want to in them." Kahuyan's shaking now. "You take the shape of someone's need, and you don't know what to do with me because what I need is—"

"You don't need me, Kahuyan," Mari interrupts, bitterly. "You have a people to return to. A family. A life that you can grow. You don't need anything from me."

Kahuyan blinks.

"You're right," she says, squaring her shoulders. "I don't need you."

"Good," Mari spits. "So I suppose this is—"

"I just want you."

It takes a moment for Mari to realize she's being kissed. Clumsily, hungrily, desperately kissed.

But she gets her bearings quick, hauls the nymph's plump, perfect thighs around her waist, and tumbles into bed.

* * *

Never before has someone needed her less.

Never before has Mari wanted to *give.*

Kahuyan's soft all over. Her softer parts are striped with stretch marks like the lenticels of a tree trunk. When Mari runs her tongue over them, the nymph makes a sound the goddess wants to etch into the mountain.

She's bossy in bed, directing Mari in position and pace. She's loose with praise, though, unlike in the rest of her day, and when her fingernails scrape over the short hair at Mari's nape and says *good girl,* Mari nearly comes untouched.

"You don't have to do this alone," Kayan whispers into the crook of Mari's throat. "You don't have to drift away. Let me ground you. Let me stay."

"I don't deserve you," Mari says, then curses her sex-loosened tongue.

"Stop that," Kayan says, so stern Mari shudders. "You are possibility and nourishment and *majesty.* You are a force of fucking nature, Mari, and you are *not* washing me out of your story."

Kahuyan pins her to the bed then, all soft hands and steady power, and Mari's mind goes stormy in the best way. The nymph unmoors the goddess as easily as she might bring a sapling to bloom, leaving her a wreck of *want* and *yes* and *why do I feel more alive in your hands than I have in centuries*, and something suspiciously like devotion.

Mari can't put her finger on it until after. The moon hangs huge in the night, and the nymph sleeps soundly beside her. Only then does she realize what the unfamiliar feeling is. Not love, though that's undeniably there.

No. It's that for the first time in her eternal life, with Kayan, *Mari* wants to worship.

* * *

The morning sun slips slow through the kapa-kapa at the window, dappling the soil-dark wood of Mari's bedroom and easing open the eyes of the nymph splayed beside her in a tangle of Mari's best sheets.

They strike an arrangement. For three months out of the year, Kahuyan returns to her people. She relieves her brother and brother-in-law, tends to her growing things.

The rest of the year, she spends on the mountain.

As for those who seek Mari's well-established services, some the diwata and the nymph attend to together, at their pleasure and whim. For the others, Kayan conjures several guest houses out of tree and root partway down the mountain, and sets to running a system that groups them in pairs or threes or more according to their needs. Some stay, cultivate the crops that have sprung up, others go off together to build fresh lives for themselves. Mari casts a diwata blessing on the wood for protection and prosperity. Not many years pass before they've got a bustling community center, for women and other disempowered islanders to build something new for themselves. Neither of them would feel right keeping Kayan from her forest for*ever,* but every year, Mari misses her like a wound for those three months.

That ache is nothing compared to how she felt before. It feels necessary. It feels good to have something to look forward to.

And neither of them have to be alone, ever again.

"Cloudbreaker" is a standalone short by Maya Gittelman. It was loosely inspired by the stories of Maria Makiling, Hades & Persephone, and, frankly, just a bit of The Ultimatum: Queer Love. Follow her at mayagittelman or bookshelfbymaya, wherever you follow writers. Hopefully by the time you're reading this, they'll have a website up.

Frog

Seanan McGuire

Sapphic Representation: Lesbian
Heat Level: Low
Content Warnings: None

I was walking back to camp when I saw motion in the reeds next to the trail. Probably a rat, I thought, even as I stopped and swung my camera around, ready to capture whatever sliver of life had somehow managed to survive in this polluted mire for posterity. Not that anyone believes the pictures we send back. Too much CGI, too many generative engines; I could fill this wasteland with bunnies if I had the right software. I think some people want to believe that's exactly what we're doing out here. Easier to give up on the world outside the cities if you tell yourself it's nothing but slime and slag.

I lifted the camera and adjusted the lens, trying to zoom in on whatever might have moved in there. Most of the pictures we get outside of camp are unintelligible to the untrained eye: I would call it a picture of a rat if I got the spiky edge of fur on its haunches, or a curve of tail, pink and hairless and scaled as a scab. It didn't matter if anyone else could look at the picture and see proof the world was healing. I could see it, and Angela could see it, and the rest of the world could wait their turn.

There was no rat. But there was another flicker of movement from the same location, and I pressed down on the shutter button without thinking about it, holding it in place as the camera clicked away in my hands, picture after picture tucking itself away in its digital memory. The camera is quicker than the eye. Even if the source of that motion was gone by the time I could look again, I could hope to have caught it. We could hold on.

Pictures taken, I lowered the camera and squinted at the reeds.

Like most of their fellows, they were low and stunted, dark green leaves leading to tan cattails already poofing out white and going to seed. There was water there, I knew, feeding the roots that hid it; if I tried to step into the green, I would find myself sinking, and those cattail marshes could be deceptively deep.

We've mostly cleaned up the surface-level water, the stuff that moves, evaporates and returns, but it'll be a while before we tap those deeper estuaries for their secret stores of toxic chemicals and mutagenic compounds. I didn't really want to follow a rat into the cattails and find myself growing extra toes. So I stayed where I was, straining for a glimpse of something that might or might not be there.

The movement came a third time and my breath stuck in my throat, my entire body locking up with shock and bewilderment as I stared. That was no rat.

There in the reeds, deep green and brown-spotted body almost perfectly camouflaged by its surroundings, a leopard frog looked back at me. Its eyes were large and golden, and there were only two of them. From what I could see, it was formed exactly as I would have expected a frog to be formed, slick-skinned and perfect, if I had still expected a frog to be formed like anything at all. Which I hadn't, and didn't, because there are no frogs anymore. They all died out in the late 2020s, when the summer heat waves expanded to last from May until September.

Some species of frog did just fine with higher temperatures, but most of them were already extinct by the time the web finally crashed, and they wouldn't have saved us anyway.

People liked to yell about the dangers of climate change and why we needed to get ourselves under control. They liked to point to tropical storms and rising sea levels, to humans with heat stroke and dangerous fluctuations in temperature and say that we had to stop this before it was too late. And the whole time, coral was bleaching and insects were disappearing and amphibians were rotting from the inside out as invasive fungus ate them alive.

Some people tried to sound the alarm, but it was like— well.

One of the first field operations I ever went on was in the early '20s, when a large swath of Northern California burned. I was young then; sturdy and tireless and capable of sleeping on the floor of the van for a week with nothing worse to show for it than a crick in my neck and a weird craving for corn chips. So I'd signed on as a biologist, intending to go out and survey the damage that had been done, to help draw a map of the recovery. There had been medics with our group, human doctors and veterinarians alike, and people whose entire job was distributing food and water to the impacted population.

We'd pulled into Paradise two days after the fire and stepped out of our vehicles into what had looked, at the time, like a slice of hell. If I saw that landscape again today, it would look like a slice of purgatory, if not paradise. It's amazing how perspective changes the songs we're singing.

But back then, it was the worst thing I'd ever seen. I was given a clipboard and a cooler and sent out to start asking questions about the native snake populations—had people seen them? Before the fire? After the fire? Where had they been seen? The usual things you ask at the beginning of a biological survey.

I'd been walking up to people who'd just lost everything and asking them whether they'd seen any snakes. I could give them bottles of water, I could make sympathetic noises, but what I was really there to do was find the snakes.

Was it any wonder I'd been sent home after two days with a cracked ocular socket and the words "heartless bitch" ringing in my ears? My presence hadn't impeded the human rescue efforts in any way. If anything, it had supplemented them, because every bottle of water and protein bar I handed out was one that didn't have to come from someone who had better things to do, but still, the sight of me had enraged some people so much that they'd resorted to violence. How could I care about animals when people had just lost everything? When the ground was still smoldering in spots, and they were still tallying their dead? How *could* I?

In the days before it had already been too late, those of us who wasted precious empathy on the denizens of our shared planet who weren't human had been shouted over, drowned out, ignored. If we'd been too aggressive in our caring—if we'd gone to the sites of disasters to help the creatures who couldn't help themselves, if we'd pushed for new regulations, if we'd gathered signatures in an inconvenient spot outside the grocery store—we'd been reminded of our place, how badly we needed to sit down, shut up, and let the people in charge get on with the business of destroying the world.

Temperatures had continued to fluctuate, now higher than they'd ever been, now lower, until not only the species at the bottom of the food chain started to disappear. And that was when the people who hadn't wanted us there with our clipboards and our jars had realized the thing we'd been trying to tell them all along:

We were never alone here. Never. But if you kill too many bugs, the bats go away, and if you kill too many bats, the owls go away, and when the temperature changes and doesn't change back, the fungus that can grow in your mulch and your middens changes, but that doesn't mean the new fungus is lined up and ready to go.

We kicked the supports out from under the environment, and everything came toppling down. Humans lived in domed cities in the high mountains now, had for the past fifteen years, ever since they'd pulled themselves past the walls and slammed the doors shut. The people who'd been too poor to make it inside, they got locked out during the worst part of the collapse, the years where nothing grew and the rain, when it came at all, was an acidic sludge that eroded skin and ate away at fabric.

But they didn't all die. People rarely do.

So now, twenty years after the collapse, when the cities are finally starting to send people like me and Angie down into the thick, poisoned air of the valleys to learn whether or not the world is starting to recover, we not only need to navigate the damage our species did to the planet, we get to navigate around the rest of our *species*, the ones who were born in the wastes and the wilds, and won't ever forgive those of us who managed to get to safety before the sky fell down.

And all of this is just to say that I couldn't possibly be looking at a frog, because there are no frogs anymore. The frogs are gone. The frogs have been gone longer than the government clerk who signed off on this expedition has been alive, and they're not coming back.

I stared at the frog. The frog looked impassively back at me. I wasn't moving, and I wasn't something it recognized as a predator; it was content to wait until I went away before it decided what was going to happen next.

Now knowing where to focus, I raised my camera again, zoomed in, and took a more deliberate shot.

When I lowered the camera, the frog was gone.

* * *

There was no further motion in the undergrowth or the reeds as I walked back to camp, following the thin, untrustworthy desire paths through the briars and the scrub. Every other damn plant in the Pacific Northwest did its best to go extinct when we started getting summers Phoenix would have been proud of, but the highly invasive Himalayan blackberries did just fine.

Their branches dipped low and enticing with bruise-black fruit, so ripe that it gleamed in the afternoon light. It had been enticing when we arrived at this site a week ago; now, after days upon days of freeze-dried rations, it was all but irresistible.

The first bite any of us took would be the last thing we ever tasted. Part of why the blackberries were so important was their network of roots, drawing heavy metals out of the soil and pressing them into the fruit they bore. We'd been collecting it all week, dropping it into deep buckets that we'd take with us on the air transport back to the city, where the useful metals could be extracted before the rest was incinerated. This would keep the toxins from being swallowed by any local wildlife that had managed to hang on so far, and also remove them permanently from the soil. In another six or seven hundred years, it might be safe for people to farm here again.

I twisted to avoid the clutching canes, trying not to think too hard about the path beneath my feet. Desire paths are formed when people—or animals—walk the same way often enough that it gets etched into the world. Well, we hadn't made these. There were four of us in our camp, no more, and the paths had been here when we arrived. Which meant either that there were surviving deer we hadn't encountered yet, or that there was a survivor's encampment somewhere near here.

H.G. Wells had it right when he said the future would be all Morlocks and Eloi. He'd just been wrong about where we'd be living, and how we'd all get there. Lowland survivors don't tend to think well of mountaintop city folk, and if they found us, we might not be making it back to base.

We knew that, agreed to it when we signed on for studies outside the city, and we counted the numbers of the dead every year, and then we went out again anyway, because some things are more important than personal survival. Some things matter more. I had no doubt that if we ever declared this land safe and usable again, the people who owned the cities would be back to exploiting it within the quarter, and still, it was worth the effort to see the world come back, a centimeter at a time. Maybe this time they'd play more gently with their toys.

I came around the bend in the path and found myself looking at a smoking ruin. I stopped dead, not quite processing what my eyes were seeing. Where the geodesic dome of the main tent should have been there was a black smear of ash and char; the smaller tent we used for storage and supplies was equally gone, and our barrels of blackberry slurry had been broken open and left to soak into the ground. There was no sign of Angela, or of our two assistants.

The desire path had betrayed us after all.

* * *

I am not a brave woman. I've never needed to be brave. I'm a middle-aged biologist who's only done two brave things in my entire life. I told the pretty girl who worked with me at the water desalination plant in the city that she was beautiful, and I agreed to leave the city for field work as soon as the people in charge gave me the option. Loving Angela was never brave. Marrying her wasn't brave, either; she had to be the one to propose, my pretty girl in her industrial gray uniform getting down on one knee next to the algae tanks, even though that had been a terrible idea with her back being the way it was.

No, I have never been brave. But in that moment, I stared at the wreckage of our camp and the absence of my wife, and I felt bravery blossom in my chest, as invasive as the blackberries, and as poisonously sweet.

First things first: I was wearing my good field boots, the ones designed to stop anything short of acid or actual lava. I had on multiple layers of reinforced canvas, and while I didn't have any rations, I had a packet of water purification tablets and a collapsible pot. I'd be able to drink before I died of dehydration. I didn't have any real weapons. Just my camera and the field knife I took with me when I went out to photograph the scant returning wildlife. I was supposed to use it if I got attacked by, say, a miraculously surviving raccoon.

In reality, I carried it because I was required to. If I ever found a raccoon, I'd let it eat my face before I'd harm something that had been able to stay alive in the wasteland we'd created. But still, a knife's a knife, and I had to count that as one of my assets.

Breathing deeply and slowly, I advanced into the clearing and looked around. In addition to the desire path I'd arrived along, three more snaked off into the blackberries, starting at different points around the perimeter of the clearing. I approached and studied each of them in turn, settling on the path that looked like it had been used most recently. Some of the briars in that direction had been snapped off, whether due to rough handling or simple gravity, and it seemed like the best of a bunch of bad options.

Silently promising that I'd bring her back, I started down the desire path, walking slow and careful, trying not to leave any sign that I'd been there. "Take only pictures, leave only memories," as they used to say. These days, I suppose it's more "take only contaminated fruit, leave only a record of your expedition," which is less pithy, but still applicable.

The ground was dry. Lushness of the blackberries aside, it hadn't rained in the better part of a month, and the dust held few footprints. Still, there was enough for me to be reasonably sure that I was heading in the correct direction, and so I kept on going, not quite sure what I was going to do when I reached my destination, only sure that I had to try. I owed it to myself, and to Angela, and to the frog whose pictures waited captive in my camera.

If the frogs were coming back, then the recovery of this stretch of land was farther along than we'd ever believed it might be. It wasn't a surprise to realize that the outside folks had moved back in, looking for safety, finding ways to use the resources we'd abandoned. They clearly knew about the blackberries; the fruit had been left untouched before our arrival and had been taken by the scout drones as proof that this area was still uninhabited.

This was their land. It might have been ours too, once, but we'd run away when things got bad. Not the assistants, maybe—they were both too young—but myself, and Angela. When the world had been burning and the gates had been open, we'd fled like all the rest. These were the people who'd stayed, their sons and daughters, holding to life by the skin of their teeth, rehabilitating a world the rest of us had abandoned. Surveys like ours had to look like the ultimate insult, the deserters creeping back in the night to sniff at the remains of the old world, looking for some sign that we could come out of our fortress and take it all back again.

I could understand why they'd be angry. I could even empathize. That didn't mean I was going to let them take my wife. I crept along, silent as only a middle-aged naturalist can be, placing my feet with utmost care, until the thinnest slice of another clearing like the one where we'd established our camp appeared. Why had we been so suspicious of the desire paths, yet so willing to believe that a large, round clearing was naturally occurring? These people had clearly carved a network of paths and resting spots into the blackberry canes. Not difficult to do, if you had the time to do it. I was still impressed, and sobered. It spoke to a degree of planning that told me this place was important to the people who used it. They weren't going to give it up without a fight.

Aware that someone could come up behind me at any moment, I held my ground and did my best to breathe silently, little, shallow breaths in through the nose and out through the mouth, until I was certain that if anyone had been moving in the clearing, I would have heard them. Only then did I straighten and proceed into the clearing.

Several tents had been set up near but not quite touching one of the sheltering walls of briar. Their nylon sides were worn and tattered, patched in so many places that I suspected they were more thread, tape, and twine than original fabric. Waste not, want not, I suppose: the old world had a lot of planned obsolescence, but it also had a lot of things built to last the better part of forever. Those tents would have been thrown away in a heartbeat if they'd broken before the collapse. Now they'd be used until they dissolved, patched and mended and handed down through family lines, keeping people safe and dry for as long as they possibly could.

Metal chairs and old-style shopping carts decorated the open parts of the clearing, and no one moved. There was no sign of my people, either good or ill. I exhaled, a long, slow sigh. This encampment didn't prove that they'd been taken this way. Their captors could have hauled them off in any direction while I was staring at the impossible frog, and I would never find them now.

There was another desire path on the far side of the clearing. Pushing aside thoughts of failure and devastation, I kept going.

I was going to bring them home.

* * *

The second desire path led to a larger clearing, as deserted as the first had been, this one dominated by a rusting RV. The door was closed. I approached, staying as quiet as I could, then knocked on the door and ran to hide around the back of the RV, where there were no windows.

Nothing happened. After several minutes of silence, I approached the door again, this time to test the knob. It turned, and I pushed it open, stepping into the dark interior.

There's a quality to the darkness you find in man-made things, a texture, almost. This darkness was textured by thin shafts of sunlight seeping through the boarded-over windows, and it filled the space inside, flitting across the faces of the people who had been tied up and dumped there, like so much garbage. I stepped over our two assistants, moving to kneel next to the only person in the world who mattered.

"Angela. Hey. Angela," I said, shaking her shoulder. "Honey, wake up. We have to get out of here."

"Yes, you do," said a voice behind me. I whirled.

The man in the doorway bared surprisingly intact teeth at me, a rusted machete in one hand, which he brandished like it was Excalibur itself.

"Creeping around here, stealing what's not yours," he spat.

"Wait!" I held up my hands. "If you kill us, they'll send another team, and another after that, until someone asks why you're protecting this stretch, why this piece of ground is so important. Killing us doesn't stop the city."

"What does?"

"Let us go." My plea sounded weak even to my own ears. "Let us take our beacons and call our transport, and go. We'll take the berries you didn't spill—they're so toxic that they'll support a report that says this land won't be safe for generations."

"Why should I trust you?"

I paused to swallow, silenced by my own hope and fear. Both were for the same thing—the future. But getting there meant finding my voice.

"I saw a frog today," I said. "All our science says I didn't. No one would believe me if I tried to tell them. But I saw a frog. Whatever your people are doing to clean up this land, it's working, faster than all our technology is projected to work. I saw a *frog*. If there's one frog, there are others. If the city comes bursting in to take this land back, the frog could be hurt."

Angela was awake; her hand closed silently over mine. I glanced at her, and she nodded.

Right. "You should trust me because I care about the frogs," I said. "Only the frogs. We have space in the city. People just want what we don't have. We just want what's forbidden. We can stay there a while longer. I can be content, knowing there are frogs in the world again."

The man frowned. "And if we kill you?"

"Another survey comes."

"If you're lying, and you tell your superiors about the frog?"

"Another survey comes. But if I'm telling the truth, you get left alone." I shrugged. "Three endings. Only one of them gives us all what we want. What do you say?"

* * *

Angela held my hand while we waited, looking up at the sky. The assistants hadn't woken until our negotiation was done; the younger still hadn't woken. I was worried about a brain bleed. We could fix that soon enough, once we were home.

"Can you really keep this a secret?" she asked.

"For you? Forever."

"But Mel..."

"But nothing." I shrugged and smiled at her. "I live in a world where there are frogs. What could be more wonderful than that?"

As the hum of the descending transport filled the air, I ejected the memory card from my camera and dropped it to the clearing floor, grinding it under my heel.

A life with the woman who loved me wasn't better than a world where there were frogs.

But it was close.

Seanan McGuire writes things. It is difficult to make her stop. She has won some awards for writing things, which disincentives stopping. She spends a lot of time in the local swamp, and mostly emerges to feed her cats and sleep before vanishing back into the rushes. Find her at seananmcguire.com

Please take a moment to review this book at your favorite retailer's website, Goodreads, or simply tell your friends!

ABOUT THE AUTHORS

Rosiee Thor began her career as a storyteller by demanding to tell her mother bedtime stories instead of the other way around. She spent her childhood reading by flashlight in the closet until she came out as queer. She lives in Oregon with a dog, two cats, and an abundance of plants. She is the author of *Tarnished Are The Stars, Fire Becomes Her, The Meaning of Pride,* and *Life is Strange: Steph's Story.*

J.S. Fields (@Galactoglucoman) is a scientist who has spent too much time around organic solvents. They enjoy roller derby, woodturning, making chainmail by hand, and cultivating fungi in the backs of minivans. J.S. lives with their wife and kid in the Pacific Northwest, along with a Flemish giant rabbit named Sir Chip Edmonton III.

Fields' writing spans across science and science fiction / fantasy. Their *Ardulum* series was a Forewords INDIES finalist in science fiction, and a Gold Crown Literary Society finalist in science fiction. Their YA fantasy *Foxfire in the Snow* was also a Foreword INDIES finalist in YA. All of their writing, from published to drafting, is available on their Patreon: http://www.patreon.com/jsfields. You can keep up to date on their work at http://www.jsfieldsbooks.com/

William C. Tracy writes tales of the Dissolutionverse: a science fantasy series about planets connected by music-based magic instead of spaceflight. He also has an epic fantasy available about a land where magic comes from seasonal fruit, and two sisters plot to take down a corrupt government. He is currently writing a space colony trilogy set on a planet entirely covered by a sentient fungus.

William is a North Carolina native with a master's in mechanical engineering, and has both designed and operated heavy construction machinery. He has also trained in Wado-Ryu karate since 2003, and runs his own dojo in Raleigh, NC. In his spare time, he cosplays with